I0831293

WELL OF TOWERS

JON PRICHARD

CP
CRITERION PRESS
DALLAS

Library of Congress Cataloging-in-Publication Data

Prichard, Jon Erik
Well of Towers / Jon Prichard

p. cm.

ISBN 978-0-6151-3641-7

1. Nichols, Jake (Fictitious character) - Fiction. 2. Archeologists - Fiction.
3. Team Babelus (Fictitious Organization) – Fiction
4. California – Fiction. I. Title

Printed in the United States of America

DEDICATIONS

Blake, Bobby and Sophie
My unlimited sources of inspiration, ever always.

Larry S. Poland
1956-2006

Whatever you're doing up there brother, it's all good!

Prologue

Al Habariya, Iraq
150 Miles SSW of Baghdad 4:33 am

Pre-dawn darkness shields the sun's rays from a desolate and dry-caked piece of earth 150 miles Southwest of Baghdad. The barren landscape offers no shade from the scorching heat in Iraq's Syrian Desert. Late spring and summer temperatures in the desert regions approach 120 degrees at mid-day and will roast skin, ruin fresh goods for market and take the very oxygen from one's lungs…life and living under the searing rays of a Mesopotamian sun for all of recorded history.

Mahmoud is a wood and clay-stone carver from the small town of Abd al-Karim, a dusty unaffected hamlet not far from the river port city of al-Hillah, the City of Hills, the infamous place where the infidels drove off the Moujahadeen and left a town in ruins, replaced by a new form of government and way of life not known in this part of the world. No matter to Mahmoud, his family has lived in this place for over a millennium and gone to market with little interruption for at least 400 or so years.

Today Mahmoud is returning from an overnight sojourn into the desert in search of heavy clay sheets, the material used in his carvings. Traveling under cloak of cool darkness Mahmoud is bringing his best work to market, carvings of elephants and warriors representing the great victories of Nebuchadnezaar. In Arabia any victory no matter how remote is cause for celebration and Mahmoud's decorated and gilded war elephants will fetch a healthy price, perhaps enough to feed his family for half a year. If only Jaffah would move along.

As far as beasts of the field go Mahmoud will take his steady donkey Jaffah over most any camel or horse. He is hearty and carries much more than other animals, often without braying in complaint. Jaffah with his white face and one twitching black ear is not so pleasing to the eye but he is a good travel companion with a pleasant disposition. Too bad the tired donkey is getting along in years and slowing considerably, leading to much consternation for Mahmoud as the sun is rising quickly, casting increasingly shorter shadows.

"Come now Jaffah, the market waits for no man nor donkey," yells Mahmoud, yanking on the distracted beast's rope and leather harness. Jaffah is passive and unmoved by his master's pleas. "Jaffah, the sun is rising the markets are set to open, can you not understand this? I will put the strap to you if you do not come along!" The full-throated appeal to reason does not stir the donkey to action so Mahmoud walks around to Jaffah's backside amidst panicked braying to prepare a sound lashing. There he notices a previously overlooked detail…the beast's back right hoof is stuck in a small hole on the dry lakebed.

No one is quite certain why this particular area is called a dry lakebed. No lake has ever existed here so far as anyone knows. But the land is cracked and caked giving the appearance of dry lakebeds found in desert regions. An odd sticky mud oozes up from nowhere during the spring months. But there are no active wells or known springs here and no water sources of any kind. Perhaps the moisture is run-off from the great Euphrates River but no one has ever detected a tributary.

The phenomenon is an unexplored mystery of geology but to Mahmoud it is merely a nuisance and now his beast of burden is stuck in one of its dry holes on the way to the most important market of the year. "Oh Jaffah I suppose I'll have to pull you out myself!" shouts the artisan as he tugs on the donkey's rope, gently at first and then with the passion of an angry man late for market. Still, the poor dumb beast does not, cannot, budge.

Finally with a ferociousness not seen since warrior elephants roamed the Mesopotamian plains Mahmoud, nearly prone to the lakebed, his anxious donkey braying in rhythmic song with each tug, manages to set the animal free in the same moment a few chunks of clay earth fall away into a deep dark chasm. As the donkey's hoof separates from its restraint more pieces fall away, then larger sections and slices until whole sheets of land break off and drop down into the abyss.

The sheer volume and mass cascading into the gorge makes the earth appear to swallow it self up, threatening to take Mahmoud and his trusty friend down to its black depths. Both run and bray for their lives, at first with Mahmoud tightly holding to Jaffah's harness, but as the earth gives way under paddling feet and hooves the two companions are separated by thick clay dust and the immediacy of saving one's own life.

Irony abounds with each turn of the globe. Here a simple carver and a humble donkey step in a hole, a seemingly neutral and harmless act that changes the understanding of everything ever known or thought over the course of the planet's history…the perfect job for a dumb ass.

1

Harpoon Harry's Bar and Grill
Seal Beach, California

The possibility of a mediocre life never entered Jake Nichols' mind upon graduation from the University of Texas with honors and degrees in history and science, although he could get used to lying about like the driftwood he often sees bobbling along the surf and sands of the California shore.

"Well, not mediocre exactly," he thinks to himself. "More of an aimless trek through life without purpose."

"But really, a sense of purpose is rather highly overrated, especially at the end of it all. Even if I had some reason for my own wretched existence what would it all mean at the end, when I have to search for my teeth in the morning and I can't even get it up anymore?" he muses with the wisdom of two good stiff drinks.

"Jackson Cooper Nichols, adventurer extraordinaire! I tip my hat and my ever empty cup to you." Jake mutters, with glass and hand raised, shoulders slouched and head tilted downwards as if toasting his own reflection in the bar counter. Jake's life is at a stage where his general direction is without form and void…so to speak. There are no grand ideas or spellbinding tours-de-thought rattling around in his once impassioned, now well-sauced brain. He's already lived a hundred lifetimes and it shows.

"I've caroused with famous people, found adventure in exotic lands, bedded more chicks than most guys!" Glassy eyed Jake, toasts him self within earshot of Jerry the bartender.

"D'ya do it with any famous chicks is what I wanna know," asks Jerry as he wipes down the counter at the other end of the bar? "And who? C'mon dish!"

"She wasn't famous exactly Jer, but she did a couple of Seinfelds and a few commercials." Jake tilts his scotch glass toward Jerry affirmatively.

"What only one semi-famous woman?" Jerry's brow furrows with inquisitive concern.

"No, but this little gal was special, she meant something to me. You know the commercial with the grandmother and the little girl with the flowers?"

"The one where the little girl brings the flowers to her grand-mamma's hospital bed and she takes a little pink pill and is cured of a wickedly terminal disease? Yeah I know that one, brings tears to my eyes!"

"Yeah! That's the chick!"

"What, the old lady?" Jerry demands, his voice rising indignantly?

"No moron, the girl!"

"You sayin' you did it with a kid you wretched asshole?" Jerry queries, his voice rising in obvious anger.

"No-oh idiot! She was a grown woman by the time I met up with her. But I see that damned commercial from time to time and I think of us together, knockin' it out with the old Magnovox playin' shitty porn all night."

"You are one sick bastard dude!" Jerry returns to his chores shaking a spatula toward Jake as if in the middle of a fencing match against an evil spirit. "Ya want another?"

"Yeah, yeah ok, why not?" Jake hunches over with elbows firmly on the counter quietly reminiscing of conquests long since passed.

2

Harpoon Harry's is a sea shack of a bar on the Pacific Coast Highway running along the California coast. The atmospherics are dark and heavy with sea-aged wood covering the walls, floor and ceiling, much like a rustic beach shanty one would expect in a Ken Auster painting.

Various nautical items clutter every surface, both offending the eye while giving the comfort of old familiar things… reminding tourists of treasured moments on the open sea with the spray of sea-salt air and rhythmic bobbing of a fishing boat…or pretty much any time getting slob-happy drunk with friends by an open pit fire on the beach. A fishing net motif dominates one wall with pink and orange starfish knotted to the sisal rope in a haphazard pattern, as if the designer purposely calculated the randomness of the presentation.

The hallway heading towards the bar's mixed-gender restroom is adorned with surfing legends of the past. Most of the pictures are apparently from the surfing Golden Era of the

1960s. There are no shots of the sort you see on today's surfing circuit featuring logo-emblazoned wetsuits, wild fluorescent colors and trick performances at the top of a wave's crest on a short board.

No, these are genuine article, black and white or Sepia-toned portraits of the sport's legends like Jack Haley, Buzzy Trent or Phil Edwards. The authentic surfer, long board planted foot-deep in the sand majestically beside its Harachi sandaled, bushy haired, Bermuda short wearing owner. Harry of harpoon legend probably knew these guys personally.

Palm fronds and coconuts hang from a ceiling covered in what is apparently a large bamboo placemat. In the corner stands an obligatory totem pole with three faces, one happy, one sad and one that looks an awful lot like people who get toasted at the local beach bar. The floor is always gritty with sand, though the actual beach is 500 yards away. Perhaps the owner carts the stuff in to provide the place with atmosphere, as if it needed an extra ounce of kitsch to qualify as a bona fide beach establishment.

The smell of fried fish, typically served in taco form, hangs in the air like a heavy fog that won't clear despite the sun's persistent rays. And though Harry's is merely yards from the ocean it is virtually impossible to detect any hint of fresh fish in the place, this despite the fact local fishermen catch everything from hearty lobster to savory pink salmon off the California coast. There's something inauthentic about serving fresh fish in a kitsch-laden beach hut of a bar. Such a commercial faux pas would offend the sensibilities of your average tourist from Iowa or Ohio.

At various epochs of the bar's existence, Harry's has served as the cool place for college age retro-beach aficionados hanging out and chatting about the Big Kahuna or the origins of the Real Gidget. It's acted as a haven for dead-enders bent on drinking them selves into the next metaphysical phase of some New Age religion. Harry's has given solace to wide-eyed masters of drinking games attempting to find the highest levels of the newest Far Eastern Quai Chang Kane thing. Even former Moonies drink here.

Harry's is also a comforting way station for locals, not quite as commercialized as other beach bars lining the highway from Surf City to Long Beach. Today it stands as a cubbyhole for mediocrities…the sort who drinks expensive single-malt scotch jiggers out of sheer boredom.

3

Jake has no idea where he wants to take his life, which to this point he deems an unmitigated failure. He hasn't failed at every task or job put before him, quite the opposite. He's achieved a level of success with each rung of his life's ladder. To Jake's mind, the problem lies in a general lack of fungible successes of the sort that makes one a media star and gets you into the best Oscar parties. Or rich. Rich would do. Failed businesses, marriages and professional shortcomings have made him weary and wary of living.

Jake is a former Navy SEAL, has a fine education and a bright scientific mind. He has known adventure the world over and lived fully in the throes of love and hate. But passion is lacking at this stage in his life. His soul is devoid of heartfelt, thirst quenching desire for any thing or any one. Nothing excites him, neither life nor living. As he slouches on his red Naugahyde covered stool, sidled up close to the bar at the local establishment providing him comfort and security about the only thing he can muster any true feelings for these days is the single-malt Dewars sitting in front of him.

He's not an alcoholic he assures himself with a long slow sip just before lunch. He doesn't have an alcohol problem it's just sometimes when he drinks he has problems. And he doesn't drink every day or hide liquor under the mattress. But lately, as self doubt and a sinking worthlessness has crept in he's sought solace in the soft denial induced and warmed by alcohol. Jake is not seeking a wall of separation from anger, hurt, danger or turmoil. He wishes to cover up the wrenching, tearing painlessness of mediocrity and put a salve on a tired and irritably useless soul.

Jake's not exactly gainfully employed at present. Scuba diving lessons don't count as a moneymaking enterprise, given his services are often remunerated with a trip to the sack of any halfway decent looking chick. Bored housewives and post college girls, never quite popular or deemed hot by their peers seeking a safe adventure constitute the better part of his clientele. Jake finds no problems getting laid as an adventure educator and protector from sharks and other ocean dangers…at par with the deeply tanned, sweaty, gin-breath, tattooed, smoke laden vermin running stomach-churning rides for teenagers at traveling carnivals.

Jake's one and only job these days is to plant his carcass on a barstool. Here at Harry's in the rustic comforts of his scotch tempered proximity there is no need for pretenses or business attire or ties, so he's dressed in the lazy shiftless clothing one expects of the relatively employed grizzled beach bum in California. Frayed and grubby khaki Bermuda shorts with pleated tool pockets and a small canvass loop, presumably to hold a hammer hang on his thin waist like a pair of hip-hop pants.

Loosely draped over surprisingly well-toned shoulders is a frazzled Pacific Islander print shirt with several missing buttons and a coffee stain roughly matching the contours of a lake with a few Easter Island monuments on its shore. His sandals are of the worn brown leather variety, the sort typically found on the bottom shelf of thrift stores or church bazaars, curled up at the ends as if worn by an elf. Jake's single diversion from form is a magnificent *Seapearl* diver's watch with its dark sapphire blue dial, seven-jewel quartz movement and screw down crown and back for maximum water resistance. As a final insult to good taste and culture a yellowed pukka-shell necklace salted by sweat and sea drapes insouciantly around a deeply tanned neck, lending considerable cheapness to his threadbare ensemble.

The introspective quietude of a nearly empty fish fry hazed rich-wood adorned bar is broken abruptly upon the entrance of a pair of gravely serious men at extreme odds with the surroundings. The two agents of an unknown type, nattily dressed with gig-lines straight and the earnest demeanor of those reeking of federal government covert operations training, strut through the portico with the assured presence of a panther meeting a goose for the first time. And the goose, sitting by him self at the bar is dulled and sedated by his Dewar's labeled medication.

"Could be FBI or State Department," thinks Jake as he warily measures the pair from a distance. "Maybe they're CIA or toadies from the NID or any number of uptight straight-laced stick in the mud agencies that would pass for an organized crime gang in most circumstances. Hell they could be jack-booted thugs from the ATF…well, without the boots."

Whatever the circumstances of their arrival, the button-down men walk into a broken down overly hyped shanty-like beach bar on the Pacific Coast Highway. They aren't here for the sand-floor atmospherics and backslapping drinks with the Beach Boys and Jan and Dean playing on the jukebox. The serious men mean business and head straight toward Jake, to his eternal consternation.

4

White House Situation Room
Washington, D.C.

"The picture is just now coming up on the forward monitor Mr. President," White House Chief of Staff Gene Lamont whispers into the ear of the freshly inaugurated leader of the free world. "General Keith is reporting from a makeshift media area at an HQ tent at the Well Site."

Barely three months removed from his inauguration on a cold crisp Washington morning, President David Hardwick Crandall finds himself seated at the 'captains chair' in the White House Situation Room. The President chats amiably, surrounded by several cabinet members, staffers and important agency heads. They've assembled to grapple with a burgeoning crisis demanding the keenest policy, military and scientific sensibilities. Some dumb beast of a mule fell into a well in Iraq, igniting a diplomatic and potentially lethal conflict likely to breach the dam of well-crafted messages and high-minded political statements.

"Of all the crises to fall on my watch," muses the President to himself, "I get Bessie's Cow."

Crandall isn't certain what to make of the potential damage brought on by this particular crisis, only that it's import has the singular ability to gather some of the world's most powerful people into one room. The foolish old donkey fell into a well of sorts, there are archeological discoveries of unknown substance and value, the United States military set up perimeter security around the area and that's what's known at this point.

"Good morning Mr. President, Warren Keith here," greets a General clad in desert fatigues. He is the head of American operations in Iraq.

"Yes General Keith and good morning to you," the President responds, "We can see and hear you quite clearly. The technology is rather remarkable!" He speaks in the deep-throated voice used during the campaign, a tone designed to impart sincerity, pride and humility.

"I'm afraid Mr. President we have a problematic situation on our hands out here and we need some direction from Washington as to how we intend to proceed in the matter." The General informs with a matter-of-fact resolution of military men who serve in the field and require quick answers without any attendant political breeze. "I'm actually on the site touring the area in question. We've set up in the communications tent doubling as a headquarters about a hundred yards from the point where we believe the man and donkey fell in."

"Well I hope you're all getting enough water out there General. I understand the heat this time of year can raise blisters." The President is still campaigning to no one in particular.

"What's the real fuss about here?" the President asks himself. "Does this meet the criteria of a full-blown national security event, so imminent the cabinet and security agency heads are forced to meet in the White House Situation Room? Maybe we should do this over a cup of coffee in the Oval Office or in one of the less threatening conference rooms in the West Wing."

"Mr. President it's vitally important Washington thoroughly understands the gravity of the situation we have on the ground here." Everyone gathered in the room, except perhaps Crandall, understands the General's use of 'Washington' as a euphemism for the President himself. "Any delay in the decision-making stream surrounding this event could create conflicts for years to come."

5

"General I'm afraid I don't quite catch your drift," an obviously confused President allows, "What sort of problems are you seeing out there?"

"Mr. President have you seen the aerials shot from the drones this morning? We couldn't get good pictures until first light after dawn but we sent what we did get and then posted additional shots from the early runs at least two hours ago. You should have that stuff there." General Keith is certain Washington is clueless as to the seriousness of the Well Site problem.

"No I haven't gotten a look at anything I would classify as a clear picture yet General but they're bringing some stuff up right now so hang on a few moments." Crandall is perturbed about not having information at his fingertips and he barks orders to staff, mostly out of embarrassment.

The White House Situation Room is a relatively tiny wood paneled conference room located in the basement area of the

West Wing of the White House. Quite unlike grandiose depictions on television of a roomy theater for the discourse of national emergencies, the actual area is akin to a conference closet. There is a large dark mahogany table surrounded by high-back leather executive-style chairs and a few seats adjacent to the table for staff. On the side opposite staff seating is a small walkway and a coffee stand. The ceilings are low, as in most basement rooms and add to its cramped atmosphere. Like most everything else in Washington the room is built for an effect and comfort is not what the designers had in mind. There is no elbowroom for heated discussions. Nor are there places to lay back in thoughtful repose or windows begging for idle daydreams. Everything about the space screams high alert. It is essential for participants in the Situation Room to work with laser-like focus and cool unrelenting resolve to handle some of the world's worst crisis moments.

Despite its Spartan accoutrements and lack of creature comforts, the Situation Room is filled with bleeding-edge communications technologies. Stuffed behind various wood-paneled doors are the latest computer aided electronics enabling real-time communications with most anyone nearly anywhere in the world, including outer space. Communications between the Situation Room and outside sources are closed-loop private networks, not the virtual variety found on the Internet, but separate secure lines with information encrypted and segmented into packet data transmissions for the highest level of security. Super resolution Plasma and LCD panels monitor events in the outside world giving the President the clearest possible picture with which to make crucial decisions, often millions of lives hang in the balance. This small conference room with its hyper-technical capabilities was built in response to the Bay of Pigs crisis during the early months of the Kennedy administration, when a lack of secure real-time information contributed to a disastrous end. Crandall and the officials and policy-makers of his administration sit apprehensively around the room's grand table, each hoping they don't meet the same fate.

6

An array of aerial pictures and clips shot from the cameras of unmanned drones flying over the Iraq site appears on a monitor to the left of the President. Clicking on a thumbnail expands and loads each image or video clip onto the 60-inch crystal clear plasma screen. Unlike satellite images the drone photography is taken, in this case from a few hundred feet to a couple of thousand feet above the site, giving the President a detailed high-resolution report.

"What are these shots of General?" The President's demeanor shifts and a hint of concern is heard in his voice. "To me it looks like Downtown Manhattan, only the city is sunk into a big hole in the ground. Am I getting this correctly?"

"Yes Mr. President your description roughly captures the site as far as the size of the structures and vastness of it all. But quite frankly size is not what I'm worried about Sir. After coming to the site and getting a first-hand look at the anomaly I firmly believe we're in dangerous territory. Whatever is down there will attract attention at some point from some of the worst characters in the region. We've got to do something fast."

"What do you have in mind General?" Crandall grows slightly alarmed at General Keith's heated demeanor.

"First we've got to get more boots on the ground up here Mr. President. I know the Iraq withdrawal orders state American troops are only allowed in the immediate perimeter of the Green Zone since Baghdad was pacified except where there is an existential threat. I believe this place and its contents represent just such a threat Mr. President and I need your authorization immediately to get sufficient forces out here."

"Now General, I, uh, I'm not so certain an archeological site is an immediate threat to our soldiers." The President blatantly ignores the advice of a General in the field. "Is anybody shooting at you? Are there insurgents trying to get at the site? I don't need to tell you…any order for large troop movements outside the Green Zone will appear to the Iraqi government like another invasion."

"And then what, do we take over the site and have television crews from the BBC and CNN running reports about the American Imperial Army running roughshod over the helpless Iraqi government? That's the way they'll spin it! The talking heads will jump all over themselves with a tale of our men occupying territory in a sovereign land. No, no, the whole notion is diplomatically impossible General, you've got to find another way."

General Keith coolly replies as generals often do when walking into Washington quicksand. "Mr. President, failing to act here will result in the loss of soldier's lives for certain but we're in a war and often called upon to sacrifice our lives. Sir, I'm a military man and I know a military threat when I see it. The possible technologies down in that hole could overwhelm any military force ever assembled. If we let powerful undefined technologies fall into the wrong hands we may as well kiss the Western world goodbye."

Irritated, Crandall addresses the General by first name showing who's in charge. "Warren isn't all of this conjecture and speculation? Nobody's been down there yet to see if there are any technologies whatsoever, certainly not enough to sound a three-alarm fire."

"We don't know a single thing about the place. I certainly don't want to damage or outright sacrifice all of our hard won gains in the War on Terror by setting off an international incident. We've got to dial this back a bit."

Noises from outside the HQ tent distract the General from the monitor. "Mr. President something is developing behind me here. I need a couple of moments." He quickly disappears from view, leaving the dark brown tarpaulin background as the only image left on the screen.

Observing the situation on the monitors along with the President are the most important elements of the nation's security and diplomacy apparatus, along with a few components of the President's own political organization. Directly to the President's left is newly confirmed Secretary of Defense, Graziella Green-Newton, America's first female to head the typically male dominated military hierarchy. Seated adjacent to her is the Director of National Intelligence, Graham Likely, former head of the Office of Naval Intelligence. To Likely's left is the Director of the Central

Intelligence Agency, Hugh Norton, indistinguishable and bland as milquetoast.

Seated directly at Crandall's right is Gene Lamont, the White House Chief of Staff, a longtime personal friend of the President. To his right is the Department of Homeland Security Director Patricia 'Patsy' Heatherton, a shrill yapping poodle of a woman. The freshly minted Secretary of State, Merton M. Malloy III sits beside Heatherton picking at a hangnail. Next to him is National Security Advisor Daniel Maney, whose generally crimson-toned face and protruding vein at his temple renders him apparently ready to blow a gasket upon the slightest provocation.

Rounding out those seated at the table is the gravel voiced Chairman of the Joint Chiefs of Staff, General Rory Broadhead. Several agency staffers occupy seats adjacent to the table along with Torie Smart, the White House Communications Director.

"Mr. President we are under attack!" General Keith heatedly reports to the group, returning to face the camera. "At the moment we don't know who or what is involved but they blew up the fuel dump and there's a lot of automatic weapons fire. Sounds like Kalishnikovs so they're probably not ours or Iraqi soldiers, maybe Syrian." The General delivers his report in a continuous stream of serious but excited tones.

• • •

President Crandall won election to the highest office in the land by the barest plurality. The campaign, one of the most contentious and frightfully nasty political battles in the annals of American history, was earmarked by massive voter anxiety, allegations and counter allegations of fraud and disenfranchisement. In some quarters blood filled American streets as a result of violent riotous clashes between partisans. After failing to earn his party's nomination a maverick Republican formed a ticket with an equally unorthodox Democrat running mate and caused great upheaval in the race, taking nearly one-third of the popular vote and nearly that much from the Electoral College.

The popular third party, newly reconstituted and inaptly named Federalists, garnered much of its support from the populous areas of California, New York and Illinois. The South and much of the Mid-west held firm for the Republicans, leaving political breadcrumbs from New England and Minnesota to the Democrats. The Democrats added two seats in the Senate to maintain control of the body but lost control of the House of Representatives as the Federalists gained seats and caucused with the Republicans. The new alliance gave Republicans control of the House but forced a uniquely American version of a coalition government.

Presidential crisis management faces heightened scrutiny after an election without an outright mandate from voters. Results are historically a mixed bag of courage and disaster. The President, a businessman and then Governor of the State of Mississippi, has no military expertise in his background. His running mate, the first female Vice-President of the United States is well versed in matters of security, having served in the Defense Department and as National Security Advisor in a previous administration but she is dispatched to Memphis, Tennessee to speak to a corporate forum on child safety products. "That's a real scheduling blunder," the President thinks to himself. For a moment he wishes for a role reversal with the Vice-President, and all interested parties operating from their natural vantage point.

7

The solemn group in the Situation room watches in horror and amazement as General Keith provides a real-time play by play of the battle erupting to the west of the Well Site. At certain points during the battle a shriek will pierce through the room followed by muffled discussions among staffers. They hear the firefight and the voice of General Keith explaining the battle but can only see the brown tarpaulin on the screens. Crandall wonders if the lack of any visuals only adds to the frightening drama playing out in front of them as if it were occurring just outside the room.

About 100 fighting Marines make up the bulk of the original contingent sent to secure the Well Site. The outbreak of an exigent circumstance putting American soldiers at great risk fills the President with resolve and he immediately orders a troop expansion to ten thousand. General Keith calls up reinforcements. They will take hours to mobilize and reach the site. As gunfire rattles in the distance no one knows if the newly mustered forces will arrive as reinforcements or as a recovery operation to collect dead soldiers.

The battle rages for over an hour as the sounds of rocket and mortar fire blast into the tiny Situation Room chamber - considerably enhanced by a state-of-the-art SRS surround sound system. General Keith, now bunkered down clad in helmet and flak gear, continues to update the group as each significant sound fills the room. A hollow THWOOMP followed by a distant KWISHBAM denotes friendly mortar fire. A concussive BAMSWISH followed by the return spray of automatic weapons fire or screams not nearly far enough in the distance signal an incoming rocket. General Keith can only wait helplessly, pacing back and forth while delivering reports to the Situation Room. Barking out orders to troops in a firefight is the job of the squad commander on the ground. In this case a heroic highly competent performance carried out by Major Mitchell Bruce.

As gunfire sounds and shouting soldiers recede a weary silence invades the Situation Room. The battle ends but not without casualties. Three Marines lay dead with another 24 wounded. An unknown group clad in Syrian military uniforms attacked the security contingent without provocation. No information thus far reveals whether or not the attackers are actual Syrian soldiers and no prisoners are caught, leaving an identification vapor trail.

General Keith returns to the screen. "Mr. President?"

"Yes General we're here." Crandall answers, appearing worn and disheveled.

"I could go on ahead and say I told ya so but ya already know so there's no point in walking through a finger pointing exercise. It looks like we're in the clear for now and reinforcements should arrive shortly. I've got a squad to tend to at present. How about we reconvene at oh-eight-hundred your time?"

"Yes General, certainly. Take care of your men. We've got a lot of work to do here on this end. And good luck." The President turns away from the monitor chastised and graven.

"Aye, aye Sir!" General Keith signs off.

Chief of Staff Lamont speaks first, his mouth dry and sticky, his voice gravelly from exasperations and anguished pleas during the firefight. The others, tired and frightful, sit frozen in rapt attention, anxious and nervous as if each had gone through the helpless terror of a cell phone call with a loved one on the other end getting car jacked.

"All of this seemed a tempest in a teapot at first glance but we now know first hand these issues carry the greatest weight and gravity. God bless the men who gave their lives and limbs today. It's painfully obvious the issues and dilemmas we face during the crisis will challenge and confound the heartiest among us. As we go through this I fully expect each of you to comport yourselves with the utmost respect for the offices, character and persons involved here today. We owe at least that much to those who have already made the ultimate sacrifice"

"This is a real problem Gene." A worn and shaken Secretary Malloy takes a turn at the table, his normally jovial manner severely muted by the day's events. "I have no idea what's down there but somebody wants it bad enough to go to war over a hole in the ground. I don't know how we're going to pull the necessary diplomatic strings at the U.N. or with the Iraqi government. Ambassador al-Nouri scoffs at our withdrawal plan. He's not about to let the Iraqis give up one inch of sovereignty. We can't even get a small defensive base there on a permanent basis. He'll never go for anything we try at this point."

"Nothing is simple in this matrix I'm afraid," continues Lamont. "We're in for the ultimate test of character and ability and a few of us aren't even moved into our offices yet. When we got the action brief on the mule falling in a well we assumed this was your garden-variety stumble into one of history's hidden vaults filled with shards of pottery or a few ancient pillars denoting a village or perhaps a palace of an ancient despot. The satellite images and pictures from the unmanned drones reveal an entirely different set of circumstances. Now we see a fierce firefight played out right before our own eyes and we have to shift gears. We've got to re-imagine the entire thing and come up with solutions fitting the new reality. We're a new team and I'm not sure we have the gravitas to get this job done right but we aren't going to let the President down."

"Let's not worry about letting me down Gene. We have no reason to go adrift over politics just now. It doesn't matter if I'm let down by some mistakes. We can't let the people who elected us down. Let's just stick to working this the best we know how without bringing in politics."

"Whatever problems arise I'm sure we have enough forces in the area to handle the situation." Secretary Green-Newton, listening intently, feels compelled to assure the President. "Our Marines on station fought bravely today and have reinforcements set to arrive at any minute and they've already re-secured the perimeter. Even though we are steadily drawing down troop levels there are still about ten thousand troops up in Baghdad stationed in the Green Zone along with another twenty thousand in Kuwait. Unless there's a nuclear weapon or a stash of chemical weapons buried in the well I don't see any contingencies we're not capable of handling."

"Madam Secretary." Lamont rises to his feet in anger. "The basic problem is we don't know exactly what is down there. We're not securing an ordinary little well out in the country. This is a vast tract of land, under ground, populated by freestanding buildings that look modern and yet are decidedly not new. We can't see everything from the sky. The Well Site is a deep dark abyss and its contents are an unknown quantity. There are secret forces out there willing to attack American soldiers with a frontal assault in broad daylight to find what's hidden in there. And whoever is trying to get at the Well Site is desperate and likely state sponsored. Insurgents never attack head on. They kill with improvised explosive devices you know…IEDs or car bombs. When I say we must completely re-imagine this I'm not kidding around. We don't know who or what we're dealing with!"

"Perhaps it's the mother of all Saddam's hidden underground bunkers." CIA Director Norton puts his thoughts in the arena to make certain everyone knows he's still breathing. "We have no idea whether or not Saddam was bluffing about supposedly having tons of weapons of mass destruction stored up around Iraq. We've suspected the Baathists from Syria acted in coordination with the Baathists in Iraq to spirit truckloads of WMD out of Iraq and into Syria's Bekaa Valley. Maybe they didn't get so far and dumped everything in a huge underground bunker that caved in when a donkey walked over. Now we have armed attackers in Syrian uniforms mysteriously showing up. It's not proof but the circumstances sure make sense for me."

"Our predicament is we don't have any answers Hugh." Lamont continues to plead for a sense of urgency. "The CIA doesn't know. The Defense Department doesn't know. Nobody knows. Your scenario is plausible…I suppose…but nowhere near any sort of slam-dunk. I don't want to put the President in an untenable political position by making grandiose statements we can't back up."

"We're not sitting here in the Situation Room over politics, at least not now!" National Security Advisor Maney rises heatedly to address the group. "What we just saw and heard on the monitors shows proof beyond doubt we have an exceedingly dangerous and determined enemy who wants or needs to get at something in the hole. I don't want to see whatever is there end up on U.S. soil, doing whatever extent of damage possible! Where will your political fortunes be with a million dead Americans splashed across the front pages of every newspaper in the world?"

"Dan, don't start with this political crap." The Chief of Staff's anger rises in his throat. "The last thing we need is turf battles and contentious diatribes. The road we're about to travel is rocky enough without creating departmental disputes between people who need to work together. So let's get together on this people. Believe me we will sink or swim on how we handle severe problems, and these qualify as severe!"

"I'm worried about protecting the American people!"

"All of us are worried about the same thing Dan." The President recomposes him self and speaks in measured tones. "Everyone here is committed to doing their job which ultimately is the protection of the American people. Now we're all a bit shell shocked by what we've seen and heard today. But we'll be ok. Let's not sacrifice the honor of those who died today by falling into finger pointing blame games. Let's concentrate on getting the job done and done right."

President Crandall ran large-scale corporations in the private sector. He's seen turf battles and inter-departmental politics ruin good debates and even better plans. Today, in the shadow of a fierce gun battle and heroic deeds he will have none of that. "I am the man for this job after all," he thinks to himself.

"Folks look at this presentation NRO put together." Director Likely interjects a new subject into the discussion in a rich Southern drawl as he loads a DVD prepared by the National Reconnaissance Organization. "As you can see in the first satellite image we're not talkin' about a dumb little ass fallin' in a well. The chasm as I call it is quite large…huge and vast. Bigger'n the city of San Francisco I'd expect. And those buildings you see there aren't designed like one of Saddam's palaces or a bunker housing a whoppin' load of WMD barrels and boxes of explosive munitions. In fact they aren't any sort of architecture we've ever seen or heard of. Oh no, this is somethin' quite a bit different. We can tell the press a donkey fell in a well to keep them at bay while we explore this thing. If the word gets out we'll have every Jihadist from Iran to Syria trying to get at what's here, not to mention the Iraqis themselves. As we know somebody already knows the Well exists and they're trying desperately to get at it. But I have a good hunch they don't want anybody else to know its there either, otherwise somebody would already have gotten their mug in front of a camera to call America the Great Satan who keeps the world's technology and the great truths to itself, for itself."

"That's all well and good Graham but the chasm as you call it is the sovereign territory of Iraq." Secretary Malloy shakes his head vigorously back and forth as he speaks. "I'm trying, God knows I'm trying, but I just don't see how we can unilaterally take over this whole vast territory, if it is indeed as large as San Francisco, at the drop of a hat without so much as a how do you do. Look at the problem from the diplomacy side. Sure we'd like to just swoop in with an overwhelming force and take over a gigantic swath of land in the dead of night. But we can't, we just can't, not that it isn't physically possible, but how many international treaties do we step on with such an action?"

"We'd need approval from the U.S. Congress before we took over territory in a sovereign country. Well, there goes your secret! Plus I'm not sure Congress is in the frame of mind to give us what we want on any of this. Another huge stumbling block is the Iraqi government. They aren't going to lie down and let us take over a tract of land this size. Especially if they believe valuable historical treasures are down in the hole. The Iraqi Army is battle hardened, well equipped and runs about 400,000 strong these days. We should know we trained them and equipped them. I don't think we want to go tangling with them just now."

"We've spent an enormous amount blood and treasure in Iraq." Dan Maney pounds his fist on the table, the much-vaunted vein at his temple starting to throb in rhythm with his statements. "Iraq owes us. Yeah they owe us for every last bit of sovereignty they possess! If it weren't for the ability of our military and the courage and fortitude of the last President the Iraqis would still live under the harsh boot of Saddam and his ruthless raping thug sons. So I ask you Malloy, why shouldn't we go in there, take charge and bust some balls while were at it? I do not want chemical weapons or worse to make their way over here to our shores. Not on my watch. No sir!"

Secretary Malloy argues the point vociferously. "Its not about your testosterone or your watch Dan. This is the way of the world. The reality. Are you saying we're supposed to just walk all over the rest of the planet to suit our needs? Are you telling us that we can't work with other countries on issues of sovereignty? If so, then where does our own sovereignty begin and end? What's to keep the North Koreans or the Russians or China from just walking into Washington D.C. and declaring the need to take over the Lincoln Memorial to protect their own interests?"

Maney won't let the matter rest. "About four thousand nuclear warheads! The nukes and the don't-tread-on-me resolve of the American people, that's what!"

Chief of Staff Lamont speaks in dulcet tones with a desire to end the debate and inspire the political troops to greatness. "All of your points are well taken. Most of them make sense to us in our mindset even as they seem to contradict each other. Secretary Malloy is rummaging through all the machinations necessary to settle certain diplomatic issues that need occur in an ordered civilization. We've been trying for decades to convince countries in the Middle East to sign on to the ideas of modern civilization. To simply run roughshod over those ideas themselves is not only hypocritical but might send the entire region back to its Stone Age leanings. Mr. Maney is right too. The Iraqis do owe us and above all else we owe the American people one thing…protection."

"Though all of these arguments make perfect sense by the logic of our world all of them fail to grasp the larger issues going beyond a nation's sovereignty or the protection of its people. The chasm is not a hole in the ground filled with a weapons cache, at least not the weapons of our era. Indeed we're not observing a hole at all. We clearly see from the drone images an ancient city that looks an awful lot like a thoroughly modern one. We're not seeing something we understand like Pompeii or the destruction of Crete."

"The city in the well didn't get swallowed up by the earth in some ancient volcanic cataclysm or all-encompassing deluge. Indeed, the land, the earth, solid rock, stone and clay grew up around the city as if covering it in ivy. The city is fully intact its ramparts unmolested by the eons of time. Try for one instant to fill your feeble human minds with this concept. The ramifications to humanity of a city, an entire civilization buried so deep its age is incalculable, perhaps in existence before the ape-men we call our ancestors. And its location is, not coincidentally I think, the place generally referred to as the 'cradle of civilization'. What does this mean for the world's religions? I expect the Islamists might have a few lethal comments in regards to the concept."

Lamont stands slowly, deliberately to preach to the choir. "This discovery is so far beyond our current understanding. I fear our capacity is far too limited to deal with the problem. I wonder, sitting here listening as our soldiers are attacked if any of you, in fact if anyone in all humanity possesses the capacity to understand just what is going on here? Do you? Ask yourselves, do you have the mental acuity to reach beyond your own understandings, your upbringing, indeed, every thing you know or have ever studied and learned through the many degree programs of higher learning to grab hold of the images and concepts we're discussing here today?"

The group falls silent in deep thought as the Chief of Staff's soliloquy settles. Sitting in the Situation Room are some of the most learned and powerful people ever produced by the United States, and yet they are stunned to silence by the gravity of what lay ahead and the understanding lacking in each of them. Clearly there is more to the story of a donkey falling in a well. And the silence of the group speaks volumes.

"We should break for lunch, though I don't believe I can eat anything myself," Director Heatherton quietly acquiesces. "We have so much to do and think about. I for one need a rest to recharge a bit."

President Crandall stands from his seat and heads for the door imploring the others to join him. "I agree, let's take a brief lunch break. Try to eat something though. We have a long haul that may last all the way through the night. We have a lot of work to do before we connect with General Keith at oh-eight-hundred hours."

As the meeting breaks for a lunch repast, the participants wearily trudge from the room in search of a degree of solace. Prayers fill their hearts for the dead and wounded and a grim determination grows to ensure America does not fail humanity.

Not on their watch.

8

Life Sciences Building at Andrews University
Berrien Springs, Michigan

Kelly Anne Carter spends the better part of her professional life debunking scientific postulations. Whenever an objectionable treatise or paper is published showering glory and the imprimatur of scientific truth on a subject such as the latest *Ardipithecus ramidus* ape-man, Hobbit people on Florez Island or Mankind's scorching of the earth Kelly Anne is on the record with contrary evidence refuting the assumptions of the discovery.

To Kelly Anne science is an ever-open door to discovery, not a set of alleged truths and assumptions tied up in a time warp of moribund ideas. In her way of thinking scientists, particularly in the fields of archeology, human development and genetics are never willing to escape conventional wisdom nor buck the tide in the world of academia. Merely questioning the orthodoxy of the scientific community leads to ridicule, obscurity and loss of income. Historically this dynamic ran in the opposite direction with scientists and free thinkers shunned by religionists, churches and neighbors for contrary views. Nowadays orthodoxy in science is a secular religion unto itself and ideas running contrary to such monolithic thoughts are viewed as insanity.

Kelly Anne's chosen profession as a medical doctor takes her around the globe from the Trauma Center at St. Johns Hospital in Santa Monica, California to AIDS treatment tents in the wilds of Uganda. No matter where she traveles in the world Kelly Anne sees the best and the worst of people as they try to deal with diseases and ailments. Whether rich or poor, alone or part of a large group any sentient being will let you know about aches and pains…generally quite loudly.

Armed with a Doctorate in Archeology from Yale and Medical Degree from Loma Linda University, she lectures at colleges and universities on the importance of keeping an open mind when dealing with science. But Kelly Anne prefers teaching. Of all her considerable accomplishments the greatest rewards in Kelly Anne's life are found in imparting knowledge and understanding to college students. She finds students in her classes generally inquisitive and serious about her contrarian's subject material giving her a deep-rooted satisfaction…somehow life is worth trudging through, good days and bad.

The time Kelly Anne spends on the lecture circuit brings her grief and ridicule for the most part. She simply can't resist putting in a cutting gibe at the scientific community and its latest pontifications on subjects ranging from Global Warming to the geologic history of the Sphinx in Egypt. Her controversial views manage to alienate her from most of the establishment scientific academia. In truth she wouldn't live life any other way. Kelly Anne revels in confounding the scientific community at every turn. She is a true iconoclast.

Although she loves teaching at the highest levels of her profession Kelly Anne's job prospects in the field are surprisingly meager. Harvard's School of Arts and Sciences rejected her entreaties, as did her Alma Mater Yale. The University of Michigan took no interest in what they perceive as a Bible thumping scientist bent on bringing a secular orthodoxy to its knees. Countless other institutions of higher learning reject Kelly Anne too with the misguided assumption she and her unsettling views would simply vanish into the night, forgotten by all. That is until she published several books on the scientific principles of the existence of God. The popular books - filled with questions science consistently fails to answer, continues to drive more than a few academics to rabid apoplexy.

"I wonder what the lefty secularists at Harvard would think of this lesson plan," ponders Kelly Anne to herself. "Another Global Warming paper goes up in smoke...ha, ha. Maybe I should send the Dean a copy. He'd have no compunction calling up the President here at Andrews and try to get me fired…again."

Kelly Anne landed in a professionally and personally comfortable place, both a forum for her views and a platform for teaching the next generation about the vanity and excesses of the scientific community. Her shingle now hangs as the Director of the Institute of Archeology at Andrews University, a Christian college cozily nestled in a rural section along the St. Joseph River in Berrien Springs, Michigan.

Berrien Springs and the Oronoko Charter Township where Andrews University makes its home is an agriculture-based community where the norms and conventions of small town living create a sense of belonging and a fond attachment to its quaintly rustic surroundings. Berrien Springs, a postcard picture town of heartily designed brick buildings and wood trim, festooned with signs hailing such grand events as the Christmas Pickle Festival, provides a thoroughly bucolic and satisfying standard of living.

Andrews University is an institution owned and operated by the Seventh-Day Adventist Church. The Adventists espouse a fundamentalist view of Christianity along with a number of controversial theologies outside the mainstream of Christian thought. Particularly contentious is the Adventist belief in a Seventh-Day Sabbath as practiced in Jewish tradition. This view coupled with an Apocalyptic focus on the last days of the earth and a belief God's Remnant Church, in effect Adventists, will suffer persecution in the last days sparks controversy and confusion among other Christian sects. Andrews is an ideal home brew of theology and living for an iconoclast of the Kelly Anne Carter variety.

Theology dominates the Andrews curriculum, representing an important aspect in Kelly Anne's career selection. Her qualifications would place her in most any academic institution or think tank in the world if she could bring herself to suffer fools lightly. Or, she could return to a dynamic and profitable medical practice but money is no longer an issue as her books generate quite enough for considerable creature comforts. Kelly Anne chose the environment of a theological seminary so she can openly teach archeology, science and history from a religious perspective.

Kelly Anne was raised in Loma Linda, California, a city founded by Adventists. All her life she worshipped on Saturday and studied her Bible daily until she memorized the entire tome, chapter and verse…testaments old and new. Her parents are Adventists, her father a prominent Adventist geologist whose discoveries uncovered truths tending to support a Biblical interpretation of history. Andrews feels like home.

One of Kelly Anne's stumbling blocks with the worldwide scientific community is her deep abiding faith in the existence of a God, an omnipotent creator of all living things, and for that matter the entire Universe. She often wonders whether her colleagues are most offended by her fiery iconoclastic nature or her unflinching Christian beliefs. Either way, the closed-minded fellowship freezes her out, ostracizing her from science academia at every juncture.

Kelly Anne is not a stubborn person so much as a determined academic. She is a true believer and her faith unshakeable. This trait dominates her personality in all aspects of life, not limited to her religious views. To the academic world faith absent of reason is the essence of closed-mindedness. To Kelly Anne theories and conjectures in science, from belief in Evolution to women's so-called reproductive rights are themselves acts of faith absent of reason. Expressions of faith have caused her numerous problems within the academic community in the past. Most of her colleagues believe she is incapable of understanding reason…the reason of science. For her part Kelly Anne believes those self-righteous colleagues fail to comprehend the obvious evidence and logic of grand design, a theory of programmed intelligence. Such professional adversity would destroy most mortals. For Kelly Anne it is the breath of life.

Kelly Anne is preparing a lecture for today's class as she sits comfortably in the warm surroundings of her generously windowed office in the Life Sciences building on the Andrews University campus. The school, founded by agriculturally minded Adventists, is rural and pastoral. The trees are in spring bloom the winter snows gone and the mighty St. Joe flows gently in the background.

"Why is it every time the weather gets a little warm someone comes out with a gloom and doom study, supposedly researched for years, assuring us the world is going up in flames?" Kelly Anne asks herself. "For years all the top scientists followed each other around with papers informing everyone of the impending onset of a new ice age caused by Mankind and, of course, curable by Mankind. Now we get these obviously overstated scholarly studies warning us the world is warming at an alarming rate and, of course, its all caused by Mankind and we only have ten years to do anything about it. Tomorrow I'll read something in the *New York Times* quoting this study. A couple of months later I'll read a science journal quoting the *Times* and then another paper quoting the science journal, all without a single objective quote from an outside party. Why don't they ever call me? I'll give them something to get hot about."

"The media has an axe to grind about climate change. It makes no difference what direction the science community picks to rampage over…if the story is breathless enough it will get ink or TV time. Over the last hundred years science mouthpieces in newspapers and television news programs have warned us of an impending global doom, they just can't decide whether we'll all die from the spine shivering cold or the skin blistering heat."

"Now, ahem, a learned scholar from NASA's Goddard Institute for Space Studies tells us we've reached a period of time hotter than 12,000 years ago. And if we don't quit driving SUVs he thinks we'll break a million year old record. Well he conveniently forgets 1930 is still the hottest year on record, and we're not getting anywhere near the record this year."

"Hmm, and it looks as if his data is spliced together from different areas of the globe and posted at different times. That pitchfork won't poke. Now he says we have ten years to fix the problem or the chance for reversal is toast, uh, so to speak. Ten years? Why not five or twenty or 180.5? This isn't science its secular religious orthodoxy pure and simple. The media eats it up. Sells papers I guess!"

Upon a thorough review of the data tossed into the 'latest groundbreaking study' feebly conducted by a guy from NASA Kelly Anne prepares for today's lecture with a renewed sense of purpose, armed with the knowledge that once again the Chicken Littles of climate change are wrong. "Looks like I won't have to burn in Hell until I'm good and ready," she clucks to herself on her way to the lecture auditorium.

9

The lecture-style classroom easily fits 200 hundred students in its stadium style seating. The walls are beige, covered in wallpaper in a burlap pattern. The ceiling of the room is high, almost lofty, and lends the space gravitas.

The lectern is situated in the front at the bottom as if the speaker were in the Roman Coliseum, fed to the lions. In this lecture hall every angle and view of the room is focused singularly toward the speaker.

A good percentage of teachers prefer the informal atmosphere of a typical classroom. Although the grand lecture hall intimidates some, Kelly Anne is in her element. In front, in charge and with all eyes and minds trained solely on her lecture.

Through a modified Socratic teaching style the class debates Kelly Anne's initial arguments. She parry's one question with humor and fends off another with raw data. She is in command of the material and knows the facts are piercing through the haze of the media-science juggernaut.

As Kelly Anne fields a question about the qualifications of a certain ne'er-do-well scientist, a pair of sharply-dressed people, a man and a woman, enter from the rear of the lecture hall. They appear serious with a determined gait.

The pair makes no announcement to the class, nor is there any sort of fanfare. A badge is shown, her cell phone confiscated and Kelly Anne is lead quietly away to the stunned expressions of students. She has no idea why she is summoned but is thrilled by the sensations of a sinking wariness as well as an excited anticipation her entire universe is about to change.

Kelly Anne walks the long hallway, arms akimbo with the silently grim agents and ponders her fate.

"Are these the Global Warming Police?"

10

The White House Situation Room
Washington, D.C.

President Crandall is devoid of expectations upon the return of the Cabinet and agency heads from a brief lunch. He foresees scant possibility of a refreshed crew happily fulfilling duties with renewed energy. The mortifying scenes they endured at the morning session were grizzly and horrific. As he sits and ponders the morning activities the President is, quite frankly, surprised no one resigned during lunch. But they remain on duty, all of them, faces grim and weary, clothes disheveled and unkempt, attitudes uneasy but resolute. A cloud of despair hangs like a curtain of darkness over the room full of sullen politicians.

New Presidential administrations enter office on the heels of adulation and excitement. Inevitably an issue or crisis reveals a monstrous inhuman face. As if the Fates decide an electoral honeymoon has run its course and the new untested team is due for a political or diplomatic challenge to get the party started in earnest.

Unprepared or unqualified teams may meet with disastrous results while an experienced group handles the crisis and comes through with minimal damage. The opposite is also true on occasion. The John F. Kennedy administration faced the Bay of Pigs crisis, an operation handed over from the Eisenhower Administration. The new Kennedy team, touted in the campaign as the Best and the Brightest met with defeat. To his credit President Kennedy took full responsibility on his own tired shoulders.

President Reagan took over the Iranian Hostage Crisis from the Carter Administration but never had to work the crisis from the Situation Room as the Iranians, in abject fear of the cowboy perception surrounding *Ronnie Ray-Gun,* released the hostages immediately upon the President's taking the oath of office.

George W. Bush's administration used the Situation Room during crisis when the Chinese Government took an entire American C-130 aircrew hostage as 'spies' after one of their fighter jet pilots recklessly crashed into them. Experienced diplomacy brought the crew home safely.

The Situation Room is designed to help the Chief Executive protect the country in time of crisis of the sort the Crandall administration now finds itself firmly embroiled. But no one has the slightest clue if the team is ready to match the lore of the room.

President Crandall is faced with the first crisis of his fresh Administration and he is unsure whether this group or any other can handle the delicate diplomacy and political maneuvering necessary to solve the crisis to a satisfactory resolution. There are no other options, this group, a new team barely assembled will make a stand here and now.

The new Secretary of State, Merton M. Malloy III, a jauntily humorous overweight man everyone calls 'Marty' sets the table of discussion arguing for a scientific mission, a strike-team of sorts, assembled from some of the brightest minds in the fields of archeology, genetics, high-technology and linguistics. The Secretary argues this point as if M.I.T. had a special-forces division within its ranks.

"Marty I just don't think that we'll be able to find and create a Delta Force out engineering professors and science geeks," offers Dan Maney, having cooled down over lunch. "I'm not sure we could field a badminton team out that type of expert. Nothing against them, these kinds of people are brilliant I grant you but to go in like gangbusters and secure sensitive technologies, in full battle gear, all with the Syrian Army and bands of wild Jihadis breathing down their necks? That's never gonna work. This is a job for soldiers, fighting men familiar with the sound of gunfire."

Malloy fully appreciates Maney's characterizations of armed geek squads but presses the idea further. "First of all we don't know Syrian Army personnel are the belligerents who attacked our soldiers this morning. We just sent ten thousand fresh Marines from the Green Zone up there so a good size force is on site to protect the area. Dan I'm not talkin' about some science professor you may have played badminton with in college. I'm thinking along the lines of a team composed of brilliant scientists with military experience or athletically inclined."

Secretary Green-Newton firmly believes her military can effectively conduct any type of operation in the field and questions the need for scientists. "Why is brilliance a determinative factor in who we send down there? All they have to do is find and secure technologies that are a possible danger to the world and us, right?"

Malloy disagrees profusely. "No Graziella, you're not quite accurate. They are charged with identifying potentially dangerous technologies first and then secure them or get them out of there. Stated in those terms the task seems simple but I doubt we're dealing with simplicity. Let's say we sent you down there. As Secretary of Defense I'm sure you could spot a missile or a nuclear reactor or perhaps a store of biological weapons. But we're not necessarily looking for things of that nature. To put this in perspective, given the age of the structures in this chasm, we don't know what to expect so there's no way to tell if an object or substance is benign or dangerous or nothing at all."

"So we're looking at the sort of people who can divine an object and infer its properties instantly or at least fairly quickly."

"What about the Islamic side of the equation?" poses Director Heatherton. "How are we going to get this aspect of the matrix secure and on board with sending a team of science experts into a sphere refuting Islam or any religion? How are we going to get them to sign on Marty?"

Malloy is prepared for such concerns. "Islam isn't a nation Patsy. I highly doubt we'll have any chance of getting a cleric or a group of clerics to jump on board anything that might upset the carefully crafted history of Islam. In fact we can't so much as let a whisper of this discovery out in the Islamic *ummah*...not if we value the lives of our soldiers and scientists and their families. Do you want the short answer? We're not gonna tell 'em."

Heatherton is thoroughly un-impressed. "Oh-ho no, we're not contemplating a massive cover-up are we? We can't cart off technologies hidden under the ground owned by a sovereign nation, can we? Please tell me the Secretary of State of the United States of America isn't offering such a perverse strategy!"

Malloy is incensed by the Homeland Security Director's inferences. "C'mon Patsy give it a rest! I remind you again, Islam is not a sovereign a nation. Iraq is a sovereign nation. It's also free and democratic. Over Lunch I hit the phones and secured an agreement with the Iraqi government, from President Adjani himself. These discussions included the Iraqi Defense and Foreign Ministers."

"They absolutely agree we need to send a scientific team of people down there to see what's what and to make certain the enemy doesn't get its hands on anything. They have a couple of requests though. The Iraqis want a couple of their own scientists to tag along and they are absolutely insistent no military force of any size goes in the Well. They're already miffed we sent ten thousand soldiers up there in the first place, though they understood why after I relayed the events of the morning."

The idea of a science geek squad makes Dan Maney restless and uneasy and he address his concerns with the Secretary of Defense. "What do you think Secretary Green-Newton? Do you see our boys standing out on the perimeter while we send a gaggle of science geeks out into a war zone? Is this the role of our military in the field? And what happens if the geeks come under attack down in the hole? Do we go down there and rescue them or watch them get slaughtered?"

The Secretary of Defense is uneasy with an impotent mission too. "My first inclination is to say no way in hell can we allow this. Our Marines are highly effective at getting the job done. We in fact do have an archeology and history contingent within the Corps. You may recall we used them in re-securing myriad priceless historical artifacts stolen from the Iraqi Museum after the invasion."

"What about sending a recon group in with some of our own military science geeks? They're smart and they can fight their way out of a jam if necessary."

Director Heatherton agrees with the Defense Secretary, her discomforting shrill voice piercing through the room, startling everyone. "Secretary Green-Newton's idea sounds like a reasonable compromise to me. This way we have experts from the military that are also equipped to fight and they're protected by ten thousand battle ready Marines on the perimeter. At least we won't have to worry about holding the hand of a timid scientist under mortar fire."

Chief of Staff Lamont had about as much as he could stand of the mini-turf battle. "The military scientists aren't equipped for this type of mission, point blank. This discovery and its attendant contents have the potential to upset the world order. Such considerations go far beyond the crassness of politics and in many aspects is a greater issue than even national security. We have no idea what we'll find down there but we need the sort of people who can interpret what they see."

"I don't expect they'll find signs in English pointing the way to the local nuclear weapons factory and I'm fairly certain the symbols and nomenclature on weapons or technologies will not resemble anything we or our scientists have ever seen or even so much as contemplated seriously. We need theoretical scientists, those who don't follow the rules."

"Our perfect candidate bucks trends and thinks way outside the box. Military people are specifically trained to stay in a box and follow orders. We don't want submissiveness on this mission."

Lamont's suggestion brings Malloy to his feet. "Absolutely correct Gene, absolutely correct! I was thinking of gathering the top scientists in their respective fields but you struck a nerve with me Gene and I'm coming around to your way of thinking. We need the guys who don't get the great peer reviews and they may not look so hot on paper but they're willing to ask the tough questions and determine what they see based on their own lyin' eyes instead of a preconceived notion rubber-stamped by the scientific community."

"We're also looking for the type who won't let you hold their hands during a dust up," reminds Maney.

"Indeed," Green-Newton nods her head.

• • •

"Mr. President we have President Adjani coming up on screen," a gasping aide informs the President as he rushes into the room. "He's set up at his office in Baghdad."

"Mr. President, how are you today?" President Crandall greets his counterpart cheerfully.

"I am not well Mr. President," replies President Adjani with a sour glare. "I understand you are planning a military exercise on our sovereign lands without permission from my government. I am seeking an explanation directly from you as

I am certain you fully understand the implications of the grave situation you are in."

Crandall sits quietly, shocked by Adjani's inferences but maintains a cool exterior. "What are you referring to Mr. President?"

"Please don't toy with me Mr. President!" Adjani gestures, menacingly, wagging his finger toward the camera. "I am well aware of the archeological discovery and the thousands of Marines you sent to guard its perimeter. Are you planning to loot my country of its rightful treasures?"

"Of course not." Crandall stares toward the monitor with a blank poker-faced expression. "I understood we had cleared a scientific mission with your government. We sent the Marines up there to reinforce a platoon of ours that came under attack."

The angry Iraqi President gesticulates wildly, shouting his responses. "Came under attack? Attacked by what army? Iraqis have no forces in the region and we've not experienced an insurgent attack in over a year. Are you claiming peaceful Iraqi citizens attacked your soldiers with table knives?"

Crandall is irritated but has difficulty stifling a laugh as he casts a disturbed glance toward Secretary Malloy. "No. The attackers wore Syrian Army uniforms but we don't know they are actually Syrian soldiers. Quite frankly we don't know who or what they are. Nor do we have any idea as to their motives or intentions."

Adjani, visibly angry offers a list of requirements. "Mr. President I am demanding your soldiers leave the area immediately and without further provocation! We will not tolerate the theft of Iraq's treasures from sovereign lands. A failure to leave the area immediately will result in an unfortunate development. The United States is not our master. You are ordered to leave the area now!"

As President Crandall sets his jaw to respond firmly the screen suddenly blinks to black. "Wha…What happened did we lose him?"

Maney chuckles under his breath as he answers. "No I think he, uh, hung up Sir."

Crandall's public game face evaporates as he explodes and lights into the Secretary of State. "Jesus, what the hell is going on here Marty? I thought we had an agreement on this thing! Now they want to chase us out with our tail between our legs? Well its not gonna happen Marty. What an embarrassment!"

The Secretary hangs his head in shame, thinks for a moment, lifts his head high and provides a defense. "We've been double-crossed Mr. President. The bastards set me up! They lied to me and they lied to you by proxy on the phone only an hour ago. The agreement was solid! I have no idea what went wrong in between the time I spoke to them and moments ago. They lied and apparently they're trying to cover something up or perhaps to improve their bargaining position. I am truly sorry Mr. President. I'm willing to take the blame but I can't vouch for lying bastards."

The richly deep gravelly voice of General Rory Broadhead, Chairman of the Joint Chiefs of Staff, overtakes the pleading whines of Secretary Malloy. "Ladies and Gentlemen, Mr. President, we need to understand the President of Iraq has just declared war on the United States of America. While it may not have been the intent of Adjani and his ministers the implications are clear. The leader of a sovereign nation has ordered our President to remove our soldiers from a theater of war without an armistice treaty. As his posturing is unclear we must treat him and his nation as an enemy with hostile intentions."

"I don't think it rises to the level of war," interjects Graham Likely, the Director of National Intelligence, "But the Iraqis have broken the treaty between our nations. The treaty calls for no threats made by the Iraq government against the American government or its armed forces. This much is clear and we're going to have to respond with lucid clarity. We don't want the Well Site Operation to escalate into war and must do whatever we can to back up despite our wounded pride."

Chastened and unnerved Secretary Malloy rushes to the anteroom and a bank of secure telephones. The pressure is mounting to work diplomatic and political magic. His country and his President count on him to do his job. He'd just been double-crossed and embarrassed by the Iraq Foreign Minister. It won't happen again, if there's one thing Marty Malloy knows its how to work the phones to get results. He digs into his work with bravado and confidence hoping for the best. In truth he needs a miracle.

The President is stunned by the latest developments but seeks to shift the subject and direction of the conversation. He turns away from politics and toward the scientific side of the situation at hand. "Bring in Doctor Kane. I want to put a scientific perspective on the problem. We'll continue to operate from the assumption we're sending in group or a team of some sort and our man Kane will lead out in recruiting the best minds available."

11

Dr. Gerald R. Kane, officially titled the President's Chief Science Advisor but unofficially respected as the sharpest mind since Isaac Newton, walks smoothly into the Situation Room. Educated at the Massachusetts Institute of Technology, earning his first doctorate in computer engineering at the tender age of eighteen, Dr. Kane commands respect from any group. His leadership during twelve years at NASA transformed the agency from a moribund bureaucracy to a fluid energetic leader of technology. His leadership in the Computer Science Lab at M.I.T. created an infrastructure ushering in a nascent Computer Revolution and the Information Revolution after that.

Dr. Kane moves comfortably among politicians having lobbied billions of dollars earmarked for computer science research and educational resources reaching every state in the country. He is a well-dressed tall and lean man with silver hair coiffed in the manner one expects from a news anchorman, a politician or businessman. His long hands and fingers offer cleanly trimmed nails. A firm grip built by glad-handing around Washington and piercing deep blue eyes give the immediate impression of a man in control of every molecule in the room. Today Dr. Kane wears a dark navy suit and a serious red stripe-patterned tie over a crisply starched white shirt. Upon entering the room the uninitiated would automatically assume he is the President.

The actual President introduces Dr. Kane as an official member of his inner circle. "As many of you know Dr. Kane is the Chief Science Advisor for the country and I think it's vital we share our ideas and recent experiences with him to gain some perspective on what we've been looking at all day. Gerry I know you've had a chance to study this thing. We've given you the aerials from the drones and shots from satellites and I believe you had a chance to look at the various action reports and we hope you've developed some answers for us. Tell us what you think this thing is and what we should do about it."

Dr. Kane, a one-time child prodigy, highly accomplished scientist, engineer and effective administrator clears his throat and remains standing to speak for effect.

"I don't know," He begins wisely.

"I have ideas about how to proceed but they are filled with my own biases and prejudices. My study of the pictures and reports proves to me we are standing at a precipice between one epoch of history and another. But the ledge we're on has no firm foundation. We may cast a glance one moment and see wondrous technologies never imagined in our own moment of history. A glance in the opposite direction reveals destruction on a massive scale so violent we cannot comprehend the resulting global upheaval. Is the discovery a treasure trove of human development, found just now to take us far beyond our own technologies or is it a gigantic Pandora's box leading to the elimination of Mankind?

"The scope and scale of the site provides no room for an answer in between the two extremes. We cannot know the answers without close exploration. Some would have us fill in the hole and forget we discovered anything. A comforting thought. Others seek to gather and exploit whatever technologies are found there. A disquieting notion. Neither option is acceptable. Humans are built to explore but somewhere inside the human heart lays the desire for destruction, killing and war, even self-elimination. Today I stand here and wonder which side of humanity we will feed."

"As a man of science I find an unexplored closure of the discovery unacceptable. As a God-believing human being, and yes I am a scientist who believes in God, I fear what we may find and how those new discoveries will affect our way of living life here on Earth. Will we find the Book of Genesis or the Book of Revelation or worse, something completely beyond our comprehension to which we have no guide whatsoever?"

Dr. Kane spreads an assortment of fresh photographs around the table for closer inspection. "Look here, look here, the pictures are remarkable. And I should tell you the shots are notable for what isn't there as much as what's shown. You can clearly see soaring spirals of an architecture never known. Obviously someone or something lived in these buildings, they're not monuments or obelisks. Oddly there are no doors or windows, no streets or signs."

"There are no markers of any kind. Except where chunks of dirt fell from our time this ancient city, buried for eons is excessively clean as if the entire area was hermetically sealed in a vacuum. What sort of technology makes this possible? Nothing we know of today. I stand utterly afraid of such advancements in physics without the context to fully understand them. And yet, the discovery is laid open for us at this moment in history. The immoral act is to deny humanity the discoveries leading to its own origins or predating them. We must explore, it is programmed in us."

"To this end I suggest the following. First we must recruit bright minds unfettered by scientific orthodoxy to competently explore this well filled with spires, this well of towers. We'll need to make certain they are a hardy lot. I can foresee numerous physical dangers in exploring an area this large. Additionally, there may exist easily misinterpreted religious texts or signs of the Gods that would seem to prove where humans received religious inspiration. And here it is, resting like a dagger through the very heart of Islam. Any misinterpretation of the evidence can force humanity to a worldwide calamity or a series of never ending wars. We need people who understand these issues and can speak to them effectively."

"Our expert team will hail from the fringes of the academy. Oh their resumes may read like applications to the science lunatic asylum but we know each has a solid foundation. I have in mind a certain type of expert for the exploratory strike force. Each team member is athletic and physically sound. They are bleeding-edge thinkers with the courage to take on established conventional wisdom. Indeed they relish a pursuit where every waking moment seems to challenge the powers of academia. We cannot afford to suffer slaves to the status quo. Due to circumstances this effort must remain covert. Indeed ladies and gentlemen, the Well's location and its neighbor's general disposition and eagerness to destroy any historical artifact not lending itself to an Islamic version of the world demands absolute secrecy."

"The possibilities are endless, but I can see we stand on the edge of discoveries as grand as all history compressed into a single cup, a time capsule of immense importance that can reveal our origins and stage the roadmap for humanity's future."

Dr. Kane quietly takes his seat as cabinet members and agencies heads consider everything from the meaning of life to the existence of God. Several want to go home and hug their kids.

"So where do we go from here Dr. Kane?" asks President Crandall.

"I have a list sir."

12

The ponderous silence of the Situation Room is broken with the breathless excited return of Secretary Malloy who runs pell-mell from his telephone command post to update the President on the latest diplomatic news.

"We have five days," he spouts out heavily, trying to compose him self. The Iraqis have agreed to a five day exploratory team complete with Marine protection on the perimeter."

An incredulous President, not wanting a repeat of the earlier embarrassment, steps gingerly into the breach. "Is the deal real this time? We most certainly don't want a re-run of the last episode Marty."

"Yes Mr. President this time its real. I called the Egyptian Ambassador who got in touch with a rebel group leader in Iran. He contacted his cousin in Baghdad who, as luck would have it, is the Foreign Minister's brother in law. Well, the brother in law's cousin just returned from what they called an expedition where they fought U.S. Marines to the death as they told it. Turns out the guy, a Syrian was at the site. This ran a huge red flag up the Foreign Minister's pole and he convinced Adjani that Iraq wasn't ready to go to war with Syria and its better to have ten thousand U.S. Marines out there at the moment so they're giving us five days to see what we can see. The Iraqi President is coming up on screen to confirm the plan right now."

"Good afternoon Mr. President," Adjani opens the discussion cheerfully, as if he hadn't declared war on the United States an hour ago. "It looks as if you're going to explore the site. We request two of our scientists join the mission and any treasures or artifacts remain on Iraqi soil. Other than these simple conditions you have carte blanche."

"Then we have an agreement Mr. President," Crandall responds diplomatically. "How are your wife and children?"

"They are doing wonderfully and thank you for asking. And how is your lovely First Lady?"

After an additional exchange of pleasantries the Presidents retire to their respective meeting groups, each confident of their own diplomatic skill. The Situation Room empties for a brief break before the task of managing the recruitment and assembly of the exploratory strike team.

Dan Maney ruminates over the day's events as he walks through the door. He can scarcely believe the diplomatic jiggety-jig danced by the two leaders. He shakes his head in earnest over the outright hubris of President Adjani, remarking out loud to no one in particular.

"I'd really like to kick that guy's ass!"

13

Naval Air Station Oceana
Virginia Beach, Virginia

A flight-weary unshaven scruffy Jake Nichols drifts off the tarmac in the hazy daze accumulated from hours of sleep deprivation, stressful worry and no idea as to one's own whereabouts. His cross-country flight featured a buffet of briefings and meetings with military personnel, government bureaucrats and spooks of all stripes. No alcohol is served aboard military transports like the C-130 ferrying him from coast to coast. His glazed eyes and dazed countenance is likely due to a hangover without the requisite medicinal hairs of the dog to slake his thirst.

Still attired in his unemployed beach-bum gear Jake, scratching a rough stubbly cheek, feels somewhat out of place among the suited spooks and uniformed military personnel running about feverishly. Feeling out of place isn't an unusual sensation for Jake Nichols, nor is he terribly aggrieved by the brief bout of self-awareness. Back in the day he'd been a Navy SEAL commander operating with a squad of efficient covert killing machines in the Gulf War. He knows the drill and wants no part of the tied down, life sucking choking hazard disguising itself as military regulations. In fact he'd developed quite a claustrophobic reaction to the tight assed military box. He is glad, no, in fact proud he is dressed in casual garb, even if he reeks from two days of swilling Dewars in the hot California sun.

Jake is free to move around and do pretty much whatever he wants for a few moments but wishes he could take a shower and put on some fresh clothes before meeting the top brass. He objects to the manner in which the government swooped in and took him from the comfort of his bar stool, led away by stern government agents. After his thorough briefing he changed his mind and thought perhaps he wouldn't want anyone knowing what's going down. The world may not be ready to get turned upside down like a flapjack.

"Maybe I've got a bit of motivation now to push on with this wasted life," Jake think to himself with a large dose of self-pity. "That is, if sitting on the edge of a government issue card table in an airplane hangar at a Naval base in God knows where is much reason to go on living."

"I'm not even wearing skivvies." Jake chuckles at his predicament, remembering the barely stifled grin on the face of a serious female agent who conducted a pat-down search as he boarded the airplane back in California. "At least the story should get me laid somewhere, sometime."

As Jake sits and thinks over the possibilities of his general location a random idea occurs to him. "Its possible I'm stuck in a freakish nightmare of a dream or part of a secret government plot to pick up former military people who act like homeless hippies. Nah, it's probably just the Dewars talking. Feels like the South here. Pitch black out and I'm sweating like I just ate a bottle of peppers. You only get humidity like this in South. Not too far south though like Miami or Atlanta. We must be in Norfolk. I know it's a Navy base, I can tell by the F/A-18 Hornets in the hangar. You only need tail hooks on birds that fly from carriers. They're Navy all right, look at the swabbies runnin' around with those silly caps. Never understood why the brass would make 'em wear those gay little teacup hats. We're probably at the Oceana in Virginia. I'm sure they think nobody knows we're here. What a crock! Big C-130 lands in the dead of night. The local rags probably have reporters waiting outside for C-130s to arrive in the dead of night. Late night reporters are probably too sauced to notice anything. Hell it all sounds like a bad movie plot. Government people are dumb as earwax."

The distinctive THWUP-THWUP sound of a Sikorsky VH-3D Executive Transport Helicopter, widely used by the Marine Corps, fills the air. Jake examines the craft landing on the tarmac. "Sounds like a Sea King coming in. I wonder what kind of stuffed shirt will step out of there and ruin my life further? That's the kind of bird they fly the President around in so whoever is on this one is important. Maybe the Secretary of State or the Director of the CIA. Could be they're delivering pizza to the top brass."

Appearing every bit official as Marine One, the President's short distance transportation, the helicopter lands just outside the hangar where Jake sits pondering the meaning of reality versus fantasy. Through the portico and on to the ladder steps an annoyingly perky woman who looks thrilled to have ridden in a helicopter for the first time. Her brown locks are swept back in a pony-tail revealing flushed cheeks, a bright engaging smile and beautifully alluring aqua eyes the color of the sea on the coasts of Tahiti. Jake recognizes her right away. "Aw hell, I'll never get laid on this trip!"

Government agents 'procured' Kelly Anne Carter in the middle of her Global Warming Refutation lecture to a science class at Andrews University. Now she's here in Virginia set to embark on an important mission. Kelly Anne's fresh and comfortable appearance contrasts markedly with Jake's pungently aromatic presence. And though her unexpected journey, long and arduous, leaves her tired and worn, a natural irrepressibility displays a woman glowing with energy. During one of the many stops and flight changes Kelly Anne borrowed a flight jacket from a male pilot obviously quite taken with her. This she wore over her usual pantsuit get-up, dark pleated slacks with legs slimming to the ankle. She feels her way down the ladder steps with her one sartorial indulgence, a pair of Bruno Frisoni black satin lace-up platform sandals bought at Neiman-Marcus.

The heels of her shoes clack on the hard concrete surface of the hangar as she approaches the out of place beach bum clinging desperately to the edge of a table. Gene Lamont, the President's Chief of Staff follows eagerly in tow.

Kelly Anne walks straight to Jake and immediately tears into his jugular slicing through flesh and bone with a low sultry voice dripping in sarcasm.

"What happened sailor, did they find you rummaging for lunch in the dumpster out behind Harry's? I was under the impression the CIA was forbidden to work with unsavory characters. Guess Congress changed the rule after 911, pity. You smell like you spent the night in a drunk-tank. Did you get another DUI or are you playing the role of embarrassing drunk at the party?"

Jake looks passively away, his head nodding in a bobble-head sort of way.

"You two know each other?" asks Lamont, surprised and somewhat amused.

"Well you never really know someone do you Jake Nichols?" Kelly Anne stares intently her eyes piercing Jake's soul.

"Hello Kayann, how the hell are ya?" Jake, peers at her from the side of his eye, head bowed ashamed, barely stifling a burp.

The Chief of Staff to the President of the most powerful nation on earth stands in a Virginia-humid aircraft hangar watching helplessly as the two main elements of the most vital mission of the millennium, perhaps in all history, banter and joust in the manner of spurned teenagers. He can barely keep from laughing out loud.

Lamont leads the antagonists to a squadron ready-room for introductions to the rest of the scientific exploration team and the top brass, wondering out loud if the government stepped into a large pile of horse crap on this mission.

14

Jake practically lived in air squadron ready-rooms during his tours in the Navy. Even now the mission maps and theater of war seating, with a Navy-issue gray metal lectern at the front, ready for a squad commander to impart a deadly mission into exotic and sometimes primitive places thrills his heart. The finest moments of Jake's life, the camaraderie of shipmates and the anticipation of dangerous adventure, started with orders given in ready-rooms like the one they're entering.

This particular ready-room, one of hundreds on a flight base the size of Oceana is home to Strike Fighter Squadron 151, the Fighting Vigilantes. Flight squadrons move around a great deal to fulfill military missions. The 151 Squadron is attached to the USS Dwight D. Eisenhower a Nimitz-class Super-carrier and is currently deployed. The ready-room is empty and inactive. An administrative skeleton crew from the 151 remains stationed at the base to coordinate logistics and family relations. At any time the ready-room, hangars and administrative offices are occupied by various Strike Force Squadrons, deployed to Oceana for six months or a year and then shipped off to another base or to sea on a carrier.

"Man this brings me back," marvels Jake as he enters the ready room. "The fighting Vigilantes, those flyboys always have a macho 'we mean business' name. I guess so the enemy knows they're coming to kill them. At North Island we had the Gunslingers and the Rough Riders. Don't think I'd want to get into a dogfight with a Rough Rider. The ghost of Teddy Roosevelt would burn me down."

Fighter squadron ready-rooms force the senses to high alert and prepares the mind and attitude for battle. Perfectly appropriate for a scientific exploration team about to venture into the dark abyss of politics, religion and a shooting war.

Seated together in close-quarters at the front of the room are two men, apparently of widely diverse backgrounds. They chat animatedly in excited, nearly quixotic tones. The fluorescent lighting, although bright, casts a whitish haze about the room and conveys the impression of a basement poker game lasting into the wee hours of the morning. The plain government-issue wall-clock reads 8 o'clock though it seems to Jake like two or three in the morning.

Gene Lamont sets about introducing the fresh recruits to each other, although an additional one will arrive later. "Folks, I just want all of you to get a chance to meet each other before we go into the lion's den. You'll meet with the Joint Chiefs of Staff, the Vice-President, the Secretary of State, the Secretary of Defense, the President's National Security Advisor, the Director of National Security among other high-powered notables. I want to introduce you as a team ready to tackle the mission at hand. Hopefully you can get comfortable with each other in the next half hour or so while we work to get everyone together."

Lamont's audience is dazed but expectant although none are particularly impressed by the list of top brass they are to meet. "To start off I'd like you to meet the lead element of this mission, Commander Jackson Nichols. His file details a distinguished military record as the Commander of Seal Team 5 out of Coronado, California. Prior to assuming command of the unit he worked in the field as a weapons specialist. His missions and decorations are too numerous to mention this evening but Jake has no trouble getting free drinks down at the VFW."

"Upon leaving the Navy Jake pursued a life of quiet academia returning to his native Texas to build a career as a professor at his alma mater the University of Texas. Not content to rest on his laurels he produced a television show called *Jackson Nichols' Big Dig*, traveling the world uncovering new excavations at archeological sites. Yes, he's that Jake Nichols. Lately he's settled down and teaches, uh, gives, well, uh instructs in private scuba diving lessons."

The hung over ill-dressed tub of guts standing before the group doesn't immediately create an impression matching the resume…with the exception of his latest line of employment.

"If I'd had some warning I'd have cleaned up a bit," thinks Jake, ashamed of his appearance and wondering how he looks to this button-down crowd. "I certainly wouldn't take direction from a yahoo like me, there's no reason they should. If any of them do listen to me I'll immediately question their judgement. I already have grave reservations about the government selecting me for this mission. What are they thinking? That's government, I always have serious reservations about the bureaucratic decision-making process."

Lamont introduces Kelly Anne affectionately. "This striking young woman to my left is Dr. Kelly Anne Carter. Currently she's the Director of the Institute of Archeology at Andrews University, though you may know her better from her many bestselling books on the subjects of ancient civilizations and interpretations of Biblical history. Dr. Carter is a Medical Doctor who has worked in trauma centers and emergency rooms as well as medical missions to the jungles in South America and Africa and dangerous hot spots in and around the Middle East. If you've ever heard one of her lectures then you know she can tip a few apple carts in the scientific community. And I probably don't need to tell you that she's a dynamic hard charger who won't quit. Well, you'll find this out for yourselves soon enough."

"At least he didn't call me a spunky little gal," thinks Kelly Anne. "I don't know if my new colleagues need to hear I'm a hard charger. Usually hard charger translates to bitch. I don't mind living up to expectations but overcoming all of the problems we're going to experience is a difficult enough proposition without having to exorcise the bitch perception. Why did they get Jake for this mission? My God he's a drunk! He looks like a wreck, not the tall tan and lean-muscled debonair Commander with the wide white smile I once new. And he stinks! I can barely breath."

The Chief of Staff continues his introductions. "Dr. Kagen please stand if you will. This is Dr. Darren Eugene Kagen a geneticist from the Massachusetts Institute of Technology. He's a world-renown expert in human development and sociology. Dr. Kagen attended Oxford University as a Rhodes Scholar, earning a PhD in Sociology. At M.I.T. he earned another PhD in Genetics. He won a Nobel Prize for his research and work in the Genetics field and is the author of the leading textbooks on the subject. The brilliant doctor will be the first to tell you he comes from humble roots, born in the slums of Watts, California and worked his way out of poverty by selling magazines over the telephone. Dr. Kagen is by far the most accomplished genetics research specialist in the world and a great addition to our team."

"Why do they always have to mention my humble beginnings," Dr. Kagen asks him self, brow furrowed and shoulders hunched. "Every time I get involved with a matter of scholarship or anything needing half a brain they always have to put me down in the ghetto with all of the stuff about selling magazines to get out of the poor house. These people probably think I got my scholarships because I'm black and I was poor. Well I was poor and I am black but I'm smart too and by the time this thing is over they'll all know it. Why did they get a smelly bum like that Jake Nichols to run this outfit? Scuba diving lessons? Lord Almighty, scuba diving lessons?

"Please be seated Doctor," Lamont directs as he finishes his introductions. "This rather large lad standing here is Kenneth Orbeson Gyllenhal. You've probably never heard of Kenny, in fact I'm certain you haven't. He doesn't hold a single PhD; in fact I don't believe he has any college degrees at all. To look at him you may wonder why he's along for the ride, what with all of those tattoos on his beefy arms and that mop of a hair-do. You might think we're sending him along for protection as your personal bouncer."

"But this is a case where you can't judge the book by its biker-gang cover. This man is an expert linguist. He speaks at least twelve languages fluently but speaking them isn't the most useful part of his talents. You see he's a virtual walking Rosetta stone. Symbols, written languages, Sanskrit, Cuneiform, Egyptian Hieroglyphs, whatever, if he sees it he can parse the meaning as if by magic. His brain is a language computer and can recognize patterns in speech and writings on the fly. We've had him stashed over at the National Security Agency in the Central Security Service working on sophisticated cryptology software to decode and translate the correspondence of our enemies in the War on Terror. His work is invaluable to the nation's security."

"Just another bunch of suits," complains Kenneth to himself. "They seem so arrogant and snotty. These kinds of people never know anything. When I started at the NSA not a single agent could reliably translate Farsi. Farsi! It's a language that's been around for thousands of years. The Iranians became our enemies when they overthrew the Shah and took our embassy workers hostage."

"You'd think one of those brainy bastards in Armani suits at the CIA or NSA would get a clue and hire someone to translate the language, but no. Even after 911 we didn't have near enough Arabic translators. Arabic speaking terrorists attacked us for over thirty years and we have no Arabic linguists? Idiots. When I think of the millions of documents from Saddam's Secret Service still left in boxes and untouched it wounds me. I don't like these people at all. About the only person I think I might get along with is the guy in the beach shorts. I should have worn shorts to this gig."

• • •

The meeting of the newly formed council starts, Vice-President Katherine Prescott Murcheson presiding over the briefing and President Crandall connected via a secure satellite uplink. Team members file into the briefing room, a gray conference room with wax polished white linoleum flooring, steel furniture, electronic equipment reminiscent of the Truman era scattered about and an aged water cooler. An enlisted man is preparing coffee that seems to take on a life of its own like a woolly mammoth rising out of a tar pit. Enlisted personnel are explicitly instructed not to use soap to wash the coffee percolators at military installations…ruins the kick from built up coffee oils.

Non-essential personnel depart the room as the acrid smell of syrupy military-issue joe wafts through the air. Vice-President Murcheson asks those present to take their seats and proceeds around the table introducing each member of the exploration team as well as the support members. A crisp rap on the door followed by a brief conversation with the Vice-President's aid, Phil Lawson, briefly interrupts the proceedings. As Lawson leaves a smart looking youngish woman with quick alert movements walks in, eyes scanning the room like a protective mother lion at the entrance of a cave. At first glance she reminds Jake of a world-class gymnast or one well past her prime, probably about 28 years old.

"Everyone, allow me to introduce the team's technology captain, Ms. Tasha Hicks," Vice-President Murcheson proudly announces. "She is a top graduate of Stanford University. Her professional career includes groundbreaking work at the Lawrence Livermore Laboratories in California working with Blue Gene/L the world's most powerful computer. I should note Ms. Hicks has a good deal of familiarity with the United States Patent Office as she holds patents for numerous inventions. Even the latest packet data encryption systems we use in our cell phones spring from her mind. Please have a seat Ms. Hicks and we'll continue with the briefing."

"This is quite a group," muses Tasha to herself. "Everyone looks so serious and tired. Heck I'm tired why shouldn't everyone else be tired too. Its days like these I'm glad I refused to take my friends' advice and get a piercing or two. The grouchy General over there would have a cow and make a big deal out a few extra holes in my head, or my lip. Then I'd be forced to ruin his credit or I'd hack into the Pentagon database and erase all of the records of those ribbons on his chest. Oh-ho I'd love to see the headlines on that story and what a scandal! I hope the team I'm joining isn't too stuck up and conforming. That's why I left the lab, too many rules. How'd a guy with a Hawaiian shirt get in a tight ass meeting like this? He doesn't look like he plays by the rules. What is that odor? Coffee and what exactly, rum punch?"

15

Tasha McTierney Hicks graduated Summa Cum Laude from Stanford's Engineering School in two disciplines, Computer Science and Mechanical Engineering. She originally made a name for herself as an accomplished track and field athlete on a full-boat Title IX scholarship at Stanford. Her world record in the 5,000-meter distance race stands to this day. As a woman in the engineering program and bona fides as a jockette with short red boy-cut locks and a lithe athletic body she attracted the attention of many men and on occasion a few misunderstandings with the lesbian crowd. Tasha always performed at the top of her class in math, physics, geometry or anything having to do with building something. She invented a suite of new processes enabling secure wireless communications while at Lawrence Livermore and holds several U.S. and international patents on her inventions. Tasha's best developed talent is the ability to construct useful devices out of nothing, utilizing technologies in ways no one ever considered.

This is an aptitude passed down from her father who as a theoretical scientist at the old Xerox Palo Alto Research Center in Santa Clara, California devised reference specifications for new technologies eventually making their way into the marketplace as new norms for computing.

The Vice President opened the briefing in serious tones. "As all of you now know we are about to embark on the gravest of missions for our country and all of humanity. From our present vantage point it is impossible to know if we can succeed, indeed, we have no idea what success looks like. The Iraqi government has given us five days to explore an archeological discovery near Al Habariya out in the Syrian Desert."

"Five days isn't long, including travel from here. Normally a trip to Iraq might take several days but we're going to transport the team overnight via a long-range black operations airplane."

"You and your equipment will leave Virginia in exactly two hours flying straight through to Baghdad on a specially outfitted 747 transport. Upon arrival at Baghdad International Airport you'll meet with a military liaison along with a pool reporter and cameraman. They'll escort you to the Iraq Green Zone via transport truck and from there you'll engage the remainder of your team…two Iraqi scientists. Are there any questions so far?"

"I have a few minor questions." Jake raises his hand and proceeds to ask without acknowledgement. "When did we start using 747s for black ops flights? And why don't we simply fly from Baghdad International directly to the Site instead of traveling through dangerous Iraqi neighborhoods on a transport truck? And why are taking Iraq scientists on this little outing?"

General Peter Hayden the Air Force Chief of Staff addresses Jake's first question. "Of course the information about black ops planes is classified Commander Nichols but to let you know the government has a need from time to time to transport large groups and equipment around the world we don't want everyone and their mother to know about. For example we captured and imprisoned large numbers of terrorists and transported them to various locations around Eastern Europe for a time."

"And nobody knew the plane was black ops? How'd the government manage that?

"The black ops planes in question don't fly under U.S. government colors."

"You mean they fly under foreign flags?"

"Uh no, not exactly."

"Well what, exactly?"

"The bird you're riding to Iraq flies under corporate sponsorship…uh in a manner of speaking."

"Corporate sponsorship, what the…"

"FEDEX Jake, the bird is painted up like a FEDEX 747 freighter. The interior space is outfitted nearly the same as Air Force One."

"Oh."

Jake is uncomfortable with the scenario but worries about the safety of the mission. "What sort of equipment are we taking down in the Well Site General?"

"As far as equipment goes, well it's pretty thin I should say. We can't outfit the team with heavy mechanized equipment…impossible to cart heavy items down to the bottom. You'll be traveling light. The aerials don't show any roads or pathways for vehicles and such so you're mode of travel is a squadron of ATVs."

"We'll outfit them with the latest survival equipment and I think they'll get you around adequately. Then of course you have a full complement of state-of-the-art electronics and communications gear with night vision goggles, mobile computers and secure radios."

"What about weapons? You're not sending us down there holding our dicks are you?"

General Hayden knows the question is coming but never formulated a good response. "The Iraqis aren't letting the team take weapons down there, Jake. It's one of the main conditions of allowing us access in the first place and we're going to have to honor it."

"I don't know about the rest of the team but I'm quite uncomfortable going anywhere in Iraq without a weapon for self-defense. There are places in L.A. I don't venture into without a pistol. You want us to go into a war zone without so much as a Pez dispenser to protect ourselves?"

"It's unfortunate and I understand your concern."

"You understand my concern? General I think we're…"

At this point Kelly Anne seethes with apprehension. She coolly and confidently interrupts Jake to address General Hayden directly, staring straight into his resigned eyes. "We're putting our lives on the line for this country the same as any soldier. Is the United States government sending us into a battle zone like a platoon of Iranian teenagers armed with plastic keys to paradise draped around our necks? General I realize the ongoing debate about sending women into battle and I understand the argument but surely the President doesn't approve of sending women into a war zone unarmed. Would you send your daughter down a dark alley without a weapon?

Men of honor don't sacrifice principles to appease the vanities of tyrants. I know you're a man of honor General and so is the President. Perhaps we should re-think the issue and outfit the ATVs, not the team, with a light arsenal to protect the equipment. We can include a handgun as well as an M-16 rifle holstered on the side of each vehicle. I would recommend storing a cache of ammunition in the saddlebags of each ATV providing enough firepower to transport the ATVs, U.S. government property, back to where Marines are stationed safely on the perimeter. Surely the government has an interest in protecting its own equipment."

General Hayden is in unfamiliar territory. Dealing with disarmingly beautiful civilians on any level is not his bailiwick. He sits back in his chair in shock and glances at the monitor where President Crandall is enthusiastically nodding his head. The General knows Kelly Anne and the team has every right to self-defense despite Iraqi objections but international politics often confound points of honor. He admires Kelly Anne's nerve and thought process.

Despite his reservations the American government is going to send women into a battle zone, unarmed and without protection. To a hardened lifelong military man nothing is less honorable.

"Don't worry, we'll outfit the vehicles with the guns you mentioned…for their own protection or course."

"Of course."

"I'm wondering," Tasha queries, breaking the tension, "Has anybody detected EMP problems at the site? None of our computers will work with Electro-Magnetic Pulse issues. Nothing electrical will function if the magnetic fields are unstable in the area. Even the ATVs won't run. Has anyone checked this out?"

General Rory Broadhead addresses the issue. "At this point we've only checked for radiation and we're happy to report there is no detectable radiation outside the bounds of normal levels. But you're right Ms. Hicks an EMP spike could shut down everything. The problem with tracking EMP difficulties is we'd need to get gear down there to conduct the tests. Radiation is easy, it radiates but an EMP is a pulse and sporadic or spikes like a tripped fuse. So we can't test from above. We'll make certain you're outfitted with the copper shielded gear we use in the field now to protect against EMP weapons. And we'll shield the spark plugs on the transportation vehicles too."

"We only have a short time left before the team takes off," informs the Vice-President. "Jake you can talk to Phil Lawson about a shower and some fresh clothes. He's just outside the door in the office next to this room. Before we break the President's Chief Science Advisor, Doctor Kane has requested a few moments to address the team followed by a brief message from the President."

Dr. Kane stands up from his chair in the corner of the room and walks closer to the team who sits attentively waiting for wisdom from the famous scientist.

"In envy you," he starts, his sharp blue eyes piercing the envelope of air between them. "Oh how I envy you. We selected each of you for your attitude as much as your expertise. You are the iconoclasts in your field. You break down walls of orthodoxy and do your level best to share your thoughts and ideas with the world no matter how controversial."

"Each of you displays a personality trait transcending science. Despite years of education and work in the field you approach science in a childlike way with wide-eyed wonder and curiosity. You ask the tough questions and seek the right answers and never settle for status quo thinking. That is why you are here about to embark on a mission for the ages. I implore you to go out there with every fiber of your being and all the enthusiasm you can muster. And if I might say Godspeed."

The team sits quietly pondering the Doctor's words, each wondering if his statements reflect their true selves. Or is the wide-eyed wonder a product of make-up in the studio for Jake? Does energy and enthusiasm sell more books for Kelly Anne? Do Dr. Kagen's expressions of amazement mark a deep-seated resentment toward the world and its unfairness? Is Kenneth's passionate language work merely a way to put one over on the suits he disrespects? Is Tasha looking for respect more than discovery? The ponderous mood is broken by the cheery voice of the President of the United States.

"Good evening everyone!" The President fairly shouts through satellite uplink speakers. "Your little talk was very well put Doctor Kane and I thank you for your words. Jake, Kelly Anne, Darren, Tasha, Kenneth, you are a wonderful group of scientific soldiers. Your mission is dangerous and yet you choose to defend your country and support all Humankind. You are the cream of the crop as they say. The American people and I wish you great luck in this important endeavor. God bless you."

The tired and weary group standing at attention gives the only response possible under the circumstances, despite their collective hatred for bullshit.

"Thank you Mr. President," they answer in unison like a class full of kindergartners.

"Ladies and Gentlemen I officially introduce you to our science exploration team," the Vice-President announces, imploring the team to stand at the front of the room. "In honor of the location of the discovery and possible contents we christen our exceptional group of scientific explorers as Team Babelus!"

The official announcement breaks an icy tension bringing everyone in the room to their feet facing the team, clapping and cheering passionately, excited for the mission and its participants but not knowing whether they will return alive or dead, if at all.

The briefing dissipates and the team trundles off to prepare for a long flight to Iraq via the modified FEDEX freight plane.

Phil Lawson points Jake toward the men's locker room and a much needed scrubbing. "Now I really need a shower after all that syrup."

16

The Well of Towers
Near Al Habariya in Iraq's Syrian Desert
100 Miles West of the Euphrates River

"This place is no Heaven on Earth," remarks General Warren Keith, Head of American Operations in Iraq. "The landscape reminds me of those pictures the little NASA rover sent back from Mars a few years ago. Desolate, nothing alive and no sign anything ever has lived here, except in the big hole everybody's so hot to get a look at."

General Keith scans the area with the flinty-eyed gaze of a warrior inspecting the battlefield. The earth is dry and caked. There are no trees or shrubs. The Well of Towers is sunk roughly equal distant between the Euphrates River and Iraq's border with Saudi Arabia, 150 miles from anywhere or anything. No palm trees or streams or lakes catch the General's eye. The terrain is flat but not sandy.

The soil casts a rusty hue giving it a Mars-like surface. To the west is a small mountain range. Not mountains like those found in the Andes or the Rockies. This range is best described as a series of small rocky hills. The General is reminded of great wastelands of the earth where there are no resources to sustain much life. The Badlands of South Dakota come to mind, as does the Great Mohave Desert. The basic makeup of many places on earth contains this same terrain and appearance and yet the General can't take his mind off of the little roving robot sending back digital pictures of a desolate faraway land.

Earlier in the morning, at dawn, a Marine platoon came under small arms and mortar fire, attacked by a band of mysterious soldiers in Syrian uniforms. The platoon lost three men and suffered another twenty-four wounded. The platoon took no prisoners during the engagement and it is impossible to know if the attackers are Syrian soldiers or band of insurgents dressed to look like them. The Syrian border is approximately 300 miles to the northwest, its unlikely an authentic Syrian incursion would travel this deep into Iraq and openly attack an American military unit. After the attack they scattered toward the south and Marine patrols have not yet located any sign of them.

"I could stand here wondering who, what and why all day I suppose." The General mutters thoughts out loud to hear him self think. He wheels around and stalks off toward the HQ tent determined make certain the perimeter of the large hole is secured. "I don't want them coming back but if they do I wanna be ready for them."

General Keith walks into the communications tent, now re-established as a battle headquarters. As he enters through the open flaps a serious Marine, a Major denoted by the oak-leaf insignia on the lapel of his desert fatigues, stands at attention and salutes. The General returns the salute.

"Major Lee reporting Sir," the young Major speaks sharply in a Southern accent. "I am the advance element of a troop deployment due to arrive here at nineteen hundred hours."

"Is that my ten thousand men Major?"

"Yes Sir, complements of General Broadhead Sir."

"At ease Major, please take a seat. We need to discuss a few of the unique parameters of this particular, and I might add peculiar mission. What you may have gotten a look at flying in here is a giant hole in the ground outside this headquarters. I hope you haven't made any assumptions as we don't know anything or have any answers at this point. Our basic mission is to defend the perimeter of that gaping hole in the earth while a group of scientists from the States goes down there and gets a good look. We aren't to enter the area within the perimeter for any reason whatsoever. Just let the scientists do their job and then we get outta Dodge."

"Sounds a bit like a babysitting party Sir."

General Keith detects complacency in the young Major and snaps at him to get his undivided attention. "That's the same mistake your Marines made earlier this morning Major! Now we're burying three good soldiers and sent twenty-four wounded over to Ramstein to sit in a hospital bed wondering what happened to their arms and legs. The enemy who attacked us, with the President and his Cabinet looking on by satellite I should mention, remain on the loose and we don't have a clue as to where they are or even where they came from. Unfortunately we have no idea of the size of force or how well equipped they are. So what manner of firepower are you bringing to this babysittin' party Major?"

Major Lee is familiar with military mannerisms and fully understands the serious nature of General Keith's tone. "Sir I didn't mean to imply the situation isn't dangerous. When our fighting men are called upon to ferry dignitaries and politicians through Baghdad the soldiers are generally at the highest risk of getting hit with an IED or gunfire. We call them babysitting parties as we're not there to do anything but protect people from harm and we can only conduct those exercises from a defensive position. It is dangerous work but our Marines are highly effective at such operations."

Having got the Major's attention General Keith continues pressing for answers. "I understand Major. Sometimes we're called upon to do certain jobs that don't carry obvious glory. It's not like taking a hill or storming a beach, but we do it nonetheless and sometimes we die. So what are we bringing to this firefight?"

"As you know General the United States has drawn down forces for over six months. Most of the mechanized equipment is already out of country. As far as soldiers, well the bulk of what's available are Military Police types but they're well trained. Lt. General Patterson has cobbled together a few assets of the 1st Marine Expeditionary Force with the 3rd Marine Aircraft Wing and the 1st Marine Division. We don't have a lot of heavy armored vehicles but we will have air cover and a long-range patrol so perhaps we can spot where our mysterious enemy makes camp and neutralize them. I should add General there is a concern that all of this is a ruse to draw the better part of our forces out here in the middle of the desert, away from our re-supply, leaving both the contingent here and the Baghdad Green Zone vulnerable."

General Keith is impressed by the Major's attention to detail and fine manners. He converses with him as an equal. "Hmm," the One-Mef, that's a positive development. They've been here a long time and know the territory. I had not considered a ruse in the threat matrix but as I think about the possibility I tend to doubt it. The Iraqis are acting a bit more fussy about sovereignty and have rattled a few of their own sabers lately, at least since Mad Man Adjani took over as President. But I can't see any benefit to attacking an army already well on its way out the door, unless there's some public relations value with Arab communities. But this seems unlikely too. The so-called Arab Street gets outraged at the slightest provocation. The Iraqi's wouldn't need to shoot our soldiers in the butt as they scoot out the door to hype up the Street. The Iraqis aren't going to risk war with the U.S. to get a nice plug on Al-Jazeera either. We've got to consider the giant hole outside the tent. It's the size of a major American city and impossible to create out of thin air, not with the resources in post-war Iraq. It doesn't make sense the entire structure could be a set-up. Then again you never know when a fool might think he's got an opportunity. We better alert CENTCOM to the possibility."

As Major Lee starts to speak the rat-a-tat-tat of automatic weapons gunfire rings out…a hail of bullets in a cacophony of shouts and the ping-ping of slugs finding a target startles the two military men. They leap from their seats and dash into the hot desert sun, eyes squinting, they observe a small truck speeding directly toward the HQ tent. The compact truck, a civilian vehicle contains a driver and another man firing an automatic weapon while perched on the truck's roof.

Marines lay on the ground in a prone position feverishly firing at the oncoming vehicle seemingly impervious to the onslaught. As the mad dashing truck closes into fifty yards of the HQ tent Major Lee tackles the General to the ground in a cloud of red dust. The Marines fire a handheld rocket piercing the truck's engine compartment, exploding the vehicle and its cargo in a large fireball. The bulk of the wreckage lands barely sixty feet from the HQ tent with bits of shrapnel raining down on Major Lee who covers General Keith. Soldiers rush to the vehicle and pull away the suicide attacker. Badly burned and already dead the failed bomber wears the same Syrian military uniform as those in the dawn attack. The Marines search for the other attacker and find nothing but limbs and other body parts in varied places around the wreckage. A left leg, black boot firmly attached is located on the far side of the HQ tent. Cleary none of the attackers survived for questioning.

General Keith stands, dusts him self off and barks loudly into the air. "Somebody knows we're here and it's startin' to piss me the hell off! We're going to see more of this Major, mark my words, we're gonna see these pukes every way from Sunday! We better get our shit in one sock or this mission will never get off the ground. Who are these yokels and how the hell do they know we're out here in the middle of this God-forsaken desert doin' nothin' but holdin' on to our freakin' dicks!"

Keith turns to Lee with fire in his eyes. "Major, has there been any scuttlebutt on the streets in Baghdad about the cave-in? Did they run it on television or something? We discovered this thing ourselves by a drone flyover accidentally off course. There's nothing out here, no phones, no buildings or structures of any kind. How in the world do these jerk-offs know we're here?"

"We hadn't heard anything Sir. Until I flew up here and saw for myself I had no idea what the whole thing was about. CENTCOM told us nothing and there's no news report I know of suggesting anything at all. We thought there was a mild earthquake which isn't unusual around here and that's the whole story from our end. None of the informants or Iraqi soldiers knew anything about this, or at least it never came up. I don't know…a Bedouin with a cell-phone?"

"I think we can take care of the fighters Major. They're mysterious but aren't sophisticated militarily…more balls than brains ya know? I'm extremely worried about reporters getting wind of the giant hole in the ground out here. The last thing the mission needs in this toilet is a bunch of those un-flushable turds clogging the drain. You understand what I'm talking about here Major?"

"Yes Sir, I believe so. Keep journalists away!"

"You betcha. Once they start shooting film and taking notes we're in a heap of trouble. Suddenly the entire whole world will know our business out here and we'll get a million of these crazed suicide bombers coming to the site to get a shot at eternal life in Paradise. We can't have any of that Major. Oh sure, the reporters will scream to high heaven about the First Amendment and the people's right to know everything but we can't let them anywhere near this thing, you hear me?"

"Oh yes Sir, loud and clear."

"Major, we've been attacked twice in one day. If the attackers know we're out here then you can bet your ass CNN and the BBC and Fox News know too. The President asked us to defend the perimeter of this hole for five days, and we can, against people that shoot at us. But not journalists, no way, we're not allowed to shoot them!"

"General I think we should increase the perimeter. We'll patrol from the sky and try like hell to keep out anything that isn't U.S. military. If we spot one of those media wagons we'll surround and detain them. I just hope it's not Lorenzo, he gets through anything."

"Make sure none of them get shot Major. I don't want to get hauled before another Congressional inquiry."

As the two American soldiers stand in the shadows of a fading sunlight commiserating about the latest events the comforting sight and sound of an Apache helicopter squadron peeks over the eastern horizon.

17

Naval Air Station Oceana
Virginia Beach, Virginia

A light drizzle descends on Oceana as Jake and Team Babelus muster out of the hangar toward a Boeing-747 emblazoned with FEDEX markings and logos. The jet's shiny white exterior flashes between lighting bursts through the dark night air. Rain increases in volume and intensity to a raging downpour in a matter of moments. A spring squall in the South is disquieting and exhilarating all at once. Such quick strike storms often dissipate as fast as they appear but are uneasily frightening upon boarding an airplane.

"I hate flying!" Dr. Kagen, the team's lone truly un-athletic geek fairly shouts over the sound of raindrops beating the tarmac pavement, his light jacket pulled up over his head in a vain attempt to remain dry. "I specifically loathe going up in a storm like this. Look at the plane the way it lights up between lighting bolts, it's a haunted house with wings. I'm not sure I really want to go up in this thing. Is it safe?"

"Don't worry Doc," assures Jake, "These storms don't last long in the South. It'll probably pass before we take off. And don't get sick over it, a 747 is about the safest way to fly storm or no storm."

"Every time I hear about an airplane going down it's always a 747 or a jumbo jet of some kind and there's usually a storm attached to the news report! I'm not as sanguine about this as you are Jake and I believe it's a bad omen to start this mission out flying through a thunderstorm. And don't call me Doc!"

Jake rolls his eyes. "What's wrong with calling you Doc? You are a doctor aren't you?"

"I'm not one of the seven dwarves! Would you like me to call you a dwarf name like Happy or Sneezy? How about Smelly?"

Jake listens to Dr. Kagen's protestations and remembers the long list of reasons he left academia but he keeps his thoughts to him self out of respect for the Doctor's reputation. "Everyone is a fussbudget about how they're addressed in the academic world. When you're on a team like the SEALS or out in Hollywood on the set of *Jackson Nichols' Big Dig* everybody wants a nickname or a handle. It gives them a sense of belonging and camaraderie. And it's easier. Academics constantly fawn over themselves with an attitude, as if to say I am the team. Except Kayanne, she's not like that at all…no she's much, much worse, all high and mighty and self-righteous. She does like me to call her Kayanne though. I can see that by the way her eyes squint softly."

"What do you want me to call you if not Doc?" Jake addresses Dr. Kagen.

"Doctor Kagen, just Doctor Kagen.

"Ok, we'll stick with Doctor Kagen."

Jake shouts his conversation through the rain as they quicken their steps toward the plane desperately trying to dodge cascading sheets of water. He ponders an epithet for the good Dock-tore, something a leaning more to the blue side…like fat-ass.

Kelly Anne, Tasha and KO are only a few steps behind as they climb the stairs taking them up to the lower deck at the forward entrance of the 747. From there they scale a stairwell into the second deck main cabin. As they enter the quietly serene warmly lit travel space sounds of the squall grow faint and distant. The soft splashes of water drops from rain soaked clothes dully land on the plastic sheeting covering the walkways and creates an atmosphere of warm comfort, as if a well-stoked fireplace flickers in the corner. The spell of relaxed quietude is rudely interrupted when KO, big burly long-haired KO shakes his stringy brown locks like a Labrador Retriever fresh from a cold creek, sending the rest of the party scurrying in a commotion of shrieks, howls and swearing.

18

The cabin of the highly modified FEDEX adorned black operations Boeing-747 transport plane is laid out roughly the same as the accommodations on Air Force One, though the accoutrements are far less extravagant. The working spaces in this configuration total about four thousand square feet with cargo decks on the lower levels. The plane is dubbed Lucky Lady, most likely due to her home port at Las Vegas' McCarron Airport, also home base to a fleet of unmarked military owned airplanes ferrying covert workers to the infamous Area 51. The Lucky Lady features a clean functional interior resembling a high-tech office suite. At the nose of the cabin is a sleeping quarters with a set of bunks decked out in military issue coverings complete with hospital corners tucked neatly under mattresses as soft as concrete cinder blocks. The motif reminds the casual observer of the type of bedding and furnishings seen in most prison movies. To the aft of the sleeping quarters is a small dining lounge, not quite to the standards of a high school cafeteria with a round blond-wood linoleum table and swivel stools bolted to the deck. Behind the dining area is a galley where meals are prepared. Unlike the richly appointed double galley on board Air Force One the Lucky Lady sports a kitchenette of the seedy motor motel variety with faux-wood paneled cupboards and a barely functional microwave oven.

Joined to the galley is a well-appointed conference room, lavishly stocked with ten flat panel communications monitors. A long conference table with speakerphones at each end sits in the middle of the room. A shelf-like workspace with hastily installed high-speed Internet jacks lines the interior bulkhead. To the aft of the conference room is a series of worktables and seating reminiscent in style of the forward dining area. At the tail of the bird is a group of twenty first-class style airline seats designed for long-range travel and fold out into passable sleeping berths.

The Lucky Lady's top deck is outfitted with a state-of-the-art communications room and in-flight command center. With its rows of computers, copy and fax machines and telephone banks the room would rival any Fedex-Kinkos store at a strip mall. That is, any outlet featuring secure two-way radios, heavily shielded electronics to guard against an electromagnetic pulse and sophisticated equipment to jam enemy radar. The nose of the top deck houses the cockpit and a small pilot's lounge and galley.

• • •

The Team, having completed their brief tour of the craft transporting them to the land of Mesopotamia in a single leg's journey, descends to the second deck where they will spend the next 18 hours. Gene Lamont greets them at the bottom of the stairs and hustles the group into the conference room.

"Everyone please have a seat," the Chief of Staff directs. "I'm glad to see you've all changed into flight suits for the trip. They're loose and comfortable and should allow you freedom of movement for the duration. We'll be going through a number of briefings over the course of our journey to Iraq and there's quite a lot of work to do so it's important you're all as comfortable as possible. After take-off we'll conference with General Keith, head of American Operations in Iraq. He's on station at the Well Site coordinating efforts there. His insights will aid us a great deal."

"I don't want to worry you unnecessarily but the Marines out there have come under attack twice today so they're a bit edgy. However, a contingent of ten thousand soldiers arrived moments ago lead by an Apache helicopter squadron so you're in good hands when you arrive."

"You know Mr. Lamont," Jake starts, wearily slumping on a leather-covered swivel chair. "I don't believe any of us have slept for, well, several days. Have you scheduled any rack time during the flight?"

"Jake I really hadn't given that much thought. I know you're not robots but some things slip through the cracks. You folks will need rest as I very much doubt you'll get any sleep at all when your down in the Well. I'll make sure we schedule some down time. The government wants your minds are fresh and lucid. We can't suffer mistakes in the field on this venture. Do the long sleepless days remind you of your time in the Navy Jake?"

"Yeah, they called it Hell Week."

"Heh, I'm sure they did Jake, I'm sure they did. Everyone take a seat in the rear cabin and prepare for take-off. We'll have a working breakfast once we reach altitude. There aren't any flight attendants to give you safety instructions to buckle up or serve you drinks on a flight of this nature. The emergency exits are clearly marked though and the restroom is in back behind the seats. Fortunately we did bring a cook along so you won't endure the force-feeding of my microwave goulash especiale."

The team trundles toward aft seats in a shuffling cadence as a tired weariness overcomes them en masse. To a person they slump in their chairs, arms hanging loose over the armrests in an exhausted stupor. Seat belts ka-clink throughout the cabin and seat backs spring in a thud to upright positions, belying the lack of flight attendant supervision. The group sits motionless, slouching deep into comfortable leather seats, with the exception of Dr. Kagen whose stiffly alert manner and sweat beaded brow bespeaks of a white-knuckle take-off about to commence.

Kelly Anne sits in the front row, as is her custom since at least the first grade. Jake positions himself strategically to her right by the starboard window. Tasha takes a window seat in the second row on the Lucky Lady's port side while KO finds the window seat in the front. Dr. Kagen sits apprehensively in an aisle seat in the sixth row by the restroom.

All four of her General Electric jet engines whine in unison as the Lucky Lady lurches forward taxiing toward the runway, rain sheeting across her wings.

After the captain signals preparation for take-off the big bird whistles forward, her engines building to a roar, a shaking vibration enveloping the cabin. Dr. Kagen, teeth clenched, knuckles glowing like sunlit snow braces him self for a sudden impact inevitably to come at the end of the runway or just after taking flight. The plane powers into the air…fifty-six thousand pounds of thrust pushing her toward the heavens. As the grandly elegant 747 reaches her take-off apex and settles into the instant moment of unsettling quavering weightlessness Dr. Kagen lets out a plaintive wail followed by a deeply inhuman moan, a haunting sound overpowered by the bellowing, mouth open, nose to the air snoring of KO Gyllenhall.

19

"This'll be fun don't ya think Kayanne?" Jake asks, leaning in his seat as would any plaid-coated traveling salesman marking a captive prey.

"I don't really know what to think Jackson," Kelly Anne allows, trying to rub the fatigue from her temples. "I know we're in for a grand adventure but I have no idea where it will lead. The whole exercise fills me with excitement, dread and fear but I am glad to have the chance. I'm still not sure why they chose me."

Jake moves into high misogyny. "Probably 'cause you're a hot lookin' babe Kayanne." He looks forward to a strenuous objection he can turn into a decent conversation, or at least a full-throated argument.

"I know what you're trying to do Jake and your little ploy won't work. I'm too tired to care about your petty chauvinism or your obvious attempt to bait me so give it a rest ok? If you want to talk about something just go ahead and carry on a regular conversation. And please don't give me your patented whipped pup look, its unbecoming a man your age."

"That's getting to the point I guess. But c'mon, that's my signature move! I always thought the puppy dog look made the chicks swoon."

"You're no longer a pup and I'm not a young chick anymore Jake." Kelly Anne awkwardly massages her left shoulder with her right hand. "I'm sure a lot of women still swoon for you but do any of them still have their own teeth?"

"Of course they do, well most of them anyway." Jake perks up knowing the return of Kelly Anne's biting wit signals an intention to talk further. "On the flight from California the briefing team suspected we've discovered the Tower of Babel from the Old Testament of the Bible. In fact they're all quite sure of the idea. What do you think?"

"Oh brother. My briefing team gave me the same stunted opinion." She's now sliding down the slippery slope of engaging Jake in a discussion. "Any time a group of dogmatic scientists and muddle-headed academics herd together on an opinion I start to suspect their conclusions. Personally I think they're full of gas. The Well and its contents are too deep, too large and probably too old to match the description of Babel given in Genesis. I'm of the opinion the Well is antediluvian."

Jake's eyes widen at Kelly Anne's reference to the great deluge in the time of Noah. "You mean older than the Flood?"

"Yes. The Genesis account puts the building of the Tower of Babel by The Mighty Man Nimrod at what, around 5,000 B.C.? Nimrod is only two generations removed from Noah and the Great Flood. Did you see the shelf on the edges of the chasm in the drone elevations? The soil on the shelf is a hundred feet deep and the structures are at least another hundred feet lower than the lip edge. How many digs have you gone on with that dopey show of yours? What was the last site you excavated forcing you to dig down two hundred feet to get at ancient ruins? Never. No way! Shliemann dug up Ancient Troy, 4,000 years old, at about twenty feet and it had nine cities built up over it. Plus the Troy site is basically on a mound. Our site is below flat ground. Two hundred feet below flat ground. Oh it's old alright, the experazzi is barking up the wrong tree as usual."

"The experazzi? Is that a real word?"

"No, but they're allegedly experts in their fields and they pack around like paparazzi – crazed cattle with a herd mentality. The whole operation severely diminishes the possibilities for scientific advancement and true understanding."

Jake is clearly pleased to enjoin Kelly Anne in a substantive conversation and moves in closer. "What do think is down there? Is this Atlantis? Valhalla? An alien ship crash-landed in ancient times? How old would you say the site is judging from the photographic evidence we have?"

Kelly Anne shakes her head back and forth in disagreement. "Ehh, it's not Atlantis Jake, get real! Atlantis, at least Plato's version of it is a civilization of the early or pre Bronze Age and far too young to lie buried deep in a hole in Mesopotamia. And if the legends are correct in the slightest Atlantis rests in the Atlantic Ocean beyond the Pillars of Hercules. In other words out in the deep water, not in the middle of a desert. Atlantis is in the ten to twelve thousand year old ranges, unless Solon, the Egyptian who told the story to Plato was mistaken in his dating and its actually ten thousand years younger. In any case Atlantis is too young for our little project if it is indeed more than fiction. If you want to find Atlantis, look around Crete or Santorini. Maybe Minoans were the true Atlanteans."

"I understand but I'm curious as to your thoughts on what we're actually looking at here. An ancient civilization never previously heard or thought of or even expected? And again, what's the age of this crater? By the way how do we know it isn't a city actually built in a crater and then later covered up? You know the sand around the Sphinx was pretty deep when they discovered it, just its head poking above the surface. About a hundred feet deep I'd guess."

"The Well Site isn't like any of those concepts Jake. The Sphinx example is particularly off base. First of all the sand around the Sphinx is just that, light desert sand blowing in the wind. I think 10 feet blows in during the windy seasons in Egypt. Our site is solid earth. Dirt composed of clay and rock, densely compacted as only eons of time can allow. The crater idea has some validity I suppose. Perhaps a band of misguided people constructed an entire city in a volcanic crater and it sunk or was covered up over time but then we have to consider the condition of the structures inside the Well Site."

"And what is your theory about that?" Jake is thoroughly engrossed in Kelly Anne and her passionately expressed ideas.

"I haven't formulated a general theory yet but I'm fairly certain the city wasn't overcome by volcanic activity…there's no evidence of ash or cinder. I don't see any signs of the structures affected by compaction. Millions of tons of heavy dirt and clay weighing on a building for thousands of years…it's like putting a soda can in a trash compactor. Everything gets squashed or deteriorates and crumbles. When we dig them up thousands of years later they are ruins. At this site the structures and paths are pristine. There is no crumbling, no fallen pillars, no scattered boulders, it's as if the city existed in a vacuum for thousands of years and then the bubble burst. But none of these ideas fit in with any known geologic or archeological dynamic."

"Yeah your right about that. None of this excursion fits into known archeological conventions. We're flying covertly to a dig in a FEDEX freighter…talk about unknown dynamics! Ok Kayanne, strain your brain a bit. We have a good idea about what the Well Site is not. Obviously it's not a typical ancient ruin and probably not less than ten thousand years old. But I'm intrigued about the potential of what the site contains. What is it and how old are the structures?"

Kelly Anne knows Jake is pressing. On any other day she might press back harder. Today she is tired but enthusiastic and curious. "Slow down Jake I was getting to your main question. We have a long flight and plenty of time to go over my feeble theories. She shifts her upper torso toward Jake. "So ok, try to follow me here. I know you don't read your Bible much but you know the stories about the Flood and Noah and the Tower of Babel, right?"

"Yeah, I went to Sunday School. Not that I believe one word of it. I'm agnostic about religious myths and stories. I can't say I believe in an all-knowing omniscient God who knows every hair on my head. I believe in scientific facts I can see and touch and tangible evidence about where those facts lead me."

"Sure fine, that's you but I'm trying to give you a basis for a theory or perhaps a hopeful fantasy about this particular dig site and its origins. I'm not trying to substitute as your spiritual guide through the Universe Jake."

"Sorry, sorry please continue, heh, heh."

"In the Bible, Genesis primarily, accounts are recorded of a highly advanced but infamously corrupt civilization existing prior to Noah's Flood. According to the stories those people are the reason God caused the great deluge. The people of the era, as related in the Bible supposedly lived exceedingly long lives…several of the lead characters in the stories lived hundreds of years. Methuselah was allegedly over 900 years old at his death. Nobody has ever uncovered a single hint of highly advanced civilization predating the Flood of Genesis."

"Maybe nothing but cavemen and yak farmers existed in the antediluvian timeframe…not to admit there ever was an earth destroying flood."

"Sure, perhaps, then again the Bible's historical record is fairly accurate and an absence of evidence isn't an absence of existence. For decades, scholars thought the Bible story of the Exodus was a Jewish fairy tale. Then they found corroborating evidence in Egypt vindicating the historical accuracy of the Bible."

"Yeah, ok."

"There're a number of historical records not canonized in the Bible pointing to accounts of ancient civilizations. For example there is a book expressly excluded as part of the Bible canon, an apocryphal work possibly scribed by Methuselah's father Enoch. The Book of Enoch is a rather fanciful tale recalling the beginnings of mankind and other beings that supported the creation effort. It comes across in style as foreboding and fantastical as the Book of Revelation and in reading you're never quite sure what is literal and what is figurative or allegorical."

"Well I see it all as fiction myself but if The Book of Enoch is so important and historically accurate why isn't it in the Bible?"

"That's a good question. Unfortunately we don't have a clue as to its veracity. Although Enoch is mentioned in Genesis himself…sections of Genesis, particularly Chapter Six, corroborates the existence of Enoch, there's no way to know if he penned the book or if later people concocted the Enoch narrative. Jews of the pre-Christian era did read and believe in the book and so did early Christian followers. But The Book of Enoch wasn't canonized for various reasons."

Jake knows from past experience with Kelly Anne that somehow the Catholics are to blame for the omission and he reluctantly poses further questions. "Why didn't Enoch get canonized?"

"As you know the Holy Bible as we know it was canonized by officials of the Roman Catholic Church…"

"Awww here it comes!" Jake slams his head dramatically into the backrest.

"Stop it Jake, this isn't my day for ranting against the Catholics if that's what you're thinking. I only conduct said rants on Tuesdays now. Jake you know I was brought up as a Seventh-Day Adventist, a Protestant's Protestant if you will and I know some of my paranoid thoughts come out from time to time but this isn't one of those times!"

"Mmm…ok. But don't start with all of the end-times apocalyptic junk featuring the Pope as the Anti-Christ."

"Ha ha, ok, I promise. This is all Old Testament so not to worry."

Kelly Anne animatedly describes for Jake the process of canonizing the Holy Bible. He manages to stay awake for the better part of her presentation.

"Try to picture the Christian Church around the Second Century A.D. Jake. At the time hundreds of diverse Christian sects worshipped under the banner of their own philosophies and for the most part each sect used a separate and distinct version of the scriptures. Typically these quote, unquote Bibles were Old Testament texts utilizing a wide range of writings.

Interestingly most Christian churches of the First and Second Centuries didn't ascribe Divine status to the writings of the New Testament, including the four Gospels of Matthew, Mark, Luke and John. So the Christian canon, in effect, the Bible that we know today didn't exist in the early Christian era.

"I thought the Bible we know today was the same one as the time of Christ's death. That's what I learned in Sunday School Kayanne."

"Nope, not accurate, not nearly accurate. The entire Bible as we know it wasn't collated in any form until the third century after his death. In the third century several movements to collate and synthesize scripture materialized."

"I'm afraid to ask but what caused the change?"

"The first major move to create a universal set of scriptures was by a church leader named Irenaeus. Now don't get upset Jake, but he's the scholar generally credited with the founding of the Roman Catholic Church."

"Of course."

"Anyway, Irenaeus wanted all Christian churches to follow a standard set of scriptures so he convened a council of bishops to decide what went in the canon and what stayed out. The bishops flocked to Rome, argued for days, voted on the God-inspired qualities of various writings and scriptures but couldn't come to conclusions and didn't canonize a Bible. They did generate a list of accepted texts, in their opinion, and implored the other Christian sects to adopt them."

"Sounds more like politics than faith to me."

"Yes Jake a lot of politics and not enough faith I think. Creating a generic Bible didn't end with the council of bishops. Other people and groups jumped into the fray. A pair of Christian scholars named Jerome and Augustine made up lists too. Both produced efforts to bring in additional books and writings as well as exclude a few. Jerry and Augi didn't utilize the council method of divination. They created lists of acceptable Biblical teachings based on their own opinions as to the veracity or divinity of various texts. They weren't historians or experts in writing styles and didn't conduct research into the history of the texts. They simply read them and decided for everyone else. Clearly this was a job to which they were singularly unqualified."

"I don't see the hand of God in any of this Kayanne."

"That part is a matter of faith Jake and you don't have any so pipe down and listen to the historical narrative."

"Heh-heh, yeah ok, sure."

"At the time about forty different Gospels of Christ, According to Whomever circulated throughout Christendom. Eventually the canonizing process whittled them down to the four included in today's Bible. Of course they left out thirty-six or so. Also there were all sorts of books called Revelations by various prophets and apostles and hundreds upon hundreds of texts proclaiming Acts of the Apostles. The Revelation of Peter was seriously considered as the standard, instead of the work by John found in today's Bible. During the era several councils convened to try and sort it all out."

"Well, who's to say they didn't leave an important Divine work out of the mix?"

"That's the point of this discussion Jake and I'm getting there."

"Ok, ok, if I fall asleep nudge me."

"I'll nudge you alright, clear to back to Virginia! Continuing the story…The Old Testament went through this process too. There were many groups working to decide the general make-up of the overall text. The Council at Nicea was convened in 326 A.D. They talked and compromised and fought furiously to include or exclude various texts. They found precious little agreement as is the case with all of these types of councils and they didn't canonize a Bible, though they suggested a list of their own. In 365 the Synod of Laodicea canonized the first actual set of texts one could call a Bible but they rejected the apocryphal books on Augustine's list, including The Book of Enoch. Later the Third Council of Carthage canonized a Bible and re-instated Augustine's list including the apocryphal books but threw out Lamentations, all by bare majority vote and a thousand prayers I'm sure. That's how the process unfolded. For one council a book like Lamentations was in for the next, whoosh, tossed out like old cheese. Eventually the current Bible with its 66 books came into being, although the Roman Catholic version contains a few different books than the bible used by Protestant Christians."

"All these machinations sound so arbitrary Kayanne and based on personalities and opinion, not faith or reason. Thanks for the history lesson…I guess. Doesn't all of the compromise and voting and religious-political intrigue go a long way in ripping apart the notion of an inerrant inspired word of God? Aren't you pushed toward atheism by eating from the tree of that knowledge? And don't even bother to pardon the pun."

"I can see why an absolutist rogue like you might think so Jake, but I don't necessarily look at today's Bible, as formulated by the various councils, as the inerrant word of God. Nor do I see it as the literal word of God like Islam views the Koran. Historical facts show us the Holy Bible doesn't represent the entire truth of God's existence. The Bible itself mentions scriptures lost to antiquity such as the Book of the Wars of the Lord and The Book of Nathan. There're quite a few texts missing from the narrative. And who knows what degree of importance we should ascribe to lost information when assessing the existence of God."

"Yeah that's a good point."

"You see Jake the Bible describes its impact on humanity through its own passages; as a set of examples to live by pure and simple. The Bible's writers claim only inspiration from God, not that God literally penned the works…well…except for Moses and the Ten Commandments on Mount Sainai. The beauty is the Bible writers left us a fairly accurate historical record bound up with laudable virtues and morals instructing us in the way God expects his creations to interact in the world and we can test the historical record through science and the virtues and morals through observation."

"You think God allows his subjects to test his words?"

"Absolutely! I can't believe in a God who gives me a brain and then expects me to shut it down when the subject turns to his history and interaction with humans."

"How can everything in the Bible be right given the historical narrative you just threw at me?"

"I don't believe every word contained in the Bible is divine Jake. As fallible mortal beings many of the writers interjected their own thoughts and ideas when they penned the works. Also a good number of the Bible's books were first handed down through an oral tradition and then written down by scribes centuries later. You can understand how information may end up like a whispering game of *Secrets* with some degrading of the message over all that time and through the numerous characters relaying the accounts. The various Bible canonizing councils acted in the same way our modern day scientific community does…like collegial pack animals with an imperious herd mentality trying to pigeonhole the truth into a concrete set of ideas to stand as their own legacy for all time. That attitude tends to obscure rather than reveal truth."

"So you're saying there's more truth out there?"

"I'm saying I have an open mind on the subject."

"You know I would never get condescending on you Kayanne, but I didn't know you were capable of this level of maturity in your thinking."

"Now if we can get you to open your mind up Jake we'd get somewhere. I have an open mind on this basis…for centuries after the death of Christ the contents and therefore the substance of the Bible changed dramatically. Our beliefs, as culled from today's Bible are based on traditions limited by the understanding of so-called Bible scholars with agendas to protect and axes to grind. There's an entire world of information out there Jake, hidden in caves, stashed in old urns or tucked away in ruins under centuries of dirt. Those secrets and answers await discovery and I think we're about to cross the chasm on this adventure."

"So why is Enoch important to us in this venture and to the rest of the world?"

"Not so much Enoch Jake but the idea of Enoch and the stories he allegedly wrote. There are a number of figures in antiquity roughly matching the character of Enoch and a good number of scholars see him as a keystone to understanding the ancient past and beginnings of mankind. Enoch is the seventh in line from Adam just as the Sumerian legends of Emnduranki place him seventh in the line of Sages. This construct is the same with the Assyrian legend of Enki. And they all had the same purpose on earth…keepers of secret wisdoms and as a liaison between higher beings or Angels and humans."

"Ok, that piques my interest a bit. What do you mean by keeper of secret wisdoms? Do you mean treasure?"

"That's the Jake I know, ever the mercenary! But yes, technological treasures and perhaps some actual fungible caches as well. The legends say Enoch buried this knowledge inscribed on a golden delta."

"Like a golden triangle?"

"I suppose so but I think the information on the item would be more valuable than the gold it's made from."

"Probably so, but getting hands on gold isn't a bad thing. What about these higher beings, what are they?"

"In some of the legends the higher beings are called Angels, in others they are spirits. All of them are 'watchers' of humans. Some of the stories have these higher beings watching over the everyday lives of humans while others make them out as glorified delivery personnel for God. The Archangel Gabriel allegedly recited the Koran to Mohamed. Enoch's white buffalo spirit is found in certain American Native legends. For Enoch the beings were trusted guides offering keys to the Universe. Obviously they're important historically but many people believe they live among us even today."

"So this is what you expect to find in the Well Site Kayanne, evidence of Angels on earth and secrets of the Gods?"

"I don't know what to expect Jake but I am certainly intrigued by the possibilities."

"Me too, by the possibility of finding gold or some usable high technologies we can patent."

Spent by her presentation Kelly Anne sinks back into her leather seat and falls asleep, her head leaning toward Jake's shoulder, with dreams of finding truth in a large hole in the middle of Iraq's Syrian Desert.

Jake stares out the window, his brow forming a deep crease between his eyes. He experiences an unfathomable sense of worry and foreboding despite Kelly Anne's obvious enthusiasm. The Well Site Operation isn't tangible like a stealthy run up a beachhead, attacking a mortal enemy at night. The former Navy warrior fears venturing into an ethereal world beyond his abilities and tangling with gods and demons of ancient times. The Bible story of Joseph's futile nighttime struggle with an archangel springs to his mind. A soldier entering a firefight carries the proper weaponry to neutralize the enemy. Jake, staring solemnly through the small portal window at the massive cloud cover over the Atlantic knows full well he lacks the necessary tools to fight a deadly unearthly foe.

"Faith and wisdom," Jake muses wistfully, "Tools you don't build wasting half your life on a barstool at Harry's."

20

Main Deck of the Lucky Lady
Over Newfoundland

A sudden jerk and severe banking maneuver jolts Team Babelus from the shadows of deep slumber. The Lucky Lady's massive engines strain and groan against the friction of the outside air as the plane dives through a phalanx of thunderheads and lightning bolts. Yellow oxygen masks drop from secure compartments, annoying, frightening and in this case utterly useless. Kelly Anne grips the arms of her seat in tense fear, her eyes fixed straight ahead. KO clutches a threadbare backpack as if to make a quick exit at the nearest opportunity. Tasha sits wide-eyed, hands clasping the sides of her face, her mouth open and face distorted, frozen and soundless in a real life adaptation of *The Scream* by Edvard Munch. Jake openly laughs between shouts of whoo-hoo! staring danger in the face with the skill and bravado of a rodeo cowboy on a Brahma bull.

Dr. Kagen, absolutely apoplectic with fear assumes the standard airplane crash position and cries out in a high-pitched mournful wail muffled by the cocoon created with his head resolutely sandwiched between his knees, "We're going to die! We're going to die! Oh Lord, oh Lord we're going to die!"

"Sorry folks," comes the calm reassuring voice of Captain James Tucker over the intercom as the Lucky Lady rights and steadies. "We thought we could save some time flying through the storm but it looks as if she's grown into a Category Three hurricane. Hurricane Myrna they're calling her. We encountered severe turbulence, as you may have noticed and there's no end in sight. We're going to climb to 45,000 feet and make our way to the north around the hurricane and then head toward the Mediterranean. There are bags in the seat backs if you need them."

"They should at least warn us when they take our lives in their hands like that!" complains Kelly Anne. "Not as if we could storm the cockpit in rebellion."

"We were asleep, they probably thought we needed the rest," Jake allows. "Besides after the United States government virtually kidnapped you right out of the classroom, confiscating your cell phone and cutting you off from all communications with the outside world. You don't expect them to ask your express permission to fly through a little storm do you?"

"Well a fat lot of good flying through the eye of a hurricane did us!" blurts KO. "I don't think I'll ever go to sleep on an airplane again."

Dr. Kagen, sobbing uncontrollably remains in the crash position, his head wedged firmly between his knees in shame and fear.

"Are you ok Doctor Kagen," Tasha asks with motherly concern as she makes her way back to his seat and gently rubs his back.

"Don't coddle him Tasha!" barks Jake in his SEAL Commander tone.

Tasha is incredulous at Jake's suggestion. Her face grows crimson and pinches in confused anger. "What? Is there something wrong with showing a little compassion? He's obviously pretty shook up. We're human beings not machines Jake."

Big KO leaps to his feet in defense. "Yeah what's your problem Jake? That little diversion scared the livin' shit out of me and I fly a lot. Give the guy a break will ya?"

Jake's been on this little trip before and knows the ropes. He lights into Team Babelus furiously. "No I won't give him a break and neither will the rest of you! This is the problem with packing a bunch of panty-waist science geeks out into the field on a mission demanding soldiers. Soft and timid academics like you aren't familiar with the dangers of walking into a war zone. And make no mistake we're going to load up all of our dainty little techno-gadgets and march directly into a fiery hell that will have you on your knees pissing your panties while you pray to God for a quick and merciful death and we'll be armed with nothing but a few pea-shooters!"

"The enemy will have automatic weapons, grenades and mortars and the fear you'll feel when the bullets fly will sink into your soul. We need to work as a single unit with all manner of cunning, guile and bravery we can muster. Each member of this team is responsible for all the other members and it's critical we walk into the fight with confidence we can count on each other. Doctor Kagen is hiding back there quaking in his boots and delivering his own last rights over turbulence that won't make babies cry. What's the little mamma's boy gonna do facing live rounds? If the bullets fly and Kagen tucks his head between his knees crying and sobbing like a whimpering fool he puts one or all of us in serious jeopardy and we could die or get seriously hurt as a result."

Jake turns ominously toward Dr. Kagen and addresses him like a man. "I'm warning you right now Doctor Kagen, straighten your ass up and fly right or I'll shoot you between the eyes myself if you freak out like a grade-school girl during a firefight."

KO is compelled to defend the distraught man sulking behind the seat. "Your he-man macho military shit is totally uncalled for!" He points a menacing finger towards Jake and moves forward.

"Damn Jake that's pretty harsh don't you think!" Tasha, fists are balled up, planted firmly on her hips. She is enraged and shows no fear in the face of Jake's verbal onslaught.

"No Tasha I don't, in fact I…"

"Everyone just stop!" Dr. Kagen, finding his manhood, sniffles, raises his head, eyes filled with tears. "Jake is absolutely right. If there are people out there gunning for us then we can't have any one of us falling down on the job. I'm embarrassed and ashamed about my reactions here so please don't try and console me though I appreciate the gesture Tasha and your spirited defense KO. I want you to know something about me Commander Nichols."

"I grew up in a war zone called the ghettos of Watts and I know the sound of gunfire. I was an out of place geeky brainy fat kid tossed out on those streets to fend for myself and I've faced the wrong end of drug dealer and gangster guns or baseball bats too many times to count. I am not a coward in facing the barrel of a gun or men of violence but I have an intense flying phobia. Airplanes drive me to apoplexy. I can't prove it by my actions here today but you can count on me Sir…yes you can…when the going is tough and the bullies come out from whatever rock they hide under."

Kelly Anne kept her silence and didn't interfere or speak out during the fracas, knowing effective leadership is often accompanied by harsh declarations and rough treatment of the timid. Jake's mean sounding statements aren't thrown out there maliciously. In fact the opposite is true. None of these brilliant science experts have endured the rigors and mind-warping team-building tactics of a military boot camp. They aren't trained to act as a unit. This group is specifically selected for a demonstrable willingness to buck the tide, not join the flow. Jake is only giving them an abridged version of the dissonant training necessary to foster the hard-edged mindset they'll need for a firefight no matter what form the battle eventually takes.

"Jake has a way of bringing out the man in anybody," Kelly Anne thinks, grinning amusingly to her self, shaking and trying to stifle a laugh.

Jake sits back in his seat comforted by the near melee. He knows character and the way Tasha and KO stood up for Dr. Kagen shows a fierce fighting spirit. And for a man of Dr. Kagen's stature his admissions and willingness to plough through shame and embarrassment to keep the nascent team glued together is a mark of an abiding solidly upstanding character. “Perhaps the makings of a cohesively effective unit are here after all if they don’t kill themselves first.” Jake smiles to himself as he dozes off, hoping they won’t slit his throat while he sleeps.

21

The Lucky Lady bobs and weaves over an airborne highway of cumulus nimbus clouds on the fringes of a gigantic storm while crossing the Atlantic. The team sleeps soundly despite inclement rough weather and brilliant lightning flashes illuminating the night sky.

Rousing people from near comatose sleep is difficult, particularly when their slumber is at the tail end of a series of long arduous meetings and monotonous briefings. But Chief of Staff Lamont is determined to succeed.

"Ok everybody its time to hup-to!" bellows Lamont, clapping his hands vigorously and sharply to stir a groggy Team Babelus. "Rise and shine, let's get movin'. We've got boatloads of work to do and no time to waste on sleep."

"What the hell?" KO complains. "Where are we? Where am I? Who are you people?" he asks, rubbing his eyes in a search of a clear view.

Lamont continues his rousting maneuvers over adamant complaints. "I have a couple of people you need to meet. You slept for six hours so we need to get moving. Go ahead freshen up and then meet me in the conference room in ten minutes. We'll have breakfast waiting."

Jake yawns and stretches and cracks his back with a twisting motion. Kelly Anne rubs a leg that fell asleep in the night and thinks about how messy her hair surely looks just now. Dr. Kagen rolls his head around on his neck to loosen the muscles and snaps his jaw open and shut wondering if he's woken up with a case of morning breath. He breathes into his hand to check. KO reaches to the ceiling and hangs on a baggage compartment door stretching his back while his pants fall loosely around his hips revealing the pride of every plumber. Tasha, a perky morning person takes first dibs on the restroom and bounces toward the door.

After washing, brushing and straightening up the team trundles forward to the conference room, each continuing their respective morning stretching and cracking rituals. No one in the group woke up in a chatty mood and little is said on the way to the meeting. On a normal day under typical conditions six hours of sleep would fulfill most needs. But after a full 24-hour day of rushed travel and meetings piled on top of briefings sixty hours of sleep seems a better plan.

"Goo-ood morning everyone!" Lamont cheerily greets the team like a politician as they enter the brightly lit conference room. "I hope you all slept well. Last night we prepared beds for all of you in the forward berthing compartment but when we went back there you were sound asleep in your airplane seat bunks. You looked comfortable so we didn't disturb you and put our briefings on the back burner. We have a chef on board borrowed from a casino restaurant in Vegas. He's an exceptional cook and has prepared us a breakfast. They'll bring our meals in here shortly and we'll work while we eat."

"Coffee," KO rasps in the voice of a man clearly used to sleeping in.

"Over there in the corner Kenneth. Half-n-half is in the ice-box underneath the table."

"The last thing I need is to cut my life-blood with cream. I should just stick an I.V. into my arm and mainline the stuff. Can we smoke in here?"

"Heavens no Kenneth."

"Heavens no? Why heavens no? Is smoking against your religion? A simple no gets the point across and I prefer my nickname KO if you don't mind Eugene."

"I'm not trying to be rude Kenneth, uh KO. Smoking on an airplane went out with oversized 80s hair-dos and Yuppies. It's passé!"

"Passé huh? Well we don't want to offend the Gods of Fashion now do we? Can't go around blowing smoke up the government's P.C. ass, can we? What's a Yuppie?"

"Well they were a…"

"What's on the agenda Mr. Lamont?" Jake asks, abruptly refocusing the conversation as he takes a seat in the middle of the conference table directly across from the Chief of Staff. We're bleary and out of sorts but anxious to get started. Though I admit the past 24-hours is a little hazy to me."

"Indeed Jake. The agenda is full and we may as well get started. Everyone come on in, take a seat and get comfortable, we'll be here for awhile."

"Mr. Lamont the mission seems a little loose at this point." Kelly Anne remarks, taking a seat to Jake's left. "Have we formulated a basic action plan yet? "

"We're efforting that as we speak Doctor Carter. There are a number of factors to consider involving a plethora of government agencies, sub-agencies and contractors. We can't afford to sacrifice mission-critical time to adjust for mistakes and contingencies. Of prime concern is ensuring the proper level of initial accuracy as the directives of each stage are executed. I have assurances sufficient mission protocols are forthcoming and we'll begin the process of implementation prior to our arrival."

KO, already miffed at the rude awakening from his peaceful slumber won't sit for government bureaucrats dancing on the table with vague and uselessly complicated answers to simple questions. He bares his teeth and snarls at Lamont. "What the…? What a load of suit-speak crap! Your overblown bureaucracy's bad enough with one government agency doing the planning. How many yakkin' suit-bots we got working this operation?" KO barks his complaints between slurps of coffee and takes a seat to Kelly Anne's left.

Lamont is put off by the hostile behavior but answers KO's questions. "About forty agencies, contractors and sub-agencies."

"Kuh-rist, they'll never get anything done! We'll be flying in this tin can until the end of the world. This bird has in-flight refueling right?"

"Yes it does KO but that's hardly the point. Can we please just continue?"

"Yeah, yeah, yeah, sorry…sort of."

Tasha and Dr. Kagen take seats to Jake's right as Lamont describes the myriad diplomatic, technological and military problems facing the mission. His presentation lays bare in stark terms the reasons for the involvement of various government entities in an archeological discovery. He reiterates the delicate diplomacy required to operate in a sovereign nation still technically at war and how the Secretary of State personally negotiated an agreement, was double-crossed and then able to secure five days of exploration from an inflexible Iraqi government. He tells the group in graphic detail the specifics of the attacks against Marines on the perimeter of the Well, an unknown enemy remaining dangerously at large.

Lamont mentions the heads of important agencies and members of the Cabinet, as well as the President himself, monitoring the mission from the White House Situation Room. The normally affable Chief of Staff imparts his personal feelings about the mission and its grave importance to the United States, the world at large and all of humanity. He emotionally pours out his appreciation for the members of Team Babelus, their dedication and sacrifice. Lastly he admits the government possesses no reliable intelligence about the site, the dangers the team faces and, in short, has no useful answers whatsoever. Any true knowledge will come from boots on the ground worn by Team Babelus.

"Awww were running up the creek lead boatload of suits without paddles and they want us to do all of the rowing!" laments KO, slamming his head back into his chair and staring at the ceiling.

22

The West Wing of the White House
Office of the Vice-President
Washington, D.C.

"Team Babelus is in the air and headed toward Mesopotamia." Vice-President Murcheson informs the small security task force gathered in her West Wing office. "The mission is a go but I have a number of concerns we need to mitigate before they land in Iraq. The President is very concerned about the security situation at the Well Site. General Keith reported a second attack, this time a suicide bomber in a truck. They took a run at the HQ tent and nearly hit the intended target, including the General himself. The politics of the operation are tenuous at best and we need this to go smoothly as possible with minimal casualties and a blackout on news coverage."

"Madam Vice-President I have several concerns too," Dan Maney pipes in. "As you know I had serious reservations about the type of people we planned to send on the mission in the first place but I don't want to give you the impression I'm a fly in the ointment on this. The decision is made and the team selected, I'm fully on board. My first concern is we haven't informed Congress about the operation. Not that we're violating any laws…there are separation of powers provisions in the Constitution protecting us. We can certainly send a scientific exploration team covertly to study an archeological site without alerting the nation. The problems are political and concern matters of national security."

"When the press gets wind of this, as they inevitably do, and starts shouting with hush-hush stories through their loud media megaphone about how the administration is hiding something from Congress there'll be hell to pay. Shouldn't we pre-empt the political fallout with an informal briefing?"

Murcheson, acutely familiar with the Washington Press Corps is dubious. "My immediate impression is perhaps we should call in the Speaker of the House and the Senate Majority Leader and give them a briefing. But I'm not sure they won't leak the information, of course not directly but through staff or inadvertently to a friend in the press."

"We could request any press entities aware of the story to hold off on going public until Team Babelus has completed the mission," suggests Secretary Green-Newton. "I know that's been done in the past and most press agencies have honored the requests."

"That all depends on which press entity gets the story," objects Director Likely. "Politics, especially in Washington are overheated since the election. Relations between the press and the Administration are dicey and exceedingly partisan, unfortunately. Press relations with the previous administration were positively nuclear. You may recall the major newspapers exposing sensitive War on Terror programs vital to national security. Director Likely throws his hands about in wild gesticulations to illustrate his point. "Breathless stories filled the front page in major newspapers detailing the inner workings of the American security apparatus. They provided the terrorists a heads up on our methodology in monitoring their telephone conversations and how we tracked their money through the international banking system. And worse no one was ever punished or hauled before Congress to answer for the crimes. I guess we don't prosecute treason these days."

"Back in the old days politics stopped at the water's edge. Not anymore. We've got to keep a lid on this or it could blow up like the Abu Graihb Prison photos brouhaha or the Islamic riots caused by mere rumors of our soldiers flushing the Koran down a toilet. The Well Site is smack in the heart of Islam. Can you imagine the Islamic reaction after the press incites them with details of pillaging Islamic treasures? And if there's anything at the Well Site challenging the Islamic historic narrative the Imams will gin up the populace and create mass hysteria around the globe. We'll have to double security because the radicals will take pot shots at the Pope and the President. Do you remember the violent reaction incited by those silly cartoons depicting Mohammed with a bomb in his turban? I shudder to think where a leak about the Well Site would lead us."

For once Dan Maney agrees with the Director. "You're right about that! The press seems to take great delight inciting terrorists and blaming America…making the country look bad even though they're biting the hand feeding them freedom of the press. If there's a leak on the Well Site Operation or the story gets out one way or another and we haven't covered the President politically by briefing Congress the atmosphere in Washington will superheat and could boil over to chaos on American streets. I'm worried about the possibility."

"Looking ahead with a crystal ball I can imagine calls for impeachment from the Democrats. I have no clue how the Federalists will react, I can never put my finger on anything they believe. They caucus with the Republicans but the relationship is on shaky ground, not to mention it's built on a platform of national security. If something goes wrong and we throw off the delicate balance, even slightly, the situation could deteriorate rapidly. We'll have negative headlines in the papers every day. The talking heads on television will screech and the Blogs will blow up like a 300 megaton stink bomb."

"Yes, and all of this while we're trying to get the President's domestic agenda through Congress," mentions the Vice-President. "I'm inclined to keep the mission under wraps completely but we've already moved ten thousand Marines out of the Green Zone, surely the press has taken note of that."

"Perhaps," allows Director Likely, "But we've been shipping thousands of soldiers out of country every day for months so they may not notice a change of any kind. Although they seem poised to jump on anything looking the least bit like the fall of Saigon when we high tailed out of there and left a disaster in our wake. All those images of Vietnamese women and children clinging to helicopter skids and crying on camera left an impression the nation didn't get over for thirty years, if ever. A picture is worth a thousand words but live video is the Magna Carta. The press is just salivating to get those kinds of shots."

"The Marines are increasing the size of the perimeter around the Well Site," informs Secretary Green-Newton, "They're specifically on watch for media trucks and civilian vehicles carrying reporters and photographers. General Keith is adamant no press enters the area, he'll detain any civilian so much as catching a glimpse of the security perimeter."

"If I know General Keith," adds Maney. "He's far more afraid of press people running loose in a theater of war than an armed enemy shooting at him. Of course as the head of operations in a war zone he has every right to control the movement of civilians, not that it will stop the press from screaming censorship and shouting claims our administration is the most secretive since the Soviets rounded up dissidents and sent them to gulags in Siberia."

"I'm worried about the domestic situation." the Vice-President redirects. "Before this past election I never believed Americans would openly fight in the streets over politics. The last administration had to call out the National Guard in twelve states to quell the rioting. Seven states instituted curfews and four declared martial law. At this juncture the country seethes from the experience and a lot of bitterness percolates under the surface. If this President is seen as hiding an important national security issue by holding the press at arms length it could trigger a new round of dissension. It's nearly unfathomable but we came awfully close to civil war last November and the stock market took a nosedive. We must walk a fine line and make certain those scenes aren't repeated."

"Perhaps we should embrace the madness in a way," suggests Director Likely. "We can embed a pool reporter with

Team Babelus. Said reporter will get strict instructions nothing goes out until we're good and ready to release the information. And we can cover the President by giving the Speaker and Majority Leader a briefing but leave out some of the details such as the location of the Well Site and an unknown enemy having already attacked it twice."

"I don't know Graham," worries Maney. "Embedding a reporter into this situation is the riskiest suggestion I've heard today. When we let them tag along on the march to Baghdad it was a hot shooting war and they were scared out of their wits so they obeyed the military leaders instructions. The Well Site is quite likely the greatest archeological find in the history of mankind and the designation might represent a scoop too tempting for any reporter to keep under a bushel. On the other issue, if we hold back information from Congress as you suggest the action will signal to them something's up and they'll turn over every filthy informing rock in Washington to get to the bottom of whatever they think we're doing. Then they'll claim a cover-up and put the President right in the cross-hairs of impeachment proceedings."

"We could keep quiet about it and hope for the best," demurs the Vice-President. "But I'm skeptical of silence as an option. As with any Washington scandal the cover-up is worse than the crime, and in many cases no underlying crime is necessary to gin up political heat to overheated temperatures. Also there is the issue of moral rightness. The American people deserve an open transparent government, but not at the cost of the nation's security. Our responsibility is to balance the county's competing interests. Then there's the whole religion problem. The Well Site could conceivably overturn the concept of a creator God and upset the faithful. We may have more to fear from angry priests and imams than we do from mad politicians. And the believers in Evolution could see some negative effects too. What if information at the Well Site shows Evolution as a false science? Entire academic orthodoxies are built on the Evolution premise. I'm not sure toppling that citadel will be pretty. The point is we can't cover up any of this. If we do the conspiracy theories will ruin us all and severely damage the country."

Murcheson decides the issue after careful deliberation. "We will inform Congress with a full briefing to the leaders of both houses. If they leak the information it's an act of treason and we'll come down hard on them. I hope and pray there is at least an iota of patriotism left amongst the political class. We have no option but to assume the two leaders are reasonable when the nation's security is at stake, a stretch in today's political climate I know."

"Embedding a reporter isn't necessarily a bad idea, depending who the person is. An independent record of the exploration is necessary and morally correct but we'll manage the information with tight controls by prior agreement with the news agency as well as the individuals involved. I fully understand the fox in the henhouse dangers and risks of positioning a mouthpiece in the middle of a sensitive operation but making the leap will aid us in the end. And yes, it's imperative we allow a news photographer to tag along and record everything. And I do mean everything. In truth the American people can handle risks to their security, intellectually and physically, so long as they see with their own eyes a greater good is accomplished."

"For us in government transparency and honesty is an act of keeping faith with the people employing us. Perhaps the Well Site crisis is an opportunity to stitch together open wounds of the recent past by bridging the bitterness between partisan groups with a common cause of survival, although even under those conditions openness is a risk."

"You're dead set on this arrangement?" Maney asks, his face etched with grave concern. "Once we cross the river it'll be impossible to leap back the other way, though I probably don't need to tell you that."

"Yes I am Dan and I'll pardon your 'dead set' expression. I'll inform the President personally. Director Likely please set up a briefing with Speaker Hartley and Majority Leader Garland. Oh, and Graham, keep Torie Smart out of the loop on this. We don't want to give the press an open door through the White House Communications Office. Dan I've made the decision and there's no turning back. I expect your complete cooperation on all matters pertaining to this subject as well as your discretion. We're blindly running through uncharted territory with every aspect of the Well Site Operation and we need all hands on deck if we hope to succeed."

"Fair enough Madam Vice-President, God help us all."

23

Conference Room on Board the Lucky Lady
45,000 Feet Above The Mediterranean Ocean

Meetings heaped on top of briefings served over conferences and mini-summits wore on the normally lively and energetic Tasha Hicks. She prefers building things, putting multifaceted gadgets together, experimenting and immersing her self in technological complexity. Tasha loathes sitting stoically in meetings while self-important windbags yak obsessively in the latest techno-jargon impressed by the magnitude of their own brilliance. She has observed a disturbing tendency of such inflated personages to mask a lack of technical expertise by exaggerating technical vocabulary.

"The higher level of consultant the more they use the baffle them with your bullshit technique." She leans over and whispers in KO's ear during a particularly verbose and wholly unproductive meeting. "I get more useful information and real expertise when I talk with garage mechanics than I do from these bozos."

During one briefing describing the utility of various technological devices a Dr. Leo J. Abernathy nearly drove Tasha beyond the edge of sanity with his incessant blather on the virtues of mobile computers. He was particularly effusive in describing the EVA-XG3100 mobile computing tablet.

"The EVA-XG3100 is a modified state-of-the-art itinerant biometrically controlled input/output access device," Abernathy drones, his dull-serious face looming large on the center plasma screen in the Lucky Lady's main conference room. "The titanium-alloy casing houses an Intel dual-core one point six gigahertz microprocessor including the M-915 GME chipset, five hundred gigabyte storage system and twelve hundred megabytes of random access memory. In addition the unit features a personal computer memory card type one and type two card slot, a revision two point three twenty-four bit card compliant integral full duplex microphone array system and a silicone bezel sealed electrostatic digitizing interface. As you can see she's a rocket."

Thoroughly unimpressed Tasha lights into Abernathy, a doctor of exactly what she has no idea. "What's the battery life on your little rocket Doctor Abernathy?"

"Approximately seven and a half hours I'm proud to report. Of course that's always dependent on your usage."

"What's the battery life under load Doctor Abernathy?"

"Well now of course that depends on the load Miss and I don't know what level of usage you have on your mind."

Tasha's dismay builds as she knows the conversation can only lead to pain and discomfort for the vendor. She continues her cross-examination, eyes narrowing and turning askance in skepticism. "What's the battery life at 50 percent resource load?"

"Oh I'd say about two hours at 50 percent but I highly doubt anyone can utilize 50 percent of the unit's resources 100 percent of the time."

"Doctor, Doctor, Doctor, using the on-board CCD camera to record events at the Well Site will utilize 50 percent of the unit's power resources all by its little self. You know full well recording video draws massive power with extensive loads on the CPU and graphics chips as well as the LCD panel. And if we use the digitizing interface and stylus to jot down electronic notes or create rudimentary sketches we'll drain even more power. In fact I can't see how we can utilize the little rocket at anywhere under 50 percent 100 percent of the time we use its functions."

"In truth Doctor most of the wireless communications technology is useless for our mission and there's no reason to discuss it given the short time frame we're working under. All those jacks are useless too. I don't anticipate going down into an ancient site thousands of years old and finding an Ethernet jack to plug into. And about the phone jack, well, we're certainly not going to go down there and get dial-up! And just how are we going to make use of biometric security? We'll record events and technologies that are probably sensitive but the chain of custody for the machine is in our hands at all times for the four days we're at the site. We don't need to spend valuable minutes putting our thumbprints up to the unit every time we boot up. And the warm-swappable nature of the battery dictates we'll have to stand there and wait while the machine reboots from sleep status. That's hardly efficient or useful in the field where mobility is crucial. How much does the little rocket weigh?

"Hmm, huh, Three and a half pounds."

"Three and a half pounds? Pounds? Oh-kayy…I suppose three and a half is light and airy when you walk from your car into the local Starbucks but our mission puts us on our feet for ten to fifteen hours a day for four days straight…at minimum. Our arms will fall off toting your cinder block around day in and day out. We're better off taking notes on a yellow steno pad with a Sharpie than to amble around with the little bomb all day long."

"I see what you mean. But the EVA-XG3100 is state-of-the-art in mobile computing."

"Unfortunately Doctor the state-of-the-art hasn't progressed far enough to fit the task. We should bring along digital capacity though. Are you familiar with the Avenexus Pocket Studio?"

"Yes, we have some Beta units of the product available but our labs haven't bench tested any of them so they would be unreliable at best I should think. Do you think they'll work for your application?"

"Quite efficiently. They're pocket-sized and only weigh about 5 ounces. The battery life is all day long at full use and it incorporates tiny cube shaped Nanotech batteries we can keep in our pockets like a bag of marbles. What I drool over is the five inch Organic Light Emitting Diode display, it's gives you a sharp view, shifts easily between light and dark environments and is very thin so we can strap the unit to our forearms and barely notice it's there. Plus they're copper shielded to guard against EMP and I can modify the removable wireless chip on the spot to conform with military communications standards."

"You know your gadgets that's for sure." Abernathy shakes his head, disbelieving a diminutive red-haired pixie runs circles around his own vast knowledge. "We'll prepare the Betas for you and good luck with your mission."

"Thank you Doctor." Tasha walks away from the screen wishing she had a Pocket Studio to fiddle around with while she sits through more meetings.

Virtually all of the technology briefings are of the same character and flavor of the mobile computing encounter. Various Department of Defense contractors and technology purveyors proudly tout their wares. Although many, if not all of them are useful to a degree none pass Tasha's discerning technology eye without modification or outright rejection. Not that Tasha is smarter than all of the scientists in all of the labs in America but they are hamstrung by bureaucratic nonsense where technology meets funding and political pork-barrel considerations. Tasha, free of government interference has learned the art of practical application of technologies. She exhibits no compunction speaking loudly and forcefully to scientists with twice her experience, not where the safety and efficiency of her team in the field is concerned.

During one briefing a Homeland Security contractor suggested an intra-communications system the police and fire organizations use during emergency responses. Tasha deemed the system impractical, its users required to bend a face toward a shoulder, pressing a button to talk into a microphone. She suggested the use of hands-free cell phone earpieces with Bluetooth for lightweight simplicity.

One agency official offered a modified bright yellow HAZMAT radiation suit with chemical exposure safety features complete with self-contained oxygen system and helmet roughly matching the design used by beekeepers. Tasha recommended packing the light chemical exposure suits used by soldiers in battle in the all-terrain vehicles while the team will wear dark navy blue flight suits with lots of pockets along with comfortable civilian commercial hiking boots. She further requested a mission patch and American flag patch affixed by Velcro.

During an earlier conversation with General Broadhead at Oceana Tasha debated the pros and cons of military all-terrain vehicles. The General suggested the Army's Prowler RTV, a Rugged Terrain Vehicle, as the best solution for safety and ease of use. He theorized the Prowler operates like a car, sports a gun mount, is constructed of heavy-duty steel with a full roll cage and rides on run-flat tires mounted on double-reinforced wheels. He specifically appreciated the Prowler's Army heritage.

For her part Tasha allowed the Prowler is a magnificently functional machine…and cute too…but bulky and heavy for the Well Site mission. She preferred the Polaris Sportsman 800 EFI with on demand all-wheel drive. Her demeanor turned positively giddy as she described the 800's attributes. The vehicle is a lightweight all-terrain dynamo with a powerful liquid cooled, electronic fuel injected twin-cylinder engine. It rides on PXT radial tires and super-light cast aluminum rims. The compact rugged 800 features a variable transmission, dual exhaust, over eleven inches of clearance, 1500 pound towing capacity, tough composite body panels and a 300 pound rack capacity. She suggested one for each member of the team with the exception of KO who she surmised could ride a Sportsmen 6x6, a six-wheeled version of the 800. It features a molded rear dump box with 800-pound capacity for hauling gear and has the same mobility as the four-wheeler. The Polaris vehicles also include a rifle holster accessory.

"And you know General Broadhead," Tasha confided in a stage whisper, "The Polaris comes in Army Green as its also an official U.S. Army vehicle."

Tasha's recommendations appealed to the General's sense of practicality and he liked the spunky gal to boot. Six Polaris Sportsmen 800s and one Sportsmen 6x6 were procured and loaded onto the Lucky Lady prior to takeoff from Virginia.

Evaluating and selecting mission critical electronics, gadgets and devices are a veritable technology candy store for Tasha. For global positioning technology she selects Garmin's eMap hand-held GPS unit that easily tucks into a pocket is a compact lightweight receiver, runs twelve hours on AA batteries and is accurate to 49 feet. She didn't select the eMap for mapping functions in the Well Site's previously unexplored and unmapped areas. Rather, she sought to install tracking electronics using the map-card bay, giving military monitors the ability to track the team's movements.

Specific task requirements and expertise dictated each member of Team Babelus select tools of their trade. Dr. Kagen orders several forensic evidence kits from the Sirchi Company to use for gathering genetic and DNA samples at the Well Site.

Jake, a former SEAL Commander selects a survival kit for everyone of the type tucked under the seats in Navy airplanes. The kit includes an 8-inch Navy issue knife with a smooth edge for slicing and a rough serrated edge for sawing, a set of distress signal flares, a compass, high-protein food bars and a reflective blanket.

Kelly Anne, a Medical Doctor, formulates the items to include in first-aid kits. She chose the basic Army issue kit with gauze bandages, anti-bacterial solution, pain medication and stick-on bandages. She insists on the inclusion of chemical weapons antidote injectors with atropine in case the Well Site is indeed a Saddam Hussein hidden WMD cache. KO, the team member most concerned with food selects a week's supply from a menu of K-Rations labeled dubiously with mouth-watering titles such as Chicken Cacciatore, Beef Stroganoff, Enchilada Rice and Beans and savory Lemon Meringue Pie.

24

"You may want to look out the windows on the port side," Captain Tucker's voice belts out over the intercom. We're just flying into Baghdad and are cleared to land in about 20 minutes. The crew of the Lucky Lady hopes you've enjoyed the trip and we thank you for flying Black Ops Airlines." His joke falls on deaf ears but at least he amuses himself.

"That's the Euphrates down there on the left and the Tigris is on the right," informs Jake, giving everyone a brief geography lesson of Iraq. The Well Site is about a hundred miles off to the left of the Euphrates but we probably can't see it from here. It's a little hazy out anyway so visibility is no more than 20 miles or so. That does make me wonder though if others can see a big hole in the ground when flying into Baghdad on a clear day."

"You see the highway down there? Our soldiers marched straight into Baghdad using the road when America invaded Mesopotamia for the first and only time. Some of those towns look a little ragged too. But nothing like Dresden or Berlin after World War Two."

"Did you fly over Berlin after World War Two Jake or did you get there by boat?" Kelly Anne teases. "You're holding up pretty well for a man your age. You don't look a day over sixty-five."

Jake ignores the sarcasm. "Of course not Kayanne. I've seen pictures. You forget I was a History major in college and I also got a good look at intelligence and reconnaissance photos during my tours in the Navy. The Captain of our ship carried around a collection of them and he used to show them off all the time to impress us youngsters."

"Those are huge rivers down there," remarks Dr. Kagen. "I was under the impression Iraq was a desert. I didn't expect to see water and all those trees. I'd call that lush vegetation down there if I didn't know any better."

"Some parts of Iraq are barren desert Doctor Kagen," Jake lectures, "But in truth Iraq is one of the most fertile and well-watered countries in the Middle East. As you can see to the far left of the Euphrates the huge farming tracts and there's a number of places with marshes and swamps."

"Why does it always look dry and arid on television?"

"Well it's not Oregon but for this region Iraq enjoys the most arable land. You can see the huge fresh water rivers from up here. Mesopotamia has looked this way since the beginning of time, or at least recorded history."

"Water, oil, land for crops and a free democratic society," Dr. Kagen marvels. "The Iraqi people are surely blessed. One would think they would use all of those natural resources and turn the entire region into a citadel for good. Instead they are forever mired in violence and chaos."

"They were under the dictatorial boot of Saddam Hussein for nearly forty years. That's gotta leave a mark on a society."

"What about before Hussein came along? Weren't they mired in chaos then too?"

"Ehh, you may have a point there Doctor. I'm anxious to get down there and see how Baghdad has fared over the past few of years of democratic government. I bet the place looks a whole lot different from the time I spent here after the first Gulf War."

The Lucky Lady gracefully sweeps into Baghdad's International Airport with a perfect three-point landing. Team Babelus waits in high anticipation for the plane to dock and release them from the captivity of a long tiring flight. Unfortunately the sights and sensations just beyond the plane's doors will make them wish they had chosen to turn around and fly straight home.

25

Searing heat taps the last gasp of air from unsuspecting lungs with the first step from an air-conditioned airplane cabin into the Baghdad summer. Having endured a grueling 36 hours of flights, meetings and government enforced captivity Team Babelus finally arrives at Baghdad International Airport, a way station to the location of a vast sinkhole potentially housing the most significant archeological discoveries in modern times.

"All of this is about the same as the last time I was here," Jake says to the group as they walk the tarmac toward freight hangar A-6 on the south side of the airport. "Its hotter than I expected, usually the heat doesn't arrive until the middle of summer. Must be Global Warming."

"Yeah right!" mocks Kelly Anne. "I was kidnapped by the government at the exact instance I started giving a refutation lecture on that very subject. I imagined they were the Global Warming Police come to cart me away for my crimes and hide me in a dungeon. Seems like a week ago or longer though I know it was only a day and a half. I've been to some fairly hot places in the world, down at the Equator, West Texas in the summer and Death Valley in California at over 120 degrees but the heat here makes my skin feel as if I we're dipped in vat of hot oil. I literally feel like bacon."

"One of the Generals told me Baghdad's high temperatures are a dry heat and I wouldn't notice it much," informs Dr. Kagen. "Obviously they were lying or trying to assuage my fears. It's dry alright, so hot my sweat evaporates before I know I'm perspiring."

"I'm Scotch-Irish," Tasha tells them. "I'm genetically predisposed towards gloomy cold weather. When the temperatures get above 72 degrees I start looking for air conditioning or a freezer to stick my head into. It was bad enough in Virginia; I was dripping with sweat every waking moment at Oceana. Southern heat is not dry I can assure you!"

"I'm comfortable in desert heat," brags KO. "All those weekend getaways riding my Hog out to Vegas conditioned me for frying pan weather like this. Maybe I'll get a good tan while we're out here."

"With my pink skin I'll probably develop skin cancer before we make it to the hangar." jokes Tasha.

"We won't be exposed to the heat once we're out at the Well Site," instructs Jake. "Not directly anyway. At 200 feet or so underground the temperature will even out. I'll guess its around 72 degrees down there Tasha so don't break out the 200 SPF skin cream just yet."

"I hope I can hold out until we get out there. I think my freckles have already turned."

"You and me both but I'm starting to think the heat isn't our only problem here in Baghdad."

"What are you talking about Jake?" asks Kelly Anne. "I haven't detected any problems around here. In fact it seems remarkably quiet."

Jake walks toward the hangar, a worried and distracted look plastered on his face. "Remarkable quiet is an aspect of what I'm getting at guys. Do you notice all of the workers here, they're wearing traditional Muslim clothes and when we walked past the public terminal the only women I saw wore the traditional *hijab*, veils and all."

Dr. Kagen's curiosity compels him to ask questions, though he may not like the answer. "What's so unusual about veiled women and bearded men in a Muslim country Jake?"

"Not unusual at all if you're in Pakistan or Iran. This place has the look and feel of Saudi Arabia. Those places aren't merely run of the mill Muslim countries. They're extreme Muslim nations under the rule of oppressive Islamic regimes operated by clerics and Saudi Arabia is the citadel of Wahabism, the most extreme form of Islam. The atmosphere around here is eerily reminiscent of the Taliban. As if Mullah Omar picked up stakes from Afghanistan and carted the whole shebang to Iraq. The people of Iraq, through all of the petty tyrants and despite neighboring extremist governments have generally lived as a secular society. If I didn't know better I would say Sharia Law found a foothold here and that's bad news. Possibly it's just the airport or I'm going loony."

Kelly Anne interjects, finding any criticism of Jake irresistible. "Maybe you just don't know any better."

"Heh, yeah maybe but I doubt it."

Dr. Kagen presses the debate further. "It's their country so what's the problem? They vote on these sorts of things don't they?"

"Yeah, live and let live Jake," KO remarks, ever the antagonist.

"Look gang, the United States sacrificed thousands of lives and hundreds of billions of dollars to liberate Iraq from a dangerous tyrannical thug. To see Iraq go from an evil dictatorial regime to an equally oppressive theocracy is the dictionary definition of a horribly wasted opportunity. As we all know Iran, an Islamic theocratic dictatorship of the first order is completely against Western values, our way of life. Their beliefs and interpretations of the Koran make them dangerous to you and me."

"Most acts of terrorism against the United States since 1979 are the result of extremist Islamic views. Not oppression or poverty…religious fascism pure and simple. If the Iraqis built their government on the beliefs of the Shia sect of Islam, the same as Iran's, then we're in for trouble…eventually the Iraqis will hate us too, if they don't already."

"We sent our troops over here to liberate Iraq from oppression. The sinking feeling I have is due to the possibility America let the situation get worse by allowing the Iraqis to write Sharia Law into their constitution. But like I said, maybe there's something going on at the airport, a convention or something or people returning from a pilgrimage to Mecca. We'll get a good look when we go through Baghdad proper and some of the smaller towns along the way out to the Well Site."

Dr. Kagen cannot grasp Jake's apprehensions and argues the point. "Jake it's immoral and hypocritical for Americans to turn a liberated country back over to its natives and then expect them to form a democracy along the same lines as ours. After all one of the greatest tenets of the West is the freedom to worship as you please. We can't force Western thoughts and ideas on a society and make them drop their own religious expressions. America was founded to get away from all of that sort of thing."

"Have you ever heard of Shintoism Doctor Kagen?"

"Can't say that I have Jake, I'm not an historian. What is it a religion worshipping the lower leg and foot?"

"Heh-heh, no Doctor. Shintoism was the Japanese state religion of the World War Two era, and of course before that. They used the religion as the basis behind the idea of Japanese supremacy in much the same way Iran uses it's state religion to promote the idea of Islamic superiority. We didn't allow the Japanese to write a theocratic form of government into the Japanese Constitution after we whipped their butts in World War Two. In fact General McArthur wrote the Japanese Constitution himself, modeled after the U.S. Constitution. The world hasn't had to face a problem with Japanese supremacy ever since…unless we're talking about micro-electronics."

"So you're inferring we should have written the Iraqi constitution too? The problem I see in your argument is we didn't go to war with the Iraqi people…they weren't our enemy. We went to war against a regime. What right do we have to impose our values on the people of Iraq?"

"There's nothing wrong with respecting their right to worship as they please Doctor but a social contract is implied in our respect. Islam does not respect people's right to practice their own religion. They lop the heads off Christians, Hindus and Buddhists all around the world. So intellectually you're right but we can't send our people to fight and oust regimes wanting to kill us and then replace them with dangerous theocracies that don't share or respect our values. At some point they will reject us and set about the business of killing us along with the rest of the radicals. Sure, we waged war with

Iraq to liberate the people but this aspect of the fight is a sidebar in the War on Terror."

Perhaps the Iraqi heat is affecting his mind but Jake is only warming up with his geo-political lecture. "You might have the idea we went into Iraq to find weapons of mass destruction or get rid of Saddam but those are only bit parts of the larger picture. The true reason we invaded Iraq was to create a magnet for Jihadists to come here and fight. They did, we killed them and we prevented thousands of American civilian deaths from attacks on our own soil."

"What is a magnet for Jihadis?" asks Dr. Kagen.

"Before the Iraq War the entire Middle East was teeming with young Islamic zealots itching to take on the Great Satan, meaning us the United States. They saw America as weak and vacillating and to them 911 was a tangible success. So thousands of young men in the Middle East, ginned up by imams teaching hate and destruction were spoiling for a fight. The President didn't want all of that hatred and negative energy directed at Americans on American soil so we went into Iraq and created an accessible battlefield where young radicals from Jordan, Saudi Arabia, Syria and Iran could easily get to and tangle with the American military in a straight-up fight. We killed thousands of radical Islamists who otherwise would have become standard terrorists doing their level best to conduct operations in America. Why do you think we were never attacked again after 911?"

"Sounds like we used Iraq and its populace like a bucket of bait worms. Why didn't the President come out and say it like that instead of taking all the grief over the lack of WMDs and links to al-Qaeda?"

"Its not diplomatically polite or good politics to say you're in a fight for ignoble and selfish reasons. Political correctness demands you claim a noble cause laced with lofty words like freedom and liberty and you only fight to exact justice from evil tyrants. The truth is we fought save our own butt, not to say there's anything wrong with that."

"I'm glad we did," admits Tasha, "I like to keep my butt intact, including my country."

"I guess we throw our principles out the window when the survival instinct takes over," allows Dr. Kagen. "Survival is genetically programmed into all species, I'm not sure values and morality are. I should write a paper on the subject."

26

Baghdad International Airport
Freight Terminal A-6
Baghdad, Iraq

The team strolls into the shadows of the freight hangar and out of the sun, momentarily sparing them from Iraq's direct blistering heat. They stand, alone for a brief instant while waiting in the hangar for a military liaison to take them to the staging area for the trip out to the Well Site. It is the first time the assembled team spends any time together without the presence of a government employee.

The over-traveled group of Americans, dressed in navy blue flight suits, stand in a hangar in sweltering heat at a place formerly known as the Saddam Hussein Airport. A small generously bearded man dressed in a white Islamic gown-like dishdasha and white kufi headwear approaches them shouting loudly and gesticulating wildly.

"He's saying cover your face, cover your face!" KO alerts the group. "He's informing us we are infidels and an abomination to Allah."

"Tell him to move along and mind his own business," orders Jake.

KO barks in Arabic toward the distraught little man but fails to dissuade him from his vociferous tirade. KO tries again, louder with increasingly serious tones. The man refuses to stop shouting and pointing, nor will he step aside. Jake senses danger and moves toward the man as several more men approach the group from the shadows of the hangar. Jake stops and the team stands frozen now surrounded by more than two-dozen shouting menacing men.

Instinctively the team forms a semi-circle with their backs toward each other. The shouting men crowd closer and their numbers grow larger. The shouts and gestures take on a rhythmic chant as the members of Team Babelus each raise their balled up fists preparing to defend themselves from the mob now seemingly breaching the edges of sanity. In unison the mob inches forward and starts grabbing and clutching at the team, tearing at clothes and continuing their frighteningly intimidating chants.

Kelly Anne punches one zealot square in the throat sending him reeling backwards clutching his neck in pain. Jake pushes men away defensively and throws elbow blows in close quarters, smashing faces with the precision of a seasoned warrior. Dr. Kagen twists back and forth swinging a heavy backpack through a sea of arms and hands. KO holds a man in a vice-grip headlock while holding the throat of another, using him to fend off the onslaught. Tiny Tasha bobs and weaves, punching, scratching and kicking in a flurry of red hair and primal screams. Throughout the melee the team holds ground in a semi-circle but the mass number and fury of the attackers threatens to overwhelm them.

The sound of automatic weapons fire echoes throughout the hangar chamber followed by the mob quickly scattering. Four battle-hardened Marines step into the breach, weapons trained on the mob as it scurries away with continued shouts.

"What are you people doing here?" demands a young Corporal

"We're with the United States Government," informs Jake. "We're waiting for our military liaison, a Gunnery Sergeant Williams."

"Well then I'm sorry to inform you Gunny Williams was killed this morning, gunned down at his desk with a dead reporter and photographer laying next to him in a pool of blood. Are you attached to a department here in Iraq?"

"That's classified Corporal."

"Well how did you get here to the airport Sir?"

"That's classified as well."

"Look mister, I could give two shits and a damn about your business or what the government has in store for you at the airport! We can't have a bunch of unarmed civilians milling around. I just want to get you to safety. You won't last long out here, especially with the women unveiled."

"How did you know we were here? Did your supervisor send you out here to rescue us from the mob?"

"We overheard some of the women talking in the terminal. They saw your group walk by with unveiled women and threw a hissy fit. Then the men started out after you. We followed them knowing trouble might ensue."

"Thanks Corporal, we flew here."

"The only plane landing here over the past hour is the big FEDEX 747 freighter. The big dumb beast sticks out like a sore thumb around here. The Iraqi government just recently started letting FEDEX fly in to Baghdad International. DHL is what we usually see. You don't look like a palette of packages so that bird must be a CIA plane or something."

Jake shakes his head in disgust as he ponders yet another round of egregious government incompetence and wonders if this experience wasn't the whole Iraqi affair played out in miniature.

Baghdad International Airport is designated as an American military base until the final elements of the U.S. military ship out of country. The Corporal summons his supervisor who in turn gets in touch with the Base Commander. Unfortunately Chief of Staff Lamont had directed the team toward the wrong freight hangar, number 6 instead of number 16, and they are lucky to have survived. If not for the prescience of a handful of Marines the Well Site Operation may have ended ignominiously at the hands of a mob offended by the mere sight of a female face.

"This whole thing doesn't feel right," Jake thinks as the team hurries to the correct hangar bay under armed Marine escort.

27

White House Situation Room
Washington D.C.

"I understand Team Babelus has landed in Iraq," informs President Crandall speaking to the Cabinet members and agency directors gathered in the Situation Room. "When will they head to Well Site and begin the exploration process? I'm anxious to get a look at what's down there."

"They've loaded up on a military truck and are headed for the Green Zone Mr. President," relays Dan Maney. "From there they'll fly by Sea Stallion helicopter, gear and all, directly to the Well Site. The trip shouldn't take any longer than two hours providing they don't run into any snags. General Keith is waiting for them with the two Iraqi scientists we agreed to include in the exploration team. I think he's anxious to get started as well."

"There was a bit of a dust up at Baghdad International," informs Secretary Green-Newton. "Apparently some Iraqi workers at the airport objected to the uncovered faces of the women and started a row."

Quick to anger, Maney reacts loudly. "You're telling us our team was attacked at the airport? Why were they in an unsecured area? Didn't they have any protection out there? By the way Baghdad International is designated a United States military base last time I checked. Are you saying a team of American scientists was attacked by a group of Islamic radicals on an American military installation? Where is Base Command all this time our people are running gauntlets?"

Green-Newton is tired of constant contretemps with Maney and tries to answer calmly. "The report relayed from Lamont indicates the team walked into the wrong freight hangar and were accosted by a group of men. I have no idea if the men are radicals or not. Apparently the Gunnery Sergeant in charge of security for the team was gunned down in his office an hour before the flight arrived. No one else on the base knew of the mission as we're keeping a tight lid on information."

Once again Maney feels anger welling in his throat. "The zealots attacked the team because the women were unveiled?"

"Yes, apparently so. An unveiled face is a grave sin in their culture and we didn't take that into account."

Maney is furious at the implications. "Make no mistake those are radicals! Since when do we take religious beliefs into account at our own military installations?"

"We can't assume the men are radicals just because they don't hold to the same religious traditions and Western

Culture, Dan. As I said the report is sketchy. Lamont wasn't with them at the time and the information comes second-hand. For all we know our people started the fracas."

"Oh yeah right! A group of science geeks on the most important mission of their lives march right into Baghdad International and within five minutes of their arrival start a bar fight! Is that the story you want to run with Madam Secretary?"

"I'm only saying we don't know at this point! I understand the women fought bravely and helped stanch the violence."

"Was anyone hurt?" Vice-President Murcheson calmly asks, apparently the only adult in the room.

"Nothing more than a few scrapes and bruises. Four Marines came upon the fight and chased the men off by firing guns into the air. Armed Marines command immediate respect. Everyone's ok."

Maney is livid with anger and vents his wrath. "I am getting dead sick of this shit! We can't allow Islamists to impose Sharia Law on our people at an American military facility. We can't allow it! This sort of nonsense has gone unchecked ever since we capitulated on the Iraqi government's demand our military women wear veils when they go off base. When are we going to learn Islam isn't peaceful and the radicals want to impose a backward 9th century religion on everyone in the entire world? Islam means surrender in Arabic ya' know."

"We're all aware of Islamic history Dan," interjects Secretary Malloy. "This is a delicate operation so why don't we quit venting our spleens and get on with the business of making sure our people explore the Well Site as completely as possible and get out of there safely, ok?"

"What about the Gunny Sergeant and the reporters, Malloy? Don't they rate anything in this? Don't you find it curious they're gunned down right before our team shows up in Baghdad? How did the killers know?"

"Yeah, they rate, of course but…"

Vice-President Murcheson wishes to move forward but is careful to address the reporter issue. "Hey Dan, I'm the one who ordered the reporter and photographer into harm's way and, yes, I feel responsible for their deaths. My guess is they told someone about where they were headed and the information found the wrong ears. Now let's move on."

"General Keith will join us on the monitor in a few minutes," informs General Broadhead. "And Lamont will pipe in from Baghdad International, we can ask him directly what happened but perhaps we shouldn't waste the time. We don't have much left."

Maney is un-assuaged but understands the need to move forward. "Ok we'll just leave it for later. I'll be coordinating the effort from Washington and Lamont is working from the Iraqi side. Malloy is engaged with the Iraqi government diplomatically through their foreign ministry. General Keith is in charge at the Well Site. If everything goes according to plan our team will go in, gather the information we need and high tail it out of there before the Iraqi imposed deadline. Team Babelus is equipped with high-tech communications so we can monitor their movements, conversations and field images from the Situation Room. If we all do our jobs correctly the mission will work. Does anyone have any quest…?"

Graham Likely, the Director of National Intelligence barges into the Situation Room unannounced, startling the group and stopping Maney in mid-sentence. The Director's smooth natural gait and easy manner belie the hint of crisis written on his concerned face. He stands at the edge of the grand mahogany conference table, hands hanging at his sides and speaks in grave tones.

He turns and directly addresses the leader of the free world. "Mr. President, We have a new quandary on our hands."

The President sitting directly to Director Likely's left stares up at the Director at an uncomfortable angle and asks the Director to take a seat.

"Yes of course Sir." Likely finds an empty chair three spaces away to the President's right between Secretaries Malloy and Green-Newton. "Intelligence we've gathered over the past several hours through satellite imagery and covert agents on the ground reveals the Iranians are conducting unusually provocative maneuvers as it relates to their nuclear power facilities. We've confirmed their activities through four different intelligence sources and CIA Director Norton is certain of the veracity of information contained in reports."

"What kind of situation are we dealing with here Graham?" the President asks as he runs all of the Well Site scenarios that could possibly involve Iran through his mind.

Likely drops the bomb. "The Iranians are preparing to test a nuclear weapon."

For what seems an eternity but is in reality a brief instant the room falls quiet. Normal rustling of papers, leaned whispering and squeaks from chairs rocking back and forth are absent. Deeply ingrained images of apocalyptic destruction, towering mushroom clouds, searing red infernos and flesh eating radiation contamination etch a perfect picture of ashen faces, creased brows and tightly pursed lips. The morbid silence breaks with the vibration ring of a cell phone going unanswered.

"What on earth are you talking about Graham?" demands the President waking from a disaster-induced coma.

"Iranian movements roughly mirror North Korea's provocative actions before they conducted nuclear tests a few years ago. They've dramatically increased activity at a missile site in Dezful. The site is in the west about twenty-five miles from the Iraqi border. They cleared the area of all automobile traffic, communications equipment and civilians, even shipped out livestock in stake trucks. About four days ago they shut down the main reactor at the Arak nuclear power facility, we believe to extract weapons-grade plutonium from the reactor's nuclear fuel rods."

"I thought we had them contained!" bellows Secretary Malloy. "The International Atomic Energy Agency gave them a clean bill of health on weapons-grade plutonium and I don't recall any briefings alerting us to this potential from the outgoing administration! Do you Dan?"

"No," answered Maney quietly shaking his head. "But you can't hang your hat, or the country's security on anything the IAEA rubber stamps Marty. Their inspections are an international joke. They never seem to stop or even slow down determined rouge regimes from acquiring nuclear weapons. They couldn't stop Pakistan or North Korea and Saddam damn near got them in the 90s. Libya built an entire nuclear weapons program directly under IAEA inspector noses. The truth is when a country wants to hide fissile material from the IAEA they will and there's precious little the agency can do to uncover the stuff. They aren't a military organization and have a limited mandate from the feckless United Nations."

"I'm just as concerned with the intelligence handed over to us from the previous administration, or lack thereof. The outgoing NSA told me point blank they were successful in putting the Iranian nuclear program in a box. If the information Graham is giving us is what it looks like then we are in for a rude awakening. Suddenly everything comes back into play. The Palestinian solution will go to the dogs with Israel in Iran's nuclear cross hairs. Iran is smack dab in the middle between Iraq and Afghanistan and we can't afford further instability in those countries. There's going to be a lot of unhappy Arabs out there if the Persians prove they have the Bomb."

"The Iranians haven't made any provocative statements or acted belligerent in any way for at least six months," Malloy affirms. "How do we know this is the real deal Graham? Do our intelligence agencies have a firm grasp on the inner workings of the Iranian government to make this sort of judgment call?"

"Unfortunately I can't answer that question unequivocally Marty. We've monitored a decided increase of cell phone communications in Farsi indicating this is the real deal as you call it. We have no way of knowing if they have the capability to test a nuclear weapon with any degree of certainty. Everything is anecdotal at this point. I would tell you to get a diplomatic envoy over there right away but, as you know, we don't have diplomatic relations with Iran and of course, no embassy in Tehran."

"How long do we have to work this thing Graham?" the President asks with despondent seriousness.

"We're in the dark here Mr. President. Any timeline is predicated on the Iranian's actual capabilities and we know too little about them. Our best intelligence normally comes through informants who contact local embassies in their respective countries. We don't have this resource in Iran and gathering reliable intelligence is difficult. We can estimate anywhere from a couple of days to a couple of weeks if the technology is already staged to conduct the test. After that it's a matter of transferring nuclear fuel, a dangerous and delicate activity but not particularly time consuming."

President Crandall addresses the Secretary of State. "I know we have action plans for this Grazzy. I'm wondering what options we have to deal with this crisis. Everything is on the table, we can't allow Iran to go nuclear."

"With all due respect Sir, we do have plenty of options but I'm not so sure we want to place all of them on the table just yet. On the less risky end of the apocalyptic scale we can run bombing sorties using Stealth bombers and take out some of the known Iranian nuclear research and power sites, causing considerable collateral damage. At the other extreme we can launch a nuclear-tipped inter-continental ballistic missile aimed at the middle of Tehran and take out the entire government in one strike Mullahs and all. The number of civilian casualties after a nuclear strike in a large urban area is unconscionable."

Green-Newton relays her thoughts as fast as they come to mind. "We can try diplomacy through the United Nation and hope to get some of Iran's Arab neighbors on board with sanctions or perhaps a blockade. The U.N. Security Council isn't much help, not with China, Russia and France as duplicitous as they are in regards to Iranian affairs. Frankly Mr. President I don't see any good options, every alternative is chock full of political and moral peril. As a nation we sat on our hands while Iran developed nuclear technologies. We should have acted years ago. Now the only choice we have is to select the least damaging horrible course."

Maney can barely contain himself. "We should have taken out the regime in 1979 when they invaded the sovereign territory of our embassy, took and held hostages for over a year and deposed our ally the Shah! Couldn't anyone see this eventuality? Now we have the entire mess unceremoniously dumped in our laps and we'll be the one's to hang for it by hook or by crook!"

"This isn't the time to fret over politics Dan," Secretary Green-Newton states derisively. "We need to focus on the immediate threat."

"I'm not worrying about politics Graziella!" Maney pounds his fist loudly on the table. "I'm agonizing about waking up in the dead of night with the telephone call informing me the State of Israel has just been wiped off the face of the earth. I live in abject fear of Iran taking control of the entire region with nuclear blackmail and sending the West into economic ruin. I'm concerned about the security of every American city and the prospect of the radical Mullahs handing over nuclear technology to terrorists to annihilate anyone within ten miles of the bombs they'll explode. I'm worried about religious zealots trying to bring about the appearance of the 12th Imam by creating ten or twenty nuclear ground zeros all around the world. At this moment I don't give a damn about the political ramifications of our decisions."

"I'm sorry, I didn't mean to imply…"

Maney in full tirade is impossible to interrupt. "And I don't see why we should take the nuclear option off the table! Are we suicidal?"

"Maybe we should take a couple of steps back from the brink," Malloy says soothingly. "The North Koreans pulled the same stunt and has never launched a nuclear weapon against its enemies. We're not even sure the Iranians can actually field a usable weapon out of the technologies they've boasted about over the past few years. And the test the NoKos conducted was barely a half-megaton. We've got conventional weapons with a bigger blast than that."

Maney is singularly unconvinced. "Marty we can't treat the Iranians on the same plane as the NoKos! Don't be an idiot! The North Korean government is quirky and dangerous but not suicidal in the same way as Iran. Their nuclear weapons program is apparently created to bolster North Korea's standing in the region not wipe out entire civilizations. In stark contrast the Iranians are religious zealots who want to use the most powerful weapons they can get their hands on to kill infidels en masse. In their war with Iraq the Mullahs sent legions of teenagers to the battlefield armed with nothing more than a plastic key to Paradise hung around their doomed necks, that is the measure of their lunatic mindset!"

Maney calms down for a moment, checking his own growing lunacy. He continues in quiet, serious tones. "For the Mullahs in Iran, the state, their own state, is secondary to the wishes of Allah. They have an expressed desire to bring about the appearance of the 12th Imam by triggering an Islamic Armageddon. Religious zealotry often trumps survival instincts and this notion is the gravest aspect of our problem today. If you need an example where devout religious attitudes overpower the need to survive look no further than the experience at Waco where David Koresh and his followers sacrificed their lives and those of their women and children in a raging inferno because they thought themselves part of an end-times prophecy. Imagine the same diabolical attitude played out by a billion screaming zealots around the entire globe."

28

"Dan you mentioned the 12th Imam a couple of times, what are you talking about?" asks Green-Newton, curious as to the nature of the reference.

"You're kidding, right? Ehh, whatever. The return of the 12th Imam is a traditional belief of the Shia sect in Islam. They believe an end-times prophet will magically appear from a well and re-establish an Islamic caliphate or empire to rule the world under the banner of Islam. An appearance of this Islamic Mahdi, meaning the Guided One, is prophesied as a redeemer figure, like Christ, and will change the world into a perfect Islamic society, a Heaven on Earth if you will."

"As you can see the re-creation of Paradise is a powerful stimulus among religious zealots and they will go to any lengths to ensure the will of Allah as they see it. The Shia believe the secret figure of a mysterious 12th Imam is brought forward through the overt actions of the faithful, and I don't mean prayer and fasting."

"Martyrdom, mass killings of infidels in the name of Islam, even the destruction of the entire human race qualify as precursors to the Imam's appearance. And who is the dominant Shia group in the world? The clerics and Islamic followers in Iran and they're about to go nuclear at precisely the same moment we're investigating a mysterious well in the Mesopotamian desert."

"I concede your point Dan," Malloy allows, "But we've got to find a way to work this crisis through diplomacy first and this isn't a turf battle on my part, it's a moral imperative. We don't want to inadvertently bring about Armageddon ourselves by provoking the Iranians. Our duty as citizens of the world is to avoid global destroying conflicts at all costs. If we turn away from the principles of shared responsibility for the world's safety, how will our maker judge us?"

"Fine, fine…of course you're right Marty and I agree with you about the need to avoid Armageddon. And yes, we must use every diplomatic tool at our disposal to ratchet the crisis down to a manageable level but we aren't morally required to commit suicide as a nation in the process. All other options are violently dangerous and likely to cause catastrophic destruction throughout the entire world. Our problem is Marty, we may have already crossed the point where there are no satisfactory diplomatic options."

"We are blindsided on this," interjects President Crandall. "But we are bound by our oaths of office to protect the American people. Marty do what you can, turn over every diplomatic stone possible. Let's pray you're successful somehow. Let me make myself clear, all options remain on the table. Maybe we'll get lucky and learn our intelligence is in error, wouldn't be the first time."

"I'll do the best I can Mr. President."

• • •

The tense atmosphere in the Situation Room subsides briefly with the addition of Chief of Staff Lamont and General Keith via plasma screen monitors. The General informs the group on the arrival of the designated Iraqi scientists as scheduled. One, a botanist named Ahmed al-Tikriti who matriculated at Oxford University in London wears the traditional dishdasha and kufi. The other, an historian and expert in Mesopotamian artifacts named Brian Saylor was educated at the University of Pittsburgh and is clad in Western style clothing. His western assimilated appearance provides a sense of relief and comfort to the group.

A conversation with General Keith allays some fears regarding the Iranian nuclear tests; the General reminds the group the Iranians often tout new weapons systems that don't exist or fake evidence such as the time they broadcast a video as their own depicting a Chinese cruise missile shown a year prior. In any event the General surmises the Well Site mission is safe from Iranian interference and should continue unabated.

Chief of Staff Lamont apologizes profusely for the confusion leading to the violent confrontation at Baghdad International and assures the President of safe transport in the future, continuously guarded by a phalanx of able Marines. His report is somewhat less than sweetness and light as he relays the re-emergence of the Mahdi al-Hadj, a key figure in the Iraq insurgency, and his elevation to Grand Mahdi shifting the balance of religious expression toward Shia practices. The newly minted Grand Mahdi is now the dominant force in Iraq. The Iraqi government, at the behest of the Grand Mahdi, implements the severest forms of Sharia Law throughout the nation including the stoning of women caught in adultery, the elimination of women's rights and strict adherence to extreme Islam under penalty of death. Lamont sees no adverse issues related to the Well Site mission despite Iranian provocations.

"The Well Site mission is a go!" informs the President to the enthusiastic clapping of those gathered in the Situation Room. "May God go with our brave and gifted scientific exploration team."

Dan Maney pulls aside Director Likely as the Situation Room empties for a brief break, grabbing him by the elbow and leading him to a quiet corner in the room.

"Graham, have the Iranians announced an impending nuclear test?

"No, not a peep."

"A press release on al-Jazeera, a video-clip on a website anything of that nature?"

"Not a single gesture, no saber rattling at all."

"When the Iranians shout from the mountaintops they have a brand new miracle weapon I take it with a grain of salt. Their record of technological achievement is spotty at best. I would expect them to make loud claims to the world demonstrating technological superiority."

"Its all quiet out there."

"Then we should be worried. The silence scares the crap out of me!"

29

Baghdad International Airport
Base Command
Baghdad, Iraq

36 hours of travel and incessant briefings followed by a brawl with a crowd of religious zealot drones will normally wear down the heartiest adventurers. Although tired and weary from their experiences with the travels and travails of the Well Site Operation thus far, knowing the close proximity of their mysterious destination infuses Team Babelus with a sense of heightened anticipation.

An unexpected calm envelops the group as they load personal gear into a Cheetah armored vehicle used by Marines to transport soldiers and dignitaries safely through dangerous Iraqi neighborhoods. The heavily armored desert tan Cheetah can withstand a blast from an improvised explosive device of up to 50 lbs. of TNT. With its blast tested restraint system and heavy-duty protection against mine explosions and bullets the rig provides a comfortably safe cocoon for its passengers. Team Babelus feels empowered and invincible riding past burned out stores and war ravaged houses in the physically aggressive vehicle escorted by tough battle-hardened fighting Marines.

The trip from Baghdad International to the Iraq Green Zone, now officially labeled the International Zone in deference to local sensibilities is a short cross-town excursion. The time apart from government overseers gives the team a chance to chat with each other and the Marine guard seated in the passenger compartment while the convoy wends its way through stifling morning traffic.

Looking for information on Baghdad since the war Jake quizzes the Corporal seated next to him. "How long have you been in country?"

"About eight months now," the Corporal replies, "But I spent a year in Kuwait before getting sent up here."

"What do you think of the place?"

"Don't like it much."

"Yeah its pretty hot here and war is hell as they say."

"The war is hell I suppose, and yeah, it's hot out here but that's not why I hate the place."

"What do you mean?

"In the first place there's no place to party. Since they came down hard on the Sharia Laws all the bars got closed down and there's no place to pick up chicks. You can't even get a look at a decent female around here what with all of the clothes they wear and the veils. My great grandfather was in World War Two, he told me stories about how they'd find girls all over Europe at bars and in drinking places where they'd get shit-faced. A lot of the soldiers married some of those chicks. Heck Pappy brought my grandmother over from France. When I signed on to this war part of me wanted to do those things too. Now I ask ya, when have ya ever heard of a war where nobody was allowed to drink and fool around with the women?"

"No whiskey-sexy, huh?" Jake asks in reference to the famous early post war attitudes of the Iraqis.

"Ha ha, no none not one sip unless you're willing to guzzle the swill they make from anti-freeze and sell on the black market. And the women, well around here you can't even look at the menu!"

"That is a sad state of affairs." Jake hopes the Corporal's information is restricted to Baghdad as a show to other Islamic states. "Do you feel like we did a good thing here liberating the Iraqi people from Saddam?"

"I was stationed at CENTCOM in Kuwait for about a year before I got up here and they pretty much have the same restrictions. Of course we heard about all of the wild times guys had in Baghdad just after the government fell, I guess it was like the Wild West or somethin'. When I finally got stationed here I was surprised at how strict they were and I thought maybe we had liberated them from one tyrant and threw 'em back in with another tyrant of a different kind."

"As I got to know the lay of the land and how the people in the country operate I started to think differently. Just after the shootin' war ended it was a bloody mess around here for a couple of years and all kinds of honor killings and what they called sectarian violence. The Shia were determined to get revenge on the Sunnis who abused them during Saddam's reign. Naturally the Sunnis reacted to Shia death squads with their own roving bands of murdering rapists."

"We'd find dead bodies piled up behind the post office or a beheaded corpse thrown out in the open so's everyone would know who did the killin'. Blood quite literally flowed in the streets. Well the whole thing reminded me of one big family feud that would go on for generations like back in the hills of Arkansas where I'm from. Then the clerics got together with the government and they put together the Sharia thing and it's been pretty quiet since. In the long run it's good for them I guess, but I ain't havin' any fun."

Kelly Anne, observing the interchange with fascination couldn't resist joining the conversation. "Joined up to get ya' some?" She asked.

"Uh, no ma'am, I am a patriot and believe in my country. I think we're doing the right thing here, it's just that glory doesn't happen only on the battlefield if ya know what I mean."

"I'm just teasing you Corporal. No need to wave the banner on my account. Anyone who volunteers to go halfway around the world and fight for their country is a patriot in my book and as an American I appreciate your decision."

"Thanks ma'am."

"When I think about how the world has gotten so completely off track morally I sometimes wonder if hard rules and strict guidelines aren't the best for society?" Kelly Anne stares reminiscently through the Cheetah's square window at a rebuilt Baghdad shopping center. "I grew up in an orthodox town…in California believe it or not. A Christian sect that kept strict rules, the Seventh-Day Adventists, founded Loma Linda, my hometown. When I was a little girl none of the grocery stores in town sold liquor and there were no drinking bars at all. I never saw a person take a drink until I went to Yale. We weren't allowed to wear make-up or jewelry or dance. The high school, called an academy, had banquets instead of homecoming dances or senior proms."

"We also had strict diet rules too. In Islam you probably know they don't eat pork. Well almost nobody in our town ate any kind of meat at all. Many were strict vegans. I knew a guy who only ate fruits and nuts and he always looked pale like a ghost and sick."

"We worshipped on Friday night after sundown through Saturday at sundown like the Jews. The entire town shut down for the Sabbath. All of this seems so quaint and restricting now but as I look back on those times, admittedly with some nostalgia, it doesn't seem such a horrible existence."

"I never once saw a woman with bruises, beaten down by a drunkard husband. Nobody ever used the N-word in my presence. The only time I ever heard it growing up was during a movie in school on the harmful effects of racism. The local police didn't run around every night chasing after gang members, armed robbers or answering domestic violence calls.

The worst incident I ever heard of during my entire childhood was a purse snatching. Citizens in the community caught the guy who was from a nearby town and made him do three hundred hours of community service. Eventually he became a Christian, went to school and graduated with a degree in Medicine."

Kelly Anne continued her trip down memory lane, partly as a knife in Jake's side. "Each Friday evening the church bells rang out and we all went to Vespers…Friday night worship services. Of course this was the perfect time for flirting with the boys and socializing with our friends. On Saturdays you would see families out walking together in the afternoon. Just think of that one aspect, families, together, out walking instead of watching television or running off to separate rooms of the house to do something on the computer."

"Saturday nights were the best times. There was always a function at the high school or University gymnasium on Saturday nights. We celebrated the end of Sabbath playing basketball or volleyball, eating buffets of goodies and generally having good clean fun. The most important part of those experiences to me is we had a tremendous sense of community and I think we and the rest of the world lost human connectivity in this day and age."

Jake can't take much more and he interrupts the nostalgic tour. "All this sounds like a real hoot Kayanne and not to burst your little la-dee-da cocoon of denial here, but did you know an unmarried woman or girl who flirts with a member of the opposite sex is committing adultery under Sharia Law?"

"Yeah, I know that."

"Well do you further know the crime of adultery under Sharia Law is punishable by death? And do you also know the manner of execution is by stoning where they bury the poor flirtatious gal in sand up to her chest and let the citizens of the community throw small rocks at her until she cruelly dies in pain and agony? Can you imagine the sheer terror she goes through and what her corpse must look like after being stoned to death?"

"I knew you'd hate me talking about my childhood. But hold on Jake I'm not trying to prop up Sharia Law!" Kelly Anne shoves both hands toward Jake's face signaling stop. "You're point is well taken. What I'm trying to say is back when I was a kid our community was looked on as weird and out of step with modern society but it was good for us and the folks of the town were generally happy. I'm agreeing with the Corporal's assessment of the Iraqis. Then again I was probably waxing nostalgic. There is no comparison between my childhood experiences and what life must be like under Sharia Law. Sorry for the confusion."

Kelly Anne sinks back into her seat chastened and thoughtful about the ebb and flows of history and how a society will live under strict orthodoxies for hundreds of years and then shift to a liberal attitude, and often back again. "Why don't humans learn from history?"

The Cheetah and its anxious passengers approach Iraq's Green Zone less than a half-hour after departing Baghdad International, though time seems to stand still as they gaze solemnly through the windows out into Iraqi society. The caravan progresses through several heavily armed checkpoints, stopping and checking with Iraqi military guards and U.S. Marines at each one for the sake of security. They pass bulwarks of sharp razor wire coils, chain-link fences of various heights, massive earthen mounds and heavy-duty reinforced concrete slabs known as T-Walls.

Bradley Fighting Vehicles, M-1 Tanks and Desert camouflaged Humvees with .50 caliber machine guns on top sit menacingly at various points along the route to the Parade Ground area where Team Babelus will meet a helicopter to take them to the Well Site.

As the group journeys inside the parade grounds, under the oft-photographed Crossed Swords Gate a chill passes among them, a realization of the evil regime once proudly boasting genocidal military might on these very grounds.

The team spills out of the transport truck into the hot Iraqi sun, fairly skipping toward the Sea Stallion already fired up and waiting for take-off, barely noticing the violent air stirred up by the helicopter's blades as it swirls around them. The military-spec helicopter cabin is designed for rugged missions, featuring none of the creature comforts found in the executive Sea Stallion models. Kelly Anne is pulled into the cabin with the assistance of a Marine on board. She sits in one of the jump seats to the rear. Tasha leaps into the cabin on her own accord and stays by the entrance to assist Dr. Kagen, who requires two sets of hands to help him aboard. KO and Jake climb into the helicopter last and buckle themselves in for the ride out to the Well Site, the last leg of a long tortuous journey.

The powerful Sea Stallion lifts from the deck and pulls dramatically backward and to the right, aiming due west toward the Euphrates river and Iraq's Syrian Desert. The team dons headsets with microphone communications to mask out the thwump-thwumping of the great helicopter's heavy rotor blades. The Stallion is joined in flight by a squadron of equally loud and powerful flying beasts all chopping the air in unison with the sound of a thousand horses galloping across the plain.

"Now this is the way to hit a beach!" Jake yells out loud. "Whoo-hoo!"

The flying flotilla heads west into the morning haze over fully developed Iraqi urban areas teeming with traffic and people. They fly over the grand Tigris River it's smooth flowing water glistening in orange hues from the reflections of a rising sun.

The urban areas below give way to smaller neighborhoods and towns, separated by vast swaths of lush green gardens. They pass over big blue lakes, mansion-sized houses and industrial areas that would fit right at home in the exurbs of Houston or Boston. They fly over the mighty Euphrates River, the subject of so much Biblical lore. To the west of the Euphrates they gawk at huge irrigated farms, well-tilled by

John-Deere combine tractors and advanced farm machinery built in the factories of Iowa, Michigan and Texas.

The lushly green farms below gradually recede into desert. Tan sands dotted with green and brown palm trees surrender their hypnotic beauty to wild and hard dirt with bits of dusty shrubbery haphazardly strewn about and no pattern or clear source of nourishment.

The team peers through the Stallion's small window ports to get a good view of the approaching desert wasteland and its rocky hard dirt landscape. The land below is stark and barren with a tinge of rust color. There are no hills or mountains to see or marvelously majestic vistas, only a tired desolate quietly haunting terrain.

"We'll be coming up on the anomaly shortly," barks a static-degraded voice on the headsets, breaking the team's trance-like state. "I'll swing around to the south side and you can get a good look out the Starboard windows as we pass by towards HQ."

Every member of the team scrambles toward the right side of the aircraft, noses and cheeks pressed against the glass, kids in a candy store. Heat rises from the desert floor giving the panorama a mirage-like quality. Toward the horizon they can see a foreboding dark shadow matching the curvature of the earth growing ever larger as they approach. Soldiers, camouflaged Bradley Fighting Vehicles, and half a squadron of Apache helicopters come into view on the ground below. The cabin grows quiet in heart palpitating anticipation.

"Oh my fucking God!" screams Kelly Anne.

30

The Well of Towers
Iraq's Syrian Desert

"Sorry Lord, sorry Lord!" Kelly Anne prays to God after abrasively ripping the third commandment to shreds. "I've never used that expression in my entire life!" She shouts breathlessly through her headset as she excitedly pats her chest in rapid staccato movements. "When I went to a Christian boarding academy a couple of boy's used the expression constantly and the next thing you know, boom they're hit by a train, one was killed. After their tragedy I always kept the object lesson in the back of my mind, certain God takes his immediate and unconditional retribution against anyone using the phrase…and I don't want to be this team's Jonah!"

Unceremoniously seized from the comforts of work and home, hauled halfway around the world in a 36-hour blur of meetings and sleepless travel, accosted by religious zealots, doubted by condescending politicians, Team Babelus finally comes within view of the object of the world's consternation: The Well of Towers.

"Lo-ok a-t th-at!" Jake shouts, drawing out his words in wide-eyed wonder. "Oh my God it's the Grand Canyon on steroids! Only I don't think we'll be getting down there by mule train!"

"That's an entire modern day city down there," yells KO. "Look at the buildings, they're skyscrapers! The satellite images made everything look flattened out but the real thing is absolutely incredible."

"How deep is the lip of the chasm?" asks Tasha in a giddy shout. "That must be 150 feet or more. I could repel down the face of those cliffs for days!"

"What manner of civilization could possibly coalesce the knowledge it would take to build all of that?" inquires Dr. Kagen. "The architecture is strangely wonderful, post-modern expressionist like an entire metropolitan city designed by Frank Gheary. Beautiful, simply beautiful!"

As the Sea Stallion flies its way around the southern edge of the great chasm Team Babelus surveys its spectacular enormity in awe and unadulterated amazement. Satellite and drone pictures failed to register the immense scale of the Well Site, it's hidden city a series of spires and undulating facades reflecting sunlight in a mirror-like finish. The team sees the tops of structures as they poke heavenward through dark shadows of the deep seemingly bottomless abyss. Building surface textures appear polished to a fine sheen in a palette of white and pastel hued finishes.

Various sculptured shapes appear from the shadows as the helicopter hovers toward the western edge catching sunlight at new and fascinating angles. Hundreds of structures appear in the light with the general values and softly muted color tones of a watercolor painting.

A towering smoothly refined skyscraper reflects light sea foam green while its equally robust neighbor shows a warm orange tint. Absent windows the edifices in a central area of the chasm seem hypnotically translucent, giant spires of colored hard candy. The only comparative reference for the assemblage of buildings, their layout and size is the Downtown Manhattan area of New York. The magnificence and splendor of what is obviously a city under ground outshines any conceivable ancient construction. The pyramids at Giza, the Acropolis in Greece, the Roman Coliseum, indeed, all of Rome, suffers by comparison. And these structures show no obvious signs of aging and wear. They are not ruins but stand as a citadel of technological advancement available for immediate examination.

Eerily solitary buildings within the chasm are sculpted with curves and bezels as if Stradivarius, the famous master craftsman of finely crafted violins personally carved the surfaces. The layout and proximity of the structures, as communicated in groups or en masse, fit together as would the elements of a symphony, its musical strains frozen in time. From the sky it is impossible to ascertain the nature of the materials and construction techniques used to raise these structures but the highly orchestrated nature of the entire presentation suggests a thoroughly master planned community on a scale never known even to this day.

Whomever or whatever built this city possessed intelligence far beyond the understanding of modern science or at least modern sciences' understanding of ancient times. Though it occurs to Kelly Anne a group of artists and musicians could readily fathom the clever intellect and astute design of this metropolis, vacuum-sealed in an underground time capsule, buried and hidden for thousands of years. "This city belongs in the Guggenheim in New York or the Louvre in Paris," she thinks, "Or perhaps they belong here!"

Parapets and stanchions decorate the façade at the upper reaches of one tower as another is glazed smooth without any visible support structure to hold a massive bulb-shaped balcony aloft. Tower spires rise from the depths in the manner of stalagmites deeply buried in caves beneath the earth's surface. Unlike a modern-day city the structures are devoid of the accoutrements and devices signifying living inhabitants. There are no radio towers, satellite dishes or metal boxes housing air conditioning units. There are no obvious ventilation pipes, no gaudy signs advertising the latest gadgets or safe cigarettes. All that is seen from the Team's vantage point are the crystal smooth surfaces of hundreds of towering structures seeming to grow organically out of the ground, a stupendously fascinating amalgam of art and architecture.

The barren acreage surrounding the Well Site is parched dry and caked as if a great mass of water once covered the area and evaporated slowly over time. A cracked-clay puzzle piece pattern typically associated with dry lakebeds spreads out from the Well Site edge as far as the eye can see. A survey of the chasm's lip edges reveals millennia of earthen strata, evidence of centuries piled upon centuries upon centuries. The lip of the abyss is the depth of large cliffs such as the Cliffs at Dover or the sheared inner walls of the Grand Canyon. The top of the lip is jagged and rough, undulating with the contours of the small peaks and valleys of the desert floor. The bottom edge of the lip is disquietingly uniform as if chiseled and refined by a computer-controlled lathe, the type used to hone parts to exacting specifications for the Space Shuttle. Directly underneath the lip edge is a continuous dark void as if the caved-in gash in the earth is but a small portion of the site's overall circumference, leaving a menacingly unstable dirt overhang shrouding previously undetected sections.

"We have got to get down there. Can't this banana crate move any faster?" Shouts Jake, breaking the spellbound thoughts of the crew and passengers. "Do they have parachutes in this bird, I'll jump right now!"

"Hold your horses Jake we need our equipment!" Tasha yells above the din out of habit, unaccustomed to life without the aid and comfort of machines. "The last thing we want to do is go down there unprepared. Don't you worry about what might be waiting for us down in the darkness?"

"I don't care if there be dragons! I want to sail right off the edge of the map!"

"You never know," remarks Kelly Anne, "From what we've seen so far I fully expect a dragon or two. At least we would know the source of dragon legends. My head is filled with fantastic things we're going to find in the hole from dinosaurs to demigods. Well, I shouldn't call it a hole in the ground anymore…it's definitely a huge and complete city. This is beyond my wildest imagination!"

"Maybe we'll find Elvis and then we'll know the source of those legends too!" Jokes KO. "We might even find a tin of my grandmother's fruitcake but I'm not sure the site is that old. Ha ha ha ha ha!"

"We could clone Elvis from material at his museum at Graceland!" Laughs Dr. Kagen. "I think we would need approval from the Food and Drug Administration, the Center for Disease Control and an act of signed by both houses of Congress and the President to duplicate your grandmother's nasty fruitcake!" His joke fills the cabin in the lame cadence expected of a science geek.

A confirmed overdose of giddiness overtakes Team Babelus as the Sea Stallion slowly banks over the western edge of the Well Site and prepares to settle down in a cloud of dust and wind-whipped fury a hundred yards from the HQ tent. They feel triumphant and eager and each team member senses they are on the brink of a life changing experience or perhaps a world changing one.

Jake sees the chance to accomplish something truly important and worthy of respect. Kelly Anne believes the discovery will turn an intransigent scientific community on its obdurate ear. Dr. Kagen will rise out of the shadows of the shy obscurity of the lab rat scientist. KO is on the greatest road trip in history and his tales of adventure will get him drinks in bars across America for life. Tasha will redeem her family's tattered technology crackpot legacy.

For a moment the world is round, the sky is blue and one group of people is perfectly happy.

31

HQ Tent, The Well of Towers
Iraq's Syrian Desert

General Keith rushes out to greet the incoming party as the rotors of the Sea Stallion wind down to a slow whip-whip-whip. Five remarkably composed scientific explorers dressed uniformly in crisp navy blue flight suits emerge striding confidently from the settling dust. The Team's high-tech eyewear, five pairs of Oakley Canteen style sunglasses with polarized lenses in polished black iridium perch robustly above bright white toothy smiles and give the impression of a championship basketball team ready to take on all comers.

Although the winds abate and noise from the helicopters quiet, the scale and openness of the desert allows sound waves to dissipate, necessitating a loud boisterous welcome from the General. "Team Babelus, welcome to the Well Site! We're glad you finally made it out here, after your little skirmish at Baghdad International I was afraid this operation might never get off the ground." His welcoming gestures are accompanied by vigorous firm handshakes with all members of the team. As they turn toward the HQ tent General Keith walks in stride beside Jake, his large bony hand smacking Jake's back soundly and repeatedly as if the prodigal son had returned to a lonely eager father.

"Ill bet you never thought you'd get into a shit-storm like this!" The General shouts with a wide smile parting his face. "I used to watch that goofy show of yours. I remember this one episode where you tried mightily to prove genetically that a Jewish girl in France was a direct descendant of Jesus Christ. I loved the look on your face when they discovered she was an Italian chick from Newark, New Jersey! Haw-haw, that was great TV!"

The group walks into the HQ tent to the shouted command, "Attention on deck!" Everyone in the room stands in deference to the top of the chain of command in the field. "At ease gentlemen," barks the General. And everyone immediately sits down, resuming previous activities. Major Lee strides over to the group still standing in the doorway and thrusts his hand forward to greet the guests.

"I'm Major Lee and I'm handling the nuts and bolts for your exploration tour down in the Well Site." He continues down the line shaking hands. "I'm sure you're probably exhausted from all the travel just to get here but I'll bet my farm in Virginia you're also as anxious as we are to see what's cookin' down there. Am I right?"

"Without any doubt whatsoever Major," Jake agrees. "I could go down there after a week of liberty in Bangkok, right this minute and without hesitation. The same goes for the rest of the crew here. What do you have worked up for us?"

"Which one of you is the technical expert?"

"That's me, Tasha Hicks," she says stepping forward. "I'm wondering what method you have for getting us down to the bottom Major. The lip-edge looks pretty unstable so I doubt you see us repelling down the sides, at least I hope that's not the plan."

"Oh no ma'am. We're gonna drop ya like bugs from helicopters with a life wire and winch, sort of a rescue mission in reverse. If you'd please report to the Gunnery Sergeant over in the corner there he'll run through the safety protocols and procedures. You can show your teammates the ropes, well, the wires after your done. Gunny! Take this gal with you and show her the bug drop plan we've put together."

"Commander Nichols, General Keith would like to brief you in conference with the folks at the Pentagon and the CIA and maybe the White House too. If you head over behind the green burlap curtain in the corner you'll find the General and camera crew. I think Keith is excited to get on television with you even if it's a closed loop. He's been talking up your *History Channel* show all day."

"You two strapping gentlemen can help coordinate the gear dump." Lee gestures toward Dr. Kagen and KO. "I don't want to leave it up to military intelligence to make sure we get all of your equipment down there. Lieutenant Jenks is the logistics officer in charge of the materials aspect of the operation.

Jenks! Lieutenant Jenks! These two big guys are going to help with logistics. Make sure everything got here in one piece, ok?"

Tasha follows a burly rough-hewn Gunnery Sergeant to the far corner of the HQ tent. Jake peeks around the makeshift tent wall and finds the General waiting for him, speaking via video-link with the President in the White House Situation Room. KO and Dr. Kagen follow Lieutenant Jenks out into the hot sun to the staging area, leaving Major Lee and Kelly Anne to their own devices.

"You look as if you just stepped out of a day spa, relaxed and refreshed," the Major flirts awkwardly. "Everyone else looks more on the worse for wear side."

"Thank you Major. You're in remarkably good shape yourself considering the circumstances way out here in the heat and dust."

32

From the moment the beautifully striking Kelly Anne stepped through the open flaps of the HQ tent Major Lee's heart raced, his checks felt hot and flushed and his normally clear concise mind clouded to a muddled fluster. His barely disguised purposeful designation of duties leaves him standing in stasis before the most beautiful woman he has ever laid eyes on. But if beauty is the initial attraction her self-assured presence fills his heart with inspiration and joy. The smirk at the corners of Kelly Anne's mouth as she surveys the HQ tent intimidates the battle-hardened Major. Her soft femininity and attention to details of her appearance despite conditions in the field reinforce his manhood. With this woman at his side he can conquer any foe, build great things, accomplish any purpose and he falls immediately, unambiguously in love.

As she entered the HQ tent Kelly Anne took notice of a man of fair skin, tall and strong. He moved gracefully throughout the space, conversing easily from the lowest technician to the top General. The Major's gentle manner and easygoing nature belies a toughness suggested by the rack of ribbons adorning his chest and his obvious leadership skills. Men in Kelly Anne's life generally come at her flaws first, expecting her to acquiesce to their failings. Often her strengths as a woman draw men of weakness towards her as if she is the queen of all mother figures. Not this man. Major Lee reminds Kelly Anne of stories about the dashing General Custer, willing to jump into the breach passionately without hesitation but with the genial manners of a Southern gentleman. Watching him move, speaking, cajoling, laughing and encouraging…leading, gives Kelly Anne a feeling of protective security. For the first time in her life she imagines she can fall into the arms of a man and live the rest of her days as he holds her in comfort and peace. She is in love too.

A rough tough battle-scarred Gunnery Sergeant Hall, the veteran of two wars in the Persian Gulf admires the spontaneous energy and technical knowledge of the red-haired sprite of a girl under his tutelage. As he observes her skill with the mechanics of the swing arm and winch he thinks of his own two daughters now grown and attending college back in the States. Daughters he barely knows as he has sacrificed familial life for the hard edges of a career in the military, overseas for over half his kids' upbringing. Smart, independent, pretty and full of beans, he thinks of the brave scientist under his wing. "Now that's a real American girl, forgot what one looked like out here in the land of veils and stern overbearing men." He vows in his heart then and there to protect her with his life should anyone dare to harm a single hair on her head.

Lieutenant Anthony Jenks looks at the pair of misfit specialists in tow and sees a mirror image. A career logistics officer, Jenks spends the better part of his day organizing, counting, collating and counting again. All throughout high school and college he fit in best with geeks and brains, mild-mannered people whose every waking moment concerned details, facts and figures. Although they appeared different as night and day his two charges are geeks of the first order. He imagines both of them seated across from him at the card table on Friday nights playing Stratego or Yhatsee, games the kids these days have never even heard of much less understand. Jenks enjoys bantering in several different languages with KO. He listens intently as Dr. Kagen spells out mathematical probabilities of the Theory of Evolution, marveling at his quick grasp of complex numbers and concepts. For his part Jenks is only too happy in helping a pair of fellow socially awkward kindred spirits shine brightly, standouts on an important historical mission.

General Keith welcomes Jake into the laughably titled Media Area of the HQ tent, a space carved out of the mass entanglement of wires and computer gear featuring a plain green burlap backdrop. "If Osama Bin Laden can shoot video from a cave in Pakistan we can do this, thinks General Keith."

The powerful General holds Jake in high esteem and is a true fan of *Jackson Nichols' Big Dig.* General Keith, himself a science and history buff, holds a warm spot in his heart for soldiers who fight the good fight on the battlefield and then make a name for them selves in the civilian world. Jake's service record greatly impresses the General. As a SEAL Commander Jake covertly led his team into Baghdad on the eve of the breakout of the First Gulf War. While there his SEAL platoon knocked out vital enemy communications facilities, making the skies above Baghdad dark to anti-aircraft guns firing at U.S. bombers flying overhead. During their retreat the unit came under intense Iraqi fire and Jake single handedly eliminated the enemy's position, enabling a safe return to base. Shot up and bleeding profusely Jake managed to destroy an additional radar tower, ensuring the safety of pilots flying over a crucial corridor.

For his efforts Jake was awarded the Purple Heart, the Navy Cross and eventually the Congressional Medal of Honor. An Admiral of the Fleet presented the hero with the awards in a secret ceremony behind closed doors. Throughout his high profile civilian life, traveling around the world for his archeology science and history program Jake never mentions the medals or his heroism in battle. It's not easy to impress a United States Army General, yet the tone and tenor of General Keith's glowing introduction of Jake to the President shows how thoroughly he has accomplished the rare feat.

Kelly Anne and Major Lee examine fresh photography from the Well Site, shot from the vantage point of a hovering helicopter an hour from peak daylight. The lighting at the noontime angle reveals clearer pictures of the Well Site's depths and the two believe they can detect the bottom of the abyss. As they huddle closely together side-by-side seated on high stools at a chaotically messy mission table their intellects intertwine in mutual understanding. Highly technical questions asked and readily answered, a thought finished by the other, phrases mingling, enmeshed as one mind expressing singular ideas. Kelly Anne's warmly soft touch on his roughly calloused hand sends shivers down the Major's spine. His rich deep voice and manly scent threaten to cut the oxygen supply to Kelly Anne's brain as her breathing grows shallow and stops for a moment.

"So this is love?" Kelly Anne thinks. "And me at the edge of the most dangerous mission I've undertaken in my life. With my luck I'll probably die in a dumb Romeo and Juliet maneuver. If I make it through this in one piece I hope he calls me. If he doesn't I'll kill him."

Chief Science Advisor Kane joins President Crandall on the video uplink. The pair engages in a congenial conversation with their counterparts on the other side of the planet. The President congratulates Jake on the effort thus far and Science Advisor Kane asks thoughtful questions about the experience of seeing the Well Site up close in person. Jake enthusiastically relates the reactions, including Kelly Anne's brief bought with taking the Lord's name in vain. He tells of the remarkable colors and brilliant sheen of many of the structures. He regales them with a highly descriptive account, filled with wild gyrations and ecstatic phrases describing the immense size of the Site. Jake is fully in his element, performing as he does for the cameras on his popular television show.

General Keith briefs those in Washington on the preparations for the initial incursion into the Well Site. He speaks of a well-planned helicopter drop, lowering men and machines into the dark abyss no one is quite sure of its depths. The General answers a question on the practicability of flying the birds down into the hole with the analysis that the rotor blades will not fit safely between the structures. He allows that helicopters fly through Manhattan every day but reminds the Science Advisor the island city in New York is not situated deep in a hole but out in the spacious open air. As the stability of the lip-edge is largely unknown the team is to restrict its movements to the open areas of the Site in case of further cave-ins. This is met with understanding from Washington, as the size of the cave-in is already too large to fully explore in the four days left on the Iraqi imposed deadline.

The four men end the video briefing with an exchange of congratulations and words of encouragement. Each man is fully prepared for the mission at hand and their respective parts to play, Jake as the leader of the mission underground, General Keith as lead coordinator between all extraneous elements, Science Advisor Kane the lead philosophy, science and history advisor and President Crandall the umbrella of authority.

33

During the briefings and abridged training sessions the final additions to Team Babelus, a pair of Iraqi scientists, return from a short flight to survey the Well Site from the air. The team greets the pair enthusiastically and without rancor or jealousy. Although the Iraqi government coercively forced the pair onto the team through political blackmail and intimidation they too are putting their lives to the hazard for this important historical exploration. A sense of collegiality envelops the group as they exchange greetings and handshakes.

Team Babelus musters outside the HQ tent with many of the on site soldiers and airmen gathered with them. Lieutenant Jenks offers a generic non-sectarian prayer to God as the hardened military men reverently hold hands in a large circle interspersed by members of the team. Jenks completes his prayer to a resounding amen along with a couple of Allah-bewillings and the group marches off toward the Sea Stallion helicopters that will drop them to the depths of history.

High Noon was selected as the best time to conduct the drop as light from the sun directly overhead creates fewer shadows to obscure the view of the bottom. Tasha fastens a safety harness around Jake as the Sea Stallion hovers directly over the center of the gaping gash in the earth. Jake is the first to make the vertically challenging trek as his expertise and physical strength is needed to help the remainder of the crew at the bottom of the abyss. Jake makes the sign of the Cross over his heart, even though he is a Baptist and Tasha gives the sign to start the lowering motion. The winch lets loose with a slight jerk sending brief pangs of panic through the crew. The dropping motion smoothes out and Jake begins the extended process of slowly lowering past the lip-edge and into darkness.

On the way down Jake admires the scenery, now well lit by the sun's rays. He sees steeply gabled spires widen to massive structures. The tones and hues change chameleon-like as sunlight plays off various angles. He notices no windows or doors and cannot detect any signs of life ancient or otherwise. As he drops deeply into the chasm the other members of the team can barely see him and he eventually disappears completely from view.

Only the sun-gilt reflection of the life wire is noticeable, swinging gently into the darkness. The air grows cooler with each fathom further from the sun. As Jake approaches two hundred feet the atmosphere grows cold and nearly frigid. At the top Jake eschewed wearing a jacket as he was perspiring in the sweltering sun at the time. But now as cold turns to frigid iciness he openly wishes for a thick polar fleece coat…or perhaps a hot-buttered rum.

At 380 feet below the surface Jake touches down, his comfortable Asolo hiking boots bouncing off an oddly spongy floor. The unexpected consistency and texture of the ground jolts Jake to his senses. This is no dream but a real excursion into the unknown and unexpected encounters with unusual sensations are understood as normal. The hard-chiseled mindset mitigates the devastating effects of surprises. Jake sends an all clear signal up the life wire and Tasha harnesses Dr. Kagen and signals to lower him into the abyss.

Kagen lands without incident, sends an all-clear signal and Tasha harnesses in the Iraqi Botanist Ahmed, his kufi headwear blowing off and floating into the darkness. Next she harnesses and lowers Ahmed's Iraqi compatriot Brian who eagerly climbs out from the Sea Stallion as if he were about to embark on a bungee jump. Kelly Anne steps into the harness seat in giddy anticipation smiling from ear to ear. Her enthusiasm nearly causes disaster as she attempts to leap out from the aircraft without the harness fully latched. She slips through the bottom support and hangs in the air attached only by her arms. Tasha fish hooks her back in and scolds profusely as she attaches the safety latches and sends her down.

KO hesitantly approaches the edge of the helicopter's open door and gingerly slides his feet into the harness. Tasha soothes and consoles him during the process to no avail. Finally she shouts out words of encouragement in the form of swearing typically reserved for sailors, the blue streak of her personality on full display. KO responds in kind, spouting colorful four-letter words in seven languages. They laugh and KO is on his way to join the rest of the team.

Tasha prepares herself for the long perilous drop below. She is assisted by an able technician and expertly slips into the harness, buckles the safety clasps and gives the signal to let the winch loose. She too is on the way to the party.

• • •

The sound of automatic weapons fire is barely noticeable above the whirring claptrap of helicopter blades but Tasha can see a cloud of dust with Marines moving a confrontation. As she hangs precipitously in the air just above the top of the lip-edge the great chopper quavers in a gust of wind swinging her wildly back and forth without an anchor. She studies the soldier's movements on the ground, slightly lower than her tenuous position. A group of enemy attackers enters from the northwest edge of the Well Site and fires toward the Marines dug in there. A fierce battle rages with Tasha hanging in the air hundreds of feet above the floor of the abyss and fifty feet below the safety of her helicopter base station.

A trail of white smoke blasts from the enemy position and closes on Tasha quickly. She retracts in wild fear throwing her head violently backward following the track of an RPG rocket as it shoots upwards past her and towards the helicopter holding her dangerously aloft. Tasha hangs still and frozen her face gazing skyward as she sighs in relief, the missile failing to meet its intended target. A Bradley Fighting Vehicle races madly across the plain parallel to the battle, a broad-shouldered bulldog of a man, expertly firing the .50 caliber gun from its roof, strikes target after target as it speeds along. Tasha immediately recognizes the marksman. "Gunny Hall you da man!" she screams wildly.

The frightening battle wages for several more minutes with Tasha's life literally hanging in the balance. The Marines drive off the attackers and pursue them through a cloud of retreating dust across the desert. The life wire and winch system jolt to life and lowers Tasha into the Well to join her team.

"What the hell happened up there?" Jake bellows as the last harness containing humans safely lands at the base of a huge spire.

"It looks as if the mysterious attackers returned while I was hanging up there in midair," relays Tasha breathing in and out heavily. "I've never been so scared in my life! I'm just hanging there with nothing to do but wait to die but our boys ran the enemy off, I'm happy to say. My God Jake is this what war is always like?"

"Ha, ha. Yeah pretty much but you usually have a gun to shoot back."

"What's that on your sleeve Tasha?" Dr. Kagen asks. "Looks like you spilled your coffee on the way down."

Tasha reaches over to her left arm and feels a stinging burn. "Oh my God I think I've been hit! That's my blood and it hurts like hell."

"Sit down Tasha," Kelly Anne commands. "We don't want you to faint from the blood loss." Kelly Anne strips the fabric from around the wound and devises a temporary tourniquet to stop the blood flowing from Tasha's arm. A bullet or shrapnel passed through the fleshy part of the underside of the arm tearing a four-inch gash through pink freckled skin. None of the gear has arrived yet so uncontaminated first aid with sterile bandages and anti-bacterial solution will have to wait.

"Are you sure you want to go forward Tasha?" Kelly Anne asks.

"Hell yeah, are you shittin' me?" comes the angry reply. "There's no way in this life I'm going to get shot while hanging in mid-air hundreds of feet above the ground and not go forward with the mission. Not with a little baby flesh wound like this!"

"You lucky dog," enthuses KO. "I wish I was the one who got shot. Just imagine the respect I'd get from the Harley club back home. A lot of those old boys have been in wars, Vietnam some of them, and they're always going on about their wounds. If I had one it would cement my bona fides as a real biker."

"Don't worry KO, there's plenty of time for you to get your ass shot off on this mission," warns Jake. "The way things are going I would expect to see a few more of these skirmishes before we're done. Good thing there's no way to get down here easily.

The team's gear is lowered into the chasm in stages. First come the ATVs, then sealed fiberglass crates holding food and equipment. Kelly Anne immediately secures an emergency first-aid kit and expertly sews 24 stitches into Tasha's wound, applying a sealer of crazy glue along with a tetanus booster shot and a dose of antibiotics. Team Babelus makes a thorough accounting of the gear and establishes audio/video communications with General Keith and the much-maligned Media Area. They don Bluetooth-enabled ear-pieces, establish a local area network of communication between each other, mount their respective ATVs and head toward a large building in the center of a vast complex in the middle of the underground city.

34

White House Situation Room
Washington, D.C.

"Team Babelus is on mission," says General Keith to the Cabinet and agency directors gathered in the Situation Room, his announcement followed by cheering, whistling and clapping. "The Sea Stallions lowered the team and crates of gear at precisely twelve hundred hours. There was a firefight caused by a skirmish with our mysterious warrior friends in Syrian garb. The battle took place with the Well Site operation underway and one of the mission specialists, Tasha Hicks, was hit and sustained a mild flesh wound. She continued on down to the bottom of the chasm where Doctor Carter stitched her up. Everything is on schedule and the team is headed toward the center of the city."

"Your telling us everyone is relatively intact?" asks National Security Advisor Maney. "We need to remember these people are civilians and not warriors General."

"I'm well aware of their status Mr. Maney. You folks surely picked a hearty bunch of civilians for this operation though. The little red headed gal was hanging on a life wire harness between the helicopter and the bottom when the firefight broke out. When it was all over I thought she'd be down there cryin' and wettin' her pants wantin' to come home straight away. No not that one. She cursed and yelled at the party suggesting she might want to go home. I love the American fightin' spirit."

I just hope we have the cajones as politicians to see this thing through to the end." The General lumps him self in with politicians to soften his intended criticism.

"The group was hand picked for just this sort of contingency," informs Science Advisor Kane. "This region of the world is hyper dangerous and the folks we sent over, though they are scientists and historians have shown courage and valor in the face of criticism and physical danger for most of their lives so I'm not surprised. I am concerned about the mysterious attackers though General, do we have any updates as to their origins?"

"Nothing from this side, Doctor Kane. Our Marine units repelled the attack this morning and chased the enemy out into the desert but lost them in some rocky hills to the west. We killed about twenty of them but took no live prisoners so there's no one to interrogate and we're still in the dark. Does intelligence have any information about any of this?"

"The CIA and the NSA have worked feverishly to trace the origins of the attackers," Director Likely interrupts. "Unfortunately our assets aren't able to identify the source or the origin of the group making life miserable for you out there. Nobody has posted claims of responsibility on the Internet, there's no cell phone chatter and we haven't heard so much as a nano-byte of information concerning the attackers. We're in the dark over here too and I'm greatly concerned."

"Perhaps you should stop worrying about nano-bytes Director and get some agents in the field!" General Keith is clearly irritated at the idea of America's intelligence apparatus solely focusing on digital streams of information.

"Your concern is duly noted General," interjects Maney. "Director Likely we need some answers and fast. I can't believe we've been working this area for all these years and can't come up with solutions about a heavily armed group brazenly attacking our troops out in the middle of nowhere, at high noon for God's sake. It seems to me this is the easiest sort of enemy to gather intelligence against and you tell us we're still completely in the dark, no clues whatsoever?"

"I'm sorry Dan we just don't know. If we had anything, a guess, conjecture a scrap of intelligence, believe you me I would fill you in on the details and I certainly would inform the President. But we don't Dan. We don't and it's a growing concern because I know the assets we have in the field, and yes we have spies stationed throughout the Middle East digging up bits of information from Jordan to Saudi Arabia and they're turning up nothing."

Maney can scarcely believe what he's hearing but resigns him self to focusing on positive developments. "I suppose we just have to cross our fingers and sit here in Washington with our flies unzipped. At least the Marines have kept the scientists from getting gunned down out in a land where you can see the enemy coming from fifty miles away. Maybe it'll all work out with our soldiers standing guard on the perimeter of the Well Site but I'm not feeling optimistic about anything right now."

"I don't say this in criticism of the Marine units on station Graham, but I hate not knowing. Why don't we know? How can we have any confidence going forward with a renegade group out there attacking from various angles at all times of the day or night?"

"I don't think we can have confidence just yet Dan. We're efforting the problem and hopefully well extract a solution from the morass of conflicting and ambiguous information we have now."

"Efforting? What the hell does that mean? Did they say we were efforting taking out Hitler and winning World War Two? Are we efforting now Director? How about getting off our suicidal ass and doing…doing something, anything about the subjugation of the world by Islamic Fascists?"

"C'mon Dan, intelligence isn't perfect. It's hard work and the people under my command are working hard to…"

"What's the status of the Iranian problem Graham," quizzes President Crandall, purposefully interrupting Director Likely in an effort to change the subject. "We need to know if they plan on testing a nuclear weapon. Is there any movement on that intelligence?"

"Nothing's changed on that front Mr. President. The Iranians are making every move and showing all indications they plan on testing a nuclear weapon. We're at the stage of trying to ascertain the scope and scale of the test."

"Are we in the dark about this too?" asks Secretary of Defense Green-Newton. "Pentagon sources indicate the Iranians have extracted nuclear fuel from plutonium rods at the Arak Nuclear Power Facility and have transported the results in the direction of the western provinces. Aren't your people picking up this information as well?

"Grazzy, when we reconstituted America's intelligence apparatus after the disaster of 911 the idea was to create an atmosphere of cooperation between intelligence agencies. If intelligence assets at the Pentagon are holding back information from my office we need to correct the situation post haste! The very idea of, ahh, the reason why my office was created is to smooth out the kinks in the intelligence process to protect the country and deliver unfettered information to the President. If you or your people are hiding valuable information the entire rationale for my presence in this room is moot!"

"What you're suggesting Graham is treason on my part! I am not treasonous and I love this country with all of my heart and soul. You're implying I'm criminally treasonous and intelligence assets at the Pentagon are traitors! I will not sit here and let you besmirch the diligent patriots at the Pentagon because your people can't uncover the most basic operations in the Middle East! I won't have it!"

"Calm down both of you!" barks President Crandall. "Neither of you is a traitor but the future of America is at stake and we must get together on these issues or get sent to the ash heap of history! Please, please, please work together on this! Your country and your President are depending on you. If any element of the United States government fails at this juncture then the entire country fails, don't you two get that? General what's the expression you Army people use for this problem?"

"Get your shit in one sock."

"Yes, yes, that's the term. And if we don't we'll all pay the price, at the polls and every man woman and child in America will suffer when the new Islamic Caliphate takes over the entire world. Is this what you two want to see happen?"

"No Mr. President," the antagonists answer in unison.

"Alright then, get me some reasonable intelligence on the Iranian problem and find out whose behind this mysterious group attacking our Marines in broad daylight."

"Yes Sir," they reply, again in unison.

"General Keith, when do we anticipate the first reports from the Well Site?

"Mr. President Team Babelus established audio/video communications with the comm-link here at HQ. We are now in constant communication with the group and will begin sending a stream of encrypted packets directly to the Situation Room momentarily. I am anxious and excited to see what comes up on screen."

"You and me both, General, you and me both."

35

The Well of Towers
380 Feet Below the Surface
Iraq's Syrian Desert

"I know the plan was to head toward the large central complex we saw in the satellite photos," says Jake, "But I want to get a lay of the land down here from this vantage point." He shines his Luxeon high-powered LED flashlight out into the darkness revealing little in the way of usable information. "I think we landed on a hill here but I can't tell for certain even with the headlights from our ATVs lighting the way. What do you think Tasha?"

"We dropped down to a point approximately 380 feet below the surface Jake. And that's accounting for the lip-edge which is about 150 feet so we're sitting right now about 180 feet below the ceiling of this thing give or take a meter. We're pretty far down."

"I could swear we landed on top of a hill. It just feels like we're higher than the bottom. When we dropped down I thought we were right next to structures but it seems they're farther off than they look. The scale of everything changes when we get right next to things. The perspective from the sky threw us off. Let's fire up the Mobilite, Tash."

Tasha works her way around behind the ATV ridden by Ahmed the Botanist to unwrap the super high-powered portable industrial light mounted on a trailer hitched to the vehicle. The three-lamp portable Mobilite features a commanding light beam reaching a full half-mile out into darkness. Tasha raises the boom tower, it's floodlights perched on top, the picture of a menacing tri-clops. She fires up the gas generator and switches on the radiant beam. The floodlights light up the cavernous area like the surface of the moon as it meets the sun's rays from behind earth's shadow. That is if the moon had an entire city on its surface.

"See, I told ya we landed on a hill. Look at the structures and towers down there. I wonder how deep this thing really is, you have any ideas?"

"There's only one way to find out. Let's go down there! The complex in the photographs is just over there, northwest of us and a pathway seems to lead in that direction. See what I'm looking at Jake?"

"Yeah I see it Tash. Let's keep the lamps on while we scoot over there so we don't run into any holes in the dark. Must be pretty far down if the sun's light doesn't get down there."

"Not necessarily Jake. Remember we're down in a deep hole. Have you ever looked down into any regular water well on a sunny day? Usually you can't see the bottom and they're only 25 or 50 feet down."

"What do you make of the ground stability here? It's spongy and rubbery. Do you think it's strong enough to hold our collective weight?"

"I don't sense we're standing on a bubble. This is probably some kind of dead groundcover liquefied and compounded over the years. Whatever's underneath is probably solid as granite. We can ask Ahmed the Botanist, he's the plant specialist on this trip."

"Nah I think you're right about the ground Tash. We don't want to use time taking samples yet. Let's wait and have Ahmed take some samples of this ground cover before we leave in a few days. Right now I'd like to get this show on the road. Alright posse, mount up!"

The team straddles their ATVs, rev engines and familiarize themselves with the feel of their new vehicles. They follow the light beam Kelly Anne jokingly dubs the Pillar of Fire down a long hill towards a complex of tall structures.

Moss-like ground cover soaks up the rough rumbling sounds of the ATVs as they wend their way through corridors of darkness. The mossy substance is not wet or moist nor is it dried out, as no dust is stirred up under the ATV caravan's wheels. The odor in the vast cavern is a mixture of dead biology and ancient stale air, as if rooting through a greenhouse where the plants have all died and no smell is detected until you dig up some soil. The route reveals no open patches of land for farming or grazing livestock. No visible source of food is seen anywhere on this excursion.

"There's no way all of these buildings were erected as monuments to the Gods," muses Kelly Anne. "These structures have purpose, to house living beings or as giant office complexes, for that matter any purpose involving life. This is a major city, larger than many modern cities. And yet there are no signs of life or living. Somewhere along the line the peoples of this place had to eat and get rid of waste or bury the dead. No sign of any of those activities so far. Ha-ha, maybe we'll find an ancient Piggly Wiggly supermarket out in the suburbs."

Twenty-two minutes later the Team arrives at the base of a central building surrounded in a semi-circle by six separate spires. The whole picture reminds Jake of the World Trade Center complex in New York destroyed by terrorists on 911. It too was stationed in the middle of a series of smaller but still imposing skyscrapers, although the Trade Center was a twin tower configuration.

"That was a longer trip than I expected," says Jake. "We motored along at around 25 miles an hour on average so I guess we traveled something like eight or nine miles. Do you know for me to drive my Hummer from one side of Downtown Los Angeles to the other is about six miles? Good thing we don't have any traffic down here."

"Eight point four miles to be exact, according to Garmin," informs Tasha. "And we're now about 3,200 feet below the surface, two thirds of a mile down, that's pretty trippy. Look up, you can barely see the big gaping hole we came through to get down here."

After an interesting but relatively uneventful eight-mile jaunt over the mossback highway the team finds itself in front of a stark icy-white spire with silvery spots or ports or depressions in the surface. It is impossible to understand what they are looking at with absolutely no frame of architectural reference to go by.

The mysterious structures and surroundings lend themselves to misgivings. Exploring a cave or unknown lands is a normal function for those with a curious nature. Walking towards completely foreign elements beyond all understanding is frightening on a completely higher level and Team Babelus stands unsure on how to proceed.

• • •

"I know these buildings look like something from a beautiful nightmare and its scary." allows Jake. "But we're here so we may as well do this thing. Let's try the door to this central building first."

They warily approach a concave recess arcing from the ground to a five-story height.

Kelly Anne walks up to the possible doorway and knocks.

Nothing.

The surface of the structure, covered in filmy dust, feels cold like steel and smooth like ivory to Kelly Anne's touch. She searches for a knob or a latch but finds no ergonomic device providing an invitation to enter. She knocks again, this time much harder, blasting dust back into her face. She sneezes…a high-pitched expulsion of air of the type emanating from your average toy poodle. The noise or air-burst of the sneeze causes an immediate reaction and the five-story depression evaporates instantly, revealing a large open interior space along the lines of a huge office building lobby.

"Oh gosh we are in trouble now!" Kelly Anne gasps. And yet despite her own admonition, she immediately enters through the portal without hesitation and promptly trips, falling flat on her face. "What the hell? Why is there a foot tall ridge in the door's walkway?"

"You ok?" asks Jake, stepping over the ridge and into the grand lobby. "Maybe you shouldn't be so eager to just jump right into places like this, let us check things out first." Jake helps Kelly Anne to her feet while the rest of the party step over the ridge and into the great space. They gawk, wide-eyed and slack-jawed their heads pivoting back and forth, up and down scanning the room's marvels with flashlights.

"We need some real light in here," orders Jake. "KO, Ahmed, you guys haul the Mobilite in here so we can get a good look at this place." The pair rushes to the still burning torch, unhitches its trailer mount from the ATV and pulls the heavy beast over the doorway transom. KO adjusts the lamp downward toward the room's center, lighting the entire room to gasps of wondrous admiration.

The immense elliptically shaped indoor amphitheater measures 600 feet by 500 feet according to Tasha's laser guided calculations. Roughly the same dimensions as the Coliseum in Rome and much larger than any modern-day football field. The floor sinks down some thirty feet to the center in a series of stepped levels. The first level, at the same elevation as the doorway is a wide hallway ringing the entire outer rim. Large seats and tables arranged uniformly around the ring are the dominant feature of the second third and fourth rows. At the bottom level in the center is a massive structure, also elliptical in shape, with thousands, perhaps millions of small indentations or holes burrowed into its surface.

"It looks like a very large bee-hive to me," remarks Tasha. "I'm allergic to bee stings so I hope there aren't any bees in that thing."

"Looks like spider holes to me," worries KO fearfully. "I'm not allergic to spiders but looking at that thing scares the daylights out of me. What if a million spiders crawl out of it and come after us?"

"Whatever's in there is probably long dead by now," assures Dr. Kagen. "But let's not jump to conclusions. The structure doesn't appear to be organic like a beehive or holes dug in the dirt by spiders. It looks like a huge ivory cabinet holding something uniform in size like wine bottles or frozen dinners in a can."

"Well what is this place anyway?" asks Kelly Anne. "Do you think it's a huge restaurant Doctor Kagen?"

"I don't know, maybe, all these tables and chairs might suggest areas for dining. The central area doesn't have a stage for performances or speeches and all of the tables are arranged where the seats face away from the center so its not an auditorium."

"Maybe it's nothing more than a big cafeteria."

"Perhaps. This place seems more solemn than a restaurant or cafeteria but maybe I'm just projecting modern-day sensibilities on what is possibly an everyday environment as pedestrian as an eating joint."

"This place is huge, I wonder how they lit it up?" asks Tasha. "I don't see a light source in here at all. I don't see any windows to let in sunlight, but those huge depressions like the one at the doorway ring the outer rim of the room. Kelly Anne go over and sneeze on the wall and see if a window opens up."

On any other day, at any other place on earth such a request would seem foolish and juvenile. Barely a few minutes prior a sneeze magically opened the front door. Today, in this place, a sneeze is science. Kelly Anne immediately walks to the outer wall and conducts the experiment. "Choo," sneezes Kelly Anne. Nothing. "Ah-chooo!" she sneezes louder with serious deliberation, again, no reaction from a recalcitrant wall. "Choo-choo!" she tries at a higher pitch, to no avail. "I guess that's not the key," she surrenders, arms dropping to her sides. "I thought my sneezes were the key to the city, how disappointing."

"They had to light the place up somehow," says Tasha. "Let's look around for a light source. I don't expect to find a simple light switch by the door but nothing would surprise me at this point."

The team searches the area in hopes of finding technologies indicating a power source or the method of lighting for the vast room. From what they can see no chandeliers hang from the ceilings nor any table lamps or candelabras sit in plain view. They scan the floors and walls, look under tables and overhangs. KO uses the Mobilight as a search lamp, directing its beam from the base of the upper level mezzanine up towards a spectacular rotunda ceiling apparently built without arch supports. A dramatic lavishly colored design seems to emanate downward from the upper reaches of the cavity, reminding KO of the multi-million dollar ceilings at the Bellagio Hotel in Las Vegas.

The furnishings around the chamber are large, forcing even KO to climb up for a seat. Jake estimates the beings using the chairs and tables in the room stood twelve to fourteen feet tall, about the height of Cro-Magon Man who walked the earth 40,000 years ago. Kelly Anne rejects the notion of a Cro-Magnon civilization as advanced as the example under their exploratory eye. "Cro-Magnon was allegedly a dumb beast. But what do I know, I wasn't there."

Tasha stands near the doorway in her standard thinking pose, balled fists planted on hips, tightly pursed lips and angrily furrowed brow. She calculates the height of the room's original inhabitants, adjusts her search parameters to meet larger scale ergonomic requirements and searches accordingly.

"Ho what's this?" she asks, striding over to the right side of the doorway. KO give me a lift up will ya? KO kneels down on one knee, leaving the other parallel to the ground, a makeshift stepladder. Tasha scrambles up on KO's knee and inspects the edge of small disc protruding from the wall. She slides her fingers across its surface, turning it left then right. She surmises the dial isn't an on-off switch but maybe a sliding dimmer switch. She tries turning the dial faster, striking it repeatedly. Instinctively she knows the dial is in this precise spot for a reason, handy to a giant 14-foot tall something or other. "Hmm, maybe they didn't have hands? There must be a key to operating this thing though."

She sneezes at the dial without success. She yells and screams to no avail. Finally in frustration she flicks the dial making it spin like a merry-go-round. The dial spins faster and faster, picking up speed on its own without any action from Tasha. An airy wheee sound whines from inside the wall followed by a beam bathing the area around the doorway in a bright luminescence.

"Let there be light," whispers Tasha, her baby-blue eyes sparkling in the bright beam. "Everybody, look around for these dials and spin them, they're probably all over the place!"

Kelly Anne finds dials next to all of the window-like depressions and spins them to life, each platter powering a beam above the porticos. Jake finds a bank of larger dials and rakes enthusiastically at each one. As the whirring WHEE grows faster bright light shoots out from rings around the chamber's perimeter, first at lower levels then moving upwards toward the ceiling. KO and Dr. Kagen discover dials embedded into the edges of the tables. Spinning them provides an eerily fascinating glowing light hovering twelve inches above the table with no visible support. Ahmed and Brian discover dials on the sconces above the seats generating light directed downwards toward the tables. For the next half-hour the team dashes madly about the great chamber, spinning dials and lighting the room.

When done the devices generate enough candlepower to light up a night game at Chicago's Wrigley Field.

36

“Hey General Keith, you getting any of this?” asks Tasha, shouting excitedly into the Pocket Studio attached to her forearm.”

“Yes, its fantastic Ms. Hicks,” comes the reply as the General’s face appears on Tasha’s screen. “I find it difficult to fathom there’s a power source down there generating so much electricity and still works after all this time!”

“I know exactly what you mean General. But the light isn’t generated by electricity.”

“What are you talking about Tasha?”

“Its luminescent General! The little dial generators aren’t burning anything, there’s no fuel source. The power modules seem to create light particles out of thin air. I don’t know what technology they used to create this kind of light but its magical and I think its completely non-polluting. Like I said the technology doesn’t burn fuel to create heat generating light. It’s amazing! I’m going to sign off and go help the crew. By the way how's Gunny Hall? Did he make it through the battle okay?"

"Yeah Gunny's ok Tasha, the ol' coot. I don't think you could kill that guy with a sledgehammer while he slept. Good luck and keep up the good work."

"Ok General, tell Gunny he's my hero! Bye."

Tasha scuttles off to join the group who had climbed down to the center well of the auditorium. There are no stairways leading down to each level, necessitating the team to scale down to each section as if climbing down from a six-foot brick wall. Tasha athletically negotiates the route down and meets with the rest of her teammates now enmeshed in a serious discussion about the massively imposing citadel in the center of the chamber.

"What's up guys?"

"We're just discussing the nature of this 800 pound gorilla in the middle of the room," replies Dr. Kagen. "Even on close inspection it's a mystery. We've agreed on the general idea that if we can discover what this behemoth in front of us is then we'll unlock the secrets as to the nature of this complex."

"What's in the holes?"

"Heh heh, we don't know. Some of us are afraid of getting bit by spiders and I seem to remember one member of our party worried about honey bee stings."

Tasha shines her flashlight into one of the holes, a smooth cylindrical indentation approximately three inches in diameter. She sees an object roughly eight inches deep that appears to be a mechanical artifact, its well-honed features suggesting purposeful design and expert construction. She reaches into the hole and tries pulling the strange mechanical device. It will not budge from its tight cocoon. She surmises the possibility the device was intended to operate within the hole and not exorcised from the container.

"If the things inside, whatever they are, operate from inside their little cubbies then maybe something comes out from the holes like heat or cold air. Maybe this is a big air conditioning unit."

"I don't know," answers Jake. "This is an awfully big use of floor space in the center of a very well-designed area. I don't see intelligent beings of the sort putting this place together using assets that way."

"And look at these angled gizmos on the ends," he continues, referring to twenty spindles, each constructed of a two foot tall vertical bar on the left and a three foot horizontal bar attached at the bottom, all arranged in a semi-circle on counters at each end of the massive structure. "Maybe we just need to find a way to coax the devices out their holes."

On Jake's suggestion the team inspects the areas around the holes in an effort to find the key to unlocking whatever lay buried snugly eight inches deep. They run hands and fingers over the surface. They poke and prod, looking for buttons and depressions, any device that might open the contents of each hollow space.

The texture and consistency of the materials used to construct the building and its contents spark intense curiosity among the group.

"What do you think is the basic material used to build all of this Doctor Kagen?" Asks Tasha. "The shapes and texture are fantastic like they were designed by Dr. Seuss."

"You're right Tasha, but the technology behind this is foreign to me. I can't tell without taking some samples and testing. It's not concrete of any type and not stone either. I've tapped around on the surfaces and the general feel isn't consistent with plastic which of course would be a great surprise given the assumed age of this place. Maybe they devised some composite materials like the kinds of chemicals modern companies use to make water skis and the like. Well, you know it could be fiberglass or something of that nature but the construction isn't hollow like you'd expect from those so I really don't know at this point. I do have one suspicion completely out of this world."

"Oh do tell. If you're wrong I promise I won't alert the media."

"Do you know about high-density ceramics?"

"Yeah, a little, the stuff they make small knives out of that keep their edge forever or o-rings that never wear out. Is that what you're talking about?"

"Yes, that's the technology."

"Don't things made of ceramic powders go through an isostatic press with tons and tons of pressure?"

"Yup and there's your problem. We can make small items like knives and such in a rubber mold that gets run through a pressure container packing the ceramic material to a density far greater and harder than diamonds but we could never compact large things…at least not to those densities. Imagine super high pressure consistently applied over a large area. How do you create and contain it?"

"Right, well we're talking about huge structures here Doctor, tables and chairs and, well, entire skyscrapers. It doesn't seem plausible to create a press as large as these buildings."

"No you're right Tasha but I'm still working on the theory. You know everyone's thinking of all of this as if aliens built the place or flew down here and gave some pathetic humans the technology to build it. I'm developing an alternate theory that all of this is homegrown and ceramics might be the ticket."

"Well good luck Doctor Kagen."

As Dr. Kagen and Tasha discuss the merits of ancient technologies, Kelly Anne continues searching for a way to free up the technology at hand. She peers into a hole situated about eye level and examines the inside edges of the opening and the surfaces surrounding the outside edge. An embossed ridge around the outside of the hole looks like a design for aesthetic purposes but it reminds Kelly Anne of the ridges on the lid of a peanut butter jar only laid out flat. While staring at the hole she places the fore and middle fingers of each hand on the pattern and turns counter-clockwise…lefty-loosey she thinks.

THOOONK! An object shoots from the hole and strikes Kelly Anne squarely on the forehead. Her recoil sends her sprawling backward landing on her butt.

"That sounded pneumatic!" shouts Tasha, oblivious to Kelly Anne's pain and embarrassment. "It didn't knock ya out so it's not a weapon I guess, unless you're trying to kill jelly fish." She helps Kelly Anne to her feet and reaches down to pick up a cylinder three inches in circumference and approximately three inches long. She runs her fingers along the sides of the object, inspecting its curves and a dial in the middle much the same as the type that turned on the lights. She gives it a whirl. The object springs to life, a soft, barely discernible whizzing sound radiating from its core. The device doesn't produce any noticeable attributes. Tasha puts it on the floor where it softly hums but doing little else.

"I have no idea what this little critter is for. It just sits there whirring at me like a top from one of those old toys where you run the gizmo across the ground and then put it in a little hole on a car and away it goes. There's no obvious use for this thing but they have what looks like millions of them here its gotta have a higher purpose than just happily humming along. It reminds me a little bit of a spinning hard drive but there're no connections to transfer data. I don't know!"

"Well that blows our theory about unlocking the secrets to what this place is all about," complains Jake. "I guess we're back to square one on that effort. What is this place? An auditorium? A cathedral? The local Jack-in-the-Box, what?"

Dr. Kagen stands apart from the group pondering the atmospherics and general arrangement of the tables and seats situated on several levels. He thinks of the massive structure in the middle of the room apparently filled with millions of small gizmos doing nothing so far as they can tell. His thoughts drift to his childhood, as he stands alone with his right elbow tucked into his left hand and stroking his chin. A nostalgic idea floods his mind.

"You know something folks. When I was a kid I spent an awful lot of time in a place reminding me of this grand structure with importance given to how the seats and tables are arranged and the primacy of the citadel in the center with millions of small canisters of, well whatever they are we don't know yet."

"This place reminds me of the Los Angeles Public Library."

37

White House Situation Room
Washington, D.C.

"Mr. President, General Keith is on screen now," informs Dan Maney, turning President Crandall's attention from a serious, hushed conversation with Vice-President Murcheson. "He's got some information on the attackers and wants to coordinate an effort to discover their identity."

"Hello General, what do you have for us?" asks the President, distracted by the previous discussion and detached from the moment.

"Yes Mr. President, hello. As you already know we came under attack again this morning. As before we haven't managed to capture anyone alive for interrogations and the attackers are obsessively diligent about carrying off their dead as they retreat. Still we have managed to secure three corpses, two of them in good condition and one, well, mostly just pieces and parts. We have an intelligence officer on site, Lieutenant Perryweather, and he's coordinating an evaluation and gathering clues as to the origins and nature of the enemy."

"Do you have any answers yet General? Graham Likely's people haven't turned up anything useful."

"No Sir, but we've gathered some interesting clues. The attackers are all outfitted uniformly. As you know they wear a Syrian uniform but Perryweather says the clothes aren't Syrian issue uniforms, rather they are merely the same style or pattern. He says the fabric's thread count is completely different and its denier number is much higher, whatever that is. Of course I don't know anything about fabrics but we're forwarding the information over to Likely's office and maybe they can track down the origin of the type of fabric leading to the identity of the enemy."

"Two other interesting clues have come out during the investigation. The first is the attackers are apparently not of the same nationality. Perryweather believes one of the corpses is Persian and another one Arab, The third one is destroyed beyond recognition but Perryweather has reasons to think the corpse is a Caucasian of what nationality we have no idea. The third important clue is the distinctive markings tattooed on the foreheads of these guys. The symbols look Arabic or Farsi but we don't have any people here who can translate what it says, if it actually is a phrase. Again we're forwarding the information on to Likely's office but I wanted to give you a heads up."

"Thank you for the information General. I'll confer with Director Likely, hopefully the CIA can get to the bottom of this."

The President turns his attention away from the teleconference back toward the group meeting in the Situation Room. The atmosphere is absent the somber quality of the past days, attitudes turning positive as news and images of fantastic discoveries at the Well Site are posted on the room's monitors.

Science Advisor Kane provides a running narrative of the foundations and implications of each new amazing find. The grainy video clip of the lighting system in the Public Library powered by a strange new technology elicits gasps and loud oohs and aahhs of wonderment.

New discoveries are met with anticipation and boisterous cheers and clapping followed by excited questions and animated discussions. For a few hours the Situation Room knows the thrill of high achievement and its inhabitants bask in a heady glow of victory.

"Graham I trust you're on this mystery attacker problem," says the President. "Do whatever you must, we need to know who or what is directing these attacks against our people out there."

"Certainly Mr. President, I'll handle the problem personally. I'm heading over to my office this instant to download the information General Keith sent and we'll analyze it quickly. We'll have some answers very soon I should think."

The heavily criticized National Intelligence Director rises from his seat and makes a dramatically ostentatious exit as a show of importance. To his mind it's obvious no one out on the battlefield can translate Arabic or Farsi. Officer Perryweather's analysis is undoubtedly flawed and misconstrued. No, only the Office of National Intelligence can solve the complex mysteries of South Central Asia. "Once again its Graham Likely to the rescue," he thinks to him self during his flourishing exit.

President Crandall turns his attention to CIA Director Norton, quizzing him on updates regarding the Iranian nuclear problem. "Do we have any news Iran's nuclear test preparations?"

"The status of our investigation remains unchanged Sir. While its true the Iranians are making preparations that seem provocative on the surface we have no confirmation they are indeed extracting nuclear fuel from the Arak nuclear facility. Additionally, our agents in the field haven't uncovered anything indicating the Iranian government's intentions to detonate a nuclear device."

"Some of our analysts think the Iranians are playing games by making all sorts of motions on the ground, getting picked up by satellite flying overhead and then causing the rest of us to scramble around in confusion. Just a big bluff to test our resolve and resources."

"Your analysts ideas are plausible. What do you think?"

"I tend to side with my analysts Sir. The Israeli Moussad hasn't picked up any intelligence leading them to believe a nuclear detonation is imminent. Of course Israel is in Tehran's cross hairs so I would expect them to exhibit hyper sensitivity on any provocative nuclear moves conducted by the Iranians. But they read nothing so I'm leaning toward the idea of a grand bluff similar to the shenanigans pulled by the North Koreans for so many years."

"But the NoKos did indeed detonate a nuclear device."

"Yes Sir, they did…eventually. But they pulled years worth of bluffs and feints first, apparently to buy enough time to develop technologies enabling them to finally pull the trigger on an actual nuclear detonation test. I'm starting to believe the Iranians are up to the same games."

"How do we know the NoKos didn't pass on their technology to the Iranians, eliminating the need for all these penny ante games?"

"We're fairly certain that didn't happen Mr. Presi…"

Dan Maney excitedly interrupts Director Norton with a loud serious tone. "Mr. President it's Speaker of the House Hartley on the line and he's pissed!"

"He's always pissed off about something, what now?"

"He says turn on Fox News."

The channel on the Situation Room's main monitor is flipped to Fox News Channel. To the dismay and horror of the Cabinet, Directors and the President images and video-clips of the Well Site Operation leap off the screen burning into the consciousness of the room.

The report filed by Fox News' intrepid reporter Lorenzo Cordoba is replete with the Team's new discoveries and technological wonders and the exact location of the Well Site. Full biographical dossiers on Team Babelus members flash across the screen enhanced for entertainment purposed with high-tech animated graphics and sound bite info-crawls running along the screen's bottom. Operation Well Site is no longer dark.

"How could this happen?" screams an emotionally shocked President, his balled fist slamming the table. "Torie get the head of Fox News on the line immediately, I'll have his treasonous head for this outrage. They're exposing government secrets, endangering Americans and threatening national security! I won't stand for this! And Lorenzo

Cordoba, who the hell is he to make the decision to put American lives in danger!"

Torie Smart, the White House Communications Director rushes from the room to contact Fox News officials. The room falls silent, all pondering the political, social, legal and national security implications of the public exposure of Operation Well Site.

The television report flickers in the background though no one in the room can stomach watching any longer, their heads turn toward the center of the table, bowed in solemn reflection.

"This is goodbye for now, live from Iraq, your War Correspondent Lorenzo Cordoba signing off…"

38

The Well of Towers
Public Library Main Chamber
Syrian Desert, Iraq

Frustration sets in as Team Babelus considers the news of the Well Site operation's public exposure while taking a break to eat dinner. Lorenzo Cordoba, once a controversial flamboyant daytime talk show host now turned war correspondent scooped every other news media organization in the world and brought the operation and personal lives of its science exploration team into America's living rooms.

"They ran an interview with my ex-boyfriend," complains Tasha. "Where did they dig him up? At least he said nice things about me. I wonder if they paid him? And Lorenzo Cordoba of all people, now I suppose we're just part of trash TV instead of an important scientific exploration."

"I met Lorenzo a few times out in the field." Jake smacks in between generous bites of delectable serving of Chicken Cacciatore. "Our show was crisscrossing the Middle East in search of one dig after the next and he was crisscrossing the opposite direction in search of one war after the next. I asked him if he was embarrassed about how he uses confrontational trash TV, like putting some Black Panthers on the same stage with the Grand Wizard of the Ku Klux Klan. He asked me if I was embarrassed about pretty much all of my show. That was the end of the conversation. You know he quit the talk show format to work the war correspondent gig after 911. I got the feeling he was a patriot underneath all the colorful bluster, even grew to like him although I disagree with all the political tripe he stands for. I guess like most people it's a mixed bag with him but the soldiers like him and he seems to have a genuine affection and appreciation for the hard work they do. I wonder how he's getting all of the technical information on the Site. He has all the video clips of everything we've done so far. Any ideas on that Tasha?"

"He's gotta be stealing our signal, I highly doubt General Keith uploaded our communications to him. Our system is a secure closed loop network but if he has access to state-of-the-art military hardware I'll bet he can hack in. I could throw him a curveball with a random signal while we skip to a different frequency but I don't know if that's the right move now with the cat thrown unceremoniously out of the bag."

"We're famous now," interjects Dr. Kagen. "Our exploration is set up like a reality TV show at this point. Perhaps we should start fighting with each other to give the ratings a boost, or maybe one of you gals can have an affair with one of the guys or better yet, one of the girls. Heh-heh, that'll bring in the viewers."

"Doctor Kagen!" Kelly Anne yells in faux anger. "What a sexist and disgusting idea!"

"See, its already starting! Heh, heh."

KO redirects the conversation toward a reality of the existential variety. "I'm starting to feel rather useless here," he admits. "About all I've been good for so far is moving heavy objects and cooking up the food. None of my expertise has come into play. I expected to find some kind of language primer in this place I could use to translate the ancient history into a story we can understand in modern times but so far we're coming up empty. We're sitting here eating K-rations in a great hall we've dubbed the Public library but there's not a single representation of language in here. There's no books or symbols or art on the walls, as if all the tangible forms of information in this underground world were swept up by the janitor after the last guy here turned off the lights."

"Perhaps the beings living here didn't communicate by the written word," suggests Dr. Kagen. "Its even possible they didn't use the spoken word either."

"You mean telepathy or sign language Doctor?" asks KO.

"Sure, why not?"

"I'll grant you the possibility but communication isn't purely a function between persons. How do these beings communicate with the environment around them for example? They used light sources so they had eyesight. But you'll notice there are no signs of any type directing whatever beings existed here to mundane everyday things like the restroom or an emergency exit. Curiously there's no art on the walls either, that's a big clue to me. The people who designed the beautiful ceiling up there obviously expressed an appreciation for aesthetics. Anywhere there is art in a society you'll likely find language and emotions to describe its wondrous properties."

"Hmm, yes perhaps but then again we may be incapable of understanding whatever form of communication they used. Maybe they just knew by intuition where the bathroom was and how to escape in case of fire. I don't know that, I'm just saying."

"KO is right about one thing," adds Kelly Anne, "If this is a Public Library as we've named it then there's most certainly a repository of stored information. The size and scope of this area suggests it houses a great deal of data, we just don't know how to access it."

Dr. Kagen searches the chamber with wandering eyes while he dissects the argument. "Yes, yes. Good point, if we're in a library where are all the books?"

The Team finishes the quick meal, stows the resulting garbage and heads back to the massive structure they refer to as the Wine Rack sitting invitingly in the middle of the chamber.

39

Kelly Anne's imagination turns toward thoughts of Major Lee as they trek the short distance back to the Wine Rack. She wonders if he's seen her biography in Lorenzo's report and if he approves of her life. She thinks of his strong arms holding her tightly against his chest, consoling her over a life laid bare for public scrutiny. Kelly Anne's emotions swell with warmth at the idea of a man providing her solace and enduring love. Her cheeks grow flush as her heart beats rapidly and her breathing grows shallow.

As the Team walks past the curious spindles at the near end of the Wine Rack Kelley Anne hears a whispering fleeting technological sound pulling at the side of her face as if a voice inside her head is trying desperately to push through her skin.

"VUH-EEEM-UH."

She gasps loudly. "Did you all hear that?"

"Hear what? You gasping for air?" responds Jake.

"No not me. That weird little noise coming from the spindles!" Kelly Anne pants in excitement and points to the largest spindle in the center of the bunch. "I know I heard something. It sounded like someone turned on an old television. An old black and white one with tubes and everything."

"Well why don't you go sneeze on it and see if it talks to you again," offers Dr. Kagen half jokingly.

Kelly Anne walks past the spindle again to re-create the sensation.

"VUH-EEEM-UH."

"There, did you hear that? It's coming right from that one only it's also in my head!"

"I didn't hear a thing. Maybe the Chicken Cacciatore is spoiled, how much did you eat?"

"No, no," interrupts Tasha. "I think I saw something when you walked by the spindle, a greenish flicker or something. Saw not heard. Walk past it again, everybody watch the spindle."

Kelly Anne walks past the spindle, closer, nearly next to the object.

"VUH-EEEM-UH."

"There, there, did you all see that flash?" shouts Tasha. "Kelly Anne just stand in front of the thing for awhile and see what happens!"

Kelly Anne stands directly on front of the spindle, her face barely eighteen inches from its base. "VUH-EEEM-MM-MM-UH, EEEEM-UH, EEEMMM...."

"Wow! Shouts Tasha obviously excited "You guys see that right?"

"Yeah," they gasp and nod in unison.

A mysterious square blank green glowing image floats above the spindle's lower bar and to the right of it's left vertical bar. The image measures approximately 17 inches wide and 11 inches tall, giving every appearance of a sheet of tabloid-sized paper in a horizontal aspect ratio floating in mid-air. Kelly Anne stands staring, transfixed at the floating image. Tears well up in her eyes and spill over running down her flushed cheeks.

"What is it Kelly Anne?" asks Tasha. "Are you crying?"

"Don't you see what I'm seeing?"

"Yeah we see a blank sheet of a green paperish looking object floating in the air," says Jake. "Its remarkable, wow!"

"Is that what you all see?"

"Yes," they answer.

"Well what do you see Kelly Anne?" queries Tasha in worried tones.

"I see what I was thinking about a few moments before I heard the weird sound. Right at this moment I'm looking at a scene with Major Lee and me taking place back at the HQ tent. We were looking over satellite photos of the Well Site, I can see his strong hands, the pictures and everything as if it's happening right now."

"Whoa!" exclaims Dr. Kagen. "It's a bio-monitor!"

"A what?" asks Jake, "You mean like the thing diabetics poke into their fingers to check blood sugar levels?"

"No, no, no, a machine tapping into a person's biorhythms; displaying them in a graphical representation. We do this with PET scans of the brain in our world. In this case I think Kelly Anne is connected to the monitor through an interaction with her brain waves although I can't see how they connect."

"Brain waves are electromagnetic," Tasha postulates, "Could be a brainwave magnet in the spindles drawing them out of her head."

"How come the rest of us can't see what she's seeing?" asks Jake, a part of him curious as to why Kelly Anne is possessed of such strong emotions for Major Lee.

"Psychodynamics are complicated," instructs Dr. Kagen, "But I think basically because Kelly Anne is looking at the image through her mind's eye and not her physical eyeballs. Her brainwaves interact with the machine and powers it on but we only see a blank slate as we're looking through our physical eyes and don't have access to Kelly Anne's brain."

"Thank God!" exclaims Kelly Anne.

Tasha knows fundamental technologies but has trouble interpreting ethereal science. "Why do you suppose Kelly Anne's brain powers up the machine while the rest of ours don't?"

"Apparently Kelly Anne's brain is in a highly emotional state, firing synapses in the frontal lobe region of the brain controling emotions. That's probably the key to starting these things up. Also Kelly Anne is the most intuitive amongst us so she probably has a greater capacity to interact with a brainwave reader. I suspect we can all do the same thing if we think strong emotional thoughts and concentrate with the idea of turning on the machines with brainpower."

Dr. Kagen's suggestion sends the rest of Team Babelus scrambling toward various spindles arranged in a semi-circle at the edge of the Wine Rack, each selecting a spindle according to personal preference.

Tasha's monitor is the first to fire up as she thinks of the heroic Gunny Hall riding furiously to her rescue, blasting the enemy with deadly accuracy.

Her thoughts conjure up memories of her father's protective nature. She misses her father dearly, his technology stories and the time they spend together inventing solutions to the world's problems. The scene at her mother's funeral and her crushed father's slumping shoulders heaving in great sobs of emotion play out on the floating platen before her eyes.

Jake searches his heart for an emotional moment that might trigger the necessary brainwaves to bring his spindle to life. At first he tries thinking of all the girls he loved in life but his dispassionate sex life didn't seem to work, although an occasional flicker appeared to float in front of him.

His thoughts turned to *Jackson Nichols' Big Dig* and the meeting with producers a few months ago informing him of the impending cancellation of the show. His machine immediately powers on, the sad moment and his embarrassing tearful reaction on display floating like a horror movie before him.

KO remembers the time the leader of the Weekend Riders Harley Club pulled him aside and informed him he was accepted into their elite fraternity, an honor for life. The mind-movie on his monitor is the panoramic open desert heading into Las Vegas for a weekend of gambling and biker carousing. The quality of sound surprises him and he wonders if he only hears the noise through his mind's ear.

His graduation from M.I.T with high honors and his parents proudly shooting a gazillion snap shots, flashbulbs popping incessantly, starts the spindle platen for Dr. Kagen. He thinks of the generous hugs freely given by his widely smiling father and the happy tears of his mother…emotion floods his heart. The time since the long ago happy day spent in relative obscurity with the loss of both parents and a terribly nasty divorce filling the void between then and now.

Ahmed the Botaninst thinks of his devotion to Allah and the spiritual instruction of the great Imam al-Takrani who nurtured him through times of death and turmoil after insurgents stormed into his father's house killing everyone including the women and children. Only Ahmed survived the massacre and he feels ashamed of the fact. His teacher's soft-spoken reassuring instructions fill the bio-screen as they did his heart in the days of sorrow and pain.

Brian the Archeologist fails to generate sufficient emotions to create the brain wave power necessary to start a spindle. He skips around to various empty monitors hoping to improve his luck but is met with nothing more than an occasional sputtering flicker.

"I wonder what the technology is behind these things?" Tasha asks out loud, breaking the trance Team Babelus worked itself into. "I understand the part about interacting with our brains like they're some sort of CPU but I'd like to know what makes the picture appear out of nothing. The picture is crystal clear and sharp. I expected something hazy and liquid like what I see in my dreams. But this is more along the lines of a high resolution HDTV and even better than that. We could make a mint if we could invent a plasma screen with a picture quality this sharp."

"It stands to reason Tasha." Dr. Kagen thinks the puzzle through. "Even the highest resolution television or computer monitor is only a replica of what your mind processes through the ocular devices we call eyes. A digital image is nothing more than a machine attempting to re-create the real thing. What you're seeing here on the bio-monitors is an accurate representation of real memories and they're not broken up into pixels."

To Jake the problem is fundamental. "How do you think these beings built all of this super high technology without computers Doctor?"

"Jake I think they did have computers just like you and I have computers. They used their actual brains."

"You're saying they used more of their brain or they had a higher capacity brain than ours?"

"Neither Jake. I'm talking about how powerful our brains actually are. The capacity of each human brain is far more powerful than any computer ever built. Scientists have calculated the memory capacity of the human brain is as much as a thousand terabytes. Now that's tantamount to the memory capacity of a million personal computers in one head. That's a lot of capacity, it just blows the mind…uh, please excuse me for saying."

Tasha knows computer science backwards and forwards and adds to Dr. Kagen's theory. "True Doctor but memory capacity isn't the real power of the human brain. The way the brain functions…that's where the intelligence lies. The human brain is far more efficient and intuitive than any hardware system ever invented."

"With a computer, even Blue Gene/L the huge super computer I worked with at Lawrence Livermore Labs, digital bits of information are stored and retrieved through a mechanical system. The brain is bio-mechanical and science has little understanding about how it stores and retrieves information. More importantly we don't have the slightest clue how the brain picks and chooses which information to process. If you compare the world's most powerful computer with an average human brain you'll find the brain more efficient and smarter by several orders of magnitude."

"Imagine if we could jack our brains directly into a computer and do the tasks we normally do on them now, how much richer and vibrant an interface with machines is that? Actually we're doing what I'm describing here…in a way. Kelly

Anne I want to try an experiment with you but you'll have to trust me ok?"

"Uh, what kind of experiment?" Kelly Anne's familiarity with Tasha's propensity to take undue risks runs through the back of her mind.

Tasha walks over and stands next to Kelly Anne in front of her spindle. "I want to see if we can fire up one of these puppies together using both of our brains. You have to trust me that I won't use any information I see from inside your head against you."

Kelly Anne, not one to open herself up in the physical world is hesitant to open the door to the thoughts and images contained in the world in her head but she thinks of the needs of science and determines to sacrifice her self and her own interests. "Ok, what do you have in mind, Tash?"

"What is your favorite kind of animal?"

"I like horses."

"Me too. So, let's stand side by side and think of a picture of a horse that we would like to ride. Just a side view of the horse and nothing else like trotting through fields of poppies or anything."

"Ok, I'm game."

The two stand side-by-side with Tasha's left arm locking around Kelly Anne's right elbow. They concentrate on a profile view of a horse each would like to ride. Kelly Anne thinks of the time when her father took her out riding on a painted pony. Tasha thinks back to her first encounter with a large dark horse who kicked at her from his stall and made her cry when she was a little girl. Together they open their minds and the green-glowing paper-sized image appears, floating inside the spindle viewing area.

"Oh God here it comes," says Jake out loud.

"What do you see Kelly Anne?" asks Tasha.

"I see an image of my favorite horse, a painted pony like the one Michael Landon used to ride in Bonanza."

"What do you see now?"

"Its changing colors, to a dark chestnut!"

"I know…I'm painting it."

"Oh my Lord in Heaven!" shouts Dr. Kagen. "The two of you are daisy chaining your brains!"

"Daisy chain?" smirks Jake. "Isn't that a lesbian porn thing?"

"No Jake you nasty tiger. Well it is but that's not what I'm referring to at the moment. A daisy chain in computers is when you string together a series of devices and peripherals and they function as one much smarter unit. Imagine the possibilities of daisy chaining human brains to collaborate on projects. The potential output is staggering."

"Why? One brain has the same capacity as the next right, so why would that make a difference?"

"Capacity isn't the only operative function of human brains Jake, there's also ability. Put together that translates into capability. As you probably already understand some people's left-brain functions better than their right and vice versa."

"Just imagine if you were able to fuse together the logical calculating capabilities of a highly developed left-brained personality with the creative intuitive properties of a highly developed right-brained intellect. What if, for example you could put together the genius of a left-brained geneticist like me, pardon the reference, and the right-brained creativity of Mozart. What beautiful symphonies could you create with genetic programming? What genetic therapies could you create by interlacing musical genius? The possibilities are endlessly fantastic or fantastically endless!"

40

The Well of Towers
Wine Rack area of the Public Library
Syrian Desert, Iraq

Team Babelus spends the better part of Operation Well Site's second exploration day experimenting with the newly discovered and freshly dubbed 'brainy-chains', an ancient technology used to tie the mental capacities of two brains together. Forming into teams of two, they fashion brain-teasing puzzles utilizing the respective talents of each teammate. Jack matches his tic-tac-toe expertise with Tasha's mechanical acuity. Kelly Anne, mentally blocked from learning a foreign language despite her photographic memory, tries to learn bits of Arabic from Ahmed the Botanist. Brian keeps at his futile attempts to brain-start the machines.

Dr. Kagen and KO work to create a rudimentary Spanish language edition of the Human Genome to little success but a good deal of laughter. The puzzles and brain challenges spark curiosity leading to inquisitiveness. Learning how to work with brainy-chaining technology is the same as learning to ride a bike…easy to see how it's done but every try at the concept gives you a skinned knee.

"Do you suppose these beings communicated through brain waves Doctor Kagen, I mean outside of these machines?" asks KO.

"Perhaps and maybe not. It seems likely given how brainwaves are pulled out of your head and graphically displayed through these machines. Then again it's possible they couldn't do this trick without consciously hooking their hardware or brains together through this common interface. I should think any being would wish to maintain some sort of privacy and have a brain wave firewall in place to keep out unwanted guests."

"Ha! Yeah that could get pretty dicey. Imagine boppin' your old lady while thinking of your ex-girlfriends nice ass and the one you're doin' jumps into your brain and sees the same fantasy. She'd kick ya' to the floor."

"Some girlfriends would kick the man away and other's might join in on the fun. The issue is you never know what you're going to get with reading each other's minds so it's better safe than sorry in my estimation. Although in a society familiar with opening doors to each other's minds I suppose the technology could increase understanding between the sexes, or it could just as well create further misunderstanding.

I'm not the one to ask KO. I have never much understood the opposite sex on any level."

"I see your point Doctor, nothing is ever clear between any kinds of people, the sexes, the races, cultures or nationalities. Even if we could leap into somebody's actual thoughts we may not gain any useful or real information anyway. A lot of things people think about are pure fantasy. Maybe using machines as a buffer is a better way to go."

Kelly Anne and Ahmed the Botanist continue to muddle through the Arabic language exercise with poor results. Ahmed has little familiarity or skill with English and Kelly Anne knows next to nothing of Arabic. Translating languages under such conditions is nearly impossible. An idea strikes Kelly Anne. "Hey KO? Why don't you come over here and join us for a little experiment, you speak Arabic right?"

"Quite fluently M'lady. I can speak any language you might think of if you give me enough time with it. I'm not much good for anything else but I do the language thing pretty damn well, just ask the NSA."

"Great, I'm trying to learn some Arabic phrases by brainy-chaining with Ahmed but his English is uh, spotty let's say. I want to try brainy-chaining three of us together with you in the middle as a translator and see what happens."

"Ok, that's sounds cool, but if it works I get the patent rights to sell to the United Nations."

"Deal."

KO sandwiches himself between Ahmed and Kelly Anne, all three of them proceed to fire up the brain reader. The tell tale green glo-screen appears, floating above the reader's lower bar. Ahmed starts out by reciting Koranic verses in Arabic in his mind. KO translates the Arabic verses into English in his head. Kelly Anne writes what she sees in mind's eye out on the glo-screen in front of them. As Kelly Anne mind-writes what she sees in her mind, the characters are viewable to the brainy-chained explorers on the green glowing platen…in Arabic script.

"Are you guy's seeing what I'm seeing?" asks Kelly Anne. "It's the most remarkable thing we've done with these machines yet."

"We see it," they respond.

"I am hearing words in English and then writing them out in my head and its coming out as Arabic! But I can also read the Arabic script I just wrote and understand every word of it. Now let's break contact and let me see if I can recite any of the verses you just translated and ported into my head."

They tear themselves apart from their brainwave connection and Kelly Anne proceeds to recite the 34th verse of the fourth chapter of the Koran *An-Nisa*, or women, verbatim…in English. "As to those on whose part you fear desertion, admonish them and leave them alone in the sleeping-places and beat them."

"Well, not the verse I would have chosen as my first foray into the Arabic language given that I most certainly don't approve of beating your wife but the translation capabilities of brainy-chaining are absolutely astonishing. I wonder if I could learn an entire language this way? KO you're our very own universal translator!"

"Not universal Kelly Anne. I don't have any clue about the language these beings spoke or even how they communicated at all. So despite your enthusiasm and the ability to help you learn a foreign language I still feel useless on this voyage."

41

As the trio makes headway uploading Arabic into Kelly Anne's memory banks Tasha's curiosity about the small cylindrical object that THWOOOMPED from the Wine Rack begs her to find a solution to its mysteries. She turns the whirring object over and over, tosses it in the air, rolls it on the ground, thumps it, taps it, spins it like a top and rubs it between her palms as if a genie will magically spring from its encasement. Nothing works. Frustrated, Tasha walks over to the brainy-chained language class now in session and stands next to them, halfway thinking to ask Kelly Anne for assistance with one of her highly effective sneezes.

"Hey Tasha I think you're causing static, are you auditing this class?" Kelly Anne asks, laughing.

"No I'm just standing here thinking."

"Uh duh, that's exactly what fires these things up Tash!" mocks KO.

Tasha takes several steps backing away from the group, leaving the cylinder on the counter next to platen. "Is that better? I didn't know my brain was bright enough to overpower you three brainiacs and cause a bunch of static on your little brainy-vision set. You'd think I was operating a hair dryer while you watched a soap opera."

"No it's still a problem, but you have the right idea. It's as if you turned on a microwave oven on the same circuit as the TV and it causes interference, step back some more," says Kelly Anne as Tasha steps further back. "No, no, still no good. I keep seeing static and white noise, although the image of a half-naked old man keeps popping up too, weird, and no gentlemen I don't have fantasies about older men."

"I see him too," says KO. "An old geezer sitting on a rock or a chair or something, looks like Moses in a toga. There's no way I would fantasize about that!"

"Yes, I see the man too," admits Ahmed. "The Koran forbids me to think of men this way. Maybe it is Tasha's fantasy."

Tasha walks over to the counter, picks up the cylinder and retreats twenty steps. The picture clears for Kelly Anne. "Hey its all cleared up, what did you do Tasha, kick the set?"

Tasha is on to something and proceeds to follow new clues. "You guys stick to what you're doing while I experiment with this cylinder thingy that tattood Kelly Anne's forehead. She navigates the cylinder around the vicinity of the glo-screen. Moving the object closer causes static and flashing images of the old man to appear, sitting majestically on a huge chair or throne. Moving the cylinder upwards decreases the static on the glo-screen and downwards increased the static and frequency of the images. "This little thing's gotta be a data storage unit."

Tasha inspects the counter space around the machine. "It has a spinning noise like a hard drive but it must capture and store brain waves instead of digital signals. Hmm, there must be a way to hardwire this thing, it doesn't seem to work too well in a wireless configuration."

Tasha searches underneath the counter and on its edge to no avail. On the counter's top surface she notices a ring-like impression similar to those on the Wine Rack. She places her palm flatly on the ring and turns counter-clockwise. As she turns a small piece of the counter spins away underneath her hand revealing a three-inch hole the shape of a circle. She slips the cylinder into the hole where it snugly nestles two inches deep.

"Whoa! Shit! Ouch!" shrieks KO as he stumbles backward holding his meaty hands up to his head and breaking his mind connection with the glo-screen. "What are you trying to do, fry my brain? That hurt Tasha!"

"Sorry KO! Heh, heh, ha, ha! Sorry! Really. Do you guys see anything?"

Kelly Anne responds warily. "Yeah Tash. I see a man seated on a huge ornate chair in a palace of some kind, he's talking but I can't understand a word coming out of his mouth. I like his voice though, deep and ominous but at the same time reassuring like I imagine for God's voice. You don't think this is God do you?"

KO recomposes himself and returns to the glo-screen with a hint of a headache. "Wow this is like watching a high-definition DVD or something. I can hear him and I think I understand what he's saying. What about you Ahmed?"

"I see him but do not understand his words, they are not Arabic or Farsi."

"Ok then I'll try to think in terms of translation like we did with Kelly Anne but this time both of you listen."

Kelly Anne is the first to speak. "Oh yeah I can understand him now. He really is a handsome guy for an older man. His skin doesn't look old at all but his hair is silvery white, though not gray like an old man. He seems very tall and strong but his features are soft and inviting with a winsome smile on his face. He has a commanding presence but maybe his appeal is enhanced with him sitting on a throne in a palace. In our world we might call him an alpha-male but he looks too nice for the designation. When I look at him he reminds me of every mythical God ever thought of by Man. He has all the appearances of a great father figure like Zeus or the Sun God Ra or perhaps a wise mature Hercules with silver hair. He's very white as if he gets no sun at all and his skin is nearly translucent. In a lot of ways he reminds me of a great big Norwegian fella. Maybe I could fantasize about an older man."

"Uhh, yuck," complains K.O. "How about if we all try to get in on viewing this, without the fantasies."

By this time Jake and the others gather around the machine, curious as to the commotion unfolding around the glo-screen. KO informs the group the man on the throne is in the middle of some kind of speech or address and wonders about the possibilities of rewinding the disc or scan…whatever.

Upon further inspection Tasha discovers a set of rings on top of the cylinder enabling them to operate the device as simply as a DVD player. Turning the top ring counter-clockwise rewinds the movie, clockwise for fast-forward. Turning the second ring counter-clockwise resets the movie. Everyone wants to watch at the same time and Tasha searches around for a larger glo-screen to without success.

She assumes her hands on hips thinking position and after several episodes of furrowed brows and thoughtful murmurs she discovers that flipping the vertical bar on the glo-screen down to a horizontal position connects the screen with the one next to it, creating either a panorama wide-screen or a series of individual images on a bank of screens. She sets the system up in a seven-screen configuration, resets the movie and joins the others in a full-team brainy-chain.

Standing in the center of the group KO concentrates on the grand old man's speech and gestures and translates them to English in the back of his mind. Everyone except Brian, who still has not managed to ignite the power of the glo-screen, watches in awe as the image of a great personage fills the ears and eyes of the mind.

"Greetings. My name is Gael. I am the last of the people of Avinen and this is my testament…"

42

Public Library
City of Avinen

Chattering and rustling noises inside the Public library chamber dissipate as Team Babelus brain-locks in to the glo-screen panorama of images and sounds. A brainwave testament in a canister plays out before them featuring a grand wise man proclaiming him self the last inhabitant in the City of Avinen. As the narrator Gael relates…eons ago a race of people known as the Avina dwelled in the city now buried nearly three-quarters of a mile below the planet's surface. Translated directly through KO's linguistically talented brain the city and its people are phonetically pronounced the City of Ah-vee-nen and its residents known as Ah-vee-nah.

Gael, a stately wise-looking man, sits comfortably, insouciantly with the ease and grace of a high level communicator on a large white marble throne-like chair. The chair sits raised on a marble platform in the central area of a grand cathedral or auditorium. The floor of the space reflects a translucent light-blue marble cast with a highly polished sheen. Its walls are covered baseboard to ceiling with majestically splendid works of art. No living thing besides Gael himself appears in the brainwave-video. No servants stand by to acquiesce to each request of a king in charge of his surroundings. There are no trees, shrubs, bushes or flowers gracing the hallways or doorways of the great hall.

Jake notes the architecture of the auditorium on the glo-screen image roughly matches the dimensions and features of the Public Library area without the throne or its pedestal. He assumes the hall in the brainwave-video is located elsewhere in Avinen, housed in one of its numerous buildings or colorful spires. And yet his latent archeological instincts tug at the recesses of his consciousness. The spaces and porticos appear so similar as to be of twin construction with the exception of the marble flooring and art covering the walls. And too the Public Library features no throne of any type, only the immense Wine Rack library of 'scan-cans', as Tasha dubbed the brain-wave canisters, stands in the center of the chamber.

KO translates the language of the Avina, a tongue he had never heard and yet found unequivocally familiar. The exotic mixture of dialogue arranged in an unknown syntax and grammar seems to the experienced linguist as if the main elements of Old English and ancient Hebrew are spliced together in a quagmire of phonetics and jargon. He casts the crazy idea out of his mind, surmising the sensations he feels while translating the language are the effects of brainy-chaining en masse.

From the majesty of his throne Gael continues, speaking in measured, thoughtful and inviting tones with no hint of guile or malice.

Gael's Testament:

The Avina are a great and proud community of creators, builders, discoverers and managers. The legacy of our aptitude stands through the ages as a living testament to supreme power and control over the physical limits of earth and firmament. Our hands are the guide of life and living in all things throughout every land.

The plan of the Avina was to create great works to shine throughout the Universe, a beacon of exemplars in technological advancement and creative prowess. In this we excelled mightily, with dominion over the genus of all living things and command of the forces of attraction, mass and light. The Avina used this knowledge to create and sustain the varieties of the world, breathing life into the void.

•

Kelly Anne immediately seizes upon the references in Gael's opening statement, thinking of descriptions of the God of Genesis in the Bible, the creator of all things, omniscient and powerful, the Great I Am or the oft used phrase I am that am. "Is he telling us through this testament the Avina or Gael himself is God?" She asks out loud.

"That is a blasphemy," responds Ahmed. "Only Allah can be God."

"How do you know Gael isn't the true Allah?" asks Jake.

"If he were Allah he would look like me."

43

Gael continues his fascinating if disturbing narrative:

Our people grew lonely in the solitude and emptiness of our abiding existence, a thousand regenerations of the blood suspends the dimensions of time for those under the application thereof, providing the Avina with everlasting life. I am, as I record this testament an age equal with 40,000 revolutions of the Sun.

•

"Uh oh, that's not too good." laments Dr. Kagen. "I think these people discovered the fountain of youth through genetic manipulation. What I'm unclear of is if a revolution of the Sun means one day, which would make this gentleman a very good looking 110 years old or does he refer to the earth's orbit around the Sun which would make him an exceedingly well-preserved 40,000 years old!"

"What does he mean a regeneration of the blood Doctor Kagen?" asks Jake.

"Jake this is what I'm most excited and worried about. A regeneration of the blood could be a simple blood transfusion. For a time many doctors in our day believed a blood transfusion could extend life. But what concerns me is the use of a thousand such transfusions. The calculation don't add up for a man of 110 years old. This means you'd be getting nine or ten applications a year. The effect would diminish after one a year, if there were any noticeable effect at all. Also, reaching the age of a hundred and ten years isn't particularly remarkable, just quite a bit over average"

"A thousand applications over 40,000 years don't make any sense either as no amount of blood transfusions will sustain life so long. The idea both exciting and worrying me is these regenerations of the blood weren't about blood at all per se. The treatments may have been full boat genetic regenerations at the DNA level where a doctor replaces your entire DNA structure. If such therapies were possible you could regenerate all of your physical parts…skin, hair, heart, all vital organs, well, everything over and over and then you could live an everlasting life…you know, if this were possible. I have no idea what such treatments would do to your brain and its stored memories. All of this is fascinating and frightening at the same time."

"What is it about the concept that has you both excited and afraid Doctor Kagen?" asks Kelly Anne.

"Oh Kelly Anne, let me tell you! I'm excited to discover this technology is possible and the theories have a foundation in science. We could cure every disease known to mankind with DNA replacement therapies. There're no limits to the lifespan we would have at our fingertips. And oh Lordy. Yes, yes. I fear this technology, not from ignorance but from the fruits of my imagination and human capabilities for mayhem. I can envision this falling into the wrong hands, those with evil intent. As a scientist I desire for all new discoveries to see the light of day and undergo thorough testing and critical examination. I'm not sure we want to enter this territory though. I mean we're talking about the power of God here…the actual power of God."

"Do you think that's what Gael means by the genus of life in his testament?"

"No, no ma'am I think this is another scientific regimen entirely, although they probably utilize the same methods. Genus of all living things in matters of creation refers to the design, at the DNA level, of every living thing on earth. Plants, animals, even humans. Those powers are another scary thought to me. Science has just now gotten around to mapping the human genome using hundreds of computers and years of calculations but we have very little understanding of how genes work in concert with their environment and other genes. These people, as translated by KO anyway, uh, no offense to your skills KO, were genus designers and life creators. In other words they programmed the original DNA of living things, everything on earth. They were grand designers. Now I guess that's ok from where we stand at the moment but these beings, whatever species, were are mortal and I'm not sure I'm comfortable with the idea of mere mortals holding these immense powers without any checks and balances."

Kelly Anne refers to her Biblical knowledge in the discussion. "Perhaps those sentiments are shared by all of the writers and theorists who came up with stories of God or the Gods. Even the God of the Bible had to have some method to create living things and your description matches, at least roughly, the story of creation in Genesis. Of course they attributed the creation to an all-knowing loving omniscient

Creator with a big 'C', not a society of mortal scientists and creators."

"I wouldn't mind the idea of a team of creators as the genesis of my existence," adds Tasha. "I'm a lot less comfortable with a dogma presupposing all of life sprang up from a primordial ooze with absolutely no design or thought process whatsoever."

Jake is curious about another aspect of Avina life. "What about this idea of loneliness Doctor Kagen? Obviously they had other Avina in their lives and women too, they must have had sex lives. How can you get lonely if you have a sex life?"

"Jake, Jake, Jake, you and your one track mind! Have you ever been married or lived with a gal for an extended period of time?"

"Uh huh, I was married for six years then we got the seven-year itch."

"Was the sex good?"

"Oh yeah, it was great, well, for the first year or so then we settled into a routine and it got kinda boring. After a couple of years we stopped having much sex at all and then we got divorced. Of course we went back to having great sex after the divorce, well, until she remarried."

"Ok, you're marriage was fairly typical sexually speaking. Now try to imagine having sex with the same person every day, or not even that often, say only once a week for over 40,000 years! I think you just might get a little bored and find sexual activity rather useless at some point. How would you react to a 7,000 year itch?"

"I think I once picked up a rash like that in Olongopo City."

Kelly Anne isn't interested in Jake's sex life and presses the conversation in another direction. "I wonder if they had children?"

"Maybe Gael will get to that if we keep watching his testament!" reminds an irritated KO who has discovered a way to pause the action while his compatriots debate the finer points of the issues at hand. "C'mon let's get back to it, I'm getting a headache and I can't do this forever."

44

The Testament of Gael continues:

The males of Avinen designed and created living beings and physical structures. Female Avina managed processes and kept accounts of the business affairs of the City. The society replicated itself through the regeneration process, creating new Avina as the need for additional creation or management needs grew. Progeny, gathered from the superior hereditary elements of males and females of the highest excellence in Avina was sent to the Great Garden until its maturation process completed. Avina young gestated in created wombs until they could survive on their own.

When a new Avina reached the age of 200 revolutions of the Sun it was introduced into the greater society with breathtaking fanfare and celebration. During their time in the Great Garden young Avina learned science or management and frolicked indiscriminately without regards to gender or status. As the process of maturation took root the young gravitated toward a purpose driven life in Avinen society as creators, builders, discoverers or managers. Physical relations between members of the Avina grows ever more rare as the day of ascension approaches and is wholly discouraged outside the gates of the Great Garden.

•

"Alright so they had orgies until they were two-hundred years old and then they just stopped on a dime and became monks?" asks Jake loudly.

"Yes it would appear so Jake," replies Dr. Kagen.

"I think I'd just shoot myself on my 200th birthday!"

"I'm surprised you lasted past your 20th Jake," smirks Kelly Anne. "You know we've been sitting at these glo-screens for most of the day we should take some time to eat dinner. I'm famished!"

Jake is already tiring of Avinen culture and agrees with the dinner suggestion. "Yeah, I guess I'm hungry too. The Avina are interesting people but I'm a little sick to my stomach thinking about all that technology going to waste."

"Going to waste?" asks Dr. Kagen. "What do you mean by that? They seemed to have built a great society far beyond our own imagination."

"With all this technology you'd think they could come up with something to provide a little relief for an overactive libido like a super duper realistic sex doll if ya know what I mean."

"Yes Jake I see, well maybe so, its likely, well I don't know. Dr. Kagen's lack of clarity grows with an increasing unease about the limits of science.

"Let's scare up some food huh KO? While you do that Kayanne, Tash and I will check in with General Keith. I know he can hear what we're saying but I don't think he can see what we're seeing, probably scarin' the shit out of him."

KO puts together a delightful K-rations buffet featuring meatloaf surprise, creamed corn, beets and mashed potato flakes. Jake, Kelly Anne and Tasha converse with General Keith. At times somberly and others laughing loudly. Ahmed and Brian sit off in the distance speaking in Arabic, gesticulating wildly, engrossed in a theological discussion.

Dr. Kagen sits off by him self pondering Jake's sex doll suggestions. The more he considers humanity and its oversexed societies, libidinous nature and evident inability to refrain from carnal pursuits the deeper Jake's idea cuts into his psyche. He sits sideways, leaning against the seat of his ATV and wonders if the Avina hadn't done exactly what Jake suggested.

Overcome by a dark sense of grief at the scientific and moral implications of all he had witnessed this day Dr. Kagen responds in the only manner appropriate for an intelligent sentient being:

He cries.

45

Pennsylvania Avenue
Washington, D.C.

Protestors pour in from all over the United States in cars, trucks, airplanes and trains, spilling onto Pennsylvania Avenue in front of the White House in a sea of human angst and anger. They fill the public square at the Washington Monument and occupy the steps at Capitol Hill. It seems every group or person with a grievance against the United States Government is out in force on single day. Washington D.C. was once burned to the ground by the British Army but the Capitol City has never known this level of rebellious tribulation threatening to spill over the dam of peace and security.

Scenes around the Capitol are the dictionary definition of vile. Placards held aloft by God-fearing Christians and Allah loving Islamists call for the beheading of the President and public stoning of his wife and children. Men of peace speak openly of mass murder. Political and religious opportunists take to the streets never missing a trick.

Bobby Joe Buckner, President of the Christian Consortium shouts flourishes of religious epithets…from Crandall the blasphemous devil worshipper to Murcheson the Lesbian spawn of the Antichrist. Percy Blankenship head of the United Churches Against Persecution lead chants calling for the President's immediate removal from office under threat of storming the castle of government: Impeach or breach! Impeach or breach! Impeach or breach!

Nader Rizzouk, Chief Spokesman for the Council on Islamic Affairs calls for the severed head of the Infidel occupant of the White house on a platter while inciting his followers to violence. Rabbi Jacob Steenburg of the Jewish Confederation of America runs from one end of Pennsylvania Avenue to the other yelling through a powered bullhorn, challenging listeners to open rebellion against the government. Other groups attending the spontaneous protests ginned up by media speculation and Lorenzo Cordoba's breaking news reports about secrets at the Well Site include Atheist's Against Religion, the People for American Socialism, several Communist front groups, South American Nativists and the oddly named Spiritual Oppressors of the Free Press. Right wingers, left wingers, centrists, moderates and radicals break the shackles of ideology to fight the common enemy: the President of the United States.

The massive protests carry the stench of a stewpot boiling with the excrement of strange-bedfellows moving heaven and earth to force the government to maintain a recognized status quo of religious and philosophical thought in America and throughout the world. The unspoken but widely understood fact…leaders of each group have a vested interest in keeping cushy jobs based on maintaining certain ratios of religious antipathy…is completely beside the point. America's mass media outlets are only too happy to photograph and videotape every lurid and shamefully excessive public act of protest, further inflaming the seething mass.

In the view of protest merchants and demagogues the President sent a team of scientists to unseal a tomb of deceit and fabrication directly refuting the existence of God, any God, even gods bearing the names Atheist or Evolution. The grand conspiracy carried forth by this President includes the military, the CIA, the FBI, white militias, Neo-Nazis and terrorists - though not Islamic ones. For this gross misuse of power, reminiscent of moves by Hitler, the emperors of Rome and old Soviet leaders, the President must hang. No one bothers to ask whether or not the President did the right thing or the veracity of the most outrageous conspiracy theories. It is assumed the President and his minions chose the wrong path, the road to upsetting the voting base powers that be.

Unfortunately the streets of Washington, D.C. make an inauspicious return to mob rule.

46

As President Crandall burns in effigy outside his own home tensions mount inside the White House Situation Room. The Well Site story informant admits her treason to the President. She declares the mistake an innocent conversation with a television news show producer and she wasn't given the memo about secrecy but nonetheless offers a tearful apology and resignation letter.

"I'm not letting you off that easy Torie," barks President Crandall to a visibly distraught White House Communications Director. "You can't just resign and go merrily along with your life."

"Wha-what you mean Sir, prison?"

"No, I won't go that route, you didn't intend to bring down this administration with your overindulgent mouth. No, no, prison's too easy any way. Most of the folks in jail would make friends with you for destroying me, not to mention the country. No Torie I'm going to put the hammer down and make you go out on the White House lawn and face the mob out front. If you survive one hour we'll let you back in the door. How does that sound?"

Torie Smart sits amongst her peers shocked and speechless, her jaw falling to meet the table. "Are you serious Sir or, or uh are you joking?"

"Neither Torie, we're in the middle of a crisis, actually two crises meeting simultaneously and they're about to crash head on over the top of my desk. Your loose lips made the situation worse but we need the expertise of the Communications Director at this moment in history. Your continued participation is vital to this county's security. But I am serious and not joking at all. I find your actions disgusting and foolish and I expect to never run across this problem with you in the future. Now let's get back to work and try to handle this with dignity and professionalism."

"Whew, uh, yeah, uh I mean Yes Sir. Thank you Sir."

"General Keith thanks for joining us." President Crandall redirects the conversation toward a monitor where the General waits to provide an update.

"Thanks Mr. President. As you know from the data feed we're uncovering some exciting but disconcerting stuff at the Well Site. Unfortunately everybody and his brother somehow captured the same feed through Lorenzo Cordoba's television news reports. Now we're starting to receive rumors of Jihadis and regular Islamic citizens flowing out to the desert in droves. And if you don't mind my saying Sir I don't think they're making a pilgrimage to Mecca."

"I understand you're plight General. How do you expect to handle the influx if there is indeed a stream of people heading your way?"

"Our situation depends on the size of the group trying to get out here. We sent an Apache helicopter patrol out an hour ago and they should be in sight of any movements fairly soon. We haven't had to deal with any overt attacks like those of the past two days. I don't know whether to breath a sigh of relief or worry about a calm before the storm but its still an element of danger on this battlefield. Hopefully we won't be mixing the two elements together. If there's a small contingent of people wandering out here then we'll cordon off the area and shoo them away. But if we see large masses of people and equipment heading our way the only tactic we'll have available to us is to try and keep them contained. We can't shoot them down if they're just curious civilians. It's hard to maintain order with a sizable crowd no matter how benign. The saving grace is they can't just walk down into the Well Site as if it's a tour at the Grand Canyon."

"I hope you don't get a mob out there General, we have a huge mass of people forming outside the White House as we speak and reports are over a million expected to fill the streets. We've had to call in the National Guard again the same as after the elections. These wing nuts seem more determined than the post-election rioters though and I can truthfully say the Capitol is under siege…its not rhetoric I hope you don't suffer similar circumstances out there."

"Thanks for the thoughts Mr. President, though I must say they're hardly comforting. We'll keep you in our thoughts and prayers out here and with a little luck and the grace of God we'll all get through this in one piece."

"You still believe in God after what you've seen over there General?"

"To tell you the truth Mr. President I'm not exactly sure what we've seen out here. Many aspects of what's discovered so far are unclear so I'll hold on to my beliefs a while longer. Truth is I'm just a too-long-in-the-tooth general in this man's army and change comes slow for an old dog like me."

"Well then General, Godspeed."

"Thank you Sir."

"Sir, Iraqi President Adjani is joining us from Iraq and Speaker of the House Hartley along with Senate Majority Leader Garland are joining us by teleconference from Capitol Hill." Informs Dan Maney.

"Ok, is Vice-President Murcheson on her way over here? I wouldn't want her to miss out on all the fun we're having."

"No Sir, she's managed to secure direct telephone exchange with the Iranian Foreign Minister through one of her old contacts in the Arab League and feels she must take the call. The monarchies and governments of the Arab League have much to lose if the Iranians test a nuclear weapon giving Persians the upper hand in the region so I guess they're cooperating."

"Alright, let's bring up President Adjani and the others."

"Good morning Mr. President." says Crandall addressing the Iraqi head of state. "How are things in Iraq? I trust you're having a better day than I am."

"No Mr. President I am not having a good day at all." Adjani replies without so much as a formal greeting to the head of the most powerful nation on earth. "You are a criminal and a thief. I am withdrawing my support for the criminal activity that has taken place on sovereign Iraqi soil. You are to remove your people from the Well Site immediately including the soldiers!"

"What is the cause for your change of mind Mr. President?"

"The expedition has unearthed many blasphemies in direct contradiction to the teachings of Allah. The devout Muslims in

Iraq are crying with one voice to destroy this madness and fill in the hole for all time. We started this mission as a search for truth but found nothing except lies. The Well Site is a piece of Iraq and its treasures are ours, we can do with them what we feel appropriate. We will permit no further exploration or encroachment onto our territories. Even now fully armed and trained Iraqi armies march toward the Well Site and the consequences of your continued criminal activities are grave. I am warning you now President Crandall to stop or suffer the wrath of Allah on the streets of your country!"

President Crandall, once again faced with a treacherous Iraqi government turns toward his Secretary of State for answers. "Do you have any thoughts on this matter Secretary Malloy?"

"Yes Mr. President I do, thank-you. President Adjani, Secretary of State Malloy speaking."

"Yes I can clearly see you on the television fool."

"Mr. President our nations signed a treaty three days ago, a treaty including your personal signature. Failure to uphold the codicils of the agreement will result in the United States exercising clause Two in Section Fourteen; Implementation of Security Forces. As you know this clause allows the United States military to re-enter any Iraqi province in force, occupy its territory and eliminate hostile forces as we see fit. This section was written into the agreement on your expressed request in case of a decapitation of the Iraqi government. Any changes to the five-day deadline or other basic tenants of the agreement will cause the United States government to assume the leadership of the Iraqi government is assassinated, held hostage or otherwise incapacitated. And let me assure you Sir we will exercise the full weight of this contract between our sovereign nations."

"You are a filthy pig and have no right to address me in this manner! I am the President of Iraq! You will suffer at the hand of Allah and blood will run in American streets! I will take this matter to the United Nations immediately and demand sanctions against the United States! I warn you President Crandall you conduct yourself at your nation's peril, at your nation's peril!"

"Nonetheless Sir we intend to fulfill the requirements of the agreement and…"

Silence interrupted the Secretary of State in mid sentence. Once again the Iraqi government acts treacherously followed by haughty arrogant blustering and ending in a petulant hang up on the President of the United States.

"I trust you gentlemen caught that exchange," President Crandall addresses Speaker Hartley and Majority Leader Garland by speakerphone. "Do you have any thoughts on the matter?"

"Yes in fact we do, or at least I do!" Informed Speaker Hartley. "I'm inclined to agree with President Adjani on this issue."

"You what?"

"We have no right to go digging through the historical sites of a sovereign nation. If Iraq doesn't want us there then we should bug on out! Our Conservative base is up in arms about all of this and they're threatening to shut down the entire Federal Government! They don't think we should dig up any of this false history either. They're gonna tar and feather us with this scandal David. Have you looked out in the streets lately? They'll hang you first with impeachment and I'll be the first to call for hearings if you don't stop and stop now!"

"I have some things to add," interjected Majority Leader Garland. "Its not just the Conservative base that's up in arms.

The Evangelical Christians are on the march, arm in arm with the ACLU, Code Pink, Mothers Against War and all manner of left wing activists. You've really upset the applecart with this mess Mr. President and managed to get all of your friends and enemies on one page and what they're getting from this is open rebellion, civil war! I'm sad to say you've lost my bi-partisan support. If the House impeaches you it's a short trip across the hallway to confirm your conviction for high crimes and misdemeanors at the Senate. You'll be the first President to get thrown out office through impeachment if you don't call off the dogs. Voters are angry!"

After the Speaker and Majority Leader shout their respective demands and end the one-sided conversation the atmosphere in the Situation Room falls deathly silent and dark clouds of doubt overtake the group assembled there. In the beginning the Well Site Operation was a simple archeological mission…in the abstract. A hole opened up in the earth revealing the actual Tower of Babel…or so they thought at the time.

The Tower of Babel narrative is a simple story as relayed through the Bible. Everyone understands its theological meanings. The simple story doesn't upset any apple carts or challenge the core of all religious beliefs held by humans. The Tower of Babel story doesn't cost anyone votes and political power. The Well Site Operation has gone from an historical curiosity to an albatross around President Crandall's political neck and a threat to his life.

"What's new on the Iranian front Mr. Maney?" Crandall asks, redirecting the conversation toward the less politically unsettling question of Iranian nuclear weapons detonation.

"Mr. President the situation has gone from negative to dangerously perilous and world threatening. The Iranian

Foreign Minister informed Vice-President Murcheson via teleconference about Iran's frightening plans. The day after a successful test detonation Iran will begin assembling a bomb for the express purpose of exploding it over Tel Aviv Israel. They claim to have the technology necessary to both build the bomb and deliver it on target. They further claim to have tonnage capabilities in excess of ten times the bomb we exploded over Hiroshima in World War Two. They gave no indication on when they intend to wipe Israel off the map with this weapon. Vice-President Murcheson is teleconferencing with Israeli Prime Minister Netanski and expects to make a full report momentarily."

President Crandall buries his head in his hands and leans over the conference table in agony. "What's next Dan, a report the Chinese have invaded South America and hold the Panama Canal? The Russians reclaim Alaska and threaten to march on Seattle? We have got to find a way out of this mess! We've got to find a way out!"

47

Public Library
City of Avinen

Doctor Kagen ambles over to the gathering outside by the ATVs. The mention of meatloaf stirs an urge to satiate his hunger. He plops down in an empty space between KO and Kelly Anne, the Testament of Gael wearing heavily on his mind. The Team makes camp in preparation for getting in a few hours sleep. KO the official camp cook hands out K-rations and heats water to a boil over a small butane camp stove. Earlier he saw Doctor Kagen off alone lost in his thoughts and expanded his duties to include Den Mother and assembled the Doctor's all-weather tent.

They sit around the cook stove in the manner of Scouts on a campout, each sharing stories and impressions from their long day of discovery between bites and slurps. Every one is too tired and worn to worry about matters of etiquette and talking with one's mouth full of meatloaf becomes a camp stock in trade.

"I'm wondering how you feel about God and religion now Kelly Anne," starts Jake, smacking through his sentences. "I guess we can put to rest all of the tired Bible mumbo jumbo about the Garden of Eden and Creation in seven days…ya think?"

"No Jake I won't go anywhere near there yet. To tell you the truth I don't know what to make of the Testament of Gael. We need to hear a lot more before we can pass judgment on the beginnings of mankind. I'm sure when we delve further into Gael's scan-can we may discover other truths leading us to completely different conclusions. And besides it looks as if there are millions of scan-cans at the Wine Rack, how do we know Gael's version of events is the truth or the only truth? Too bad KO got a migraine or we'd still be interfacing with the historical record right now and we could very well be on to the next chronicle."

"Yeah sorry," KO apologizes. "You have no idea how much that mechanism hurts. I feel like I'm growing a tumor in my brain or my skull is growing by the minute and my head's getting fatter than a record setting watermelon. And you need to eat anyway Kelly Anne. I won't let you work yourself to death." He waves a spatula toward her.

"Thanks KO. I suppose you're right but our conversation with General Keith caused me a great deal of anxiousness. Apparently the Iraqi government threatened to pull the plug on the Well Site Operation and there's supposedly thousands of Iraqi soldiers headed our way. I don't know if we have much time left for exploring and discovery much less eating and sleeping."

"You won't get much exploring done if you're passed out from hunger or sleep depravation either. We can all use a little of both so eat up."

Tasha returns to the circle of explorers from a short investigation of the structures surrounding the Public Library. "I don't think we have nearly enough time to make sense of any of this. We only have two days left as it is and there're six other buildings in this complex alone. I guess it's a good thing we found a library the very first thing. What if we had stumbled onto a bakery or the local dry-cleaners? We'd know absolutely nothing at this point."

"We didn't come to this place by accident Tasha." Jake informs. "We knew it carried some importance to the people who built Avinen."

"How'd we know?"

"When intelligent beings design buildings and do city planning they place primary structures in central locations and more often than not the most important building is the largest or tallest. We just went for the biggest penis on the block, that's all."

"Hmm, right, the phallic symbol principle, works every time."

"I'm wondering if we shouldn't split up when we get back to exploring," interjects Dr. Kagen. "At the moment we're all witness to the same information and technologies and its redundant. What do you think Jake?"

"Not a bad idea Doctor but I don't think we should separate too far apart in case anything dangerous happens. We won't split into more than two parties. We need to watch each other's backs. And besides there's plenty of discovery left inside the Public Library for the entire team. Tasha did you see anything worth exploring on your brief tour?"

"Yeah I think the tower next to the library is some kind of science lab, inside it looks like the Chemistry building from my college and maybe Doctor Kagen can make sense of it and find out what's up with there. By the way Ahmed and I took several readings from the mossy covering on the ground as well as some from the structures themselves. We ran them through the computer to get Carbon 14 readings and came up with some interesting dates. And did you realize there aren't any rocks or dirt in Avinen?"

"Uh no I haven't had a chance to look at the ground much. So are you saying you've dated Avinen?"

"No, but we have Carbon 14 readings. The mossy stuff reads out at 25 percent Carbon 14 so the groundcover must be somewhere around ten to twelve thousand years old. As you can see its not fossilized or petrified but its definitely dead. I'm thinking all of Avinen existed in a hermetically sealed chamber until it broke open just recently and that's how botanical elements are well preserved but no longer alive."

"I'm not brushed up on dating systems. How do you date something through the presence of one element?"

"Uh, ok, let me give you the Carbon Dating Techniques for Morons version. When an object or element is new it contains a ratio of Carbon 14 and Carbon 12 with a high level of Carbon 14 and a low level of Carbon 12. As an element ages the Carbon 14 level decays but the Carbon 12 level remains the same. So when as an element grows older its ratio of Carbon 14 lowers in relation to Carbon 12. The half life of Carbon…"

"Half life? Whenever a scientist starts speaking in half-life I start tuning out. What's a half a life? And no wisecracks about my life Kayanne!"

"A half-life is how old something is once it's degraded to 50 percent of its original strength. Now, continuing the Moron's guide to the Universe, the half-life of Carbon 14 is 5,730 years. Meaning, every 5,730 years Carbon 14 decays to 50 percent of strength. So if the presence of Carbon 14 is at a ratio of 25 percent to Carbon 12, now at 75 percent then you can calculate the Carbon 14 has decayed two half-life cycles. The first 5,730 years it decayed to 50 percent. Over the second 5,730 years it decayed 50 percent from the first half-life cycle, now it's at 25 percent. At 25 percent Carbon 14 an element is approximately 11,000 years old, roughly what we see with the mossy substance. D'ya get all that Jake?"

"By those calculations I think this meat loaf is older than the moss."

"Oh, obviously you get it then."

"So you're dating Avinen at around ten thousand years old Tasha?" asks Kelly Anne trying to engage in a serious conversation.

"Ohh no…its much older. The Carbon 14 levels from organic materials on the structures come in at less than five percent, we're not exactly certain how much, these are preliminary readings but there is some Carbon 14 remaining, putting the structures at least older than 40."

"You mean 40,000 years old?"

"Yeah, approximately, give or take a millennium or two. I can't get any control data because like I said there aren't any rocks or dirt anywhere to be found for comparisons. But the accuracy is probably fairly certain given the presence of Carbon 14 in everything under the bubble."

"The bubble?" asks Jake.

"Yes definitely, a huge bubble. If you look at the ceiling under the edges of the opening you can see it's a smooth concave curve all the way down to the ground. It's nearly as smooth as glass. I think Avinen existed under a giant bubble."

"The dating is a reasonable assumption," allows Dr. Kagen. "But how do you explain this bubble idea? Are you saying a bubble covered Avinen for over 40,000 years? A bubble made of what?"

"I can't fully explain the bubble idea Doctor, it's a nascent theory at this point. I expect if we took core samples from dirt at the opening of the top continuing down to the base we'd find an accurate geological record running from present day back to 40,000 years. Obviously the Avina utilized some kind of unknown power and energy to form these huge structures. Maybe they used the same technology to put a bubble over the city to protect it from outside riff raff or the weather. And one more thing, I think Avinen is built on a base made of the same materials as the structures."

Dr. Kagen believes Tasha may have flipped her lid. "Heh heh that's rather fanciful Tasha! Why would they construct a city-sized disc and put the city on top of it? Why not just build the city on solid ground?"

"Ahem, hmm, uh, so they could move it."

"Move it? Ha ha…move it? Move an entire city around? How? On giant rollers like the Egyptians moving blocks to build the pyramids?"

"Mmm, no. I uh think they floated it around on a bed of whatever technology they used to create the bubble over Avinen."

"Ha ha ha…they floated an entire city around on a bed of solid energy. Ohhh Tasha that's stretching things, ha ha, but thanks for the laughs, I haven't laughed much lately, heh hee hee!"

"Don't mind them Tash, do you have any ideas about what possible technologies could do the fantastic things you describe?" asks Kelly Anne as Dr. Kagen and Jake slap each other silly with floating on air jokes featuring flatulence as the dominant theme.

"Yeah I'm developing some ideas Kayanne, but I need to think about the subject a little longer and I'm having a difficult time coalescing all of the elements into a unified theory…especially with these laughing hyenas and their fart jokes stinking up the joint."

"Yes well we should give the guys a break, they've been through a lot as we all have."

48

After a hearty supper and several hours of fitful sleep the Team rousts each other, sips hot steaming coffee whipped up by chez KO, turns on the communications gear and sets off on separate paths of discovery to three different locations in Avinen's central complex. Jake, Kelly Anne and KO trundle back to the Library to continue investigating the Testament of Gael. Dr. Kagen heads toward the newly christened Chemistry Kit location with Brian eagerly in tow. During her earlier tour Tasha discovered a series of labs and machines reminding her of an experimental prototype fabrication facility back in her own world. After an agreement from the Team she and Ahmed the Botanist head there to uncover its secrets.

Dr. Kagen immediately recognizes the general purpose and intent of the lab upon entering the Chemistry Kit building. Benches covered in an array of science apparatus from autoclaves to microscopes at least give the appearance of a state of the art science lab. For Dr. Kagen the lab was always home and walking through the portal brings him to the place he is most comfortable. If the Avina used pipettes, bulbous glassware, beakers, flasks, funnels and test tubes roughly matching the equipment in his home lab then perhaps they aren't so foreign after all. The notion creates a sense of comforting calm within his heart.

Kagen uses the intercommunications function on his wrist-borne Pocket Studio to contact Jake and describe the surroundings of the Chemistry Kit. He points out the particular configuration of the equipment as well as its basic layout suggesting the lab was used for biology and genetics experimentation. The Doctor informs Jake he's found scan-cans similar to those at the Wine Rack and booted one up on a glo-screen at the lab. He confirmes his suspicions about Avina technology and the capability to design or program genetic effects in living beings.

As he relays to Jake, the Avina didn't use cloning methodologies to create biological change such as injecting information into a genetic stew to ensure a baby is born with blue eyes. The Avina programmed genetics to impart adaptable intelligence in their creations, passed on from generation to generation.

"Ok so you're saying the Avina programmed adaptability into living things?" asks Jake. "Doesn't your idea fly in the face of all our understandings on Evolutionary theory and development of species through genetic mutation?"

"Of course, it completely overturns Darwin's theories of Evolution. Obviously the Avina possessed the capabilities to assume climate and atmospheric change and were then able to program adaptability in all species. You see Jake they programmed their creations to ebb with the ebbs and flow with the flows and if you examine the biological history of our planet through this prism you come up with the clear fact biological history is not linear as Darwin postulated. Animals and plants adapt to the conditions in which they live but they never adapt themselves into a new species capable of adapting to a new set of conditions. This is why the fossil record doesn't include the thousands, well no, millions of gaps in the Evolutionary timeline. When you study high school biology textbooks you see drawings of a fish sprouting legs and then it walks up on land and through five or six more drawings, bam, it's an elephant. But it couldn't possibly work that way not in a trillion years."

"What we're discovering here is evidence of an alternative theory...the genus species of all living things were created in a short period of time by the process of intelligent design, like a bunch of programmers collaborating on a piece of software. All those species populated throughout the earth and adapted to the conditions around them. So an elephant may have morphed into a wooly mammoth and modern day sheep might have started out as a goat but you'll never find evidence of a hippopotamus growing into a wolf or a fruit fly miraculously changing into a chimpanzee. Not even over millions of years, its mathematically impossible. Genetic science and the fossil record don't support those conclusions. In reality they never have.

"Alright Kagen, let's say your right about all of this. What happened to the dinosaurs? Did they die off millions of years ago in a worldwide cataclysm or did they evolve into a completely new species? Neither scenario fits with what you're telling me about the capabilities of the Avina."

"As I'm standing here this moment Jake I don't have any answers for you about dinosaurs or any paleo-species for that matter. All I can say is the genetic history of mammals, including humans doesn't support evolutionary theories. If we could trace the genetic history of every living thing on the planet today I'd be willing to bet they all lead back to a relative handful of genus species created, oh, about 40,000 years ago."

"Obviously your hypothesis fits with what we're uncovering here at Avinen Doctor but I need more answers than what you've come up with so far to shift my thinking toward intelligent design or a God controlled evolution or even the thought of a God. Besides Doctor, if you find evidence of God, Kayanne will never let me hear the end of it."

"I'll keep digging Jake, I'll keep digging. I need answers too."

49

The Erector Set Building
City of Avinen

Tasha and Ahmed the Botanist climb over a moss-covered transom to enter a large warehouse style space in a squat building situated at the right of the Library Building. The chamber houses machines and contraptions and gives the appearance of a manufacturing plant for the assembly of large items. Tasha finds a light generator dial at the entrance and searches for ways to bring the dead as rocks machines to life.

As a mechanical wunderkind Tasha wows crowds at science fairs and technology conventions with her obvious prowess. She demonstrates her abilities by examining new machines and helping inventors fix flaws that would otherwise show up in the marketplace. Tasha's combination of mechanical talent and intuition gives her unique insights into the ways humans interact with machines. She knows mechanical objects the way others know their favorite pets, intimately as if they can carry on conversations with her. In the recesses of her mind Tasha feels confident she can master use of the machines at Avinen.

As Ahmed and Tasha explore the site they engage in a theological discussion on technology. "What do you think of all these technologies Ahmed? Does your faith get in the way of science when something new is discovered?"

"Yes at times. Not my faith but certain kinds of people who practice my faith are rigid in their understandings."

"And yet you chose to get an education and work as a scientist?"

"Yes Miss Tasha, I don't see this as a contradiction. Some in Islam do."

"How do you balance your faith with reason? Especially when you're faced with the criticism of having reason at all?"

"In the early days of the faith Islam was the world's leader in the sciences. People traveled from all over the world to learn at the centers of knowledge where Islamic scientists and theologians offered the fruits of the universe. People of our faith lost ground to the West over time and grew embittered. I am a scientist to rebuild the original promise of Islam."

"I've never heard that concept from a Muslim. Are there many like you in the *ummah*?"

"No, not at this time but I am hopeful. Many want to blame others for the pains they produce themselves."

"Hmm, I understand. Christians have gone through periods like this too. I wish people who don't know God would quit telling the rest of us what he thinks!"

"Hey come over here Ahmed. Look for a power dial on this big gizmo. I don't know what this thing does but it looks cool and I want to try it."

The two pore over every inch of a complicated mechanical device sitting atop a large cylindrical base standing about four feet high. On top of the base rests a twelve-foot long horn-like object attached to a swivel. One end of the horn curves down into the swivel, apparently running a pipe through to the cylindrical base. The other end of the horn tapers to a point. The contraption looks like a water cannon on top of a fire truck, but substantially larger. Tasha thinks the device probably shoots something from its spout…exactly what she doesn't know. "The only way to find out is to turn the blame thing on!"

The machine's cowlings and larger pieces are constructed of similar material to the large structures, possibly high-density ceramics according to Dr. Kagen's theory. Gears and knobs are fabricated of a variety of metals and ceramic elements. The design protocols of the machines in the Erector Set are simple and elegant. None of them seem elaborate and certainly not ornate but they express beauty in simple clean lines. Tasha supposes the Avina built their machines for function, not as charming works of art. The machines' cleanly interacting shapes and movements remind her of the basic design principles of form and function found in Swedish furniture.

Ahmed, excited and gesticulating exuberantly motions for Tasha to join him on the other side of the water cannon machine. "Look, I have found a dial similar to the one's at the door," He points at the bottom of the cylindrical base. "I know it's quite large for an on-off dial but it looks the same, do you agree?"

"Yes Ahmed, good job! I'll try to start the machine up this way. I hope it doesn't blow us up. Can't imagine why this dial is so large compared to the others, maybe its big circumference generates more power somehow." She kneels down and gives the dial a shove in an effort to get it spinning but it refuses to move. She places both hands on the dial's edge and shoves with all her might, grunting and groaning, her face pinched and glowing a bright crimson. Nothing moves.

Tasha sits back on her heels breathing heavily as her shoulders raise and lower with each inhale or exhale. She notices a hand-sized knob perpendicular to the dial. She gives it a twist, creating a loud THUNK. "Oh, safety feature. Yeah down here you could easily kick start this puppy by accident with your foot. Whatever comes out of that cannon must be dangerous."

Having removed the safety latch Tasha gives the dial a hearty shove with one hand. A WHOOSH blows from the dial's portico…loud humming echoes through the chamber. Droning vibrations fill the cylinder as the machine whirs to life. Tasha and Ahmed scramble to the top of the base and study the interface.

"Ahmed these things on the sides are handles." Tasha refers to a pair of rams horn shaped controls on either side of the gun's base. "Now all of these knobs do something but I have no idea what. We don't have the manual for this beast. His name is Chuck by the way. I'm just going to start pressing these knobs and flipping switches so stand here next to me and stay out of the way of the front of this thing. We don't know what Chuck will spit out."

Tasha presses firmly on an easily accessible button popping up from the right handle. The swivel the pair stands on spins dramatically clock-wise, sending Ahmed and Tasha flying through the air. They crash land in a heap at the base of the cylinder. "That's obviously the right actuator!" Tasha laughs loud and happily as she stands dusting herself off. "Are you ok Ahmed?"

"Yes I believe I am unharmed. Please Miss Tasha do not do that again!"

They climb atop the cylinder again, wary and wizened. Tasha grips both handles and lightly depresses the same button. The swivel turns slowly clockwise. She lightly presses a similar button on the left handle sending the swivel in a slow counter-clockwise motion. She discovers the motion of sliding her hands north and south along the handles causes the gun to move up and down. Her fingers reach around the inside of each handle and find a series of small buttons. She presses one lightly but nothing happens. She presses one on each side simultaneously and still the machine remains silent and inactive. Finally she squeezes the handles in anger and frustration. A bolt of green glowing matter shoots from the cannon, firing a hole into the side of another machine all the way across the football field size room.

"Whoa Chuck, now that's a cannon!"

Tasha and Ahmed scramble down from Chuck the Cannon, and make their way over to the offended machine. The damage reveals a hole two inches in diameter cleanly burrowing through to the other side of a twenty-foot thick dense ceramic base. They discover no filings or remnants of the material once filling the hole. The edges of the hole cut through with no obvious sign of stress or serrations.

"What was that? A laser gun?"

"No I don't believe so Ahmed. Laser cannon fire is a constant beam, that thing was a bolt of energy or raw matter of some type. We don't have technology like this in our world, at least not yet. They were doing some experiments at Lawrence Livermore Labs before I left having to do with a new kind of plasma fusion but I…well I, ohh I just don't know but I uh, well an idea is filling my brain and this could be the greatest…or the most dangerous, oh man. We better check in with Jake, I need to tell him about some of this…"

50

Jake, Kelly Anne and KO reboot the Testament of Gael at the same spot left off from the evening before. Gael's softly mellow deep voice invades the group's mind's eye once again, capably translated through KO's brain. The imposing figure relates the history of Avina creative pursuits, describing in exacting detail the wondrous flora and fauna springing from the intelligence and imagination of the designers.

Gael explains:

The creators drew knowledge from their own existence and sought to bring forth living things to comfort and please the Avina. In early times they designed and created photosynthetic organisms, they grew of their own accord into lavishly beautiful presentations. Fueled by the rays of the Sun and water the plants and flowers occupied every empty corridor in Avinen. The Avina treasured these works of art and kept them in homes and workspaces. The Creators discovered methods for self-replication of the plants and flowers and designed a system spreading the art throughout all lands outside Avinen then called Novinen. The Avina were pleased with the work of the Creators but found the art static and uninteresting after a time. The lack of overt stimulus from their creations pushed the Creators to new avenues and concepts. They pursued the creation of beings with rudimentary sentient properties.

Using the substance of their own blood the Creators introduced small creatures who replicated through the fertilization of eggs. The Avina loved the creatures so full of life and more than a little mischief. All the Avina kept the creatures as companions but they were not loyal to particular Avina and also weak and lived only for short stretches of time. The Creators pressed further with experimentation and produced many wondrous works of living art, each successive production displayed heartier constitutions and greater loyalties to their owners.

The Creators desired to extend their art outside Avina to populate Novinen. They designed and built ever-heartier creatures who could withstand the rigorous elements in the Novena. A competition grew between the many creators, each devising their own application of the master designs. They created and built a vast population of great plumed creatures. Gradually the creatures grew apart from the Avina, building their own nests and replicating at will. At first the creatures fed on the plants and flowers populating Novinen but they consumed too much and turned to each other as sources of nourishment. The creatures grew to enormous dimensions but a design flaw proved fatal as each successive generation degraded in quality and threatened even the existence of the Avina as they feasted upon flesh indiscriminately.

The Creators in consultation with the Avina decided to destroy the creatures to keep them from destroying every thing else. The Avina churned the earth and meted instantaneous destruction upon the creatures, completely eliminating them and their progeny from Novinen. After this destruction the Creators grew solemn for a season and then proceeded to experiment once more with new designs absent the fatal flaws of the previous works of art.

The Creators sought to design creatures who would form emotional attachments to the Avina for the sake of security and companionship. Their new creations were truly remarkable and varied by the hundreds. Again a competition between Creators flourished and spurred them to greater achievements. The creatures seemed to love the Avina and of course the Avina loved them in return. Once again the Creators sought to populate Novinen with the substance of their creations. They worked in concert to develop systems of support and nourishment. The new creatures carried offspring inside of their bodies during the time of gestation, replacing the system of delicate vulnerable eggs out in the open; this provided a better method for survival and replication. The new gestation system forced the male and female creatures to work together and ensure survival. The Creators modeled this system from the basic design of the Avina, with the exception the Avina did not carry progeny to term but transferred it to created wombs. The new design functioned well throughout Avinen and Novinen.

As time passed the Creators challenged themselves to greater works, each new plateau featured species with greater capacities for emotions and survival. Unfortunately a programming design flaw surfaced within the population of creatures and they again turned toward each other as a source of nourishment. The Creators anticipated the problem beforehand and mitigated the flaw with new design patterns allowing the feeding on other creatures in concert with the needs of the greater populations. The Creators were well pleased with their intellect and the manner in which they solved the problems of a self-managing ecological system covering the whole of Novinen.

Eventually the Creators grew tired of building creatures on existing design platforms. They sought to elevate their work to the highest levels imaginable. They tirelessly pursued a plan to build creatures in the image of Avina design patterns. Thousands of creators gathered at the great hall of knowledge to collaborate on the design of new creatures and impress the Avina. They strove toward the creation of sentient beings capable of forming loving and loyal relationships bonding with the Avina. These new creatures were provided with high-level capacities for learning and survival. Their design surpassed old patterns by orders of magnitude.

The day of the first introduction of the new creatures, called Avinenev as a tribute to Avina brilliance, was a day of great celebration. The Avina came from all quarters of Avinen and Novinen to laud the Creators and their magnificent art. The Creators designed a strong desire within the Avinenev to replicate and their numbers grew rapidly throughout Avinen. The Avinenev creatures loved the Avina, showing great affection and loyalty, returned enthusiastically and without reservation.

During the early time of the Avinenev knowledge was freely shared. They received sciences and philosophies with wide-eyed exuberance and spent many hours and days at the Great Hall filling themselves with the secrets of the Avina and Avinen. As their knowledge grew the Avina placed on them responsibilities for the governance of the affairs of the Creators other works. They worked tirelessly and happily, connected with the Avina like no other creatures before them.

The relationship between the groups grew into a bond of shared responsibility and mutual affection with the Avinenev learning the ways of the Masters through appointed Avina guides. Each Avinenev was given a personal Avina to instruct them in science and the proper manner of living. The Avina enjoyed this exercise and relished the duty of watching over the development of their charges."

•

"Hey guys my head's about to pop!" complains KO. "I don't know if it's the strain of the interface or if I just can't handle the arrogance of this guy Gael. What a schmuck!"

"Yeah ok let's break connection." agrees Jake. "I'm getting tired of this guy's gas too. Besides Tasha's beeping so she probably has a report about the Erector Set location."

"You two think Gael is arrogant?" asks Kelly Anne. "He comes across as matter of fact and to the point as far as I'm concerned."

"You would think so Kayanne because you're just like him…matter of fact, to the point and all business 24/7. Hell he could be your Dad."

"Thanks for the personality profile Jake but I've got nothing on you in the arrogance department. I can't believe you're still pouting because I wouldn't date you when I was a college student and you an associate professor."

"I'm not pouting about past history Kayanne. I'm just wondering why you didn't get any of the desire for replication gene Gael was talkin' about."

"I have a healthy dose of that gene Jake but I also have other knowledge like how to avoid getting mixed up with a professor while you're still a student. Obviously they built in some selection genes too."

"Ok, ok, let's get off this point. Let me answer Tasha. Hi Tash, what's up?

"Hi Jake, Ahmed and I are over here at the Erector Set and we've discovered some unique scientific information. It segues with my theories about power and energy at Avinen. I'd like to get together to discuss this with you and the rest of the gang. I need everybody's input, especially Doctor Kagen's."

"Roger that, I'll get in touch with Kagen, let's meet in the Library in fifteen minutes."

"Alrighty, see you there!"

51

Public Library
City of Avinen

Tasha and Doctor Kagen arrive in the Library chamber at the same time and make the climb down to the Wine Rack all the while chatting furiously about Avina power and energy. At the bottom they meet the rest of Team Babelus and sit on the tall stools at the counter to discuss and debate Tasha's latest discoveries and general theory on the technologies used to build the magnificent structures at Avinen.

"I'm glad you guys came over here," KO tells Tasha. "Every time I hook up to the glo-screens and do the translations I get a splitting migraine headache. We needed the break. Besides I'm starting to think the Avina and this yahoo Gael are a bunch of posers."

"Only too happy to help ya out there KO. I don't know if the Avina are posers or not but the technology is first rate and its far advanced beyond anything we've got in our world. You should've seen what I just saw. We shot Chuck the Cannon and he evaporated a hole through twenty feet of this ceramic stuff with a single blast. It was so cool!"

"Chuck the what?" asks Jake.

"Oh I name all of my mechanical friends Jake, pay no attention to that. I called this little gathering for a reason. After firing Chuck and inspecting the results I've formulated a theory on the manner of power and energy in this place. I think it explains everything, the large seamlessly built structures, heavy items in places you couldn't move without a huge crane, light from pure darkness, screens and monitors floating in mid-air and unlimited power, perpetual energy."

"Ok fill us in, we're all ears."

"I'll start with the screens as the technology has some connection to a similar thing in our world. Obviously we've all noticed the green glowing light operating as a screen interface. I pondered the whole concept at great length and something clicked when I shot Chuck. I thought green light, what makes green light? And why green? When I fired Chuck a green bolt of lightning shot out only it was tightly formed as if it were a beam but it was a bolt so it was like a section of a beam. And then it struck me…plasma!"

"Plasma, like on my flat-screen TV at home?" asks Dr. Kagen.

"Yes Doctor the same basic element but a very different method of harnessing its properties. One of the most universal elements of all matter is plasma. It's also one of the least understood. Scientists in our world already know, theoretically at least, harnessing the power of plasma produces far greater forces and more useful applications than the power of the atom by nuclear fusion. First of all plasma is by far the most plentiful matter known, it makes up 99 percent of the visible Universe. That's 99 percent of everything we can see or touch. Are you all following me so far?"

"Yeah," they answer thoughtfully, nodding in unison.

"Plasma is not a solid a liquid or a gas but in some ways it seems to operate like a gas. Gasses are electrically neutral but plasmas are made of the essential ingredients that go into creating every form of matter. That is, every single form of matter we know. And the magic ingredient is electrically charged particles spinning around at high energy. But the plasmatrons are hot little buggers and so energetic they float around independently and don't form together. But if you cool them down they start to coalesce and form gasses, liquids and solids. The green glow we see on the glo-screens is plasma coalescing to form what I think is a semi-solid gaseous state."

"But plasmas are benign," remarks Dr. Kagen. "I don't quite see how they could ever be induced to form up in an ordered way, I'm just not grasping this."

"Hold on there, Doctor," interjects Jake. "I'm not science whiz but I had an experience once in the Navy. My unit was attached to the USS Ranger aircraft carrier and the ship hosted the Premier of China on board. We gave him a presentation of our sea and air power and we had two F-14 Tomahawk Fighter Jets fly by just at the moment they breached the speed of sound. The boatswain's mate's voice comes over the loudspeakers warning us to prepare for a sonic boom so we covered our ears with headsets and watched the planes fly by shaking us with a huge sonic blast. The thing is I saw a sonic boom. I mean I saw it with my eyes. As the jets flew by, just before they breached the speed of sound green glowing rings formed around their wings and then disappeared with the boom. I asked a pilot what the green rings were and he told me they were a plasma displacement caused by the energy of the jets. I wondered then what harnessing the power of plasma might mean but the pilot thought it took too much energy to create the displacement and could never be of any real use. Is that the power you're talkin' about Tash?"

"Uh yeah, precisely, very good Jake. Only the Avina found a way to harness the power efficiently so it uses less energy than it creates. The nature of plasma is quite more complex than liquids, gasses and solids. Plasmas carry their own electric currents and they're influenced or can be manipulated by electromagnetic forces. Also they're practically immune to gravity. The most important property of plasma is its fundamental state. Its hidden technologies can explain the dynamics of the entire Universe and harness elements in the material world. Our own science isn't quite there yet but the Avina may have discovered the secrets."

"Um ok, I can follow that," allows Dr. Kagen. "But how do the Avina do it? How do they harness the hidden powers of plasma?"

"Of course I can't state the specifics Doctor but I believe they use a combination of sound waves and magnetic waves to create a targeted beam of a type we can't appreciate from our limited vantage point. I believe the sound waves, which are nothing more than a disruption of matter, excite the plasmatrons into a different state, expanding and contracting their size with the various sound frequencies. This process also heats or cools the plasma, making it more or less dense as it coalesces into other forms of matter. I think the magnetic or electromagnetic waves order and manage the shape of coalesced plasma particles into functional properties. I call the combined energy the Avina Wave."

"You're losing me here Tash," whines Jake.

"Ok, back to Plasma for Morons 101. Close your eyes and imagine a one-foot cube of air right in front of you. There's nothing at all, you can't see or feel a thing. Now, Avina sonic displacement waves are injected into the space of the cube, they excite the electrons inside plasma particles, causing each particle to expand to ten times its normal size and turns them a green glowing color. Normally the expanded plasma would leap out of the box and dissipate but the Avina electromagnetic waves form containment fields on the six sides of your cube and the expanded plasma can't escape. Now you can touch the cube floating in front of you. At ten times expansion it might feel squishy like cotton balls, at a hundred times it might feel wobbly and semi-solid like jell-o, at a thousand times expansion your cube may now be as hard as stone but its still plasma and it remains floating there like air."

"Hey, yeah this starts to sound plausible," allows Dr. Kagen as he feels around in the blank cube of air in front of him. "But I don't know how you can have a sound wave appear in the middle of a cube in one spot without disturbing the air on the way there. How is that done?"

"Actually Doctor that's one of the least technically difficult problems. Even now consumer electronics companies create home theater sound systems targeting sound waves to specific areas of a room. The wave is sent out at one frequency and then morphs to an entirely different wavelength once it reaches the targeted destination and only then is it detectable by the human ear. Its pretty cool."

"How is all this light generated out of darkness?"

"Good question Doctor. I think once the power dials are spun they generate the Avina Wave, expanding plasma in a small chamber, which produces the ability to keep the disc spinning perpetually or until it is stopped by outside means. The spinning disc generates an Avina Wave of a different frequency targeted at specific lighting locations. The wave then excites the electrons in the plasma molecules and, well lights them up. When you stop the disc from spinning the plasma returns to its original state and dimensions. Throughout the entire process nothing burns or is fused together or creates any kind of dangerous radiation. It's a completely non-polluting perpetually self re-supplied system of energy."

"Hmm, maybe your theory is correct but I don't know. We've seen lights and the glo-screen but those interactions could occur in other ways. I haven't seen anything remotely suggesting or proving the existence of densely coalesced plasmatic forms managed by electromagnetic fields. Can you pull one of those out of your pocket?"

Tasha assumes her universally recognized thinking posture and briefly searches with her eyes around the chamber. She walks over to the Wine Rack, kneels at its base, twists a safety knob and spins a huge power dial using both hands and all the might her tiny but powerful athletic body can muster. The dial spins exasperatingly slow at first, emitting a deep hollow groaning sound. As it turns faster, violently increasing speed under its own power, the groan grows to a loud moan and then to a high pitch whine and finally at a key so high it fades from the range of hearing.

As the dial spins faster and faster an eerie green glow forms over the entire vast floor of the Library chamber and around the legs at thigh level of the frantically startled Team Babelus. The gaseous green glow starts to solidify and team members make a mad dash wading towards higher ground. The green glow transforms to a dark blue hue and solidifies further, the pressure of its increased density expelling objects from its targeted dimensions. As the plasmatic surface of the floor solidifies the team simply pops up out of the dense mass and lands on a soft surface that coalesces to a hard marble-like texture within moments.

"Oh my God!" shouts Jake as he lay on the hard blue marble floor panting, trying to catch his breath. "That was the most amazing experience I've ever had in my life! It felt like fog. Then it was like quicksand and then like jell-o. What an amazing ride! Let's do it again!"

"Ha ha ha, ha ha ha," Tasha laughs maniacally. "Ha ha ahem, I was so right, I was so right!" She stands on the plasmatic marble floor and jumps a few times to test its firmness like a kid jumping on her parents new mattress.

"Heh heh heh," laughs Dr. Kagen. "Tasha you make me laugh when I think you're wrong and when I think you're right. This time you are definitely right, my hat is off to you young lady!"

The rest of the team stands up laughing and jumping in rhythm. General Keith, monitoring the events via the Pocket Studio communications link laughs and jumps too with Major Lee by his side. President Crandall, watching from the Situation Room jumps along with his Cabinet and agency directors. Regular citizens watching the Lorenzo Cordoba report around the world laugh and jump too.

"Well I guess we should get ourselves back to work here gang," alerts Jake breaking though the levity. "There's no doubt we've discovered one of the great mysteries of the Universe but we need to gather as much information about all of this as we can. We only have two days left at the site. I wonder what we'll find next. Maybe Elvis really is down here. Ok, everyone back to the places you came from. We'll meet back at the camp for a late lunch."

Doctor Kagen and Brian trek back to the Chemistry Kit location in search of technologies enabling the Avina to design and create complex life forms from DNA building blocks. Tasha and Ahmed the Botanist make their way back to the Erector Set location to discover as many applications of plasmatic displacement technology as possible, Tasha fairly skips along the way.

Jake, Kelly Anne and KO resume a fascinatingly disturbing mind trip through Avinen history as relayed through the Testament of Gael. Somehow watching the story unfold brings forth a grim sensation. The narrative is lively and interesting but the three moviegoers sense they've seen this movie before, like watching the Titanic luxury liner launch stoutly from its berth attended by cheers and fanfare but knowing the story ends in disaster and sadness…and a sunken ship.

52

The Wine Rack, Avinen Public Library
City of Avinen

Gael reappears on the glo-screen, continuing an historical narrative of the people of Avinen from his singular point of view. KO's headaches subside sufficiently to continue translating dialogue in the language of the Avina through his increasingly muddled brain. Through headaches and recovery he finds increasing difficulty organizing his thoughts clearly and wonders if the effects are permanent. "I'll sacrifice my mind to science," he thinks. "Not for the people of America or the President of the United States. For my friends, Team Babelus."

From Gaels Testament:

From the day of their creation and introduction to society the Avinenev lived in harmony with the Avina, happily industrious in peaceful coexistence. The Avinenev grew in knowledge and understanding and studied regularly at the Great Hall of Knowledge. They appeared as smaller replicas of the Avina but lived under different societal norms and conventions. The Avinenev were designed by the Creators to go forth upon the lands of Novinen and flourish by their own accord, mating to continue life. They were given the talent of intelligence and gifts of intuition and free will and made wonderful companions for the Avina. Unfortunately the relationship exposed dark truths among the Avina.

After the maturation process in the Great Garden the Avina replicated itself through scientific means. Avina offspring are the product of scientific research and construction by a team of expert Master Creators. Genetic material is culled from perfect Avina males and females transformed into new Avina in created wombs at the Great Garden. The progeny is raised and educated in the Garden by groups of Avina Builders, Creators, Discoverers and Managers. While in the Garden Avina offspring practice mating rituals as a matter of course without regard to gender or status. Unintended offspring are eliminated. The urges to practice such pursuits dissipate after the first hundred and fifty years or so and are never practiced after introduction into the greater Avina society. This is especially true of female Avina.

The Avinenev creations are designed to replicate at will and populate wider Novinen as do all other Avina creations. They happily consume themselves in mating rituals without regard to gender or status. This activity reminds the Avina of their days in the Great Garden and they grow miserable at the sight of creatures mirroring their features but acting on impulses in free will with reckless abandon. The misery led many Avina males to sample the mating rituals with Avinenev males and females, causing jealousy and distrust throughout the Avina population. No record or account of Avina females sampling mating rituals with the Avinenev exists.

Other problems surfaced with the constant interaction between the two societies. Although the Avinenev are encouraged to study at the Great Hall of Knowledge to learn sciences and management techniques necessary for survival in Novinen they are expressly forbidden from seeking knowledge of the higher sciences as practiced by Avina Creators and Builders. At first the arrangement suffered no ill will from either side but as Avinenev knowledge grew so did curiosity and they longed to achieve the lofty status of the Masters. The Avina possessed the power of regenerated memories to retain knowledge after regeneration treatments. The Creators designed this power out of the Avinenev.

The Avina took on many Avinenev vanities such as the growing of white hair as a sign of respect and the dominion of male over female. Avina women rejected these practices as manifestations of the lower beings. Avina females existed as equals to males in all respects. The Creators designed Avinenev females as subservient and physically weaker than their male counterparts. This process was not for the sake of malice but to ensure the desire of males to stay in close proximity to the female and continue the species. Avina females rebelled against the notions of carrying progeny to term or accepting lesser roles in society. They were as strong as the males and intellectual equals and neither side prevailed in the matter.

Both societies suffered from the interactions and a grand council of Avina Masters was formed to debate the fate of the continuing relationship. As the council met many solutions were offered but none accepted. The Creators desired to maintain the relationship or destroy the Avinenev and start fresh with new recipes. The Builders argued for massive changes, to expel the Avinenev from Avinen, to exist and thrive in Novinen alone, beyond our protective shields. The Managers demanded destruction or expulsion. The Discoverers plead for mercy on the naïve creatures. No faction or group carried the argument until my friend, my close friend Luhhan, the Grand Master Builder whose dominion included mastery of the sonic technologies integral to the higher sciences rose to speak.

At this point in the narrative Gael converts his memories to a graphically displayed presentation of the meeting of the Grand Council and viewers watch through mind's eye images of the Grand Master Builder rising to speak. Gael's friend Luhhan is a grand presence of a man, tall and strong with dark hair and the countenance of a god. His voice is deep and rich, hauntingly beautiful and mesmerizing. His deep blue eyes shine from their sockets and hypnotize all manner of creatures unable to resist his gaze.

Luhhan stands to speak:

"Fellow Avina, friends and colleagues," he begins softly. "I rise on this occasion to argue on behalf of the Avinenev, creatures made, nurtured and educated by our own hand. As I see our society diminishing with each moment of interaction between the creatures we designed and our own people I am saddened and fearful. We are a proud and brilliant people of the highest order in the Universe and our actions here today will reveal us either as competent managers or shameless hypocrites. We designed these fair creatures with free will and curiosity. We gave them talents and gifts, emotions and beauty. We gathered these attributes from our own blood and made them in our own image in much the same manner as we bring forth our own progeny. The only difference is we leave our creations in darkness, devoid of all knowledge of the high sciences. We provide them with the tools of understanding but fail to complete their education by hiding the substance of knowledge. What do these actions say of our brilliance as scientists? How will other beings in the Universe perceive our actions? Are they based on fear, a lack of courage to face our own creations? If we destroy these creations we are rending apart the gift of the life force, tearing it apart on the altar of fear."

"Today I argue on behalf of the Avinenev." Luhhan continues, speaking in rich harmonious tones. "I speak from courage, knowledge and understanding. Today I call for the full and complete assimilation of the Avinenev into Avina society with full rights and access to the fruits of knowledge. I call for this arrangement in the spirit of love and harmony so we may progress in our scientific understandings. The Creators have designed creatures equal to our own existence and they deserve their rightful place at our side. Denying the Avinenev this right will lead us on a path to our own destruction for if we can destroy these fair creatures we can devour our own progeny with equal indifference as we do in the Great Garden. I respectfully submit these remarks for consideration and leave this grave decision to the infinite wisdom of the council."

After his pronouncements Luhhan sits quietly in his seat observing the thrusts and parry of argument after argument. The council drifts toward the destruction of the Avinenev only to get pulled back by vociferous arguments from a faction formed by the new followers of Luhhan, impressed by his impassioned and merciful pleading. The debate rages for hours. Opinions lean one way and then the other swinging wildly with the winds of thought and expression. During the proceedings a new member joins the discussion activities of the council, the Grand Master of the High Sciences, Shedaii.

•

"Listen guys I've got to take another break," informs KO. "And we need to break connection quickly."

"Another headache?" asks Kelly Anne with concern.

"No! Gotta pee, gotta pee, gotta pee…right now!"

53

Over at the Erector Set location Tasha and Ahmed the Botanist continue a voyage of discovery through the wonders of plasmatic technology. In the far northeast corner of the chamber they uncover a gigantic forming machine measuring 200 feet by 150 feet according to Tasha's laser guided measuring tool. The forming machine operates as a massive isostatic press capable of generating pressures in excess of 300,000 psi in Tasha's estimation. The press consists of a high-density ceramic bed, a glo-screen interface device and flues for materials to spill into high-pressure plasmatic forms. The forms are generated by Master Builder operators brain-jacked into the glo-screen where brain aided design directs the forming of plasma molds in mid-air. Powdered ceramic or metal materials flow from the flues into the molds where the plasma density is increased to create otherworldly pressures, packing the powders into huge densely constructed parts. "So this is how the Avina can build Rome in a day." thinks Tasha.

...

The Gael Testament Task Force returns to the glo-screen presentation after KO's untimely potty break resuming at the point where Grand Master Shedaii enters the debate. Shedaii, who appears in the visage of a mirror-cloned replica of Luhhan remains seated at the table as he addresses the High Council.

Shedaii's Commentary:

"Friends and colleagues, beloved Avina," Shedaii begins, his supreme authority emanating throughout the council chamber, "My dear brother Luhhan presents us with a compelling and merciful argument, his wisdom has grown to rival the brilliance of the entire Avina. Like my brother I too love the Avinenev and appreciate their obvious zest for life and thirst for knowledge. I cannot fathom their destruction and share Luhhan's desire to spare them elimination. I part with my friend and brother only as to the extent of the interactions between our societies."

"The differences between the groups create discordance and threaten the harmony of Avinen. Not by the hand of the Avinenev but through our own inability to cope with their presence and the disruptions it causes. As we know the Avinenev are designed for a richly rugged life outside the protective shields of Avinen. They are built to thrive amongst the creatures of Novinen and I suggest we consign them to the destination of their first design. As merciful creators we must not leave our creations without sustaining powers and knowledge. We will assist them in building a community of their own creation to dwell in harmony as we do at Avinen.

We can and should allow limited interaction with our society to keep abreast of their developments and assist them in building a stable society. They can continue study in the Great Hall of Knowledge in pilgrimages of no more than twenty individuals at once with the restrictions previously accorded them. Some elements of this arrangement may seem abrasive and discordant to some while others may look upon the plan as an action taken in undue haste. No doubt we are forming a compromise. Some of our brothers reject compromise. But we must focus on the problem at hand and seek to restore the peace and harmony of the great society of Avinen."

The other members of the high council stand in applause, a tribute to the power of Shedaii's arrangement. Luhhan sits with deeply furrowed brow and thoughtful repose. As the applause dissipates and the council retakes their seats Luhann stands again, addressing the chamber but staring directly at Shedaii.

"How can you so easily undercut me with this treacherous arrangement my brother?"

"I mean no disrespect Luhhan. Surely you know of my great affection for you and appreciation of your skills. I wish only to save our community and its harmonious nature. You must know this in your heart."

"I know only that you are betraying me before the council. I see how you have elevated yourself over all of the other Masters of the Sciences. I have known you since our education at the Great Garden and am witness to your changing spirit and treachery. I cannot support you or your proposed arrangement. I beseech this council to reject the plan of Shedaii and accept my ideas of full assimilation of the Avinenev. I demand this of you. It is my right as a Grand Master and the keeper of wisdom of our power. We are wrong as a people to cast aside these creations on the whims of our own indifference. This cannot stand, it must not bear fruit."

"I see much wisdom in the plan of Shedaii," replies the Chairman of the Grand Council to an additional round of applause.

"I cannot accept this direction and find myself at odds with my friends and brothers," answers Luhhan, "There are no limits to our arrogance as a society if we seek to destroy the innocent. I am compelled to act accordingly upon my convictions and do everything in my power to throw this effort to the magma to burn forever in the flames of rejection."

"I am truly sorry my brother." Luhann directs his remarks toward Shedaii. "Together we could have built a great society, the model of the entire Universe."

Luhhan turns away from the High Council and storms dramatically from the chamber determined to destabilize Shedaii's arrangement.

•

"That's enough for me at the moment," sighs Kelly Anne. "Let's break this connection before I fall down in a heap of exhaustion."

"This is getting to you?" asks Jake. "I know your religious background and your beliefs but why does this story knock you for a loop? It seems like a bunch of politics gone awry to me. Does Gael's Testament smack your beliefs out of the ballpark and undercut everything you think you know and understand?"

"No Jake, quite the contrary. Gael's Testament roughly mirrors the stories of a great controversy as laid out by theologians, scholars and prophets over thousands of years. Some of the lost books of the Bible or at least the apocryphal books describe a similar conflict between what they termed as God and the Supreme Archangel Lucifer. Perhaps Gael's story undercuts the divine nature of the other accounts but I'm open to the interpretive manifestations of Biblical thought. My problem in listening to all of this, no, seeing it as if I were a fly on the wall at the beginning of time makes my skin crawl and a feeling of deep sadness fills my heart."

"Well why? It doesn't bother me. I think I saw the same argument take place on CSPAN between members of Congress during the run up to the Iraq War."

"But see there's the point Jake. This isn't a story about debates and arguments over a particular war or fight. This is fight for the future of the whole of mankind. The fate of humanity is in the hands of a chamber of indifferent beings. Here we are witnessing two brilliantly intelligent men claiming to love each other as well as their creations and they are at odds with each other about how to deal with a problem of their own making. The innocent humans are in the middle of the power play. And the Avina women…well, they wanted to maintain their so-called rights and lifestyle at the expense of the entire society!"

"Whether these figures are God and Lucifer of the Bible or competing Grand Masters of the High Sciences in Gael's Testament they stood there eons ago, face to face full of pride and arrogance and had the opportunity to lay aside that pride and humbly resolve the situation. It deeply saddens me they managed to piss all over the world and the innocent humans they created."

"I see your point but at least they didn't accept the plan the Builders faction put out there and eliminated the humans."

"Its coming Jake, oh it is coming, Gael's Testament isn't done yet."

54

Babelus Base Camp
City of Avinen

"Step right up and get your mac-n-cheese a la KO!" bellows the den motherly camp cook. "The dish isn't hot but it will fill you just the same, step right up over here. I've got coffee brewing too."

Tasha and Ahmed have not arrived yet but the other hungry members of the team single file past KO as he hands out K-ration box lunches to the famished crew. They sit in the now familiar circle on folding stools, chewing, sipping and chatting. Conversations turn from casual yakking to serious scientific and philosophical debate as each team member eats and gains strength for the fight.

"Have you uncovered any more genetic secrets Doctor Kagen?" asks Jake. "I'm still wondering how the Avina managed to program DNA at the sub-cellular level. Don't you need electron microscopes and sophisticated equipment for these types of nano-sciences?"

Dr. Kagen starts an answer with his standard rejoinder, "Well yes and no. You see Jake the science of genetic manipulation isn't all that difficult once you get past the math. The lab here does have powerful microscopes but I don't quite understand how they work. They're easy to operate though and when connected to the glo-screen through my own brain, mapping and manipulating various genetic patterns are a snap. The tools here are every bit as sophisticated as those back home but they use technologies I'm not familiar with. The most serious obstacle for our scientists in manipulating genes is we don't know what most of them do and we're particularly ignorant on how genes work together to generate specific behaviors and character traits. The Avina obviously knew how every single gene fit into the larger schematic, well heck I think they invented the programming. I must say their mathematical skills are far superior to our own. One of the most important aspects of…"

Doctor Kagen's explanation is interrupted by the sudden arrival of Tasha and Ahmed the Botanist. The pair zoom toward the Team on floating platforms holding tightly onto a handlebar configuration.

"Hi gang, meet Jack and Jill," Tasha happily greets them as she and Ahmed float a foot above the ground on air scooters. "We found these laying around at the Erector Set factory and thought we'd try them out, cool huh?"

The other team members stand up and marvel at the scooters floating with no strings attached. Jack and Jill are configured much the same as a *Segway* Scooter without the wheels. At the base is a disc two feet in diameter and approximately six inches thick. A pole juts out from a triangle shape resting on top of the disc and a set of ram's horn shaped handlebars top off the device.

"Ok well now we know why there aren't any roads or sidewalks in Avinen," remarks Jake scratching the back of his neck in wonder. "Are they easy to ride?"

"Yeah, piece of cake, give her a try." Tasha steps down from Jill and hands the floating machine over to a grinning Jake. "Her handles adjust for your height automatically just be light on the touch with the girl."

Jake steps up onto the platform as Jill wobbles slightly and then self-corrects her horizontal plane. Jake, a broad white smile planted on his face, jumps up and down vigorously to test the scooter's stability. He leans left and right, to and fro while Jill remains stable and motionless. "Alright I'm gonna give 'er a go!" Jake squeezes the handlebars tightly but merely stays in the same position.

"How do you make her go?"

"Think of the handlebars as a joystick. Forward is forward faster, back is slower, left is left, etcetera."

Jake shoves the handles firmly and Jill leaps forward. Unfortunately Jake stays behind falling squarely on his ass. Luckily for him the dried mossy substance on the ground cushions his fall. Jill comes to a stop twenty feet away and Jake stands to try again.

"I told you to go easy with her, she's temperamental."

"Yeah, yeah yeah, it's a woman thing right?"

"Mmm hmm, but I think its ironic Jake is the one who comes tumbling after in this epic poem."

Jake remounts Jill, this time tenderly and proceeds to scoot around the encampment joyously, laughing and screeching like a schoolboy at recess. Ahmed hands Jack over to Kelly Anne who is careful to mind her manners with the scooter and takes off steadily. Jake reluctantly hands the scooter to Dr. Kagen who has minor difficulties with his balance while mounting the unit. Nonetheless he manages to scoot around happily. Brian and KO take turns with the scooters racing each other to the end of the complex and back.

"So do the scooters ride on a bed of plasma?" Jake asks Tasha.

"No I don't believe so, not exactly anyway. Plasma displacement is the technology but it's used differently for levitated locomotion. This isn't the same as our air cube illustration. In our air cube everything is made of light plasma particles immune to gravity. But Jack and Jill are made of heavy solid material, as are the people who ride them and they are most definitely not immune to gravitational pulls as I'm sure the bruising on your ass can attest. In this case plasma displacement is used to create or replicate thrust and lift. The plasma particles directly underneath the units are excited in a way that makes them cool and coalesce and form a semi-solid state, expanding the plasma in the area underneath. This creates displacement, like a ship on water and pushes the unit upwards. At the same time the plasma particles directly above the sides of the disc are excited to heat up and thin, creating a vacuum above the unit or lift if you will. The same principles are applied to the directional movements. Theoretically you could apply this technology to send large objects through space at rates near the speed of light. Its genius!"

55

Dr. Kagen sits with Jake for a few moments while the others take turns on Jack and Jill. "Do you like what you've seen so far at Avinen Jake?"

"You kiddin' me? I love this place! The technology is fantastic."

"That it is, that it is. Do you think we're ready for all of this in our world?"

"I always take the view, if you discover a thing use it to the benefit of humanity."

"Sure is a nice sentiment Jake but I don't know. Some of these technologies are incredibly powerful and I believe destabilizing."

"What, you mean like the oil companies getting pissed off because we have free energy?

"No, nothing along those lines. Nothing simple. I discovered the Avinen trick for retaining memories throughout generations of self-replication. They code recessive memories directly into the genes! They programmed recessive memories out of their creations but I believe we retain bits and pieces of the technology."

"How so Doctor?"

"You know how every once in awhile a super-genius pops out of nowhere, I mean from a completely unrelated background? Like a high level mathematician suddenly comes on the scene despite his plumber father and waitress mother. No education, just knows math out of the blue."

"Hmm, yeah I've heard those stories."

"There's all manner of genius from nowhere stories Jake and I believe, since the Avina Creators used strands of their own DNA to make creatures in their own image they may have left a little code in there and is the reason humans discover anything at all."

"But we're naturally curious Doctor, we would discover things on our own."

"Perhaps yes and perhaps no. Humans always talk about how they invent things but that's a mischaracterization of the process. We discover things. Imagine if we actually had the power to invent. In the wrong hands…"

"We invented computers and such."

"Nope. Your brain is a computer…not invented by humans. We replicate some of the brain's functions as we discover how they work. We don't invent anything."

"I see what you mean but the distinction doesn't bother me. Who cares if we have the power to invent?"

"You know those fools who send out computer viruses crashing your system?"

"Yeah I hate those guys."

"Humans have a tendency to kill for sport Jake. Imagine a new-genus human with the power to invent thinks up a force starting out the size of a pea and grows to the size of the entire Universe, destroying everything in its path. Does that bother you?"

"That's sick Doctor, you need to get out more often."

"I suppose so Jake, but that's when the trouble usually starts, hah."

56

The lunchtime festivities break apart on Jake's orders. The Team hikes back toward their respective duty stations with the exception of Tasha and Ahmed who air scoot to their destination. Dr. Kagen heads for the genetics lab seeking information unlocking the myriad secrets of intelligent adaptation; his sidekick Brian excuses himself to go to the restroom. Tasha and Ahmed decide to concentrate on discovering the methods the Avina used to transport heavy objects across great distances or high into the air. Jake, Kelly Anne and KO resume their foray into Avinen history.

"This time guys if I start to get the headaches again I'm going to break the connection right away," warns KO. "I'm worried this technology is affecting me permanently, you know, like too much cell phone usage can cause brain tumors or makes men infertile. The last thing I need against me is infertility, I have enough trouble pickin' up chicks as it is."

"Consider us fairly warned KO." Kelly Anne replies. "But you're famous now what with all those flashy Lorenzo Cordoba reports pasting our mugs all over creation. Pretty women like famous men, look at all those beautiful fashion models who go out with ugly rock stars."

"I guess Kelly Anne but those guys are rich not just famous."

"Mark my words KO your fame will bring you fortune too."

KO reboots Gael's scan-can and the trio continues to experience the dawn of history. They return to the point where Luhhan loses the battle of wills before the High Council followed by his quick and dramatic exit from the chamber.

Gael's narrative continues:

An angry and saddened Luhhan left the Council chambers and sought to rally his fellow Avina to the cause of the Avinenev. He traveled furiously from home to home, workspace to workspace and to the places of recreation. At each stop he pleaded with his fellow Avina to accept his plan for full assimilation and reject the compromise of Shedaii. In some quarters his ideas were met enthusiastically while in others skeptically. By the end of his campaign Luhhan had managed to convince nearly a third of the Avina his arrangement was best for harmony in society. Another third sided with Shedaii and his ideas of separation, the rest stood between the two factions unwilling to decide.

Avinen had never known a breach of confidence of this magnitude. Its citizens found themselves unable to resolve the situation amicably. Lacking fortitude the Avina allowed events to unfold on their own accord and during this time they lost control of the future, the fate of the Avinenev and even their own destiny.

Luhhan worked mightily to impede the progress and implementation of Shedaii's plan. Once it finally took a foothold throughout Avinen he fought to undermine its goals and to subvert its character to prove to the Avina he and his plan are the proper course to maintain a harmonious society. With each success of Shedaii's plan Luhhan found ways to countervail its effects and passed rumors of unrecorded failures. Luhhan, a Master Builder assisted the Avinenev in the construction of a city to mirror the image of Avinen. They named the new city Neniva. He toiled mightily to raise the skill and knowledge of the Avinenev to be at par with the Avina. This is where the protestations of Luhhan crossed the chasm into open rebellion against the Avina.

Luhhan used the authorized pilgrimages of the Avinenev to the Great Hall of Knowledge to educate them in the high sciences. He offered them canisters containing the archives of the foundations of the powers of Avinen. The Avinenev, designed and created with the capacity and desire for learning grew in knowledge quickly. And for a time the secrets of the Avina laid bare in the hands of its own creations. When this treachery was discovered a great upheaval overtook the City of Avinen and the struggle took on a physical dimension previously unknown to the Avina.

A great battle raged throughout the city for an hundred revolutions of the Sun. Creators fought Builders, Managers battled Discoverers, all to no end. No side or faction could prevail over the other, the powers and ingenuity of each from the same foundation. The Avinenev presented no help to the forces of Luhhan. They ran and hid in shame of their lack standing under the shields of Avinen, their ungrateful rebellion lay naked before the Avina. Eventually the Avina grew weary of the stalemate and sought to end hostilities by banishing the fuel of the rebellion. All Avinenev within the shields of Avinen were cast away forever to dwell in Novinen. The banishment itself caused much upheaval as Avinenev companions were torn from the Avina who loved and cherished them. The sight of children and loved ones restrained and chastened, marched out under threat of imprisonment through the corridors of Avinen ripped through the consciousness of all Avina and threatened to force a continuation of hostilities.

Sadly Luhhan and his followers were cast outside the shields of Avina, in an effort to help the banished Avinenev adjust although each was free to return at will and partake of Avinen society. The Avina set out watchers to Novinen who continued to guide the Avinenev. Sadly Luhhan and his followers viewed the guides as spies for the Avina. The activity became covert and less frequent. Over time tensions cooled and open hostilities ceased but Luhhan set himself as ruler of the Avinenev and sought to build a society to rival Avinen. Many of the followers of Luhhan took female Avinenev as their own and bore offspring, neither Avinenev nor Avina. The design of many of these oddities failed. They grew large but mute and unable to retain knowledge. Their strength made them dangerous and though they could barely fend for themselves in Novinen they were cast away from the Avinenev.

During the time of tranquility Luhhan and his followers used the good graces of the Avina and access to the Great Hall of Knowledge to their advantage and increased the understandings and power of the Avinenev ten-fold. Shedaii and the Avina saw the rival city grow in strength and knowledge but did not move against it for fear of breaching the harmonious arrangement under which both societies lived. But the talents and capabilities at the city of Neniva grew to a point where Avinen's survival was put to the test. The Avina sought to destroy Neniva and chose the Festival of Ascension from the Great Garden as the appropriate time to conduct the annihilation. The whole of the Avina attends and celebrates during the Festival. Luhhan and his followers would join the celebrations of a hundred moons.

As the Festival of Ascension reached its peak celebratory time the Avina opened the controlling gates upon the Avinenev and deluged them with the waters of the earth. For a time waters covered the whole of Novinen until the Avina churned the earth once more and the waters receded. The action enraged Luhhan and he and his followers thundered out beyond the shields of Avinen in search of the Avinenev remnant. Many Avina creations survived the deluge. All the creatures of the sea lived. Most of the great species of land creatures survived though in small numbers in pockets throughout Novinen. Handfuls of Avinenev survived and took comfort upon the breast of Luhhan who vowed to rebuild the lost city of Neniva.

A thousand revolutions of the Sun passed and the creatures of Novinen grew in knowledge and strength once again. Although their progress was limited by a design implanted into their blood limiting the number of their years. And yet the strong desire to replicate, capacity for adaptation and their hearty constitutions enabled them to thrive even in barren lands. Luhann and his followers retained the high sciences and lived beyond the time of the new Avinenev and they led the creations to build a new city to rival Avinen. Luhann gave the Avinenev the secrets of the Master Builder and they learned the powers of the high sciences. They constructed a city, again a mirror image of Avinen with a Great Hall of Knowledge at its center. The city grew mighty in the land of Novinen and its inhabitants began to use the powers of the Creators, the Builders, the Discoverers and the Managers. Once again the survival of the Avina came under attack.

Shedaii and the Avina witnessed the rapid rise of knowledge and strength of the Avinenev and grew concerned at the new use of powers never known outside the shields of Avinen. The Avinenev gained knowledge to create their own shields, design creatures of their own hand and regenerate as in Avinen. The Avina thought to destroy the Avinenev once again but worried another churn of the earth would cause calamitous destruction beyond their capacity to control. So they conspired to destroy the new city and erase the knowledge built up by its inhabitants. To do this they used the sciences of the Creators enmeshed with the sciences of the Builders to send forth a vibration taking knowledge from Avinenev heads, even erasing the ability to think clearly. The Avina destroyed the new city with a bolt of the powers of the Builders and desolated the nearby lands. The effects of the destruction sent the Avinenev scurrying to the four corners of Novinen.

Once again Luhhan flew into a heated mindless rage and he sought to destroy the City of Avinen by his own hand. As a Master Builder, Luhhan possessed the knowledge of the high sciences, his talent and skill in these areas unparalleled among the Avina. He summoned the forces of the earth and firmament and directed them toward Avinen. The powers of Luhhan were great and he managed to destroy the powers of Avinen outside its shields but he could not penetrate them. Avinen lost its support beyond its shields and fell to the earth, a mutilated shell of its former glory. The followers of Luhhan dispersed to assist the scattered Avinenev. The Avina dispersed as well to the resting place of the Seven Mountains and I was elected to remain behind to maintain the City of Avinen until they return.

• • •

The Testament of Gael ends and its three bleary-eyed viewers break contact with the glo-screen interface. They sit in a starry-eyed silence for a few moments uncertain how to proceed. According to the Testament the stories of the Bible are true, only not quite as presented over the past several thousand years.

Kelly Anne ponders the implications of what they learned through Gael's story. Whether creatures are created or evolved from genetic soup the tides of history always end up the same…in tragedy and destruction.

From Gael's limited perspective the story is devoid of deliberations involving even a hint of morality. In his account the two warring societies are relative and the entire affair is shown as a mere matter of survival. No one seems to make judgments as to who is right or wrong throughout the great battles and controversies.

"If that's all there is where does our sense of morality come from," she asks herself. "There's got to be more to this story…I hope."

57

Wine Rack, Avinen Public Library
City of Avinen

"There's something I'm not getting here Kayanne," says Jake, finally breaking a long discomforting silence. "We're uncovering sciences and technologies no one has ever heard of before. If the Testament of Gael is accurate in any way at all then we should see evidence of the technologies in the archeological digs over the last couple thousand years. I've been all over creation myself with *Jackson Nichol's Big Dig* and I've never seen a thing giving us a hint of any of this. If there was a Diaspora of the ancients such as Luhhan and his science freaks they would have passed at least some of the information down to humans and we would see incontrovertible evidence don't you think?"

"We may very well have seen a lot of the evidence of the very sciences we've been discovering here Jake but we may not have known what we were looking at. In the first place we always view history through the prism of our own times, myopic and closed to certain ideas. We tend to look at the entire history of the human race as a linear pageant progressing through time and ending where we are today at the pinnacle of progress. But any competent study of recorded civilization reveals history as a series of ebbs and flows. Empires rise and fall. Technologies flourish in one century and are lost in the next. Science and technology flourishes in one epoch and is hidden or destroyed in the next one."

"This arrogant linear thought process is true if you're an Evolutionist or a Bible believing creationist. The Evolutionist sees everything starting out as microorganisms and then progresses through to complex creatures and finally ends up here at us the primate of primates. But if evolution were factual science it would operate the same way as everything else in history. Beings would rise and fall with the conditions around them and conditions would dictate mixed capacities among creatures."

"Why, for example, hasn't a talking zebra evolved or math genius frogs? Simple, every living thing develops to the limits of its original programming, including humans. When we live through our lives we believe in our hearts and minds our generation is the first of its kind, the next level of, well, whatever. The basic pattern of a human life today is identical to the pattern you can find in ancient China or Babylon. Those people thought they were the first whatever too. An intelligent being designed the programming with limits for every living thing. That's why we don't learn from history Jake. We're programmed to start fresh with each generation. And I would also say we have the capacity to start over with our lives too. We can cast aside our own personal history and rise above our failings or we can rise to the top of society only to fail miserably in the end. The Theory of Evolution stands in direct contradiction to these obvious facts of life.

If Evolution were factual science progress would march on and then suddenly stop in its tracks and then recede but the theory holds everything marches on in a straight line, always upward and forward. It's possible we humans aren't the primates of primates in evolution. We might be dumb as sand and rocks compared to creatures living hundreds of thousands of years ago.

Unfortunately I must say religionists suffer from the same egotistical perspective. For them everything starts with the creation of Adam and Eve and then we march forward in a linear fashion to get where we are today. Theologians try to shoehorn the Bible into this thought process. But the Bible isn't the be all and end all of history. There is a history before Adam and Eve. And there is a history to come after mankind's time on this earth. Even the Bible states this clearly. If you read the Bible's overall concept it starts with a perfect society, morphs into a sinful one and then back into a perfect one...ebbs and flows Jake, ebbs and flows.

One of the problems we have in discerning history is the validity of any written word. In the Bible we find numerous stories and tales I find too simplistic for reality, most of them, actually. There's always more substance behind the simple narrative. But how do we choose what the writer's meant by any particular passage? We try to prove something scientifically or through observation. The Bible writers use the term Heaven but the concept may have been merely a highly advanced prehistorical society floating on Tasha's bed of plasma energy as we see with the story of Avinen.

So when we go searching the globe for evidence of lost civilizations we come at it from two angles, first, we believe today's humans are the most progressed beings in history and second, whatever technologies we've developed are the pinnacle of science. What's the dominant technology of today's world? Well there's digital technology, computers and information exchange and then our societies run by machines powered largely by fossil fuels, oil and coal. We also have nuclear fusion serving the dual purpose of energy supply and mass destruction. In our myopic arrogance we go around looking for signs of progress in ancient societies by seeking evidence of machines powered by fossil fuels or digital technologies to exchange information. What's more we never, ever expect to find anything so much as approaching our own superior advanced knowledge…so we don't.

Now look at the power and sciences of Avinen. If we dug this place up as a ruins and it wasn't well preserved we would find what we always find, broken down structures and shards of pottery, the remnants of a civilization but not a highly advanced one. If we found one of those scan-can devices and it was no longer functional we would assume it was a religious artifact or a way to carry water, we wouldn't even bother to imagine it contains brainwaves! These glo-screens we are using like computers would look like broken picture frames or some benign spindly object at an archeological dig. And all of this technology of brainy-chaining and brain-jacking, well, its far more powerful than any computers our society has invented and none of it is digital, not one bit…heh, there goes one of my silly puns.

In short Jake the reason we don't find evidence of highly advanced societies is we have no clue what to look for and if we found something we'd discard it as a practical artifact or religious relic. We're just stupid that way."

"Yeah you're probably right technology doesn't necessarily have to be digital or powered by fossil fuels to be effective or even more advanced."

"Hey Jake," Tasha's voice blares over the Pocket Studio comm-link.

"What's up Tash?"

"You know the pile of little barrels over by the side of the Wine Rack?"

"Yeah, what about them?"

"Go pick one up and give the power dial at the bottom a little spin."

Jake walks over to a pile of small cylindrical objects that look like coffee mugs without handles. He picks one up, finds the power dial and gives it a spin. The object WHIRRS to life and suddenly jumps from Jake's hands floating about six feet off the floor and emitting a bright light suitable for reading or working on a project.

"Cool huh? I call 'em Punkin' lights."

"Heh-heh, yeah thanks Tash."

"What a timely illustration," observes Kelly Anne. "If we dug those up at a site and had no other context we probably would have labeled them as olive oil jars."

"Totally true Kayanne. We should use the time before dinner to interface with another scan-can. Maybe we'll run into the Testament of Luhhan. I'll bet it's completely different from Gael's. KO why don't you pick one out?"

KO saunters over to the Wine Rack and selects a port close to his eye level. He wonders what secrets might rest inside. As his thoughts grow stronger a lighted label in the characters of the Avina language appear just above the hole. "Whoa what's this? Kayanne, Jake come here, look at this it says The Wars of Shedaii!"

"I don't see anything KO."

"You have to look at the hole and wonder in your mind what it contains and then the label will appear."

Jake studies the hole and queries the back of his mind. A green glowing label in strange characters he can't decipher appears. "Ok that is amazing! Let's call up Tasha and tell her about this."

"Hey Tash?" Jake barks into his wrist.

"What?"

"We discovered a labeling system at the Wine Rack. When you move close to the hole where the scan-can is buried and think hard about what's in it. The label lights up telling you what the scan-can contains."

"Really? That's too cool! Hey I have an idea. Jake walk over to one of the walls in the chamber and think hard about art and see what happens."

"Why?"

"Bill Gates has something like what I'm thinking about in his house, try it out."

"Um ok." Jake walks toward a wall at the east side of the chamber. He stands in front of the wall thinking about beautiful seascape oil paintings he enjoys viewing at the Laguna Beach Art Festival back home in California. As he visualizes the fine art in his mind the entire wall lights up in a series of seascapes and marine paintings. "This place is incredible, I could die here."

58

The group boots up a scan-can labeled the Wars of Shedaii and stands transfixed in concentration, watching the beginning of a presentation of the historical record of battles between the forces of Shedaii and Luhhan. In their focused state the trio never hears footsteps or noises behind them. Suddenly without warning burlap bags are shoved over their heads. Jake and KO are slammed in the head with a blunt object knocking Jake unconscious and KO senseless. Kelly Anne screams and fights to no avail with her arms and head restricted by the heavy sack. She kicks and screams some more, her muffled shouts barely audible through the thick fabric. She is struck on the head and everything fades to black. Unknown assailants carry the group away to another location.

Kelly Anne comes to, woozy and disoriented. She peers through the haze of semi-consciousness and sees the other members of Team Babelus tied up and thrown to the floor of a non-descript empty room. To her left sits Dr. Kagen, glaring toward the center of the room and to his left KO lays motionless on his side. Ahmed the Botanist sits tied together with Tasha. Jake lies still and seemingly breathless to her right. There is no sign of Brian. "Maybe Brian got away and he can go find help," she thinks. "I hope Jake and KO aren't dead."

A group of five armed men clad in uniforms and black headscarves covering their faces hover above the team. One of them, possibly the leader steps heavily over to Dr. Kagen and yells, "You, stand up!"

Dr. Kagen, hands secured behind his back and feet bound together with plastic ties struggles to his feet awkwardly. He stands tall with a straight back and his chin up facing the armed man squarely. Another of the men walks over to the Doctor and cuts the ties at his feet and unbinds his wrists.

"You are free to go." The leader says firmly.

"Free to go? What about the rest of the team, are they free to go too?"

"No they are filthy infidels and will suffer for their crimes!"

"Perhaps you misunderstand. I am not Islamic so I'm an infidel too, right?"

"Yes you are an infidel but you are a black and so cannot help it, you are free to go. Go now!"

Thoughts of easy escape fill Dr. Kagen's mind. If he leaves he can go get help but his wrist still bears an active Pocket Studio with a direct comm-link to General Keith. The authorities already know what's happened to the Team. Kagen's thoughts run back to the bullies in his Watts neighborhood during his childhood. He knows the type. They will do violence to the others. He can see the evil in their eyes. He knows he can't stop them but he will not abandon his friends. By his honor he will stay and suffer as they suffer.

"Put the restraints back on I'm not going anywhere."

"You are a fool, a stupid nigger. Do you not know how you will suffer today?"

"Yes I know, put the restraints back on!"

The armed men rebind the Doctor's hands and legs. They throw him against a wall and proceed to beat him mercilessly. The first blow comes from the butt of a Kalishnikov rifle sending the proud man dropping to his knees. The group's leader backhands the kneeled man across the face shouting epithets and slogans. He kicks the defenseless Doctor in the groin, doubling him over. The terrorists kick and punch Dr. Kagen as he lay helplessly on the ground screaming in pain. Kelly Anne and Tasha shriek and shout for the men to stop the attack. The beating goes on for ten minutes until Dr. Kagen drifts off into silence.

• • •

General Keith immediately contacts the President in the Situation Room and addresses the stunned group. "Mr. President you can see our team has been kidnapped, we need to send a rescue force in there immediately and get them out of there!"

"Yes I see General but we have a treaty with the Iraqis and we're not allowed to send military people down in the Well for any reason whatsoever. Just a few hours ago we strong armed the Iraqi President over the words of the treaty and shamed them into honoring it. We can't now turn our backs on the treaty. We've given our word. Not my word but the solemn promise of the United States government. I have Secretary Malloy getting in touch with the Iraqi government to authorize a rescue mission and that's the best we can do at this point."

"Mr. President we have a duty to ensure the safety of our fellow Americans. The Team is helpless down there and I think the situation will get out of hand very quickly. We don't have time for diplomatic dances. The kidnappers are seriously evil men. We can't just stand by and watch a tragedy play out like this."

"That's all we're authorized to do at this point General if you can't stand to watch it turn off your comm-link!"

The President's intemperate remark touches a raw nerve in National Security Advisor Dan Maney. He leaps to his feet, face red hot with anger and his vaunted blood vessel throbbing against his wide bald forehead. "Mr. President this decision is unthinkable!" he shouts as he pounds the table. "Those are innocent civilians we sent down there on a mission of peace. They are our envoys, representatives of the United States of America. Failing to adequately protect them in the first place is an outrage! Leaving them in this situation over treaty language is a vile despicable act of evil at par with the terrorists!"

"Sit down and shut up Maney or I'll fire you on the spot! Can't you see what's at stake here? Can't you see the bigger picture?"

Maney slumps in his chair, disbelief and sorrow painting his face. "Yeah I see the bigger picture," he mutters under his breath. "We sacrifice every principle and point of honor we hold dear to appease evil."

59

Unknown Location
City of Avinen

KO wakes from his stupor lying on his side, bound by his wrists and ankles, his face sticking to the floor in a drying pool of blood. A few moments pass as he gathers his thoughts to get his bearings. "What happened and why am I here?" he asks himself. "This is some kind of surrealistic nightmare brought on by connecting to technology I don't understand? No, those are real screams and this is a real headache."

He squirms around in an effort to get a better look at his surroundings, prying his face from the floor. His eyes gaze around the dim-lit room and finds his team tied up in various configurations with Dr. Kagen enduring a vicious beating. There are five men, each armed with Kalishnikov automatic rifles. A large scimitar is tied at the side of the tallest man and KO suspects him as the leader. He wriggles his way to an upright position seated against a wall, from this vantage point he directly faces Tasha whose hands are tied behind her back, apparently bound up with Ahmed. The thuggish leader strides over to KO and kicks his leg.

"You are awake filthy pig? You are not a worthy adversary. We took you without a fight, even your women put up a struggle. Do you know why you are here?"

"No I don't." KO breathes out hoarsely.

"You are here to pay for the crimes of the Infidel United States and its little puppet Israel."

"Yeah, whatever."

The terrorist leader viciously backhands KO across the face splattering the floor and Tasha with fresh blood. "Don't disrespect me you filthy American pig. What is your religion? Are you Jew? Are you Jew?"

"No I worship at the Church of the Holy Harley."

The terrorists spits in his face.

"You are a non-believer! Today you will submit your life to Allah and surrender to Islam!"

"No I won't. Islam sucks."

The terrorist slams the butt of his rifle against the side of KO's face bouncing his head off the wall. "Shut up pig! When you have surrendered to Islam you are free to go."

KO raises his swollen and bloody face toward his attacker meeting his eye. "I won't do it. Just go ahead and kill me."

"We shall see fat man. You have no idea the pain you will suffer at our hands upon your death. We shall see."

The terrorist leader turns toward Tasha and glares at her pausing to study her face. Tasha purses her lips tightly and glares right back. She is angry and unafraid. "What is your religion you filthy whore?"

"Roman Catholic."

"You are a cheap American whore for the Pope! You will surrender to Islam today as well. Any of you infidels who surrender to Allah today are free to go and join the *ummah*. Are you going to surrender today filthy whore?"

"No."

"Do you realize the danger you have put yourself in? My men will rape your filthy whore carcass and we will sever your head from your body and send it to your mother in Atlanta by Federal Express!"

"How do you know my mother lives in Atlanta?"

"That is none of your concern whore but you must understand if you do not surrender to Allah you will force a Jihad against your family and we will hunt them down like the filthy infidel dogs they are!"

The terrorist grabs Ahmed by his hair and jerks his head backward, spitting in his face. "And you, what are you doing with these infidels?"

"I was sent here by President Adjani to watch over Iraqi treasures and make certain the Americans leave without stealing."

"And so you reject them as infidels?"

"No, they are good people."

The terrorist jerks Ahmed up by the hair and kicks him in the midsection three times. "You are going to take the side of infidels against your Islamic brothers?"

"What you are doing is not representative of Allah! You are the infidel! The prophet wrote prisoners are to be unharmed and yet you beat and torture them! You do not speak for Islam and you do not speak for me!"

The terrorist summons one of his men. He jerks Ahmed's head backward by the hair, stretching his face and leaving his mouth open. The other terrorist drops his pants, pulls out his penis and proceeds to urinate in Ahmed's mouth and on his face. "You will suffer the same fate as your new friends my little brother." He throws Ahmed's urine-soaked head forward in disgust.

The terrorist walks over to Jake lying in a dark corner motionless. He kicks him but Jake does not stir. He kicks him harder and screams for him to wake up. The angry man violently lifts Jake's head up by the hair, inspecting for signs of life and then slams it to the hard floor. "He is dead."

The terrorist thug turns to Kelly Anne, propped up against the wall, bound by wrist and ankle but clean and unharmed. "You are a beautiful woman. I would take you as my wife and shower you in fine jewels and silks. What is you're religion?"

"I'm a Seventh-Day Adventist."

"What? What is this? Like a Mormon?"

"No, Protestant Christians who worship on Saturday."

"Ha, ha. You are a Jewish Christian?"

"No idiot," we believe in the Seventh-Day Sabbath but we're Christian."

"What do you think of Islam?"

"Personally I think it's a vile false religion invented by a bandit named Mohammed who wanted to control people and build an empire. Islam grew by the sword, over the centuries…either convert or die. Pretty much the same way you express Islam right now."

"Allah will punish you for your lies!"

"Mohammed was the liar! The imams and clerics who preach hatred and violence around the world…they're the liars! Maybe nobody gets it but my country and all Western countries are at war with Islam. So I hate the filthy religion…but that's just me."

Kelly Anne has a way of sending men into burning rages. The terrorist slaps Kelly Anne across the face in a feverish flurry of stinging blows. He tears at her flight suit and rips the collar. His anger grows white-hot sending him into a flood of kicks striking the defenseless woman again and again. The thug clutches her by the hair and slams her head against the floor screaming infidel whore! Infidel whore! Infidel whore! Today you will surrender to Allah or lose your whore head!"

The enraged terrorist stands above a crumpled sobbing Kelly Anne and spits on her head.

He calms.

The terrorist serenely walks over to Ahmed, cuts loose his bindings and jerks him to his feet by the hair dragging him forcibly to the center of the room.

"Will you reject these infidels now? They disrespect the Prophet. They blaspheme against Allah." He speaks into Ahmed's ear with a tone almost too low to hear, dripping in a cloak of banality.

"They are my friends and good people. You are the one who puts the evil face on Islam."

The other members of the terrorist gang begin chanting in a slow rhythmic canter. *Allahu Akbar. Allahu Akbar. Allahu Akbar. Allahu Akbar. Allahu Akbar.*

The thug swings his rifle at the back of Ahmed's knees, forcing him to the ground in a kneeling position.

The chant grows louder and increases in ferocity. *Allahu Akbar! Allahu Akbar! Allahu Akbar! Allahu Akbar! Allahu Akbar! Allahu Akbar!*

Ahmed's head is slammed to the floor and his hands rebound behind his back. The leader yanks his hair away from his neck.

Tasha, unbound leaps to her feet shouting, "No! No!" A terrorist slams his rifle into her chest sending her to the floor flat on her back. He grinds his boot into her throat incapacitating her.

Chants grow faster, louder and furious. *Allahu Akbar! Allahu Akbar! Allahu Akbar! Allahu Akbar! Allahu Akbar! Allahu Akbar! Allahu Akbar! Allahu Akbar! Allahu Akbar! lAlahu Akbar!*

Ahmed feels the cold steel of the scimitar at the base of his neck. The terrorist thug begins a sawing motion in rhythm with the chants. *Allahu Akbar! Allahu Akbar! Allahu Akbar!* He saws deeply and Ahmed lets fly a blood-curdling scream starting with a manly growl and gradually raising to a high pitched shrill shriek of a woman. The terrorist saws back and forth to the chants *Allahu Akbar! Allahu Akbar! Allahu Akbar!* Ahmed's scream never pauses for breath and it ends in a gurgling noise as the scimitar slices through his windpipe. The terrorist raises Ahmed's head to the sky in triumph to the joyous chants of *Allahu Akbar! Allahu Akbar! Allahu Akbar! Allahu Akbar! Allahu Akbar!*

The murderous thug, carrying Ahmed's severed head by the hair strides quickly over to Kelly Anne, presses the head against her cheek and screams at her. "This is the price of your blasphemies you infidel whore! These are the wages of your disrespect to the Prophet! All of you must now surrender to Islam this day or suffer this death!" The terrorist joins in the chants and dances joyously around the room. *Allahu Akbar! Allahu Akbar! Allahu Akbar! Allahu Akbar! Allahu Akbar! Allahu Akbar!*

• • •

The atmosphere in the Situation Room shifts from grim to murky darkness. Secretary of Defense Green-Newton sits in her chair sobbing a wretched pitiful mournful cry. General Broadhead buries his head in his hands, his great shoulders heaving in despair. Science Advisor Kane turns away from the table and kneels down in quiet prayer. President Crandall sits stiffly, a blank stare of shock filling hollow eyes. He cannot move and drool falls from the sides of his mouth.

In his gut Dan Maney rages but he bottles his fury and expresses his anger without emotion. His resolve will get revenge. His righteousness will move mountains and sweep through in the night destroying every murdering terrorist fuck face in its path, but not at this moment. For now his mindset is cool determination. Resolve gets things done.

"It looks like you've got your big picture Mr. President." He spits as he walks out of the room staring directly through Crandall's soul.

60

White House Situation Room
Washington, D.C.

After a brief period of shock the White House Situation Room springs to life as agency directors, Cabinet members, their aids and staff scramble to phones, fax machines and computers in response to the unfolding hostage crisis and an on-screen display of a brutal cold blooded murder. The broadcast network blocked the images of the slaying, played live in a Lorenzo Cordoba report but the haunting scream and last gurgles of Ahmed the Botanist is forever branded in the consciousness of all who heard its plaintive, mournful wail.

President Adjani roars on the monitor, railing against President Crandall and his inability to protect the innocent Iraqi scientist along for a peaceful exploration. He threatens his armies will drive the Americans out of Mesopotamia forever. Secretary Malloy's protestations of Adjani's own malfeasance in denying the immediate deployment of an emergency rescue squad is cast aside as whimpers from a dying giant. The incident forces the Iraqi President to address his nation on television to both defend Islam and his decision to allow an exploration mission uncovering blasphemies against Allah. He is embarrassed by the public exposure of his decisions. In a world of moral relativism and white-hot 24/7 media coverage the quickest way to start a war is by embarrassing a despot.

Although the Iraqi President already sent his troops toward the Well Site a half day before the incident he uses the publicly aired murder as a bludgeoning sledge hammer against the Crandall Administration hoping to exact concessions and monetary reparations. The Iraqi Army marches on the Well Site and promises war against the Marines stationed there.

The Iranian President takes to the airwaves and uses the media bullhorn to address the entire world, informing all watching that Iran is ready to test a 15-megaton nuclear weapon the next day. According to the country's President, Iran will launch a nuclear tipped missile at Tel-Aviv and completely destroy the State of Israel in the days following the test. The Iranian government is to carry out this plan unless President Crandall meets demands including recognition of Palestine as a sovereign state with dominion over Israel, complete American withdrawal from the entire Middle East and the destruction of the blasphemous Well Site and Team Babelus.

Members of the United States Congress openly call for the President's immediate removal from office. Two thirds of the congressional delegation from all political parties stand on the steps of Capitol Hill and proclaim the President guilty of high crimes and misdemeanors. Several members call for holding the United States Constitution in abeyance to dispense with a time-consuming impeachment trial. The Speaker of the House angrily denounces the President as a devil worshipper. The Senate Majority Leader requests a sanity hearing in an effort to remove the President as incapacitated. Overt demagoguery and outright lies ignite an exploding inferno, turning the United States Congress into the most frightening force since the Blitzkrieg: A televised lynch mob.

Protesting factions breach the gates outside the White House in a sea of human angst and anger. The dire situation demands the protection of the nation's symbol of American freedom and liberty by force and the National Guard responds by mowing protesters down in a hail of gunfire. The protestors, most firm supporters of the 2nd Amendment of the Constitution bring stores of weapons of their own to the tea party. They fire back, killing many soldiers in the skirmish. The two sides form lines, dig trenches and threaten all out open warfare. The White House is under armed siege for the first time since 1812.

Media organizations pour jet fuel on the raging inferno with minute-by-minute reports on every aspect of conflict. Breathless excited interviews from armed protestors fill television screens around the world, as do the mad ravings of the Iranian President. Lorenzo Cordoba feeds from the Well Site are cribbed and edited to reflect the direst points of view. Newspapers print special editions and deliver them directly to the middle of teeming masses of angry people. Web logs from both the left and right extremes of the Blogosphere scream epithets across the Internet, enabling huge lightning-strike protest gatherings in public places throughout the country. In every corner of America citizens are up in arms ready to take their country back, by force if necessary.

President Crandall tugs at his hair and rubs his chest uncomfortably as he watches his Cabinet try to tamp down the flames of dissent burning from coast to coast. Each minute he loses confidence in the American system of government, his administration and himself. The bubble of invincibility collapses around him. All situations are boxed in and no options present a way out. And the boxes keep closing in tighter, squeezing the administration in a vice grip of indecision.

The Cabinet works mightily to find solutions to each complex problem and finds little comfort in the options presented. The President suggests a telecom conference between himself and the Presidents of Iran and Iraq. Secretary Malloy reminds the President the United States has no diplomatic relations with Iran. Crandall answers that he doesn't care about diplomatic niceties at this point. The myriad problems must get solved right now and without artificial roadblocks.

Despite deep reservations Malloy arranges the summit. The leaders of Iran and Iraq join President Crandall on-screen in the Situation Room. The Cabinet and agency directors look on with worried anticipation as Crandall addresses the two leaders.

"Gentlemen we are standing at the precipice of a grave threat to our very existence," he begins. "I can put politics, diplomacy and electoral considerations aside but I cannot abandon my country in this hour of crisis. I've asked for this unprecedented meeting to work with both of you face-to-face. In return I ask for your honesty, both in assessing the crisis at hand and as to the true needs of your respective countries. What do you need to wind our people away from world war and out of this grave time of tribulation?"

The Iranian President responds first. His eyes sit deeply in their sockets, surrounded by weathered dark circles and thick brushy black eyebrows. Mr. Crandall the crisis is indeed grave and disturbing and I have no interest in saving you or your people from destruction. I have no interest in backing away from the destruction of Israel, the West's Bastard puppet state. My interests lie only in those actions advancing Islam and against activities attacking the Prophet or Allah. I can temporarily halt testing our nuclear weapons and destroying Israel but in all frankness these things are inevitable and will take place now or in the near future. The question is what can you offer me in return for my restraint. From my point of view you hold nothing over the Iranian people."

"What is your most pressing issue regarding Islam Mr. President?" asks Crandall.

"The most pressing threat to Islam is the blasphemies and lies coming out of the hole in the ground in Iraq. Since you have chosen to open that secret box and allow the world to see its lies through your reporters the whole of Islam is disquieted and seeks a remedy for your crimes. We cannot shut the memories of the open box but we can bury its message and its messengers for all time. You're willingness to do this is crucial to our decisions. If you sacrifice a small part you can win a larger part. This is simple."

"You're telling me you want to shut down the Well Site and let the terrorist thugs kill our people down there?"

"Many people are lost in war Mr. President. Consider them soldiers for the cause and move on. Religious faith is not typically lost in war. Indeed, it is generally strengthened. Islam cannot abide a threat to its existence by ancient lies and perversions. I should think the same is true for the many Christian faiths and the Jews as well. Though I have no interest in preserving them I imagine you might. A destruction of this grand blasphemy and false witness will go a long way in re-establishing the time honored traditions of these faiths."

"Yes, many of the angry Americans outside the White House at this very moment seem to agree with your assessment. President Adjani do you have any thoughts on this?"

"Mr. Crandall you have handled each phase of this operation poorly. Your activities are criminal and like the Iranian President I have no interest in saving you from political destruction. And while it is true I hold a soft spot in my heart for America I do not hold the same affection for Israel. For me Islam is the most important consideration in this crisis. The Iranian President is correct in his assessment on this point. We must destroy the blasphemies and lies of the Well Site before they take root in the public consciousness and destroy our world of faith and devotion. Your people are already lost so this no longer a concern. I would go one step further than my compatriot…we must cut off the head of the media snake in this business. I am speaking of the rabble-rousing infidel Lorenzo Cordoba. He is a conduit to the people and his influence has grown beyond reasonable proportion."

"What do you want us to do, assassinate him?"

"No Mr. Crandall we can happily eliminate this problem for you, no need to dirty your own hands with these matters. In return for the destruction of the Well Site, the science messengers and the head of the media snake, Iraq will withdraw its armies to a base inside the Euphrates, giving your Marines time to make an honorable retreat."

"Gentlemen thank you for your input. Please allow me a few moments to consult with my Cabinet on the grave matters before us. I thank you also for your candor and I trust in your continued discretion. If we decide to go forward with this compromise suggestion I'll appoint Secretary of State Malloy to contact your offices with confirmation. Are we in agreement as to the procedures?"

"Yes, agreed," answered President Adjani followed quickly by an agreement from the Iranian President.

The telecom monitors go dark and President Crandall turns his chair to look upon the angry red faces of his Cabinet and agency directors. "It's a simple plan really. It solves most of our international problems and will put out fires domestically. Why are you all looking like someone just stole your wallet?"

"We can't sacrifice innocent Americans like this Mr. President," shouts Secretary Green-Newton. "And all that important history and technology. We can't just dump it in the sewer to appease Islam. I know the Iranians are making serious threats but we have ways to eliminate the nuclear aspects of those threats with surgical strikes. We're the most powerful nation on earth we can't let them walk all over us like this!"

"You're worried about Islam Grazzy," replies Crandall. "But all the great religions of the world are up in arms about this. The Pope himself called me yesterday to tell me the Vatican is considering raising a standing army. Can you imagine? A new Catholic army marauding around the world?"

"Mr. President there's no honor in this plan," states Secretary Malloy. "If we go through with this we'll be held hostage any time Islam gets its buns in a bunch. The country won't even need a Secretary of State if we're going to refuse to try diplomacy in every crisis. And what's next on the Islamic agenda, Sharia Law in the States? We can't go down this horrendous path Sir!"

"I'm worried about not having a country at all Marty. A few scientists and some sketchy history archives aren't worth sacrificing every thing this nation has built for over two hundred years. I don't see we have any other choice and I'm not hearing any good options from any of you! By the way where are Vice-President Murcheson and Dan Maney?"

"The Vice President is meeting with members of Congress to try and mitigate the issues with them and I think Maney might have resigned when he walked out of here an hour ago," suggests Science Advisor Kane. "Mr. President I understand the way you are feeling at this juncture with everything in a box you can't seem to escape. But I urge you to consider what we truly sacrifice when we give up the innocent and all of the knowledge they've uncovered. We throw away the soul of this country is what we accomplish. You spoke of what people died and sacrificed to build for over two hundred years. Well that's not just the physical aspects of the country or its wealth. America is an idea or a set of ideas and beliefs including liberty, freedom and self-expression. The Islamic powers seek to eliminate this grand experiment from the face of the earth. Capitulating to them here on this issue will take us down the slippery slope to our own destruction. In fact America will cease to exist, as we know her. What becomes of the notion of give me liberty or give me death?"

"This is an existential crisis Mr. Kane and I don't believe in the principle of slippery slopes. We have a crisis now…needing solutions applied now. We can't ponder a future we may never have if we fail to solve the crisis at hand."

"But Mr. President," interjects General Broadhead. "I'm an old soldier and I know something of honor on the battlefield. Those innocent scientists aren't soldiers but I'm certain they would not appreciate their own government sacrificing their lives for this no good cause. They live to bring history into the light. They won't appreciate being sacrificed in the name of darkness. If they got killed while we fight for our principles I believe they would rest easy with that. In the larger scope I think the American people would rather us fight for those principles too rather than stand down, betray our fellows and hide our heads in shame."

"Yes I see your point General Broadhead but have you looked outside the window lately? The American people are calling for my head expressly because I decided to send a mission in search of the truth. They don't want the truth…not if such truths challenge their provincial notions of God and history. They're more interested in maintaining religious and science traditions whether or not they have a basis in fact. If you look out on the White House lawn you see trenches of war dug into the grounds and guns aimed at fellow citizens in anger. That General is the measure of American resolve! Those are the principles by which we stand today and I can't see those dynamics changing anytime soon."

"I've listened to you esteemed people and heard your concerns. I understand your commitment to this country and our shared principles. That is why I selected each of you to serve in the first place. But I haven't heard any arguments offering any real solutions to the crisis at hand. Secretary Malloy, please inform the Iraqis and Iranians of my decision."

"Is this your final word Mr. President?" asks Malloy.

"Yes it is."

"Then I respectfully resign my position."

"Ahh Marty you sentimental fool! You can't simply dismiss the wishes of your President. You'll never work in politics the rest of your damn life!"

"On second thought Mr. President, I withdraw my respect!" Malloy rises, stares bitterly at Crandall and stalks from the room, red-faced and heartbroken.

"Secretary Green-Newton the task falls to you."

"No. There's no way, I resign too Mr. President."

"You people don't have the stomach for governance! You're all weak fools. Fine, I'll make the calls myself."

The Cabinet members and agency directors along with staff and aids stand up and leave the room en masse. No one wants to witness the treacherous event. Good people don't enter the rigors of government service to give in to terrorists or sacrifice the innocent. Even in Washington there's no way to spin betrayal.

The President mutters to himself, rubbing his hands together nervously as the group files out of the room like marchers in a funeral dirge. "What a pack of idiots! They're clowns in a circus. In the end all of them will see I'm right. Hell, I am right!"

61

HQ Tent, the Well of Towers
Iraqi Syrian Desert

Private First-Class Steiner runs quickly to General Keith with information about a man from Washington on the comm-link. The hard-tack General scrambled his men to high alert after the slaughter of the Iraqi botanist by terrorists. He was furious with the people in Washington and their vacillating inaction and lack of regard for the safety of Team Babelus and the Marines stationed at the Well Site. The last thing he wants in this dire situation is more gaseous wind from impotent bureaucrats at the Capitol.

"What do they want private? Don't they have any idea we're in the middle of a situation here?"

"I don't know Sir but the man is insistent he speaks to you and only you otherwise I would have gone straight to Major Lee with this."

The two quick-step to the media area of the HQ tent where Major Lee and Gunnery Sergeant Hall are already engaged in conversation with the man from Washington over the comm-link system.

"What's going on here?" General Keith barks at the monitor. "Is everyone in Washington an idiot? We're up to our short hairs in shit over here! Doesn't Washington know we're about to walk right into World War Three?"

"Hello General, National Security Advisor Dan Maney here. In my opinion we've been in World War Three since 911."

"What? The President sends out his flunkies to give us more diplomatic proposals and forward thinking long-range plans cooked up by the weasels at the CIA and the State Department? Where is that dickhead?"

Maney, a former Naval Commander is comfortable with such disrespectful talk and pays no attention to the General's heated bluster. He understands the need to blow off steam toward the top of the chain of command. In the past he's blown a gasket or two himself.

"The President is in communications with the leaders of Iraq and Iran so he's tied up at the moment and you get me."

"Pardon me if I don't give a flyin' fuck about the President's busy schedules Mr. Maney! What the hell are you doing on my comm-link?"

"You are authorized to form and deploy an emergency rescue task force to enter the Well Site and get our people to safety immediately and without reservation."

"We can use deadly force?"

"Without reservation General."

"That comes from the top?"

"Again, without reservation General Keith."

"Major Lee form up immediately!" shouts the General as he turns from the comm-link monitor and puts his new orders into action. "That was just about the strangest communication I've had in long time," he thinks. "They must be getting desperate in Washington. I would have expected General Broadhead at the very least. Orders are orders so I guess it doesn't matter what level of the administration delivers them. But there's something different about that Maney guy, he's not the usual Washington fruitcake tap dancing around ten dollar words and diplomatic protocol."

"Major is your team mustered and ready to get moving?"

"Yes Sir, has been all day!"

"Obviously Washington is bit slower on the trigger Major."

"With all due respect Sir, fuck Washington!"

"I wholeheartedly agree with your sentiments Major Lee but I seem to recall your ancestors pretty much did that once and it didn't turn out so well. The problem is when ya fuck Washington it fucks ya right back only with them it's a gangbang. Move on out Major and keep the communications open!"

"Aye Aye Sir!"

Major Lee leads a squad of ten Marines including Gunnery Sergeant Hall and Lieutenant Jenks out into the sunlight, boarding a Sea Stallion and heading over the top of the Well Site. As they fly toward their destination no one knows the size of the enemy's forces, no one cares. This is a killing mission and they're going to do their jobs with cold efficiency.

• • •

Dan Maney unhooks his lapel microphone and turns toward the White House communications technician manning the comm-link gear. "Son if anyone asks tell them I had a gun pointed to your head and you had no choice."

"That communication wasn't authorized Sir?"

"This is America Son, the land of the free and the home of the brave. We don't stand by to watch while innocent people are slaughtered so we can appease tyrants. There are times when a patriot must do his duty and disobey orders. This is one of those times. In a way it's the only real American ideal we have left."

62

Undisclosed Location
City of Avinen

The haunting blood-curdling scream of Ahmed the Botanist wakes Jake from his near-comatose state. His eyes blink open and shut rapidly, flicking away the fog of unconsciousness. He lay there unable to move but his mind is alert and lucid. He hears loud chants of Allahu Akbar, then a scream of unvarnished fear followed by cold silent death. He hears men dancing around the room in celebration and he struggles to move his limbs. His hands and feet are free and unrestrained by ropes or ties but his muscles refuse his brain's requests to move. Jake felt this way before, when waking up from a long night of partying.

In the background Jake can hear a man with a Middle Eastern accent screaming epithets in English. The man screeches at his victim, "Do you like this filthy whore? Do you like the blood of this man running down your face?" Jake manages to turn his head toward the loud shouts and sees Kelly Anne, bound by hands and feet, shoved against a wall, a man rubbing a severed head over her face and breasts while he laughs lustfully.

"You're unclean!" Kelly Anne shouts as she turns her head away.

Kelly Anne's seemingly benign statement sends the shouting man reeling backwards on his feet. He throws the severed head at the wall next to the helpless woman where it strikes with a dull thud and rolls a few feet away. The man now engulfed in overpowering anger spits into Kelly Anne's face. He grabs the lapels of her flight suit and throws her body against the hard wall over and over again all the while spitting out furious shouts in a language Jake doesn't recognize. Jake's adrenaline begins to well up and the feeling returns to his extremities.

A rhythmic chant rises from men standing guard over Team Babelus. *Allahu Akbar. Allahu Akbar. Allahu Akbar.* It begins slowly in a soft tone. The furiously angered man seizes Kelly Anne by her long hair and brutally drags her across the room scraping her body along the rough floor. She kicks and screams mightily and fights bravely but her restraints keep her from escaping the terrorist's clutches.

The chants grow steadily louder and increase with intensity. *Allahu Akbar! Allahu Akbar! Allahu Akbar! Allahu Akbar! Allahu Akbar!* The terrorist spits phrases in English at Kelly

Anne, "You filthy whore! You filthy whore! You will pay for your crimes with your life! I will hoist your head to the world and prove the power of Allah!"

Chanting grows louder and insanely furious, *Allahu Akbar! Allahu Akbar! Allahu Akbar! Allahu Akbar! Allahu Akbar! Allahu Akbar! Allahu Akbar! Allahu Akbar! Allahu Akbar!*

The terrorist throws Kelly Anne to the floor face down. He sits on her back and pulls her head up by the hair exposing her throat. Kelly Anne feels the cold steel of the scimitar against the front of her neck. The chants grow to a feverishly wicked incantation. *Allahu Akbar! Allahu Akbar! Allahu Akbar! Allahu Akbar! Allahu Akbar! Allahu Akbar! Allahu Akbar! Allahu Akbar! Allahu Akbar! Allahu Akbar!*

63

The first kill is deadly silent. An expert killing machine blasts through the room like a wind from the chilled black breath of the Grim Reaper. The terrorist leader is the first to fall, his throat slit from ear to ear in a perfect happy face swoosh, the blade of his scimitar falling harmlessly clinking on the hard floor. The four remaining terrorist thugs freeze in stunned shock as Jake Nichols continues his deadly work. The terrorists move toward him, leaving their captives and the former Navy SEAL Commander proceeds to rip them limb from limb.

Jake delivers the first blow in an upper cutting motion, his Navy issue survival knife piercing upwards into the lower jaw, through the mouth and into the brain of an onrushing terrorist. He falls to the side, dead in an instant. Jake wheels around, his right elbow meeting the face of another attacker sending him reeling. Team Babelus springs into action. Tasha, freed of the boot on her throat leaps to the aid of the team and uses her own knife to free them of their plastic tie bonds.

Dr. Kagen rushes into the fray tackling a terrorist against a wall. He holds the terrorists arms to his sides kicking him furiously while KO grabs him by the throat and chokes the life out of him. Jake throws his arm around a terrorist's neck and flips him onto the ground in a single motion, his head crashing to the ground in a loud THUNK, blood draining out onto the floor. Jake straddles his prey, sandwiches his head between his powerful arms, twists like a cowboy wrestling a steer and snaps his neck to the muted crackling sound of bones breaking underneath thick skin.

Tasha slashes her knife at a terrorist as he backs away. She rushes at him and he falls backwards over Kelly Anne. Screaming a Rebel yell Tasha springs onto the terrorist's midsection and repeatedly thrusts her knife into his chest. With both hands clutching the knife handle she raises the weapon high above her head and pounds it into flesh bone and cartilage while Kelly Anne simultaneously slams the terrorist's head against the floor screaming uncontrollably. The man is dead after several blows but the furious women continue their operation. Kelly Anne pulls the headscarf from the terrorists face and recoils at the sight, falling backward on her butt.

"Brian!" she shouts. "Its Brian Saylor!"

Tasha pauses from her deadly work and immediately recognizes the traitor. She stands over him, quietly at first. Then, overcome with emotion she starts kicking the dead traitor's sides. "You led them to us you fucking traitor!" she screams as she kicks madly. "You're supposed to be an assimilated Muslim you fucking fag! You were our friend! You killed Ahmed! You killed Ahmed!" She continues mindlessly kicking the lifeless corpse lying on the ground over and over again shouting obscenities and taunts as her steel reinforced toes slash into dead flesh. "That's the power of Allah, I'll show you the power of Allah you fucking degenerate bastard!"

KO wraps his beefy arms around the emotionally charged redhead nearly enveloping her in his strength. "Its ok now Tasha," he whispers tenderly in her ear as she squirms to get free. "It's ok, it's ok, he's dead now, you can't kill him any deader." Tasha slumps, surrendering her fury to KO's strength and manly tenderness, tears streaming down her cheeks. "I don't care how dead he is KO. I want the cameras to pick this up. I want every mother fucking Islamic asshole to know they can't take over the world. Ahmed was our friend. He was the bravest one of us all. I wish the world made a lot more Muslims like him."

The Team backs away from the bodies and stands in the dim light, a band of survivors dripping in blood and sweat, bruised and battered but still alive. Kelly Anne, hair mottled over her face walks over to Jake and thanks him for his lifetime of saving other people from harm. She drapes her arms around his neck, leans her head against his chest and sobs. Jake looks around the room wondering about the general location and the possibility of other terrorists.

"I don't know exactly where we are Jake." Informs a heavy breathing Dr. Kagen. "We didn't travel very far to get here. My guess is we're in the same complex. I have no idea if there are others down here. Why didn't anyone warn us they were coming?"

"They probably didn't see them until it was too late," allows Tasha, the cameras on our wrists would only pick up things in our immediate vicinity. I can't tell you where we are either Jake I lost my GPS. But if the doctor's right then we should find our camp not too far away from here."

Footsteps and chatter in a foreign language from an adjacent area invade the Team's space. "We need to get out of here fast!" warns Jake as he leads them through a long passageway. "Let's go this way, maybe we'll get around them without being seen. KO what's that language they're speaking? It sounds like Arabic but I don't recognize a single word."

"Ehh, its Semitic for sure but not Arabic or Hebrew. I think its some kind of Aramaic or a modern adaptation of the ancient language of the Assyrians."

"Aramaic? Isn't that a dead language KO?" asks Kelly Anne.

"Apparently not anymore. The Assyrians conquered the lands around them and forced the language on the captive populace. It was spoken in Babylon and a lot of the Bible is written in it. The only time I've seen it in modern times is in that Mel Gibson movie about Jesus Christ."

"So it's the language of the conquerors?" asks Tasha.

"Yeah, pretty much."

"Oh perfect, that's just perfect."

64

The team races toward an opening at the building's exterior followed hotly by at least two-dozen Aramaic speaking pursuers. They spill out into the plaza of the central complex and run toward base camp where they keep the ATVs and guns. They approach the camp, find their gear intact and mount the ATVs in preparation to make a quick escape. Shots ring out and Dr. Kagen is struck in the thigh and knocked off of his vehicle. The team scrambles to the ground while grabbing M-16 rifles from the holsters on the left sides of the ATVs. KO crawls around to the trailer hitched to his six-wheeled ATV and pulls two ammo boxes over to the hunkered down explorers. They dig in and prepare to face the enemy in a straight up firefight.

A fusillade of bullets darts into the mossy ground around the Team and they fire back into the dark void. Tasha wriggles over to the Mobilite and points it in the direction of the gunfire bathing the enemy position in a bright searing light. They fire volleys into the heart of the enemy's position felling one or two with each round. Shrapnel from an enemy grenade blast falls perilously close to the team's position and they scramble backwards behind a high-density ceramic balustrade in front of the Library Building.

Bullets bounce off the ceramic parapet as the Team continues to fire on the enemy position, the location of which grows ever closer. The enemy makes futile attempts to shoot out the lights at the top of Mobilite pole. Having failed they shoot at its base, striking its half-full propane tank and igniting a brilliant explosion lighting up the dark underground city.

The team's position between the balustrade and the building offers no escape route. They continue firing at a vicious desperate pace, each vowing to fight to the death for the lives of their teammates. The enemy suffers casualties and gives none back but they continue to close in on the team's position with superior numbers and plenty of firepower, threatening to overwhelm them in a matter of moments. "We can't kill these suckers fast enough," yells Jake over the din of gunfire and grenade blasts. "We need more firepower! Kelly Anne it's time to pray for a miracle if you still believe in them!"

"Of course I still believe in them Jake! In case you haven't noticed we're still alive and I haven't personally killed you yet!" she yells as she prays furiously to her God in Heaven.

A continuous volley of gunfire rings out from the team's left flank raining a hail of bullets down on the enemy position. Bullets stop hitting the area around the Team as the enemy adjusts to the crossfire, training their guns at the flank.

"It's the Marines, it's the Marines!" Tasha shrieks in delight. "Whenever you pray for a miracle I'll be damned if the

Marines don't show up on your flank to save your ass! Talk about the right hand of God!"

Three soldiers make their way through the gunfire to the Team's position and motion for them to head for the ATVs. They crawl on their bellies and elbows, rifles firmly in hand, to the escape vehicles. Kelly Anne mounts the back portion of the seat on an ATV piloted by Major Lee. She jams her feet squarely against the safety lights on the back as she faces the rear of the machine, her back snug against the Major's back. Tasha takes a similar position on an ATV driven by Gunny Hall. Lieutenant Jenks lays on his belly aiming a continuous stream of cover fire toward the enemy position. The rest of the team mounts ATVs, starts them up and they ride off down the mossy highway toward the open gash in the earth…now an escape hatch.

Enemy forces follow the Marine's retreat, each side continuing the firefight. Kelly Anne and Tasha fire their M-16 rifles from makeshift turret positions while Jake, KO and Dr. Kagen ride ATVs with one hand on the handle and the other firing at the enemy. The fury of battle quiets the further they ride into the darkness until the only sound around them comes from the whining engines of the ATVs.

As the sounds of armed conflict fade off in the distance the Team holsters their weapons. The men can now concentrate on the road ahead. Tasha and Kelly Anne swivel their bodies around and straddle the ATV seats in considerably more comfortable positions. Kelly Anne wraps her arms around the Major and presses the side of her head firmly into his shoulder blades. Despite all she'd been through in the past several hours she feels safe and secure holding tightly to her hero.

Tasha stands on the back foot pegs of the ATV, wraps her arms around Gunny Hall's neck and speaks into his ear. "You are one crusty old jarhead Gunny but I love you anyway!" Though he'd fought in countless battles the world over this is first time in his life the old Gunnery Sergeant believes he's done something good for his country. For once he is in the right war at the right time.

Dr. Kagen hollers out to Jake that he isn't feeling too well. The team stops and Kelly Anne walks over to take a look at the thigh wound the Doctor suffered early in the battle. She unzips the top of her flight suit, removes her undershirt, tears it in long strips, dresses the Doctor's wound and ties a makeshift tourniquet to his upper leg. "I'm sorry we don't have better bandages to dress your wounds Doctor, we left the first-aid kits back at the camp. This should hold until we reach the surface."

"That's perfectly Ok Kelly Anne, I'll manage. And please call me Doc. All of you call me Doc from now on!"

On the way to the opening Jack thinks about the spiritual journey of Team Babelus and how they progress and stick together through thick and thin battling terrorists and bureaucrats alike. He appreciates the journey of discovery for himself as well as the crew. It took a lot for Dr. Kagen to let people into his heart and his gesture is duly noted.

65

Well of Towers Opening
380 Feet Below the Surface

A convoy of ATVs rolls up a hill to its crest. Weary riders dismount the rumbling machines, flexing and stretching tired and stiff muscles in an effort to loosen them up. The team arrives at the spot where their epic underground journey started, at the bottom of a vast gaping hole in the earth. They stand in the sunlight beaming down into the deep cavity. The warmth is exquisite as they hadn't so much as seen the sun for a few days and its rays fill them with energy.

While they stand at the crest of the mound conversing on the plan to get to the surface they hear the sound of a massive crowd of people gathered around the Well Site barely a football field length away. They look up to see Iraqi citizens lining the outer rim of the Well, shouting, screaming and gesticulating wildly toward the group below. A flurry of rocks and stones begin to fall around the group, first as light thuds into the mossy groundcover then increasing into a hail of missiles landing heavily. The Team stands for an instant, unable to process the danger. A spark of recognition catches up to them and they bolt down the hill in search for cover.

"Oh shit what now?" Jake cries out. "Where's the Marine helicopter that's supposed to ferry us out if this hell hole Major?"

"I have no idea Jake, those people weren't up there a few hours ago when we dropped down here. I'm trying to raise General Keith on the comm-link but I'm not getting through to anybody. Its as if they're not there at all, just disappeared!"

Rocks, stones and now boulders continue to rain down on the sunlit area while the Team sits behind a large tower edifice trying to figure a way out. Escaping through the hole is impossible with thousands of angry Muslims trying to stone them to death. Bigger boulders and large chunks of earth begin to rain down into the space. "Maybe they're trying to fill in the hole," offers Kelly Anne. "Obviously they don't want the technology and historical ideas down here to make it to the surface."

"And I'm sure they don't want us coming up there either," adds KO. "We're famous alright Kelly Anne…infamous!"

As Major Lee works his communicator over in an effort to raise a signal the other Marines of the rescue team come into view and race up the hill, firing their weapons to the rear. Lieutenant Jenks makes it to the Team's position first and breathlessly reports most of the enemy got killed in the firefight at the main complex but the Marines ran into a fresh group on their way back to the rendezvous site. Although they took no casualties the enemy reinforcements number over a hundred and have the Marines on the run. "I apologize for leading them here," shouts Lieutenant Jenks. "I expected you folks to be rescued and gone by now. We thought we'd have our own set of reinforcements to help us out of here."

"No you're wrong about that Lieutenant," Jake barks. "Not only do you have hostiles firing at us from the rear but our escape route is cut off by thousands of Iraqi citizens. And they're raining hell down on our parade!"

Rocks, boulders and sections of earth continue to fall in a continuous dusty barrage. Enemy fighters gather behind a low-slung ceramic deck. Team Babelus and the Marine contingent dig in behind a steep escarpment in front of a tower with a concave depression creating a fort against attacks to the rear and on their flanks. The arrangement allows them to fight on one front but this time the enemy boasts vastly superior numbers and escape routes are nonexistent.

While the two sides exchange sporadic gunfire challenging each other's defenses a voice rings out through the din coming from the general direction of the Team's right rear flank. "Jackson Nichols! Jackson Nichols! Over here!" cries a loud male voice.

Jake turns to the direction of the voice but sees nothing through the dust. "I hope that's not the voice of God calling me home!" he wonders out loud.

"Its ok Jake you only have to worry about the other guy's voice calling you home," Kelly Anne jokes, maintaining a sense of humor through dire conditions.

"I'm gonna go check it out you guys stay put."

"Jackson Nichols! Jackson Nichols! Over here!" Cries the voice. Jake follows the sound of the voice through the ever-thickening cloud of dust. He rounds a building. A pair of outstretched hands reach out and pull him into a portico.

"Hey buddy, how ya doin?"

"I'll be damned," stammers Jake. "Lorenzo Cordoba! What the hell are you doing here?"

"I'm saving your ass Jake," answers the television reporter. "Don't tell anybody though I don't want to ruin my reputation and watch my ratings slide."

"Yeah ok Lorenzo, I'm gonna go get the others, I'll be right back."

66

Jake bolts to the Team's position and informs them Lorenzo Cordoba is down in the Well and he has an escape route. Team Babelus and the Marines stand there with puzzled looks. "Lorenzo Cordoba?" asks Kelly Anne. "You sure he isn't sending us into a worse situation so he can film the whole massacre? How did a TV reporter get down here? This just keeps getting more surreal by the moment!"

"Look I told you, Lorenzo is a patriot deep down inside. He's got an escape route and we're gonna take it. Is everybody with me?"

"We're with you Jake!" shouts Major Lee, "But we'll need a diversion so the enemy doesn't follow us to wherever we're headed."

The Marines devise a makeshift cluster bomb built on the spot out of an ATV loaded with grenades and the fuel tanks of the other ATVs. Tasha rigs a firing mechanism to automatically pull the pins from the grenades at roughly the same time. "I like the way you overcome and adapt young lady," says Gunny Hall with fatherly pride. The Marines set the deadly ATV toward the enemy's right flank where it explodes in a huge fireball a mere five feet from the enemy position. Team Babelus sneaks through the hazy dust in the other direction meeting up with Lorenzo at the entrance of a tunnel.

"Hi gang!" greets Lorenzo. "I'd like you to meet the author of your escape and for that matter your entire adventure. This man beside me is Mahmoud al-Karim and the beast next to him is his loyal donkey Jaffah. They discovered this place."

"Wow, you're alive?" asks Kelly Anne. "Everyone assumed you died in the cave-in!"

"Yes, yes we are alive," answers Mahmoud. "We fell into the hole and landed on a chariot of fire Allah left for us. We found a tunnel leading us away from the hole and this is the tunnel. But we must hurry there are many dangers afoot."

The group makes its way through a long tunnel hollowed out from bedrock. The scrapings and structure of the interior walls appear man made. As they trek through the long passageway the ground starts to shake in a low far off rumble. The jostling and shaking continues to build to a violent crescendo.

"Earthquake!" someone shouts.

They all run towards where they first entered the cave to avoid getting trapped if its roof collapses. They gather at the entrance while the ground continues to shake violently. Vast sections of dirt crash to the base of the hole along with thousands of people who lined the rim at the surface. Rivers of black crude oil gush over the north side of the city wall.

"We better not stay here!" yells Major Lee as the chaos continues. "Our chances are better in the tunnel!"

The group runs back into the tunnel as the City of Avinen finally falls to the elements, its protective shields no longer useful or operational. The Team, its rescue contingent and Lorenzo Cordoba's camera crew run for more than a mile through the tunnel's dark path led by a surprisingly speedy woodcarver and a braying donkey. The ground stops shaking before they reach the surface and an eerie silence pervades the area. The sounds of running people gasping for breath, along with the whining brays of a donkey, echo through the cave. They follow a small light in the distance growing larger as they run. The entire contingent literally springs from a hole in the ground like ants from a hill and into the hot Iraqi sun.

A short distance away Lorenzo Cordoba's modified military helicopter sits waiting to take the its eager passengers to safety, away from the mysteries and dangers of Mesopotamia. Everyone crawls into the 1960s version of the Sea Stallion transport helicopter as its rotor blades start spinning. The transport is painted in the bright colors of Cordoba's TV network, the bird's nose featuring a large logo painting of Snoopy flying his Sopwith Camel doghouse…ready to splash the elusive Red Baron.

The giant transport lifts from the ground slowly and heavily. They fly over the Well Site to get a look at the destruction. Massive sheets of earth sink in along the sides of the city and dark sticky oil floods the metropolis-sized chamber. They fly across the breadth of the Site with the crew and passengers looking out the sides and through windows. Below them the ground heaves and bellows creating a thick dusty cloud. The ground seems to swell for a moment growing upwards toward the helicopter and then settles down again slightly higher than its original surface depth.

"Hey Jake look down there," whispers Tasha as they fly over a small section about the size of an acre. "Do you see the green glow in the hole? I think someone's turned on the shields. Perhaps Avinen isn't destroyed after all."

Jake glances over at Tasha and notices a pair of scan-cans glistening through an opening in her back-pack along with a mysterious gold-tinted triangular object. Let's keep this to ourselves Tash, we may need the information in the future. And quit looking back there you might turn us all into a pillar of salt."

67

Cordoba One Transport Helicopter
En Route Towards the Euphrates River

The huge old helicopter slowly lumbers away from the Well Site ferrying its weary passengers toward Baghdad International Airport and the Company owned FEDEX airplane that will take them home to their lives. Lorenzo Cordoba, normally energetic and animated, sits exhausted slumping down in his plush swivel chair. His nature begs him to ask grueling questions of the passengers but as he looks toward them, tired and torn his compassion gets the better of him and he refrains.

"These are some digs Cordoba." Jake addresses Lorenzo. "I don't think the President flies around in a rig so opulent. Is this Corinthian leather on the seats?"

"C'mon Jake, give a reporter his due. And no, there's no such thing as Corinthian leather."

Jake sits next to Tasha. The pair chats quietly about the twists and turns of their adventure and what awaits them back in the States. KO and the freshly christened Doc sink into comfortable side facing seats barely saying a word. Doc nurses his festering wound and readjusts the soiled bandages but cannot abate the searing pain. He hopes Kelly Anne can re-dress the gash with supplies on the Lucky Lady. Kelly Anne and Major Lee slump together on a bench seat basking in the warmth of their bodies. They sit with melancholy expressions of the type expected of teenagers in love.

As the great bird works its way over the horizon towards Baghdad the voice of the pilot blares over the intercom system. "Everyone look out the port side there's something you really might want to see."

Having seen plenty over the past few days nobody scrambles immediately toward the port side windows but eventually get there. Staring through sand pocked windows they see two darkly morbid mushroom clouds soaring into the Eastern heavens.

"Is that what I think it is?" asks Jake.

"Yes I believe so." Lorenzo answers wearily. "The blasts probably caused the earthquake. While you guys were down in the hole the rest of the planet was going through one of its periodic world changing epochs. I hate to tell you about all this but I suppose I'm as good a reporter as anyone so here goes. You should know President Crandall traded your lives and the Well Site to appease Islamic radicals and the leaders of Iran and Iraq. He also tacitly approved of my own assassination but that's a story for a different day and believe me I intend to tell it, loudly."

"Anyway, Crandall struck a deal with the Iraqis and the Iranians calling for the destruction of the Well Site. All the religious orders around the world started rioting in the streets as my reports became public. Not because the reports were inaccurate but they got torn apart and recast as the Devil coming up from Hell or some such thing."

"Muslim leaders especially wanted to destroy Avinen and the very idea of its existence. So Crandall went along with this, allegedly for the sake of peace. The Iraqis would stand down their armies and the Iranians would suspend their intended nuclear tests. Well of course it didn't work out that way at all. The Iraqis betrayed the agreement first and continued to march their armies toward the Well Site. They were met by ten thousand Marines and the battle continues somewhere below us up to this moment."

"So that's where our rescue team ended up." Major Lee shakes his head.

"Well listen to this news flash. President Crandall was at the Situation Room watching this global betrayal unfold right before his very eyes and he had a heart attack. He fell dead, right there on the spot. Paramedics worked on him for an hour but he was dead as dead gets, gave up the ghost. You know, he was under considerable strain. The White House, under armed siege by American citizens of every stripe at the time, managed to escape damage. Islamic radicals threatened to undo all the sacrifices we made in the War on Terror and Iran openly confirmed they were about to lob a nuke over Tel-Aviv. I think Crandall's heart just gave up. And I mean the heart in his soul not only the physical one."

"There's nothing worse than your soul giving up!" Doc shakes his head back and forth.

Lorenzo continues his news report. "I'd feel sorry for him being the elected leader of our country and all but you know, with the assassination thing and giving you and the Well Site up like in a corrupt bargain… You see, I think when you start a proposition out with a betrayal you're liable to get the same courtesy slapped back in your face. So I don't really feel all too sorry about his death."

"Who had the balls to launch the nukes?" asks KO.

"I'm getting there, I'm getting there. So Vice-President Murcheson takes over immediately and gets down to brass tacks. She is one tough bird that one and I don't think the Iranians knew what they we're in for. Sure they blustered like they always do but Murcheson laid down the law and took no prisoners. First she ordered 100,000 troops to relieve General Keith and his 10,000 Marines and made a big public spectacle about it on TV, right from the Oval Office. Then she ordered two carrier battle groups into the Gulf of Oman. If you've never seen a carrier battle group close up, well, you haven't known fear. I guess no one backed down though as you can see the nukes went off. Maybe she simply said enough is enough. Now the Iraqi Army is down on the ground putting up their dukes in the open desert …the pitiful fools. I would have thought we trained them better. They make a nice fat target from the air out there."

"So anyway, Murcheson, now the President negotiates with the Iranians. Well I shouldn't exactly use the term negotiate. She gave them an ultimatum; stop the nukes or get nuked. The Iranian President went on worldwide television and mocked her, actually taunted her thinking he was calling her bluff I guess. Obviously the Iranians mistook Crandall's vacillating nature for the resolve of the American people, big mistake. As you can see out the window we sent a couple of nukes their way…one to the Arak Power Facility and the other to the Dezful test site. From the positions and size of the mushroom clouds I would guess the bombs weren't the largest we had in our arsenal. These appear to be tactical nukes, probably launched from a submarine out in the Gulf. And the location suggests we probably took out the nuclear testing site by the Iraq border and the Arak nuclear power plant in northeast Iran. Murcheson is smart, I think she knows she doesn't have to go full-bore to scare the bejeezus out of these saber rattling tyrants. I wonder what the North Koreans are thinking about now?"

"I'm sure the tensions around the White House and in the streets of America will subside with Crandall's death and Congress will quit calling for his impeachment, uh, maybe."

"They've vowed to hold hearings though and I suspect all of us will get subpoenas and have to testify before some select committee. That'll be a joke I can assure you. They'll ask questions that come across more like scolding speeches, preening for the cameras the whole time. Eventually they'll produce an exhaustive report exhausting nothing but the reader's patience and all the King's men and all the King's horses will go on with life…status quo."

Jake remains curious how a television reporter knew where to find Team Babelus. "How did you know about the Well Site in the first place Lorenzo?"

"My ex girlfriend told me all about it after the Gunny Sergeant and reporter were taken out in Baghdad. She sent me here to both report the story and to protect you guys."

"What is your ex, a government official?"

"Well, yeah…her name was Kate Ross then but she goes by Murcheson now."

"Murches…you mean the Vice President, uh, I mean, ha ha, the President of the United States is your ex girlfriend, Lorenzo?"

"Heh, heh, yeah brother you know I do get around some."

"You dog! Does this mean you'll get invited to Christmas Dinner at the White House?"

"Hey Pal, remember, she's married now and she's responsible for saving your lives so give her a break."

"She's also responsible for giving you the scoop of your career…you lucky dog. I should follow you around more."

"Hey Lorenzo do you know who or what the people were that attacked us at the Well Site?" asks Major Lee. "They all wore a Syrian style uniform but according to KO here they speak in a modern form of Aramaic. Have you heard anything about that?"

"Oh yeah and its not good news. Here's where the world may need to make a stand…though I doubt the resolve of most Western nations."

"The bunch you're talking about are formed by the world's united Islamic governments. They're called the *Protectors of the Guided One*…something to do with the 12th Imam legends. They're building an army of Jihadis made up of soldiers from every Islamic country in the world. In the future you'll see these fighters in every conceivable flavor, Indonesian, Persian, Arabic, Chechen or whatever."

"They also recruit from countries with large Islamic populations so you'll see French, German, Australian, British and possibly American fighters join their ranks. They modeled the force after the United Nation's blue helmet peacekeeping forces, only they know how to fight."

"What's more they claim they have a right to do this, that is, form their own international body and supply it with an army. In that context it's hard to argue the point. Of course we may have to go to war with them."

"This army is a lot more dangerous than al-Qaeda or fringe terrorist groups because its state-sponsored, powered by all that oil money, and it will grow much larger as the Islamic governments are going to require service, like a draft. Now these fighters will grow to a vast international army and they hold no allegiances to their host countries. That's why they speak Aramaic, the language of the conquerors. They get indoctrinated to fully surrender to Islam and all the Muslim states of the world will use them for the benefit of the greater *ummah*."

"Didn't the CIA know about these new fighters?" Asked Major Lee.

"Uh no I guess not."

"How do you know so much about them?"

"I'm a reporter Major Lee and I'm not restricted by Congress or some fool judges on what I can investigate or whether or not I can work with unsavory characters. The CIA and other intelligence agencies are bound by the codes of political correctness. If you've seen my show you know that sort of foolishness doesn't tie me down. I found out about them through their tailor in Venezuela."

"Their tailor?"

"Heh, heh, Yeah, sort of…they have their uniforms made in Venezuela to get them done cheaply and I know a guy who knows a guy."

Jake listens to Lorenzo's narrative with mild amusement. Nothing in the story surprises him in the least. "I've always wondered if Muslims would ever wise up and get together. The only reason we could defeat them from the days of Darius until now is they're always fractured and fighting amongst themselves and the West can pack together on occasion. I hope the West hasn't lost that spirit."

"Yeah right! Send those pukes to Texas, we'll brand a Lone Star on their Aramaic speakin' butts!" shouts the diminutive redhead from a seat in the back.

If the Rebel Yell of a saucy girl-sprite of a scientist isn't crushed easily, perhaps the West has a little juice left in the tank.

68

Dirksen Senate Office Building
Committee Room 226
Washington, D.C.

President Murcheson signed Bill SR4237 calling for the creation of a select commission to study and report on the Well Site Operation. The newly enacted committee, named the *Origins Commission*, is composed of four members from each major political party; four Republicans, including a sitting U.S. Senator, a former U.S Senator, a former Chairman of the Joint Chiefs of Staff and a Christian Theologian; four Democrats, a Science Ethicist from Dartmouth University, a Geneticist from Harvard University, a sitting U.S. Senator and a sitting U.S.

Congressman; four Federalists, a Sitting U.S. Senator, an Islamic Theologian, a leading Archeologist from the University of Minnesota, a noted Atheist Paleontologist. The Republican former Chairman of the Joint Chiefs, Admiral Euless Foster, Ret., grandly serves as Commission Chair.

The *Origins Commission* hearings travel the route Lorenzo Cordoba originally predicted. Politicians, religious leaders scientists and retired military professionals lobby, politic and fight to get on the newly formed committee; Witnesses get subpoenaed, some fight to quash and others gladly appear; blowhard politicians read pre-approved speeches doubling as lectures, complete with media-friendly sound bites; affinity groups trot out experts to support wholly unrelated agendas. The Washington-style circus surely suffers by comparison with seedy carnival sideshows and bothersome street mimes. America's less than dignified modern-day system of governance once again stands on a pedestal proving to the world its similarities to a drowning ship of fools.

Commission members and witnesses preen for the cameras, the media breathlessly reports every hair out of place, the attire and attitudes of the witnesses and political leanings of all involved. American citizens tune in to view the televised spectacle via special network telecasts, featuring top anchors and network dandies, 24/7 cable news coverage with all-day talking head analysis and squabbling guest experts. Print media joins the fray with overly written above the fold front cover news features and stories. As the hearings get underway Americans watch with genuine anticipation but as participants sink into partisan bickering and finger pointing exercises public interest falls into a state of bemused apathy.

At the end of the proceedings the *Origins Commission* produces a tri-partisan report, 30,000 pages in length. The massive tome contains exceptionally verbose paragraphs detailing vague arguments and ambiguous conclusions. In the end the huge book is whole cloth, barely discernible from the intellectual heft of the local yellow pages. By the end hardly anyone outside Washington cares, most barely remembering the furious anger and open rebellion nearly felling the Federal Government a year before. Public interest grows dramatically for the last few days of hearings as the Commission summons members of Team Babelus to appear…followed closely by a phalanx of television cameras and news reporters.

Team Babelus dutifully responds to subpoenas, arriving together as a unit, presenting Congress with an impenetrable fortress against ignorance and intolerance. On their arrival Stateside the team was met with skepticism and distrust. But as they calmly and forthrightly answer questions and cut through the hypocrisies and blusters of the political windbags in Washington a clearer picture emerges and the American public comes to see them as true heroes, brave, honest and strong. As usual Americans shift distrust and frustration toward the government and away from the 'regular as you and me' folk filling their television screens with first hand tales of an ancient civilization and its ramifications.

Members of the *Origins Commission* sit in ornately gilded large stuffed leather chairs and aim questions, shout conclusions, start rumors and lecture from on high in a lofty position at the front of the grand wood-paneled committee hall. Witnesses endure ceaseless hours of questioning under the bright spotlight of withering examinations. Many witnesses, unused to such harshly public criticisms and accusations wilt under the pressure, others simply returned to obscurity. Team Babelus, each member having built up a tolerance for bluster and bullshit over a lifetime of iconoclastic behavior weather the storms with remarkable alacrity. As Jake would later remark to a fresh reporter intimidated by Washington ballyhoo, "Hell, we've lived our entire lives to get pounded on a big stage like this by politicians and experts!"

Examinations and cross examinations of members of Team Babelus stretch over the course of four days. Each endures hours of accusations, criticisms and lectures but all hold their own, fending off rhetorical thrusts while bludgeoning the examiners with clear concise truth. Americans take notice of the truths told and wisdom dispensed by Team Babelus and never forgive the government for its lack of respect and decorum toward fellow citizens sent by the same government to do a dangerous job.

69

"America is the greatest nation on God's Green Earth," lectures the Republican Senator from Georgia as he presses Jake for answers. "I believe this in my deepest heart. We have the best form of government ever devised, at least the best I know. Are you going to explain to the long suffering God-fearing Americans who have struggled for two hundred years on the Judeo-Christian principles of freedom and liberty their sacrifices are built upon the sands of a fairy tale?"

"Senator there is good and evil in all parts of the world, even in America," answers Jake. "Our experiences at Avinen prove the maxim true throughout all of history and in all societies. While I agree democracy is the finest form of human self-governance on the earth today I cannot say this is true as weighed against all forms in all societies throughout history. I've never lived under any of those systems and neither have you. All we know about them is what writers of the age left us…providing they came from the winning side.

If you're asking me to pass moral judgments on any other society I can only do so while at the same time examining the systems we live under today. America is not perfect nor is its system of governance. Perhaps history can give us better guides than the limited knowledge we have today. It's entirely possible other forms of governance in the ancient past are a higher vision than what we live today. By all accounts Avinen was egalitarian and held no specific hierarchy. No one was elected to office and no person was beneath another, ever. In theory, American democracy tries to replicate an egalitarian form of governance with a government built by the people of the people. In practice it is something altogether different."

"How dare you impugn the American form of government in this way, it is an outrage! Democracy is the highest form of governance that has ever existed!"

"I don't know about your assumptions Senator. Would you say the system in what you call Heaven is less than that of the United States? There's no democracy in Heaven. It is time we disabuse ourselves of the notion that our time, these modern times are the pinnacle of all thought and reason. History is not a linear pageant played out in a straight line from one point at the beginning of time and progressing through to the present day. History churns over time. One society may grow highly advanced in technology and philosophy and then get destroyed by a less advanced group, its technologies washed away by the sands of time. All we think we know right now may be less than what another society knew long before us. Its possible the people of the world today are the degraded end of the line and this includes the forms of government we choose to live under or are forced upon us."

"Are you inferring the American form of governance is forced upon the people?"

"No Senator but over time the government has instituted practices protecting the survival of the government often weighed against the freedoms of the people. Vast unelected bureaucracies form the better part of the U.S. government nowadays and I don't believe the Constitution contains a Bureaucrat Branch. The American government is a shell of its early promise of a system for the people and by the people. Why is this? Government seeks to create an impenetrable fortress impossible to overthrow. Now Senator, I love our land and its people but our system of governance, chiefly through the Federal Government has grown bloated, fat and complacent in its own power, no matter the political party in charge at any given time. The beings at Avinen grew complacent in their time in much the same manner, eventually using their wonderfully creative gifts to produce a race of slaves who spiraled out of control. In so doing they lost the soul of their people. I believe there is a valuable lesson in the story Senator if we choose to listen to the music of history."

"America was founded on a unique set of ideals but until the government is once again of the people it will continue to grow in power like a cancerous blight on the nation's soul. Only as we seek the wisdom of the Founders, ideas laid out over 200 years ago, do we stand a chance of re-vitalizing the sacred promise of our nation."

The Republican Senator rails against Jake for an hour, proclaiming him a traitor to the nation and a fraud as an historian, but his remarks fall on deaf ears and he sits back after his tirade, spent and disconsolate. He never again raises his voice in a public forum.

Other Commission members steer clear of patriotic pronouncements. Instead they attempt to paint the Well Site

Operation as a drag on the country's domestic agenda or a religious fraud of the highest order.

• • •

"I fear the American people will not soon forget the expense this operation cost taxpayers and the degree to which we must now find or create new resources for the Federal budget to cover expenses," drones the Democrat Senator from New York as she queries Dr. Kagen. "How will we pay for health care for the 75% of American's without Insurance? Have we not sacrificed the greater good of our people with our diversion in Mesopotamia?"

"Madame Senator you speak of health care for the poor when you are well advised to consider the spirit of a nation and its people," answers Dr. Kagen with the authority of a Nobel Prize winner. "What we learned at Avinen can fill entire university libraries with life saving and extending sciences, completely eliminating the need for perfunctory articles of the mundane such as health insurance. Our examination of the sciences of the past reveals great and grand potentials for the sciences of the future. But we also learned science without morality is a fool's gold of epic proportions. The Avina practiced science at such an elevated height they lost touch with the meaning of life. The ability to extend life beyond all bounds, to recreate themselves over thousands of years established a sense that life itself is merely a specimen in a glass jar."

"And so you mean to imply our seniors shouldn't waste time on prescription drugs with the potential to heal their ailments and extend their lives? You're saying the morally upright position is for American children to go without health care? What a sick set of principles!"

"Of course not Senator. I'm telling you we can't play God without possessing the wisdom of God. For all of us sitting here today everlasting life by our own hands is difficult to imagine and yet we see the Avina perfected methods to make the end of life non-existent. But what are the ramifications to the soul? Of course I wish to live a long and fruitful life myself but I don't want to lose my soul in the process. I wish my parents were still alive, enjoying the benefits of my success but I would not want them to live so long they lose the meaning of life…the spark living within us. The Avina once had that spark but lost the joy of being alive. They replaced the physical body through genetic replication and passed their own memories through recessive genes, living thousands of years with the same set of experiences. Eventually this created in them a sense of moral apathy permeating all aspects of society."

"I don't see how this relates to denying children health insurance!"

"Senator, like many you miss the point of human existence entirely. Yes we want to alleviate suffering, we want our children healthy and seniors comfortable but these issues are quite beside the point. We are walking down the same path as the Avina, where the physical being of the individual transcends the soul so we nurture the body and starve the spirit. We go out of our way to eliminate any form of suffering to the extent we outlaw children's games of tag at recess so no one gets a skinned knee but we throw away millions of preborn lives by aborting their nascent spark and toss them out with the detritus. We do this in the guise of a woman's right to choose. To choose what exactly? Not her own life but her convenience in life. This ethos has put us on the selfish path followed by the Avina."

"We place political correctness over correcting bad behavior. We don't hear bad words used against us but suffer the sticks and stones of gang violence or killings in the name of religious faith. We celebrate the carcass and toss aside the meaning of our existence. Like them we will lose our soul too."

"Doctor Kagen you are a scientist not a theologian. What qualifies you to make judgments as to the existence of a soul in the first place?"

"Senator I am perhaps better qualified than the theologian. I see the inner workings of the genetic code and I have come to the understanding certain things are not possible through genetic manipulation. No manner of mathematics or programming can create morality. That is given to us by other means. The Avina didn't program morals into humans but they built up just the same. You may disagree and believe morals are only social constructs but I beg to differ. As a scientist I find proof of a higher morality as humanity's moral compass recedes. Bad things, horrible things occur in its absence. This deadening of the human spirit reveals itself throughout all aspects of our society where the spark of life is expendable. With each new generation we find a greater capacity for senseless killing, not in battles against evil or physical attack but as a result of our narcissistic approach. We view the life experiences of a single being as more valuable than life itself, preserving the former and destroying the latter. The Avina made no room for moral suasion in their pursuit of living forever and impressing the rest of the universe. How is this principle so different from how we live today? I submit it is not different at all. This mindset, free of morality allowed the

Avina to cull parts of their own genetic code and manipulate it to create what they perceived as lesser beings for purposes of their own happiness. But they saw their creations bring new lives into the world, through pain and tribulation yes, but also with joy and a protective spirit."

"Now we find ourselves as a society degrading life in every manner possible, feeding our prurient interests and ignoring the wellsprings of our soul. You can lecture me all day long about health insurance Senator but you miss the moral point of our existence. We work and procreate and build to nurture the soul living in every one of us…the one part of our being that could never get erased by attempting to eliminate it in our basic programming. There is a greater good and a far richer life than we know and none of it is fostered by a better HMO."

• • •

The Senator from New York poses no further arguments nor asks other questions. She sits back and ponders the meaning of living, perhaps for the first time since childhood.

Religion experts and Atheists on the panel stand in lockstep on the wrong headedness of Tasha's dating Avinen at 40,000 years old. The religious theologians decry the date as too long, the Atheists as far too short.

"We know through Biblical timelines the age of the Earth," scolds one theologian raising a bony finger toward Tasha, "The record is unequivocal and our faith demands a retraction on your part. And it's not only Christians who believe this but Islam as well. How can over two billion people be wrong and you, one little woman, be right?"

"I'm not an expert in Biblical lore Sir," answers Tasha calmly and deliberatively. "But I am an expert in science despite my tender years. The radio carbon dating system is dead spot on and irrefutable despite your faith. The organic mossy material at Avinen died approximately 10,000 years ago. Carbon 14 tests confirm the timeline. Organic materials on the structures at Avinen died and ceased to generate Carbon 14 somewhere around 40,000 years ago. I'm not trying to challenge Biblical timelines one way or the other. I only report what the data is telling me. I leave it to others to make interpretations about how this affects the timelines of respective faiths whether religious or secular."

"But radio carbon dating is highly unreliable missy. As you know scientists regularly get readings of millions of years old on items we absolutely know to be less than five thousand years. I can quote example after example of these false tests."

"You wrong about my application of the science Sir. The radio carbon dating system is often misapplied to create dates fitting in with prevailing wisdom in various scientific disciplines. If we know the original atmospheric and climate conditions then we can infer the exact rate of degradation for Carbon 14, that part is irrefutable. Calculating half-life cycles on C-14 is simple math. Avinen existed for thousands of years hermetically sealed in a bubble. We know the conditions so the Carbon rates are probably very accurate. I will stand by the science under those restrictions."

"Where you might get confused is in the application of carbon and isotope readings providing the basis of claims by scientists an artifact or fossil is millions of years old. Or the earth is billions of years old. I don't stand by such conclusions, as we have no idea of the conditions at the time the artifact was buried. Carbon levels are not absolute constants in the atmosphere and conjectures about those conditions are un-provable. That's not objective science. I would categorize those claims as matters of secular faith."

"Ha ha ha, you are indeed a fool," bellows the Atheist Paleontologist. "Evolution and the age of the Earth are no longer a collection of conjecture and theories. Science has proven them unequivocally!"

"No Sir, science has done no such thing! For example let's examine the prevailing wisdom about the age of Planet Earth. Scientists believe it is 4.5 billion years old according to radiocarbon and isotope testing. But that age is impossible. Let me offer just one scientific example that can't be easily explained away. The Moon moves away from Earth at a rate of about a quarter inch a year and the distance is a constant observed over thousands of years and a provable fact. If the Earth and the moon started out touching each other, which is highly unlikely, then the rate of separation would only give a maximum Earth age of one billion years."

"Frankly I don't think provable science puts it nearly so old. Scientists don't know the exact or even approximate conditions of the planet at any given time in ancient history so dating norms are built on un-provable conjecture and then theories are formed with more conjecture and finally a firm date is established built on the murky foundation of pure conjecture. There's no way around this Sir."

"Even if the Earth is only a billion or so years old that's plenty of time for Evolution to occur so I fail to see your point."

"Evolution is a completely different ball of wax Sir. A billion years is enough time for Evolution to occur if you buy into the theoretical process of Evolution. The problem with the argument is no actual scientific basis exists to support the theory. Again, it is all conjecture built on false or un-provable premises."

"Today's prevailing wisdom holds Evolution as a fact. But it is impossible for species to evolve unless they do so over millions of years. So the Earth must be millions or billions of years old, right? It's a circular argument without supportive facts. I tend to agree with Doctor Kagen…evolution would take millions upon millions of mathematical miracles to occur naturally. We always hear about discovering the missing link but this is an extremely narrow view on what's necessary to prove Evolution as a scientific fact. What's necessary is the discovery of millions upon millions of missing links to make the connections between species plausible. Science views Evolution as a series of mutations and changes from microorganisms all the way through higher primates such as humans. Sounds simple in the abstract, right? The problem is a simple chart showing how to get from point A to point B includes millions of species but that's only the slightest tip of the iceberg. Each change requires millions of evolutions between them. The fossil record does not support the theory, at least not on this planet. I can only put out there what the science actually tells me and reject conjecture."

"The theory of a being or a group of beings programming the genetic code is much more plausible to me as a scientist than the religion of Evolution. We saw examples of high-level genetic programming at Avinen. We saw how they grew large complex structures with hard smooth surfaces, like teeth. We were witness to the technology of transported objects via the science of plasmatic stereo-lithography. These are great and wondrous things beyond our current understanding but they are only scientific practices. As an objective scientist I don't ascribe religious divinity to the act of creating physical beings so don't you dare paint me as a religious wing nut. They were scientists and spoke my language. I leave it to you folks to argue over meaning and theology."

• • •

"Mr. Orbeson," asks the Commission Chair, directing his questions to KO. "I am curious about the nature of the many languages we have in today's world. Do you see the myths surrounding the Biblical story of the Tower of Babel as manifestations of true events? Is the science behind the story even possible?"

"Mr. Chairman it is true that I am a linguist," allows KO. "But that is not the extent of my knowledge or experience as it relates to the Avina or how languages came into being. In my capacity as a translator during our brainy-chaining exercises I was often overcome by severe headaches and had no idea why. Several months after our return to the States I began to experience vivid dreams about the Avina and their technologies. None of this made sense to me as we had not seen or experienced the substance of these visions while at Avinen."

In discussions with Doctor Kagen we ascertained my work as a translator opened a conduit to my brain, enabling the free flow of information into my head. In a way my brain acted as a back-up disc for lack of a better term. The rapid dump of data caused the headaches. I believe what transferred into my head is the Avinen Encyclopedia of sorts. I can see and experience their history and the powers they used to control the elements around them including the manipulation of the Earth's crust and ordering of the weather. There are a number of human activities that attempt to replicate the power of the Avina…albeit rather crude copies."

"Such as?"

"Take mummification as practiced by the Egyptians for example. We now know the Avina recreated themselves over and over with genetic replacement therapies. The process consisted of wrapping the aging carcass in a mummy-like cocoon, dumping memories into a scan-can and re-energizing the physical body. Egyptians crudely replicated this process as an attempt at eternal life."

"Is there anything enlightening about languages in your data dump son?"

"Yes in fact there is a treasure trove. Avina Creators designed creatures in their own image, that is, from strands of their own DNA. A competition developed between them and they sought to create the most beautiful and exotic varieties possible. This is how the races were formed, each beautiful in it's own way but carrying basically the same capacities offered by the new programming. In other words they looked different but possessed the same mental and physical abilities. Now whether you believe in God or Evolution all languages come from a common source, either the ugga bugga of the cave man or a complete language such as that spoken by the Avina or Adam and Eve if that's your belief. What I see in these visions…as humans grew and populated Novinen they developed languages, first as dialects of the common language and then as complete and separate tongues. In the days before the Tower of Babel all people could communicate through a common interface established throughout the world by the Avina. The interface was powered by electromagnetic and sonic waves through a series of beacons built and placed strategically around the globe. As the Avinenev, or humans, grew in knowledge and power they threatened the existence of their creators so the Avina destroyed the…well, the radio network enabling universal communication, not only between various tongues but over great distances."

"Ha ha. So you're saying the Avina built a radio network operating as a universal translation device and as a cell phone network? Ha ha ha!"

"Yes. They didn't use radio waves as we know them but the electromagnetic-sonic waves did bounce off the atmosphere in the same manner as our radio systems do today."

"Heh, heh. So where's all the radio towers and beacons and transformers used to make this global network?"

"Ahem. Well, I think sitting right in front of us Mr. Chairman. The technology is simple and ingenious. First you need a large chamber to amplify the wave before you send it out, then you need a directional device pointing the beam up toward the atmosphere. The Avina built structures with a large base and a long shaft reaching out towards the sky."

"You say these are right under our noses, can you tell us where they are?"

"Ahh, yes, well, uh, ahem. A, uh, good example is the, uh main pyramid at Giza in Egypt."

Everyone in the chamber laughs. "Ha ha, heh heh. Ok that's funny. You're telling us the Egyptian pyramids are ancient radio towers?"

"No, not all of them, but at least one of them. I think most of the pyramids there are copies of the original, an effort by people to replicate the powers of the ancients. If you search around the world you'll find pyramids all over the place, from Machu Pichu in Peru to places in China, Japan, all around really. One thing you'll notice is they roughly match the distance you need to circumnavigate the globe with a radio wave or an Avina beam skipping off the atmosphere. I think they used this system as a global positioning network too, enabling them to navigate around the earth without getting lost."

"But scientists have dated the various pyramids around the world and they're not all from the same time frame."

"Well actually what they've dated are the structures and coverings built up over the originals. I know all of this sounds fanciful but logically the idea stands to reason. All of the pyramids around the world are seen by the local populace as ways to reach out to heaven whether dead or alive. How could this occur independently among diverse societies who supposedly never had any sort of contact with each other? Well, that's not likely but a global communications system erected by an ancient civilization? That's plausible, but I admit I can't prove it you Mr. Chairman."

"I guess we'll just have to leave it at that but I doubt the Egyptian tourist trade will have any good feelings toward you after this."

The Chairman relaxes in his high-back leather chair chuckling and shaking his head. The Atheists, Christians and Islamic members of the panel proceed to grill Kelly Anne about the spiritual nature of the Well Site and its implications to religion and the existence of God.

70

"Dr. Carter," lectures Congress' lone Socialist Senator, an avowed atheist. "I understand you are a religious woman and fully believed in the myths of the Bible before your adventures into Mesopotamia. Am I to understand you have changed your tune in this regard and reject the foolish notions of God and a divine omniscient creator?"

"No Sir, you are sadly mistaken if you hold conceptions of any such thing."

"How can this be? We all saw absolute refutation of a Divine God. Those weren't Gods acting out the Bible stories. Are you an idiot or are you going to give the American people some mumbo jumbo about how all of this is a matter of your faith?"

"Senator the stories of the Bible are written over thousands of years. Some of them start out as an oral tradition handed down through the generations. Others are written as the impressions of the writers and then given provenance by other scholars hundreds and sometimes thousands of years down the road. Most of the Bible stories are written in such a way even simpletons, as your self can understand them. Often the full stories behind the easy to digest narratives are saturated with remarkable science and understanding. Sometimes the stories are practical recitations of history and are deified over time.

"Give us an example of this so we can better understand your meaning, after all I'm a simpleton and need edification."

"Certainly. There are numerous examples. Let's take the story of Cain and Abel as a reasonably understandable example. As the story in Genesis relates, two brothers offered sacrifices to God. One, Abel, offered the fruits of his labors tilling the soil and the other, Cain, offered the fruits of his labors in animal husbandry. According to the text God loved the fruits and vegetables along with Abel but rejected the animals and chastised Cain. As the Bible story goes Cain killed Abel in a fit of jealous pique."

"Taken in the context as passed down through the ages the Cain and Abel narrative is a story of a petulant God who favors one of his creations over the other to suit his own whims and tastes. During our interface with the Chronicles of Avinen we were entreated to a story roughly matching this tale but with some important differences."

"The Avinen story is about two brothers who operate a foods distribution network. Sort of like a farm co-operative. One brother raised crops and offered these to the Avina as food. This was part of the social construct of the day. The other brother raised animals and offered up items such as milk and sheep wool. The Avina used these items too. As time passed and the population of the Avinenev grew the brothers found it difficult to supply both the Avina and their own people the Avinenev. So the animal farming brother slaughtered herds and offered the meat up as food to the Avina. This was a disgrace and an abomination to the vegan Avina and they rejected not only the meat but also the person who came up with the idea. In their experience every set of creatures they created started down the path of eating flesh to survive but in the process destroyed the delicate ecosystems…or balance of life. The brother who offered flesh to the Avina killed his crop-growing brother to take over the farming side of the enterprise. The Avina never practiced killing and had no remedy for the crime so they banished the perpetrator."

"Ok, so the Avina story is like the Bible story but what's the point, it doesn't prove the existence of God or Biblical truth!"

"No…no it doesn't but like all of the Bible's stories there are object lessons to learn, based on practical occurrences in life. We see most of the object lessons contained in the Bible for humans as mirrors of actual occurrences in Avina life. In the Cain and Abel story taking the life of another of your fellows is against the principles of life and stuffing your face with meat is ultimately bad for your health and eating flesh rips apart the delicate balance of life. Everything in life is designed to protect it from passing away, from dying out. Even the relationship between men and women is a strategy to maintain the species."

"In the Bible story we read God placed an enmity between man and woman due to Eve's eating of the tree of knowledge. I personally don't believe in a God or a designer who would arbitrarily tear relationships apart before they get started so I look for practical examples to gain full understanding of what this passage might mean to humans. Of course I can clearly see how this could come about by studying Avina lifestyles."

"We know the Avina relationships grew stale over time and the sexes were absolutely equal, they were almost identical. If an Avina woman wanted a man's strength she could easily order up the genes at her next DNA replication cycle and voila! She's Martina Navratalova. I believe the designers or God-designer knew this and sought to change the dynamic so humans would live in a constant state of tension. Today we call this passion and it is what makes the sexes yearn for, fight against and build loving relationships with each other."

"My wife will certainly appreciate your ideas Doctor Carter. I can understand the need for object lessons but I fail to see how this proves the existence of God. In fact your story seems to contradict the concept of a God in Heaven. And yet you seem to infer you believe in God despite your own evidence to the contrary. Are you going to tell us your faith rules over all and we should discard hard evidence and the facts?"

"Oh no Senator, far from it. The faith you describe is blind faith unsupportable by reason. The faith I carry is fully supported by pure unadulterated logic."

"How can that be? The Avina showed us exactly how they created humans and all of the other creatures on Earth. How does your concept equate to the existence of an all-knowing God?"

"Senator the question suggests myopic and unchallenged thinking. Of course that's the easy route especially in today's world where science looks only for the process and without absolute proof of the process refuses to contemplate what isn't understood. Science buries its collective head in the sand whenever it can't prove something. And worse, it uses conjecture and at times lies to show proof of a process. This sort of thinking does a disservice to all of humanity."

"The truth is if we suddenly found out how God created the Universe the knowledge would become science and no longer require any faith whatsoever. So faith must not be a design feature made to keep us blind to science. I believe faith exists to keep us striving for goodness and a better life or way of living.

The key to the existence of God is found in the existence of morality. Our faith is created in us to help us continue believing in morally upright principles."

"Morality doesn't evolve from primordial ooze. There is no mathematical calculation compelling thinking beings to sacrifice their existence for a greater good. If there is no authoritative foundation underlying the principles of life and indeed, the entire Universe, there is nothing to stop me from jumping up on the dais and slitting your throat at my whim…other than armed guards who would subdue me or in a meaner world slit my throat. A force stops us from moral breakdown, keeps us at bay, shames us when we err."

"Faith is the mysterious element Senator. Generally we view faith as a result of our lack of understanding…our way around inconvenient facts. But this is a mischaracterization of faith. You see, Senator, faith is the precursor to belief, the element compelling us to seek understanding."

"DNA programming doesn't create faith. Even in times human morality breaks down on a massive scale, such as the Jewish Holocaust during World War Two, a part of our soul is hurt and we feel intense remorse. Those breakdowns are a measure of an absence of faith. If there is no authority behind morality, and we have no faith in a better existence all of us can simply go on without a care, like psychopaths. But the human race doesn't give up. It continues to persevere, fighting evil and destruction, all the while hoping for a better day and finer place to come."

"All of this is un-provable psychobabble as far as I'm concerned Dr. Carter. Isn't there any tangible proof of God's existence? And what happened to the Avina…where did they all go? Did they simply vanish into thin air?"

"I can't say for certain where the Avina went Sir. I have no idea if they died out or still live among us. Perhaps they are the Angels whose guidance so many millions of humans claim to have experienced. As for proof of the existence of a grand designer God I offer the Well Site and Avinen as tangible, physical evidence."

"Dr. Carter your blustering is not proof of a God. Avinen is evidence only to the technologies and powers of the Avina, that's all…nothing more. I see no Divinity in such evidence."

"That's a fair point on the surface Senator, but if there is no omniscient God who designed the entire Universe in his infinite wisdom then what created the Avina?"

Epilogue

Studio Set of *Jackson Nichols' Big Dig*
Hollywood, California

After the *Origins Commission* hearings ended Team Babelus set about the serious business of rebuilding their lives. Jake, re-energized about life after his experiences got a contract from a major network to produce *Jackson Nichols' Big Dig* for a lavishly funded extended run. His experiences pushed him to focus the show on technologies and societies before time began. The fascinating new format was met with financial rewards and critical acclaim. Jake was never again forced to give scuba diving lessons to bored housewives and lonely young women a few years out of college…not that success stopped him from the activity.

Tasha, KO and Doc joined Jake as cast members on his show, world-renown experts in their respective fields. The reconstituted Team Babelus make an entertaining and informative group, fighting like family, traveling around the globe and bringing a new sense of imagination and fun to history and technology for millions of viewers each week. New dig sites are picked apart, poked and prodded for relationships to the wider world and possible lineage to Avinen roots. Video games, action figures, toys and books follow the show's success enriching everyone beyond even KO's wildest dreams.

Former National Security Advisor Dan Maney joined the cast as an advisor although his first reports are filmed from his jail cell after a conviction for treason against the United States. Following a huge public outcry he received a full pardon from President Murcheson and joined the show as a permanent fixture, the serious sidekick to Jake's bon vivant style.

Mahmoud the Woodcarver and his trusty donkey Jafaah, now an Iraqi icon, are seen every day around the world on television, print media, billboards and web sites, the new spokes-creatures for Iraq's leading olive oil brand, *Avinen Olive Oil.* The company's slogan: The World's Oldest Can of Oil.

Gunnery Sergeant Hall and Lieutenant Jenks retired from military service and joined *Jake Nichols' Big Dig* as head of security and logistics coordinator respectively. Gunny Hall found time to spend with his family who moved to Southern California. Tasha became great friends with the Gunny's daughters and they treat her as a member of the family.

Lorenzo Cordoba received the Medal of Freedom from Congress, the highest medal awarded to civilians. His legacy as a cheap thrill television talk show host transformed into that of a knowledgeable world traveling expert in foreign affairs. Now the world sees him for what he is, a patriot.

Kelly Anne went back to teaching and writing books, joined often, as his military schedule will allow, by her new love Major Gettysburg Lee. She rejoined the scientific lecture circuit and fights tooth and nail with academics and scientists around the world only on this go around she is the acknowledged expert and many of her ideas are finding acceptance as the prevailing wisdom in the scientific community. Kelly Anne is unsure whether she likes the newfound respect but it opens doors for new ideas and a fresh look at the world and its history.

Occasionally Jake gazes out on the set of his popular show, seeing his friends and compatriots enjoying financial and personal success in the limelight. He'll think back to the dangers they endured and the criticisms they met with fierce replies. Through every pestilence, toil and trauma they remain unabashedly loyal to each other.

Then he will shake his head and smile ear to ear, "Oh yeah, brother, its all good!"

www.ingramcontent.com/pod-product-compliance
Lightning Source LLC
Chambersburg PA
CBHW030822310726
48980CB00006B/596/J
* 9 7 8 0 6 1 5 1 3 6 4 1 7 *